Table Of

Albert Pierrepoint Casebook
[1932-1955]
Vol 3

1) <u>Mahmood Mattan (1952), Butetown, Cardiff – WALES</u>
2) <u>John Greenway (1953), Swindon</u>
3) <u>Thomas Eames (1952), Plymouth</u>
4) <u>Harry Gleeson (1941), Marlhill, nr New Inn, Co Tipperary – IRELAND</u>
5) <u>Frederick Parker & Albert Probert (1934), Brighton</u>
6) <u>Patrick Kingston (1942), Lewisham, s-e London</u>
7) <u>Andrew Brown (1945), Arundel, Sussex</u>
8) <u>John Leatherberry (1944), Birch, nr Colchester</u>
9) <u>Herbert Mills (1951), Nottingham</u>
10) <u>James Lehman (1945), Rathmines, Dublin – IRELAND</u>

11) *James Robertson (1950), Govan Hill, Glasgow – SCOTLAND*
12) *Max Haslam (1937), Nelson, Lancs*
13) *Bernard Kirwan (1943), Rahan, nr Tullamore, Co Offaly – IRELAND*
14) *William O'Shea (1943), Ballyhane, Co Waterford – IRELAND*
15) *Harold Trevor (1942), West Kensington, w. London*
16) *William Hepper (1954), Brighton*
17) *Leslie Green (1952), Barlaston, Staffs*
18) *Thomas Williams (1942), Falls, w. Belfast –IRELAND*
19) *John Dand (1951), York*
20) *Joseph Brown & Edward Smith (1951), Addlestone Moor, nr Chertsey, Surrey*
21) *Styllou Christofi (1954), Hampstead, n-w London*
22) *Daniel Raven (1950) Edgware, n. London*

23) John Young (1945), Leigh-on-Sea, Southend-on-Sea
24) James McNichol (1945), Thorpe Bay, Southend-on-Sea
25) Eric Norcliffe (1952), Warsop, Notts
26) Dorothea Waddingham (1936), Nottingham
27) Alfred Whiteway (1953), Teddington, s-w London
28) Horace Carter (1952), Birmingham
29) George Kelly (1950), Liverpool
30) Albert Jenkins (1950), Rosemarket, Pembrokeshire—WALES

COVER – James Robertson Case 11

From Vol 1 – See Amazon

1) **William Appleby & Vincent Ostler (1940)**
2) **John Lynch (1954) - SCOTLAND**
3) **Rupert Wells (1954)**
4) **Rex Jones (1949) - WALES**
5) **Robert MacKintosh - (1949) - WALES**
6) **Robert Blaine (1945)**
7) **James Virrels (1951)**
8) **Milton Taylor (1954)**
9) **David Mason (1946)**
10) **Ernest Couzins (1949)**
11) **Ralph Smith (1939)**
12) **Backary Manneh (1952)**
13) **James Rivett (1950)**
14) **Frank Burgess (1952)**
15) **William Watkins (1951)**
16) **Dennis Moore (1951)**
17) **Alfred Reynolds (1951)**
18) **Nicholas Crosby (1950)**
19) **Stanislaw Juras (1953)**
20) **Peter Johnson (1952)**
21) **Paul Harris (1950) - SCOTLAND**
22) **Zbigniew Gower & Roman Redel (1950)**
23) **Thomas Houghton (1952) - EGYPT**

24) *John Godar (1952)*
25) *Horace Gordon (1945)*
26) *Richard Hetherington (1933)*
27) *Arthur Clegg (1946)*
28) *Gerald Roe (1943)*
29) *George Shaw (1953) SCOTLAND*
30) *James Corbitt (1950)*

<u>*From Vol 2 – See Amazon ….*</u>

1) *Jeremiah Hanbury (1933)*
2) *Charles Gauthier (1943)*
3) *James Inglis (1951)*
4) *Ronald Mauri (1945)*
5) *George Semini (1949)*
6) *Harold Courtney (1933) – NORTHERN IRELAND*
7) *Thomas Thorpe (1941)*
8) *John Mathieson (1946)*
9) *Michal Niescor (1946)*
10) *James Farrell (1948)*
11) *Sydney Chamberlain (1949)*
12) *Walter Worthington (1935)*
13) *William Collins (1942)*
14) *Dennis Muldowney (1952)*
15) *Terence Casey (1943)*
16) *Thomas Bancroft (1956) – Reprieved*
17) *Ronald Atwell (1950)*
18) *Stanislaus Myszka (1948) - SCOTLAND*
19) *Marion Grondkowski & Henryk Malinowski (1946)*
20) *Kenneth Strickson (1949)*
21) *Daniel Doherty (1941) - IRELAND*
22) *Edward Woodfield (1950)*
23) *John Livesey (1952)*
24) *Czeslaw Kowalewski (1954)*
25) *Eugeniusz Jurkiewicz (1947)*
26) *Sidney Smith (1946)*
27) *Ernest Moss (1937)*
28) *Arthur Boyce (1946)*
29) *Ajit Singh (1952) - WALES*

30) Philip Henry (1953)

Albert Pierrepoint (1905–1992) was the most prolific hangman from Britain in the 20th century – he was certainly the most famous – but how many people did he actually hang by the neck until they were dead. Although he kept a diary, he did rewrite it at certain points. In one at the end he wrote: " .... engaged in approx. 606 executions. approx. 173 reprieved." Thus this figure would be 433. In terms of the figure from others sources, e.g. the Official Execution Sheets, he executed 433[1] people between 1932 and 1955 ….

---

[1] Removed Walasek – he is on some sources as having been hanged by AP – he was, in fact, shot by firing-squad at Hamelin Prison in Germany ….

Case 1
"Butetown's Shop-Murder And A Miscarriage Of Justice"

Mahmood MATTAN
MURDER
Of
Lily Volpert
[1952]

-The Last Execution At Cardiff Prison-

In September 2022 the Mattan family finally received an apology from the police force for the wrongful conviction and execution of Mahmood Mattan in 1952. Although they

had already received compensation from the Home Office back in 2001, the apology had taken 70 years ….

In the living-room behind her general outfitter's shop – *Volpert's*—in Cardiff's Butetown—Tiger Bay as everyone locally called it - district, 41-year-old Miss Lily Volpert was chatting happily with her mother, her sister Doris and Doris's 10-year-old daughter, over their evening meal. It was 8 o'clock on **Thursday, March 6th, 1952**, and the Bute Street shop at 203-204 was still open, for Lily also sold cigarettes and often left locking up for the night until later, although 8 p.m. was her stated closing-time. At 8.05 the shop bell tinkled, and Lily put down her knife and fork. "Someone wants cigarettes," she said as she left her family and went to attend to the customer. As Lily opened the living-room door behind the counter, her sister glimpsed a tall black man waiting to be served. Five minutes later Lily's mother, sister and niece heard the shop bell ring again. "Someone else wants cigarettes," sighed Lily's mother. Well, at least Lily was still out there to serve them. The new customer was William Archbold, a seaman living a few doors away. Seeing Lily's shop door open had reminded him that he was out of cigarettes. Stepping inside, he tapped the counter. Nobody came, so he walked hesitantly round the other side …. to see Lily Volpert lying face-down in a pool of blood. Without a second glance he hurried off to fetch the police, while Lily's family continued their supper, unaware of the shock awaiting them in the next room. A few minutes later Archbold was back with the police. He went behind the counter to reveal Lily's blood-soaked body, and when the officers opened the living-room door they and the family stared at each other in stunned surprise. While an ambulance was called to take the hysterical family to hospital Detective Chief Inspector Harry Power looked down in disbelief at the dead shopkeeper. Lily Volpert's throat had been cut four times with a razor by an assassin who had attacked her from behind. One of her wounds was eight inches deep, severing her jugular vein, almost severing her spinal column, and causing almost instant death. And nobody had heard a sound ….

The shop's stock had not been touched, but Doris said that about £115 was missing from the till. This was confirmed the next day by Lily Volpert's assistant, Miss Dorothy Brown, who had left the shop at 6.30 the previous evening. "Lily always worried about break-ins and thefts," Dorothy told the police. "If there was a regular customer in the shop and a stranger came in, she would often ask the regular one to stay while she served the stranger." The chief inspector reasoned that Archbold had come upon the body so soon after the killing that he might have seen someone. With only five minutes between the two shop bell rings, he could almost have met the murderer coming out of the shop, and the detective asked him to think carefully. "When I came out of the shop to go to the police station, Bute Street was empty," Archbold recalled. "I hurried down the street and then I saw a black man aged about thirty. I'm sure he was a Somali. He was wearing a dark coat and suit, had a moustache, and was about five feet nine inches tall." Seeing a Somali man in Tiger Bay was not unusual, but it was the only lead Power had. For the rest of that night police combed lodging-houses frequented by seamen ....

A few hours after the killing a road-sweeper reported that he had seen a bundle of bloodstained clothing in a lane not far from Lily's shop. But when police went to the lane, Bute Terrace, behind Cardiff Central Boys' Club, they found that most of the clothes – a pair of brown trousers, a blue shirt and what looked like a jacket – had disappeared. All that was left were a few small items, none of them bloodstained, and a leather belt with a small loop, which could be used for carrying a knife. Power's men managed in two days to interview every crew member of the ships docked in Tiger Bay. But they drew a blank, and all that remained was to pin their hopes on finding the mysterious Somali man. The chief inspector learned that on some Fridays, Lily would bank the weekly takings, if she thought the amount was too large to be left in the shop. She was killed on a Thursday night, and the family knew that the following day she was going to bank the week's takings. As a considerable sum was missing, Power sent detectives into the pubs, clubs and bars of Tiger Bay to find out if anyone, particularly a Somali man, was splashing money about. Again and again one name came up: that of Mahmood Hussein Mattan, an unemployed Somali seaman. Tall and slim, in

Cardiff dockland he was known as "The Shadow" because of his silent way of moving about. Officers had already questioned him briefly late on the night of the murder, during their check on occupants of Tiger Bay lodging-houses, and on the day police decided to keep him under observation he stole a raincoat from a department store and was arrested ….

On March 15th, nine days after the murder, Mattan appeared before the city magistrates on the theft charge. The police asked for him to be remanded in custody because of "another serious matter," which they were not required to divulge for fear of prejudicing their inquiries. The magistrates consented. By now Power had two more witnesses who claimed they had seen Mattan in the Bute Street vicinity between 8.20 and 8.50 on the night of the murder. One of them, Harold Cover, said he saw Mattan leaving Lily's shop at about 8.20 – probably five minutes or less after Archbold had left to fetch the police. Power believed that when Archbold turned to leave the shop, Mattan was still inside it. The chief inspector suspected that Mattan had seen Archbold enter, and had hidden behind a tailor's dummy. When Archbold saw the body and turned and ran out, Mattan slipped out into Bute Street. The other witness, Mrs. Mary Grey, the owner of a second-hand clothes shop, said Mattan came into her shop between 8.30 and 8.50 to buy some clothes. Mrs. Grey, unimpressed by his appearance, suggested he might not have enough money to pay for what he wanted, and Mattan had then produced a roll of banknotes – about £100, she reckoned. He was, she said, "excited and agitated, and appeared to have been running." Interviewed while on remand in prison, Mattan said he was nowhere near Bute Street that night. He had been to a cinema, leaving at 7.30, and had then gone straight back to his lodgings in Davis Street ….

As the investigation continued, detectives learned that Mattan had a reputation as a heavy gambler. He was known as someone who always wanted to borrow cash at greyhound meetings, but after the murder he was suddenly flush with cash. And on Mattan's right shoe there were 87 bloodstains, and 18 more on his left shoe. The blood could not be identified as Lily Volpert's, but it was definitely human. Mattan remained defiant, shrugging when Power said that he had interviewed Mattan's landlord, Ernest Harrison. Power had discovered that in a conversation with Mr. Harrison on the day after the killing, Mattan said that Miss Volpert must have been attacked from behind – and he had then given the landlord a demonstration of how it probably happened. Power believed that the killer pushed his knee into Lily Volpert's back, then pulling her back by the hair and slashing her throat. Her shoulder was bruised and her scalp below her hairline was inflamed. The detective was now confident that although all his evidence was circumstantial, there was enough to charge Mahmood Mattan with murder. Taken before the magistrates, he was asked if he wanted a solicitor to defend him. He replied: "Defend me for what?" "Defend you on the charges for which you appear before the court." "I don't want anything and I don't care anything," retorted Mattan. "You can't get me to worrying." ….

The magistrates sent him for trial before Justice Benjamin Ormerod at Cardiff Assizes in July, where Mattan's defence was simply that he was not Lily Volpert's killer. For the Crown, H. Edmund Davies QC said that if the jury were satisfied with the evidence given by Harold Cover, who saw Mattan leaving Lily Volpert's shop at about 8.20 p.m., then that was the end of the case. Undoubtedly a large sum of money was stolen from the shop. Mrs. Grey said that shortly after the murder she saw Mattan with a roll of money. Was she mistaken? Mr. Davies asked. Was the witness who saw Mattan at the dog track the following night, with between £15 and £20, also in error? And was the witness who said he saw Mattan losing £7 in a game of poker the next night lying or mistaken? T. E. R. Rhys-Roberts, defending, said that while his client was "half-child in nature and a semi-civilised savage," he was also unfortunately caught up in a web of lies and suspicion. Mattan had bought his bloodstained shoes only days before the murder. They were salvage, and he had paid only four shillings for them. They were already battered and could easily have already been splattered in blood, since no one could be sure of their history. After Mattan's landlord had shown how he claimed Mattan demonstrated the killing, Mr. Rhys-Roberts said: "If there is anything crystal clear in this case it is that the demonstration of the way Mattan described the murder was not the way Miss Volpert was murdered." ….

There was no evidence of any bloodstains on Mattan's clothing and, on the night of the murder, police officers had made a thorough search of Mattan's room and found nothing to connect him with the murder, Mr. Rhys-Roberts continued. There was no money there and no weapon that might have inflicted Miss Volpert's wounds. Mattan's mother-in-law told the court that he was at her house at 8 o'clock on the night of the murder. Giving evidence on his own behalf, Mattan said that on the afternoon of the murder he went to the cinema at 4.30 and left at 7.30 to return to his lodgings, where he arrived at 7.40. He did not go down Bute Street that night, so Mr. Cover couldn't have seen him coming from Miss Volpert's shop. He denied that he went to Mrs. Grey's shop to buy clothes at any time that day. Asked whether he had obtained any money from any source on the day of the murder or the following day, he said he had received £2.3s. public assistance. With that money he went to the dog track at Newport and placed some bets ….

Mattan denied ever having been in the habit of carrying a knife or a razor. The jury took 95 minutes to find him guilty of murder, and he was sentenced to death at the end of the three-day trial on July 24th …. An appeal was rejected on August 19th …. After his execution at Cardiff Prison on Wednesday, September 3rd, 1952, by Albert Pierrepoint and Robert Stewart, his family were not alone in still believing him innocent. Years later an attempt to have Mattan's conviction reviewed was made by Ted Rowlands, then MP for Cardiff North. James Callaghan, who was Home Secretary, found there were no new grounds to justify reopening the case. Two years later, in 1971, Harry Power, who had retired with the rank of detective superintendent, told a reporter: "Mattan was feared by local shopkeepers because he used to demand money from them. Some would give way because of his wild character. He was vicious. He was hanged on circumstantial evidence, but it was the best possible circumstantial evidence. At the request of the Home Office I went to see Mattan many times while he was awaiting execution and he put up many stories. They were fully investigated, and none of them had any foundation at all. I interrogated him many times, and we both knew what he had done. I've had no sleepless nights at all over this case. I've never had the slightest doubt whatsoever that he was guilty." ….

Others were not so sure, and the belief of Mattan's family in his innocence remained unshaken. They persevered in their attempts to clear his name, and on February 24th, 1998, their efforts were rewarded after the Court of Appeal heard evidence which put Mahmood Mattan's case in an entirely new light. For the Crown, John Griffith Williams QC accepted that the testimony of the two principal prosecution witnesses could no longer be considered reliable. Evidence which had only just become available indicated that another Somali sailor, Tahir Gass (34), had at the time of the murder been identified by Harold Cover as being at the crime scene. Not only had Mattan's defence lawyers not been told of this, but two years later Gass had been convicted of another murder! Gass arrived in Newport, Monmouthshire, in 1949 seeking work as a sailor, taking lodgings in Ruperra Street with a Somali man called Egah who with his wife ran a boarding-house for his fellow-countrymen. Gass spoke little English and his behaviour was odd enough for him to become known as "the crazy Somali," both in Newport and in Cardiff's Tiger Bay area. Apart from his clothes his sole permanent possessions were two knives and a grinding stone which he used to sharpen them. Early in June 1954 the seaman told his landlord that he had no work and his unemployment money was insufficient. At first Egah tried to help him, but on June 8th he told him he must leave his room. Gass spent the next two days in a wood near the village of St. Brides between Newport and Cardiff, building himself a shelter with tree branches ….

On June 10th, however, the villagers became concerned about him and called the police, who found him asleep in a hedgerow. He told them he was part of nature and wanted to live in it. But he added that he had to go to Newport to collect his unemployment money, and he was due to be in the town on **Saturday, June 12th, 1954** …. He had committed no offence so he was allowed to go on his way, and on June 11th he returned to Egah's boarding-house, pleading to be allowed to reoccupy his room. Egah wanted him to leave, and as Gass was carrying a hatchet the landlord called the police. A detective constable asked Gass to leave. After explaining that he used the hatchet to chop wood, Gass departed. The next day was a Saturday, and Granville Jenkins, a 45-year-old wages clerk, was helping his friend Thomas Nicholas on his St. Brides farm. Shortly after 11 a.m. Mr. Nicholas asked Jenkins to lead a horse from the farmyard to an outbuilding a mile away. Jenkins was then to wait at the outbuilding for the farmer to pick him up in his lorry. Mr. Nicholas was driving towards the outbuilding when he saw the horse approaching him unattended. He stopped his lorry, caught the horse, and called out for Jenkins. Receiving no reply, he looked around and saw a haversack on the roadside. Then he found a scrap of paper which turned out to be a letter from the Newport unemployment office. A trail of trampled grass then led him to a stream where he found his friend's dead body. He rushed to Coedkernew where he alerted the police, who that afternoon saw a foreign-looking man acting suspiciously near a local farm. They recognised him as the Somali they had encountered two days earlier, and when he began to run away as they approached, they pursued him. On being cornered, he produced a knife. But when the officers drew their truncheons he dropped his knife, collapsed and was taken to Newport police headquarters. There the police surgeon refused to allow officers to question him as he believed the man had suffered a fit. Another knife was found at the murder scene ….

Granville Jenkins had received 32 stab wounds to his head, face and back. Many were superficial, but his left ear had been cut through, he had a deep gash across his forehead and the main artery in his throat had been severed. He had not been robbed, and his murder had no apparent motive. When Gass was fit to be questioned he denied killing Jenkins, but the knife found at the scene was identified as his, and two farm workers had seen him shortly before the attack. His overcoat, with his name inside, was also found near the stream, together with a tea cosy to which he was known to be attached ….

When Tahir Gass's trial began at Newport Assizes on November 8th, 1954, his defence counsel sought a verdict of guilty but insane. The court heard that while in custody he claimed that the police were giving him electric shocks. For that reason he could not be left in a room with electric fittings, for he destroyed them. Asking for a room without a door, he said that an intruder was going to kill him. When he was placed in a padded cell he said four men were going to rape him and he then wrecked the cell, trying to get out. A medical witness testified that Gass was schizophrenic and had been for many years. Another doctor said Gass claimed to be the son of the King of Somalia, and to have killed 2,000 white men and 1,000 black men while fighting for the British in the Second World War. Concluding that the prisoner was insane, the doctor said Gass was obsessed with the idea that he would be raped and it was a reason for his carrying a knife. The prosecution called no medical evidence and the jury found Gass guilty but insane and he was committed to Broadmoor on the next day [November 9th, 1954] ….

A year later he was deported to his native country, and the authorities thought that was the last they would hear of him. But in February 1998 Gass's name surfaced as the Court of Appeal considered Mattan's case after it had been referred to them by the Criminal Cases Review Commission [CCRC] a body set up in 1997 to investigate potential miscarriages of justices – old and new …. Michael Mansfield, QC for Mattan, said the hanged man's lawyers had discovered fresh evidence while examining documents not made available to his defence counsel in 1952. They had found a note which revealed that Harold Cover had told Detective Inspector Loudon Roberts that he had seen two Somali men at the scene. One of them, seen coming out of the shop, was five-foot-10, between 30 and 40, tall and slim, and had a gold tooth. The other, aged 25 to 30, was a few yards away, near the shop window. Inspector Roberts's note indicated that Cover identified the man leaving the shop as Gass, but in court the witness named Mattan as the man coming out of the doorway, and had not mentioned Gass. "The note was of crucial importance," said Mr. Mansfield. "It showed that a senior officer twice recorded the fact that Gass was thought to be the man in the doorway and not Mattan." Mr. Griffith Williams said that further inquiries had been made about Gass, and the Crown Prosecution Service had learned of his subsequent murder conviction. A description of Gass circulated at the time of the investigation was similar to that given by Cover of the man he saw emerging from Lily Volpert's shop doorway: "Somali, 5ft 7in, of slim build and with a gold tooth." That tooth, said Mr. Mansfield, was the final piece of the jigsaw which proved Mattan's innocence ….

Outside the court Mr. Cover, now 78, said that if Mattan was innocent, then he was pleased for his family. "I never accused him. I just said what I saw." Among those present in court was Mattan's widow, 22 at the time of the murder. The family had heard the presiding judge, Lord Justice Rose, quash Mahmood Mattan's conviction as unsafe. Sitting with Justice Holland and Justice Penry-Davey, he said: "It is, of course, a matter for very profound regret that in 1952 Mr. Mattan was convicted and hanged, and that it has taken forty-six years for that conviction to be shown to be unsafe." The judge added that the case showed that "capital punishment was not perhaps a prudent culmination for a criminal justice system which is human and therefore fallible." But for Mahmood Hussein Mattan that realisation had come too late. Instead, he had acquired the distinction of becoming the last person hanged at Cardiff Prison ….

Case 2
"Swindon's Coronation Day Murder"

"The Courts had gone to bed and were woken up at 11.45, from which it was obvious that Mrs. Court was wanted. Greenway taxed her with having given such food that his friend had left, and he showed her the letter" ….

"He knows that doctors have seen him with a view to showing he was not responsible when the act was committed. He still remains absolutely determined to plead guilty" ....

John GREENWAY
MURDER
Of
Beatrice Court
[1953]

The body of landlady Beatrice Court was found in the kitchen of her College Street, Swindon, home. A heavily bloodstained hatchet lay where it was dropped by the assailant – the victim's skull had several fractures consistent with having been inflicted by an axe …. "I have murdered Mrs. Court, the landlady. I don't think I got any chance. I killed her. If Chris gets in touch with you ask him to forgive me, but I missed him so much" ….

The day was eventful for everyone, and for two 27-year-olds in particular. One was crowned Queen of the United Kingdom of Gt. Britain & Northern Ireland and her Dominions. The other also made headlines – but of a different nature. It was **Tuesday, June 2nd, 1953**, and it started well enough for John Owen Greenway, who in 1952 had moved from his home town of Pontypridd in South Wales to a new job as a machine operator at a factory in Swindon. He had seemed quite happy when he returned to Wales for Christmas and the New Year. Although he tended to be quiet and reserved, preferring his own company, from what he told his family they gathered that he'd found a good friend in Swindon, and was enjoying life. But he didn't have much to say about his accommodation; in fact he seemed reluctant to say where he was staying. He had found lodgings at 22,

College Street, the home of 68-year-old Mrs. Beatrice Ann Court and her invalid husband, who suffered from heart trouble. The Courts took in lodgers not by choice but through financial necessity. They had two spare bedrooms, and soon found a lodger for one of them – Arthur Polsue, a commercial traveller from St. Albans ….

Then John Greenway arrived at the same time as another young man seeking accommodation: Christopher Percy. Mrs. Court was reluctant to turn either away, but she had only the one vacant room. Greenway and Percy told her that it was no problem – they'd be happy to share the room and its double bed. If the landlady had any misgivings about this arrangement, she didn't display them. The two newcomers seemed to take to each other straight away, and it soon became apparent that theirs was something more than just a casual friendship. Gay relationships at that time were illegal, and Mrs. Court became concerned about what her neighbours might think – and even whether Greenway and Percy might attract police attention. But she contented herself with asking the two to be discreet. She needed their money. Life continued happily enough at 22, College Street until spring, when Percy began complaining about the food. First he said there wasn't enough, and then he criticised the quality. Greenway kept quiet. Fearing that Mrs. Court would tell Percy to leave, he asked him not to complain any more ….

The trouble seemed to blow over, but when Greenway returned from work on May 29th Mrs. Court told him there was a letter for him on his bed. Assuming it was from home, he went upstairs to get it, and was surprised to see that the envelope bore only his name. Even before he had opened it, he knew it was from Percy. "Get out from here as quick as you can," the letter concluded, "as it is the worst food we have ever had in our lives. I have gone. God knows where. Broken-hearted – Chris." In tears, Greenway read the letter again. It told him to phone Percy's sister for his new address. He did so the following day, phoning again on Monday, June 1st, and a third time on the evening of June 2nd. He also telephoned his own married sister, telling her of Percy's sudden departure, and talking of suicide ….

What happened after that was described by P. F. Y. Radcliffe, prosecuting, when Greenway subsequently appeared before Swindon magistrates, when charged with his landlady's murder. Mr. Radcliffe told the court that two of Mrs. Court's lodgers, Greenway and Percy, "had a strong affection for each other. Of their own volition they occupied a double bed in a room upstairs." Mr. Radcliffe went on to say that on May 29th Percy left a note for Greenway "and went back to Wales, from where both these men came." After making a third phone call to Percy's sister, Greenway returned to his lodgings at about 11.30 p.m. on June 2nd. "The Courts had gone to bed and were woken up at 11.45, from which it was obvious that Mrs. Court was wanted. Greenway taxed her with having given such food that his friend had left, and he showed her the letter. According to the defendant, she said it was not her fault, and thereupon she was, on his own admission, attacked with one of the hatchets kept in the kitchen for ordinary use in the house. This caused a good deal of commotion. Mr. Court came out into the passage, and the accused ran and attacked him, though in no serious way. He was injured in the hand. Polsue had also come down, and by 12.15 a.m. a passing police officer was in the house." ….

Mr. Radcliffe said that Greenway later asked Detective Sergeant R. F. Cuss, "How is she? What have I done? Is she dead?" Dr. G. W. D. Henderson, a consultant pathologist, told the magistrates that the cause of Mrs. Court's death was "destruction of part of the brain by violence with resultant bleeding." Her skull was slightly thinner than normal, and it had several fractures consistent with having been inflicted by an axe. A heavily bloodstained hatchet found at the scene was then produced in court; a forensic scientist testifying that hairs found sticking to it were indistinguishable from those of Mrs. Court. Arthur Polsue said, "I went to bed about 11 p.m. on June 2nd, but was woken up by noises. It sounded as though someone was moving furniture. After a bit I got out of bed and went downstairs. I saw Mr. Court lying on the floor at the foot of the stairs. He was wearing pyjamas and was shouting. I fetched assistance and then helped Mr. Court to his bed. In the kitchen I saw Mrs. Court on a chair. I saw the accused sitting on a chair by the sideboard." In response to a question from Mr. Radcliffe, he said the food at the lodgings was "appalling." In the dock Greenway sat back and smiled.

Inspector S. J. Young told the court that on entering the kitchen at 22, College Street he saw the dead woman ….

A hatchet lay on the floor and Greenway was sitting in a chair by the connecting door to the scullery. "He had his head in his hands and was crying. I said 'What has happened?' "At first he did not reply and then he said, 'Don't let me see her.' "I repeated my question, and he said, 'It's that letter. I will tell you all about it.'" The inspector said that Greenway then stood up, but was in a state of collapse and repeated, "Don't let me see her." Taken to the police station and charged with Mrs. Court's murder, he said, "There is nothing to say." On being asked if he understood the charge he just shrugged his shoulders. A neighbour told the magistrates that he had been called from his bed on the night of June 2nd. On going next door to 22, College Street, he saw Greenway put his hands on the sideboard in the kitchen. "Was there blood on them?" asked Mr. Radcliffe. "There was blood on the right hand." Detective Sergeant Cuss testified that in a statement Greenway said, "I had it in for her because she made Chris go away. I was worried last night because I did not hear from Chris. I had a few drinks and it was on my mind that she had made Chris leave me. I do not even know where he has gone. I got hold of her round the throat and said, 'I could kill you for the way you have treated us.' She screamed and I heard Mr. Court shouting, 'Murder!' I got frightened then, and got a hatchet from the back kitchen and hit her on the head with it." Sergeant Cuss then read out a letter which he said Greenway had written to his sister ….

Senior officers had considered it too crude to be forwarded, the sister meanwhile having been notified of the situation. The letter said, "I have murdered Mrs. Court, the landlady …. I don't think I got any chance. I killed her. If Chris gets in touch with you ask him to forgive me, but I missed him so much." Giving a Cardiff address, Christopher Percy told the court that he had known Greenway for about six years, and they had both gone to take lodgings at Mrs. Court's home in April. "We shared a room with one double bed. The food was very, very poor. It was so poor that I left on May 29th. I left a note for him. I said I would ring his sister on Saturday night. I rang later but cannot be sure if it was Saturday. I had decided to leave Swindon until I had settled some of my domestic problems in south

Wales." Cross-examined by J.D. Morrison, defending, he said, "I left because of my domestic affairs, and because of the food. The accused did not know about my domestic affairs." It transpired that Percy was married and seeking a divorce ....

Greenway's sister told the magistrates that John had lived with his parents until September 1952, then moved to Swindon, and one evening he phoned telling her to expect a call from Percy, who telephoned on the Monday. That night her brother phoned again. "He seemed upset. He said if Percy did not come back he would take his life. My brother rang a third time on Coronation Night, expecting a message from Percy. But Percy did not ring. I told him that Percy had not rung, and there was no message. My brother seemed rather upset." At the conclusion of the hearing Greenway was remanded in custody to await trial at the Devizes Assizes, where on October 2nd, 1953, he *pleaded guilty* to Beatrice Court's murder. "This is an unusual type of case, and an unusual course for a prisoner to take on this particular charge," his defending counsel, A. C. Munro Kerr, told
Justice Hubert Parker. "I have seen him, the other defending counsel Mr. Inskip has seen him, my
instructing solicitors have seen him, and two doctors have seen him. Although had the plea been one of not guilty there would have been an issue as to his state of mind at the time of the alleged killing, I am not in a position to say that he is unfit to plead. Nor am I in a position to say that he does not understand the effect of the plea. He seems to be wholly logical about it. He seems to wish to die. That is why he wants to plead guilty. I have explained the matter to the best of my ability, and other people have explained the situation. He knows that doctors have seen him with a view to showing he was not responsible when the act was committed ....

He still remains absolutely determined to plead guilty." "Do you appreciate what you are doing?" Greenway was asked by the judge. "Yes." "Is that your final decision?" "Yes ...." "Then there is only one sentence which this court can pass upon you," Justice Parker concluded, proceeding to sentence John Greenway to death. Having told his solicitor that he did not wish to seek a reprieve, the killer with a death wish wrote no letters from the condemned cell, and refused to see any visitors – not even his parents or sister. On Tuesday, October 20th, 1953, he was hanged at Bristol Prison by Albert Pierrepoint, assisted by Harry Allen ….

Case 3
"Murder In Northumberland Terrace"

Thomas EAMES
MURDER
Of
Muriel Bent
[1952]

Ordinarily, Muriel would have melted Thomas's anger. But this was no ordinary confrontation. It had gone too far. Instead of *burying his face in her chest he buried a knife in her back …. "As she was kissing me it flashed in my head, 'Now is the time. Now I must do it.' I drew the knife out of my pocket and stabbed her in the back while kissing her" ….*

Withdrawn, moody, depressed. Thomas Eames was all these, and never more so than on **Wednesday, February 27th, 1952**. That morning he asked a workmate to lend him his file. The workmate watched in surprise as Eames used it to transform a table-knife into a dagger. If Eames had shared his troubles at work, what happened later that day might have been averted. The possible significance of his filing that knife to a stiletto-like point might have been recognised. But Eames kept his problems to himself. He'd always been quiet and reserved, and his colleagues had noticed no great change in his demeanour. His troubles could be said to have begun a decade earlier when Britain was at war and he was called up for the army. His wife, already disgruntled, told him she would have nothing more to do with him and left their home, taking with her their baby daughter, who had been born in 1940. He was 26 when he returned to his native Plymouth seven years later to live with his parents. Finding work as a labourer was easy as wartime bombs had devastated the city. During work hours and after, Eames seldom socialised, but Christmas Eve, 1947, was an exception. He enjoyed a beer or two with his workmates at the building site where he was employed, agreeing to see them again in the city that evening. Knowing he was shy, they catered for this in their arrangements. When his three workmates met him in the first pub that night each was accompanied by a girlfriend. And for Eames they had brought along Muriel Elsie Bent, an attractive 21-year-old ….

No great conversationalist, Eames told her she looked too young to be allowed in a pub. Then he blushed, realising this was less than tactful. Muriel laughed, put her arm round him and told him she liked him. This put him at ease. He no longer blurted out the first thing that came into his head and his gentle nature soon shone through. At the end of the evening he asked Muriel for a cinema date.

She said yes and kissed him on the cheek. They saw each other every night for the next six weeks, then Muriel happily accepted his offer of marriage. He omitted to mention that he already had a wife and a seven-year-old child. When he suggested a quiet wedding Muriel put this down to his shyness. She was unaware that he had told none of his relatives he was to be married, and he failed to realise that for her part Muriel would observe no such secrecy. Inevitably, news of her "marriage" subsequently reached the authorities and Eames was charged with bigamy ….

The court took a lenient view after hearing that for the past eight years he had neither seen nor spoken to his wife. This saved him from prison. He was given a nominal sentence of two days in custody and he and Muriel later left his parents' house, moving to 3, Northumberland Terrace in the Plymouth district of West Hoe. Neither, however, was destined to live happily ever after. Their relationship soured and the birth of a child did little to improve it. Although Eames remained devoted to his common-law wife, she told him she no longer loved him. She preferred the company of the girlfriends with whom she went out, and at weekends she stayed with her parents, who lived nearby. Muriel subsequently left Northumberland Terrace altogether, and as 1951 drew to a close Eames began to suspect that it wasn't just girlfriends she was seeing. Early the following February he saw her arm-in arm with a man in the city centre. He went back to Northumberland Terrace and wept. Then in an act of self-torture he returned to the city centre and again saw Muriel with her companion. This time he summoned the courage to confront them. Muriel told him to grow up, and he slunk home to brood. He stopped eating and his few friends became concerned about him. One of them was his brother-in-law on whom he called on Saturday, February 23rd, asking to use his telephone to call the NSPCC because he was worried about his child ….

For the next three days Eames visited his brother-in-law each evening. The man thought he looked very ill, and noticed that his hands were shaking. On the Wednesday, however, Eames did not visit his brother-in-law. On the previous day he had seen Muriel and her man friend again. He told her a letter had arrived for her at Northumberland Terrace and invited her home to collect it. She told him to get lost, adding that she would pick it up the next day. It was February 27th when Eames arrived at work with the five-inch table-knife which he filed in front of a workmate. This took 30 minutes and was virtually completed when the site foreman ordered Eames back to work. Saying he was ill, Eames slipped the "dagger" into the front of his overalls and left the building site. Shortly after 6 p.m. Muriel arrived at Northumberland Terrace and asked for her letter. Eames begged her to stay for a few minutes. He asked if she intended to marry her boyfriend and she said she did. "You will not!" the normally quiet Eames suddenly screamed. Hitting her, he shouted, "If I can't have you, nobody will!" Moved by fear or by the depth of his distress, Muriel began kissing him passionately. Ordinarily this would have melted Eames's anger. In tears, he would have buried his face in her chest. But this was no ordinary confrontation. It had gone too far for Muriel's act of submission to work ….

Instead of burying his face in her chest, Eames buried his knife in her back. "I love you," he groaned as he thrust the blade home. "Goodbye," she gasped as she slumped into his arms. As Muriel fell to the floor Thomas sensed she was still alive, so he stabbed her again. Then he went to see his brother-in-law. "Well, the pain has all gone now," Eames said, telling him what he had done. They went together to Plymouth's Octagon police station, where after reporting the killing the brother-in-law told officers that Eames said he hadn't eaten for four days, had severe stomach pains and hadn't slept for weeks. Noting that Eames was now smiling, the brother-in-law added that he was the gentlest man he had ever known and the last person he would have associated with violence. Returning from the scene of the crime, Superintendent W. A. McConnach told Eames: "I have been to your home where I have seen the body of a woman who has been stabbed in the back and in the front. She is dead." At 1.40 a.m. Thomas Eames was charged with Muriel Bent's murder. Later that day Plymouth magistrates were told by Superintendent McConnach that Eames had made a statement in which he said, "Yes, I killed her. I want to tell you all about it. I have nothing to hide." ….

"A deliberate killing born out of jealousy," was how the crime was described by the prosecution when Thomas Eames appeared at

Exeter Assizes on June 23rd .... He pleaded not guilty. For the Crown, the Hon. Ewan Montagu QC quoted a statement in which Eames said that he and Muriel quarrelled throughout the time they lived together. At the time of the killing he told her that if he couldn't have her, "nobody else will." "She kissed me. As she was kissing me it flashed in my head, 'Now is the time. Now I must do it.' I drew the knife out of my pocket and stabbed her in the back while kissing her. She said, 'Goodbye.' I thought she was not quite dead so I stabbed her again so that she would not linger." Several witnesses called by the defence testified that they had always known Eames as kind and gentle. His brother described him as "a decent fellow," while a woman neighbour said he had always been "affectionate to his family, quiet in his manner and clean-living." Eames was now 31, and his daughter by his marriage was 12. Muriel Bent had been 26. Eames's brother-in-law told the court that the defendant called on him at 8.30 on the night of the killing, saying that the pain in his stomach had gone. "He was smiling and was his normal self again." Eames then told his brother-in-law what had happened ....

Questioning the witness about Eames's previous visits, N. F. Fox Andrews QC, defending, asked: "It was quite plain he was beside himself?" "He was," the witness replied. The defence counsel then submitted that if Eames did not know what he was doing when he thrust the knife into the victim's back, it did not matter if he contemplated doing it or if realisation came to him afterwards. "The question," Mr. Fox-Andrews told the jury, "is whether at the time he struck the blow he knew what he was doing. If, looking at the whole of the evidence, you take the view that at that moment he did not know what he was doing then you will be entitled to, and it would be your duty to, return a verdict of guilty but insane." Summing-up, Justice George Lynskey reminded the jury that two doctors had testified that Thomas Eames was sane, but they had said it was possible for people who were worried, sleepless and had not eaten to commit an act of violence without knowing it. However, the judge pointed out, the jury must take into account the fact that Eames had stabbed his victim twice. After a brief retirement of 15 minutes the jury found Thomas Eames guilty of murder. They coupled their verdict with a strong recommendation to mercy on the grounds of provocation and diminished responsibility ....

As the death sentence was passed Eames made the sign of the cross. His solicitor, Cecil Howlett, said that in view of the jury's recommendation an appeal would be made to the Home Secretary for clemency. But in view of the evidence there would be no appeal to the Appeal Court. There was no reprieve, however, the Home Secretary deciding that there were not sufficient grounds for interfering with the due course of law. Consequently, on Tuesday, July 15th, 1952, hangman Albert Pierrepoint placed his hand on Thomas Eames's shoulder in Bristol Prison. "It's time to go, son," he said. "I know," Eames replied quietly. "I am quite happy to go." …. But Eames did not go quietly to the gallows with Pierrepoint and his assistant Robert Stewart: he had to be dragged with help of prison-officers fighting and kicking as he struggled all the way to the drop …. Then in a fraction of a second he was dead ….

Case 4
"An Innocent Man Executed"

Harry GLEESON
MURDER
Of
Mary McCarthy
[1941]

For some reason the Garda wanted Harry Gleeson convicted of Mary McCarthy's murder and anyone, like Tommy Reid, who had other information was to have it knocked out of them ....

No one saw the murder of Mary McCarthy. No one, not even the experts who filed in and out of court, could even say which day it happened. No murder weapon, the actual shotgun, was ever identified. No direct evidence could be laid at the door of any man in the village of New Inn, near where Mary lived, in rural Co Tipperary. But someone, the Garda decided, had to hang for it. Almost like sticking a pin in the electoral roll, they picked farmer Harry Gleeson, who was also known as Henry .... "He's Mary McCarthy's nearest neighbour," their argument ran. "He's single, she's promiscuous, so he must have been having an affair with her." That was the start of what must rate as one of the greatest modern travesties of Irish legal history, a travesty in which the real culprits were a parish priest, corrupt police, an incompetent judge, and a bunch of villagers who erected a wall of silence around the death of Mary McCarthy. If there is such a thing as an unlikely candidate for the gallows, Harry Gleeson fitted the bill. He was born in 1903 only 20 miles from New Inn, one of 12 children who grew up on his parents' prosperous farm. He was almost six feet tall and in his youth he was a notable athlete. But his two favourite pastimes had little to do with athletics ….

The first was his fiddling. The Gleesons were a musical family and Harry was given a fiddle almost as soon as he could walk. From his teens he was the star musical turn at the New Inn community gatherings. He was, said one of his fans, "exceptionally gifted." His second pastime was his passion for breeding and training greyhounds. Gleeson was also a much admired farm manager, described as "efficient, industrious, even meticulous," in his work, forming a partnership with a friend to carry out farming operations across Co Tipperary. In the 1940s when there was a crisis people went at once for guidance to their local priest. Harry Gleeson was no exception. He lived a God-fearing life, went to church every Sunday and was highly regarded in the diocese. How then did this paragon of so many virtues find himself at the centre of this New Inn murder and on trial for his life? The answer, needless to say, was feminine. It was one of the extraordinary paradoxes of Irish rural life that good, socially-minded men like Harry Gleeson could live in the same tightly-knit religious community as flame-haired Mary McCarthy. When she moved to Marlhill, near New Inn, she had already started a brood of children, each fathered by a different man, in open defiance of the rules and conventions that bound the rest of rural Ireland ….

By 1940 she had seven such children, but there had been others who were stillborn and others who didn't live long. Six of the seven reputed fathers of the children born alive were local residents, the other being from outside Tipperary. On a two-acre field next to her cottage Mary kept a greyhound, a donkey and a herd of goats. On three sides her property was surrounded by the farm of John Caesar, Harry Gleeson's home and workplace for most of his adult life. Mary's lovers came mostly from the agricultural community, but at least two local police sergeants were regular visitors to her cottage. She was reported never to consort with more than one man at a time and she didn't ask money for her sexual favours. She put it about that she expected the local farmers to leave firewood, feed for her animals and potatoes for her children by her back door. If they didn't, well, she also put it about that she kept a visitors' book in which names were named. Mary taunted the respectable village women, who were scandalised by her. She told one of them: "I'll have as many men as I can get in me bed, and I'll never be married and respectable like you if I live to be a thousand years." The wives turned their back and crossed themselves, aware that at least seven among their number had betrayed them with "Foxy Moll" as she was known. The wives hated Foxy Moll. As for the men, the innocent among them shifted about uneasily whenever her name was mentioned, while the guilty, who were in the majority, thought of her with lascivious and secret fondness. Although she was nearly 40, Moll was very attractive, and she could spread out a pair of loving arms that could make most men shudder ….

Moll McCarthy, as she was also known, was "the devil's disciple" according to local parish priest Father Edward Murphy. He denounced her from the pulpit and refused to condemn whoever it was who one night burnt the thatched roof of Foxy Moll's overcrowded little cottage at Marlhill. The cottage – it was more of a hovel really – had only two rooms. When visitors arrived the seven kids were huddled into one of them while the other room was given over to "entertaining." For all the lowness of her reputation, Moll McCarthy held her head high. She fought back at the village wives. She went to the school to pick up her kids and proclaimed from the pavement that she was every bit as good a mother as any other mother in New Inn. Her kids would have agreed with that too – they adored her. Her nearest neighbour, 38-year-old Harry Gleeson, lived 400 yards away, but superficially at least their worlds were miles apart. Or were they? There were dark whisperings in New Inn that the father of Foxy Moll's latest child was none other than Harry Gleeson. He had been seen visiting her at night, he had been seen arguing with her after the child was born. Someone even said she had been heard to say she would set the police on him. "Rubbish!" replied Harry Gleeson when he heard about it. "It's all village talk. And there are some liars in this village." Harry had known Moll for about 15 years. He moved into the farmhouse where he lived in 1920, when his uncle, John Caesar, owner of the 75-acre farm, offered him a partnership in it. The Caesars were childless and saw the likeable Harry as a sort of vicarious son. When Uncle John decided to put his feet up in 1938 he knew he could leave the farm management in the safe hands of Harry ….

Also living in the farmhouse was Harry's cousin, Thomas Reid. Harry and Tommy frequently worked together and this they were planning to do when they awoke on the morning of **Thursday, November 21st, 1940** …. Harry was the first to get up. While Tommy stayed on slumbering, Harry went downstairs in his stockinged feet, so as not to wake Mr. and Mrs. Caesar sleeping in the ground-floor bedroom, lit the fire in the kitchen grate and prepared breakfast, which would be taken later. When all was ready he went back upstairs to wake Tommy. That was a year, it should be said, when Western Europe was in the terrible turmoil of war. Although Ireland was neutral and her menfolk were therefore untouched by the conflict, the world situation created a general shortage of food in the country and home-produced food was vital for the survival of the Irish. Although that Thursday morning was bitterly cold and it had been raining all night, they set out with a will to do their chores. The time was 8.30. They took a milk pail to the "crib field" where each milked six cows, returning around 9.30 to the farmyard. They left the full pails in the dairy for Mrs. Caesar, then separated, each to do his various jobs alone. While Tommy stayed around the farmyard Harry put one of his greyhounds on a leash to take it for exercise through the fields. This was something he did every morning, always following the same route. As he went from field to field he counted his uncle's sheep, lest any of them should have gone missing or strayed. He also collected a straying bull, which had wandered on to a neighbouring farm. In the third field he crossed he unleashed the greyhound, as there were no farm animals around ….

By 10 o'clock he was passing Moll McCarthy's cottage. They were good neighbours, although he frequently chided her for the damage her goats did to the Caesar farm. He never had a second thought about taking his dogs on a short cut across her land to get back to his farm. It was then that his eye caught some bushes. He had planted them some days earlier to block a gap in a stone wall to the next field – now someone had pushed them to one side. He climbed a little way up on the wall to determine the cause of the problem. As his gaze swept the immediate vicinity he froze. Lying in the field – called locally Dug-Out Field – in front of him was the body of a woman. He could see that her face was badly mutilated, so he couldn't recognise her, although he suspected from her clothes that it might be Moll McCarthy. But further investigation was prevented by a small black dog, sitting on her chest, snarling and snapping at him. Harry ran back to the farm and roused his aunt and uncle, then ran to the police station. Breathlessly he reported having seen a woman lying in the field. He did not know for certain who she was …. He brought two officers, Garda Vincent Scully and Sergeant Anthony Daly, back to the field with the body in it. Daly recognised it at once as Moll. He could tell at once that she was dead, and was later to say that he was amazed that Harry hadn't recognised her. The police covered the body with a tarpaulin and began questioning the villagers ....

It wasn't until 10.15 a.m. the following day, Friday, that pathologist Dr. John McGrath arrived to make a preliminary examination of the body. This was 24 hours after it was found, and it was still lying in the same position in the field. Later Dr. McGrath conducted a more detailed examination, revealing that Moll had died from the effects of two gunshot wounds to the head. Her skull was fractured in several places, her jugular vein had been punctured, her spine had been fractured. One whole side of her face was missing, from the chin right up to her eyebrow. Pieces of bone and two teeth were found nearly a foot away from the body. After the examination Dr. McGrath became violently ill. His assumption of the time of death was at best unhelpful. He thought Moll died at any time from 1.50 p.m. on Wednesday – the day before she was found dead – and 9.30 p.m. on Thursday, which was almost 11 hours after Harry Gleeson went to the police station. The body, it was believed, had been moved after she was hit by the first shot, and dumped in a way that suggested it was lifted over the stone wall. Despite the prolonged rain of the night of Wednesday to Thursday, the grass and stones under the body were dry, suggesting that she might have been killed before the rain set in on Wednesday evening ....

That didn't prevent Superintendent Mahoney from deciding that she was killed after 8 a.m. on Thursday, just a couple of hours before the body was discovered. Superintendent Mahoney reasoned that if she had disappeared any earlier than that it would have been before her children went to school, and they would have raised the alarm. Had he known Moll better, he would have been aware that she frequently disappeared for long periods with her men friends, and her children had long since grown accustomed to these absences. Every male in New Inn was a suspect, but very soon it emerged that the Garda had decided that someone from the Caesar farm was more suspect than others, only because their farm was closest to Moll's. When Mahoney had decided to eliminate Tommy Reid and John Caesar, that left only Harry Gleeson, "When did you last see Miss McCarthy?" Mahoney asked him. Gleeson said that it was on Tuesday afternoon some 200 to 300 yards from him in her own field.

There was no conversation between them. "I see you're not a married man," the superintendent observed. By this time he had been briefed on the nature of the victim. "How long have you known her?" "For fifteen years, eight years after I first arrived here," replied Gleeson. "We allow her to draw water from our well every day." "And her children? Are you responsible for any of them?" "No, I am not." ….

One by one Gleeson itemised Moll's children, telling the officer who was the father of each one – a complete list probably not known to anyone else in the village. Given the character of most of the villagers, that was perhaps information that could have made him some enemies. Mahoney left deep in thought, but three days later he came back with Sergeant Daly. This time they wanted to see some of Harry Gleeson's gun-cartridges and some of his clothes. Mahoney didn't make it much of a secret that he suspected Gleeson of killing Moll. Daly had told him that according to local gossip Gleeson was the father of Moll's last child, a claim always strenuously denied by the young farmer. Even if it were true, it would hardly make him a murderer, a fact which seemed to pass over the superintendent. "When did you last use your uncle's gun?" Mahoney demanded to know. "That would be back in the last harvest time." The last harvest was two months previously. The only use the family made of the gun was to clear vermin from their land. "I hear you give potatoes and firewood to Miss McCarthy. Is that right?" "Yes, that is so." "Did you tell your uncle about that?" "No, I did not." Much of a to-do was later made of the fact that Gleeson didn't tell John Caesar that he gave a few potatoes to Moll. But Moll was the recipient of a number of similar gifts from other farmers, and the majority of them were not her sleeping partners ….

Many of these gifts were simply left at her door as an act of kindness to the less well off. While Harry was being questioned, Tommy Reid was in New Inn, delivering milk. As he passed the Garda station, Garda Frank Gralton, standing at the door, called him inside. Tommy's heart sank, for Frank Gralton was a feared policeman in New Inn. He had once been a member of the Royal Irish Constabulary, and his brutal reputation made him a man to be avoided at all costs. Suffice it to say that Tommy Reid delivered no more milk in the village that day. Thirteen hours after reluctantly entering the Garda station, he left with a black eye – certified in a doctor's report as "a two-inch abrasion in front of the left ear, consistent with having been struck by a fist," and a puffed and swollen face. His aunt, John Caesar's wife, was furious when he arrived back at their farm at Marlhill, and she complained bitterly to Superintendent Mahoney. He replied with astonishing candour: "Sometimes you have to knock out of a fellow what's in him." What was "in" Tommy Reid was the exact whereabouts, the precise movements of his cousin Harry Gleeson on Thursday, November 21st, when, the Garda had decided, Moll was killed. For some reason they wanted Harry Gleeson, who they knew was innocent, convicted, and anyone like Tommy Reid who might stand in their way was to have it knocked out of him. This was by no means the only unorthodox act performed by the Garda in this case ….

Long before Gleeson's arrest they were already trying to bring influences to bear on getting him to change his defending solicitor, John Timoney, to one of their own choosing. When they wanted to find out something about John Caesar's ammunition store, two detectives visited Feehan's hardware store in Cashel, where most of the ammunition used in the New Inn area was purchased. They inspected the firearms register and pointed out to the staff that it contained no record of any sale to John Caesar, on a particular date that they mentioned. They also identified the type of ammunition that should be entered. As they left, they said threateningly to the staff that on their next visit they expected to find such an entry in the register. And they did subsequently find it. The firearms register was amended to show that early in July, John Caesar purchased ammunition at the store. To make the entry, the staff crossed out another purchase by someone else and wrote the John Caesar "purchase," cramped between two lines, above it. When Harry Gleeson was arrested for the murder on November 30th he answered using a form of speech he was to use several times subsequently: "I had neither hand, act, or part in it." As he was committed for trial from the district court he remarked to a friend, "They'd hang you with lies here." The way the Garda would present their case against Gleeson was that in their view he did meet Moll on Tuesday and they agreed to meet again the next day, Wednesday, when he would return to her a bag she had given him on Tuesday, now filled with potatoes. At this second meeting at dusk, it would be alleged, he killed her, and the next morning he "discovered" her body ….

This of course was at odds with Superintendent Mahoney's view that Moll was killed on Thursday morning, but truth to tell neither the Garda nor the prosecution at Gleeson's trial could decide on which day Moll was killed – the Wednesday or the Thursday. They started off by charging Gleeson with killing her on the Wednesday, then amended the charge on the day of the trial to read Wednesday or Thursday, shifting the "evidence" about accordingly. The motive, they decided, was that Gleeson didn't want it known that he had fathered her last child. Their theory was that should the Caesars be convinced that an immoral relationship existed, Gleeson's prospects of inheriting the farm would be gone. So he killed her. The Garda built this idea up from interviews with three of Moll's children, one of whom was said to be backward. Of the other two, one, Michael, was 12 and the other, Patrick, was scarcely into his teens. They mostly relied on the youngest boy, Michael, who couldn't count beyond 10, couldn't read a clock, and made a statement which was riddled with glaring inconsistencies. The tenor of his story was that in June he had seen Harry Gleeson and his mother arguing – he called it "fighting" – over the paternity of her last child, and his mother told Gleeson that "she would put him up to law to pay for the child." ….

To further the Garda case, Superintendent Mahoney took Gleeson to the McCarthy home on November 26th, and confronted him with Paddy and Michael in their farmyard. The two boys accused Gleeson in no uncertain terms of being the father of their mother's last child and at one stage Gleeson said, "Your mother was a liar – the Lord have mercy on her soul." It is difficult, when studying the transcript of the conversation, not to believe that this confrontation with the two boys was deliberately orchestrated. Nonetheless, Michael was the principal prosecution witness at the committal proceedings. He told the district court that he last saw his mother at six or seven o'clock on Wednesday evening, when she had gone out into the fields with their dog. When she did not return he and his brother Patrick went to look for her. Although she had not returned by bedtime, the older children were not unduly worried because they all knew about their mother's "strange" behaviour. His mother, he said, would often spend the night away, and she often met Harry Gleeson. Whenever he came across his mother and Gleeson talking together, she would tell him to run off home. On one occasion he saw the pair go into a farm outhouse near the water-pump which his mother used every day. The prosecution agreed that all this "scant" evidence was purely circumstantial, but it seems it was enough to commit Gleeson for trial, despite a protest by his barrister that the prosecution had not provided a case for him to answer ....

When Gleeson finally came to trial at the Central Criminal Court in Dublin on February 17th, 1941, in what was to be a 10-day trial, the prosecution ploughed on with a case so fragile that they still couldn't settle on the murder date. Prosecuting, Joseph McCarthy said Gleeson's attempt to pretend not to know the identity of the dead woman when he went first to the police station was "the first of many steps taken by the accused to conceal his association with the cold-blooded and black-hearted act that he had done." Now, suddenly, the prosecution decided that Moll was killed on Wednesday after all. They claimed that Gleeson left his farm at 6.30 p.m. on Wednesday and went out into the fields. Another local farmer heard two shots at this time – although he was the only person who did. Gleeson, said the prosecutor, was trapped by Moll's demands. "He contrived an ambush, trapped and shot her, and attempted to mutilate her beyond all recognition." Gleeson's counsel, Sean McBride, said that on this paltry evidence he found it difficult to believe that his client was standing trial for his life. He claimed that the evidence indicated that Moll was murdered on the Thursday morning, when Gleeson could account for all his movements. This in fact was the view of his own medical expert, who completely discounted the idea that Moll could have been killed on Wednesday ....

In a book about the case, *Murder at Marlhill*, published in 1993, Irish barrister Marcus Bourke points out that to establish evidence of an improper relationship between Gleeson and Moll McCarthy the Garda had only to ask around among the villagers, because everyone knew everyone else's business in New Inn. No such evidence was ever produced. Author Bourke is particularly scathing about the trial judge, Justice Martin Maguire. Several times the judge lost patience with 12-year-old Michael McCarthy, described as "diminutive and timid" – so timid, evidently, that on many occasions he did not reply to the judge's questions. When Dr. McGrath took the stand, "McBride's probing queries seemed to have irked the judge, unaccustomed perhaps to hearing McGrath's views challenged. He frequently intervened (as indeed he did with several other major witnesses) in what to a reader of the transcript years later seems an unjudicial manner." Bourke is almost as critical about Sergeant Daly. "His gruff manner and unco-operative demeanour come through even from the transcript. He gave the impression of a man constantly on his guard, even from the state lawyers. He appears to have been a domineering, even bullying personality, accustomed to getting his own way, economical with the truth, and suspicious of lawyers. Several times, when pressed to amend his account of a conversation, he said bluntly, 'I only heard what I said, that is my answer.' In disagreeing with his own [police] colleagues from New Inn, he went close to calling them perjurers." ….

Bourke insists that Gleeson's trial was seriously flawed – more than that, he claims from start to finish the entire conduct of the court case was biased. He says: "Important portions of the evidence given against Gleeson were presented in an unfair, deceptive or dishonest way. Vital evidence was deliberately concealed, withheld or suppressed by the prosecution. Most serious of all, by his handling of the trial the trial judge, mainly (but by no means exclusively) through his address to the jury after the evidence had concluded, behaved so partially that he effectively denied Gleeson a fair trial." During the 10-day hearing Gleeson conducted himself in an exemplary fashion. On day nine he must have realised that the judge was vehemently against him; he must have recognised the liars among the witnesses. As the court adjourned on that day he passed a friend from Co Tipperary who greeted him. "Say a prayer for me, Billy," Gleeson whispered urgently. While the jury were out, defence counsel made a whole series of objections to the judge's summing-up ….

On the final day of the trial – February 28th—the judge had completely failed to put to the jury the defence submissions about the paternity of the last child. He had also failed to tell the jury that the scene in the farmyard between the two boys and Gleeson had not been put to either boy in the witness-box, and was based entirely on Superintendent Mahoney's account. There had been no reference at all to the defence theory that Moll died on Thursday morning and not on the Wednesday evening. The judge evidently listened, for he recalled the jury and made some new points to them based on these objections. This brought the defence no satisfaction, however, for when the jury returned – after 2 hours and 34 minutes deliberations—they found Harry Gleeson guilty of murder, but added a strong recommendation to mercy. It was an odd verdict. If Gleeson was guilty, the murder was clearly premeditated, and hardly deserving therefore of a mercy recommendation. Were the jurors hedging their bets by trying to ensure he would not hang because the evidence against him was so sparse? "I had neither hand, act or part of it," repeated Gleeson, when asked if he had anything to say. He was sentenced to be hanged ….

In the interval between sentence and appeal, a tailor was found in the village who would say he heard two shots on Thursday morning. The implication was that they could not have been fired by Gleeson because he was then doing his chores with Tommy Reid. This information was conveyed to Father O'Malley, whose comment was "not to bother about it, as it was of no importance, and it was on the Wednesday she was killed." Several other people, it now seemed, had heard shots on Thursday morning. But none of the responsible authorities was interested. The 4-day appeal predictably failed on a raft of technical reasons on April 7th, and despite a local petition for a reprieve, signed by 7,000 people, Gleeson was hanged at Mountjoy Prison, Dublin, on Wednesday, April 23rd, 1941, by Thomas and Albert Pierrepoint at 8:30 am …. The verdict and sentence were a grave betrayal of the meaning of justice, and the trial was horrifying in its clumsiness as much as for the omissions as for the half-truths and untruths told by witnesses. One of the omissions was that Patrick "Paddy" McCarthy, brother of Michael, had gone out searching for his mother on Wednesday night with a lantern, and he was certain that neither her body nor her dog were at the spot where they were found by Gleeson on Thursday morning. This evidence would have supported the defence submission that Moll was murdered on Thursday morning, but Patrick was never asked about it in court. After the trial the youngest of Moll's children were committed to state care. John Caesar died 10 years after his nephew was hanged. Tommy Reid left the area in a state of ill-health. Many years later he revealed that the Garda beat him up because he could not tell them what Gleeson was doing after 9.30 that Thursday morning – they wanted him to say that Gleeson had been back to the body before 10.00 am .... Moll's cottage is a ruin today, with only a couple of walls still standing ....

So who might have killed Moll McCarthy? Author Marcus Bourke says: "From the day her body was found the people of New Inn closed ranks so solidly that the efforts of the guards to find the real culprits were hampered, even thwarted. It was as if, now that she was gone, the local people wanted to blot out all memories of her from their lives." At the end of a conversation with Gleeson's solicitor, John Timoney, for instance, the local blacksmith, John Ryan, said: "I don't want to be mixed up in this case. I know nothing and I don't want to say anything. I have enough to do to mind my own business. I don't want to have anything to do with it." Was that important? It was, if Bourke is to be believed. "I am convinced," he says, "that Ryan withheld vital information." Gleeson's defence team met the same solid conspiracy of silence across the village and it even embraced the parish priest. John Timoney obtained a helpful statement from Father O'Malley, then read it over to him. The priest agreed it was correct, but refused to sign it. According to Timoney's note of the interview, "He did not wish to have anything to do with it." What, one wonders, must these village people have felt on the day their good friend and neighbour was executed for a murder many of them knew he didn't commit? In the years that followed Harry Gleeson's execution the controversy about the case never died – one theory is that the victim was a police-informer and that the IRA killed her .... In the 1980s Gleeson's friend Bill O'Connor published *The Farcical Trial Of Harry Gleeson*, in which it was claimed that Gleeson was framed. Reading O'Connor's work was what inspired Marcus Bourke to write his own book about the case, with evidence supporting Gleeson's innocence. The never-ending doubts brought about the creation in more recent years of the Justice for Harry Gleeson Group, supported by his family. Their research was so detailed that the office of the attorney-general in Dublin appointed a senior counsel to review the conviction ....

Hopes were raised that Harry Gleeson would be pardoned after 74 years. On December 19th, 2015, Gleeson became the first person ever to receive a Posthumous Pardon by the Republic of Ireland. The pardon order, signed by the President Michael D. Higgins, was presented to the Gleeson family at a ceremony in January 2016. Some family members reportedly complained that the document used the name Harry rather than Henry. Whoever really killed Mary "Moll" McCarthy is now almost certainly dead and will never be brought to justice. The hanging of Harry Gleeson must remain as an indelible stain of shame on New Inn – the village that turned its back on justice. History will, though, now at the very least recognise Gleeson's good name and his innocence of a brutal unsolved murder ....

EVE OF EXECUTION: "Gleeson did not mind dying" ....

The day before Gleeson was hanged, Tuesday, April 22nd, 1941, he asked for a last visit from Sean McBride. That evening the lawyer arrived at Mountjoy Prison for an experience he remembered for the rest of his life. In a letter McBride sent to solicitor John Timoney, together with notes he wrote down outside the prison in his car, McBride described the last meeting with his doomed client. "He asked me to let his uncle and aunt and friends know that he did not mind at all dying, as he was well prepared. He was quite calm and happy. He assured me several times that he would not like to change places with anyone else, as he felt sure he had undergone his purgatory in this world and that he might never have such an opportunity of being so well prepared to meet death. He was quite cheerful and chatted freely about his execution. He asked me to specially thank you (John Timoney) for all your work you had done on his behalf and said he would pray for you. At the end of the interview he stood up and said, 'The last thing I want to say is that I will pray tomorrow that whoever did it will be discovered, and that the whole thing will be like an open book. I rely on you then to clear my name. I have no confession to make, only that I didn't do it. That is all. I will pray for you and be with you if I can, whenever you, Mr. Nolan-Whelan and Mr. Timoney are fighting and battling for justice.'" Mr. McBride continued: "I took a note of these words afterwards. He uttered these words with feeling and a certain amount of emotion. As you know, he was not usually very fluent or eloquent in speaking. He was on this occasion. That was the last I saw of Harry Gleeson. I understand he remained quite calm and happy right to the end." Many years later Sean McBride said he had been "shattered" by this meeting ….

Case 5
"The Button
On
The Shop-Floor"

Frederick PARKER & Albert PROBERT
MURDER
Of
Joseph Bedford (80)
[1934]

At first it seemed like an accident. Joseph Bedford was 80, and his small, run-down shop in Portslade, Hove, Brighton, was poorly

***lit.** So it was no great surprise when one November night in 1933 he had a fall in the premises, where he lived by himself and was seldom seen outside ....*

Joseph Bedford was a taciturn type, rarely greeting his customers, seldom smiling and said to be a bit of a miser. And now, it appeared, he had stumbled in his dimly lit shop and hit his head. That was the first impression. But when he arrived by ambulance at a Hove hospital and the caked blood was swabbed away, it was found that his wound was almost in the middle of the top of his head. He was too dazed to say how he had fallen, and he died a few hours later, the next day .... "It looks as though he received a blow on the top of his skull," Detective Constable Robert Holt told Chief Inspector Arthur W. Askew of Scotland Yard, who had been called in by the East Sussex Police. "Let's go and have a look at the shop," said Askew. As they entered, a tinkling bell on the door announced their arrival, as it did for every customer. The gloomy interior was crammed with an assortment of cheap goods, liberally coated with dust. "The old boy's sight wasn't all that good," said Holt. That might explain the dust, thought Askew, but not the "accident." "That doesn't account for his falling on top of his head," he told the Sussex officer. "That would take an acrobat and at his age it isn't halfway credible. Someone cracked his skull like an egg. Now let's see if we can find anything in this jumbled mess." Their search at first revealed little, apart from an old dented box which seemed to have served as a till. It was lying open on the floor, on which some copper coins were scattered along with a grubby display card and a few packets and tins which could have been knocked over when the old man fell. The coins included a large number of farthings, and the detectives thought that perhaps every time Joe Bedford received one of these in change he tossed it into the box without realising how many he was accumulating. Also among the coins was a button. Had it come from the box or from somewhere else? Turning it over in his fingers, Askew decided that it wasn't from one of Joe's jackets. "Let's see if he had any buttons missing from an overcoat," he said. The detectives checked through Joe's clothes and searched the room where he would usually dress in the morning. But no overcoat button appeared to be missing from Joe Bedford's meagre wardrobe ....

Then their renewed search of the shop revealed something else: a piece of thick plate glass, matted with blood and hairs, almost hidden in the shadows on that dull November day. The hairs were later found to match those of Joe's grey head. They also found his hat – a faded and discoloured bowler stained olive green in places. It had been battered almost into the shape of a trilby. "It's murder all right," said Askew. A post-mortem examination was ordered, and the East Sussex Police announced that an elderly man had died in "suspicious circumstances." Joe Bedford's last years as a recluse emerged as having been a dull day-to-day routine, save for one bright thread. It was established that, despite his reserved nature, he had time for the children of the neighbourhood. "All the kids in Portslade," said one woman, "liked old Joe. He didn't have much money, but he was always ready to stop and talk with them, ask how they were getting on at school. He was always ready to listen to their chatter." The detectives learned that in his younger days Joe had managed a music shop in Brighton, where he had taught himself to play several instruments. He had moved to the Portslade area of the town in 1906, then on to Worthing to open a hardware shop, where for a time he was known to the residents as "Tin Tacks." ....

But his wandering days apparently came to an end when he met a widow. She was 26 at the time, and Joe proposed marriage, only to find himself rejected. He had continued to write to the widow of his fading dreams. Indeed, he had a lawyer draw up a will leaving all his furniture and £1,000 to her. He also wrote a poem, found in a mound of musty papers at the time his will was discovered. On a single sheet of paper, and written in an old-fashioned script, the lines ran: "No one cares if I live or die, the hurrying crowd is passing me by. I yearn and I long to stop and think, to gather white raiment of thought, to drink at the fountain of wisdom and light – but .... there is no one who cares if I die outright." ....

One of those who read it was Sir Bernard Spilsbury, the famous Home Office pathologist. Another was Dr. Roche Lynch, the Home Office analyst. They had been summoned when the case became one for the Yard. It had been after 10 o'clock on the wet night of **Monday, November 13th, 1933** when a policeman had stood staring at the light in Joe Bedford's shop window, wondering why the old man had not taken down some of the articles he usually had hanging on display. The constable rubbed clear a misty patch of the window and observed Joe staggering about inside the shop as if he were drunk. But the old man was known to be a teetotaller. As the policeman watched, Joe tripped and lost his balance. He struck his head on a glass case and dropped. The officer rattled the handle of the shop door, but found it locked. With a heave he broke in, found that the door had been locked on the inside, and phoned for an ambulance. Because Joe had been seen staggering about in the shop, the first report was that he had suffered a heart attack. Now, however, the police were taking a different view. Chief Inspector Askew had an urgent message relayed to all the county's police stations, and within a very short time reports were coming in. One of these concerned two men in their 20s. One was a fitter from Dover, the other a labourer from Hove. They had met barely two weeks earlier, but they had lost little time in teaming up after deciding that there was little likelihood of getting a job when so many were unemployed. So they turned to considering their chances of getting some easy money ….

The little general shop at 1, Clarence Street, Portslade, in the Hove area of Brighton, appealed to them as one they could "do." It was away from the bright lights, so they would be running little risk. The only person they could see through the murky window was an old man arranging some goods. They decided that he might have savings and would give them no trouble. As they watched him unobserved, they noticed several articles in his shop that suggested he dealt in second-hand goods. "We could offer him that old vacuum-cleaner you found," said the elder man, Albert Probert (26) …. "Then while he's looking at it, all we have to do is knock him down." Frederick William Parker, a 21-year-old labourer, squinted through the window as he nodded. "All right, Bert," he agreed, "you do your stuff talking about Hoovers. He won't suspect a thing. It'll be dead easy." As they walked away from the shop, Parker said that the best time to surprise the old man would be when the street was clear of people. "Do it quick, no hanging about," he urged. "And let's get away quickly – say as far as Worthing." Then, looking at his companion, he added: "If you're not careful, you're going to lose that button on your overcoat." But Probert appeared preoccupied. They retraced their steps along Clarence Street, doubtless pondering how much they would have to share out after they had dealt with the old man. In the event their haul was little more than a paltry £6. They were about to become cut-price murderers ….

Now occurs one of those curious coincidences that happen much more frequently in the pages of fiction than in the more subdued annals of true crime. Safe, as the killers thought, in Worthing, they were to become unstuck through a chain of events that were truly stranger than fiction. On the day after the murder a senior detective chanced to look out of a window at Worthing police station. His eye focused on two men behaving in a strangely furtive manner. Heads together as they whispered, they frequently glanced around as though to ensure that they were not observed. "By God, that's a shifty-looking pair!" said the detective to a junior officer. "I'd bet my pension they're up to a bit of no good. Better follow them and see where they're making for." So, unknown to Probert and Parker, their movements were observed. They were seen lingering at a men's outfitter's where they finally went in and bought a couple of suits and two shirts. Just before the sale was made, the elder of the pair pointed to a button missing from his overcoat. "Oh, allow me, sir," said the shopkeeper. "I can fix that for you." He selected a suitable button, sewed it on Probert's coat, buttoned it up, and wished his customers a smiling good-day. The purchases had been paid for by the murdered Joe Bedford. The policeman who observed the sale reported back to his superior. A note was made of where the men had gone to earth in the town ….

Then, some hours later, the Worthing CID received the report from Brighton concerning two men who should be stopped and held for questioning following an attack on an elderly man in Portslade. The Worthing detective scanned the message. "I knew they were wrong-'uns," he said. "All right, let's have them in." So a very surprised and agitated pair of wanted men found themselves picked up for questioning. When they were asked to empty their pockets a number of farthings fell to the floor. The police officers stared as though they were seeing gold sovereigns. "You on a saving spree?" asked one. "No, I – I –" stammered the younger of the pair. "Shut up!" muttered his companion. "They can't pinch us. We've done nothing." "You sewed a new button on your coat, chummy. How about that?" Probert was asked. The detective pointed to the button. Probert looked at it uncertainly, but Parker was unnerved. "I didn't do it," he muttered. ….

"You didn't do what?" asked the Worthing detective. "I told you to shut up!" snapped Probert. The detectives sensed that this was where thieves were about to fall out. But Probert had intimidated his younger companion, and it was some time before the investigators made their breakthrough. It came when Parker suddenly jumped to his feet and yelled: "All right, so we did it!" As soon as he shouted this admission the pair were bustled away before Probert could become violent. Then a fresh round of questioning began. Askew and Holt produced the farthings retrieved from the old man's box, together with the lost button, and the Scotland Yard detective went to Worthing to continue his inquiries. Parker was now claiming that it was Probert who had struck the fatal blow. The button discovered on the floor of the shop was found to have some snapped threads that matched the torn threads on Probert's coat, and the detained men were charged with Joe Bedford's murder. At the committal proceedings on December 15th, 1933, Sir Bernard Spilsbury informed the magistrates that the victim had died from shock due to multiple injuries to both the head and the face. While the pathologist was giving evidence, Parker collapsed. Aroused by the clatter, Spilsbury turned and nimbly ran round from the witness-box to give the young prisoner attention in the dock ....

Sent for trial at Lewes Assizes, Probert and Parker appeared before Justice Adair Roche on March 14th, 1934 in a trial that was to last three-days .... Tension in the court intensified when Spilsbury was being cross-examined by J. D. Cassels KC, defending Parker. Handing the witness a skull, the counsel asked him to point to the precise spot where the fracture in Bedford's head occurred. On the instructions of the judge, the battered bowler was placed on the skull. All who could craned forward and saw that the long dent in the creased bowler corresponded with the middle of the skull injury as

Spilsbury pointed. The defence then asked: "Could a man, after receiving these injuries, walk about a very crowded shop, shut the door, lock it, put the key in its place, climb a ladder twice, put his hand over a partition, in each case turning out gases, get down, pick up a paper, carry it into a room and put it on the table, go up the stairs, which are very narrow and winding at the bottom, get into bed, come down again – all these things he would do after receiving a blow which you say caused his death?" There was a short silence. All eyes were on Spilsbury. "Yes," he replied finally, "if, as in this case, the surroundings were familiar and the acts were ones he did daily. He might automatically go through all these." Parker claimed that he had held up Joe Bedford with an unloaded revolver, but that Probert had struck the killing blow. Then Parker's words suddenly drained away. He stumbled and fell, tumbling out of the box and into the well of the court. He was carried out, attended by doctors. Then Probert went into the witness-box and denied Parker's story ….

On March 16th, after retiring for 35 minutes the jury filed back to their seats. None of them looked towards the pair in the dock as the foreman gave their verdict: "Guilty." Parker tried to protest, his mouth opening and closing several times, though no words came. But Probert said firmly: "I am entirely innocent of this." Parker's jaws were still moving when Justice Roche settled the black cap over his trim wig. The prisoners' appeals were heard on April 18th. It was argued that a policeman's lamp shining through the shop-window on that fatal November night might have startled the old man and so caused his fall …. But the Crown insisted that what happened was "murder or nothing" and the appeals were dismissed. On Thursday, May 4th, 1934, Albert Probert and Frederick Parker were hanged at Wandsworth Prison by Thomas Pierrepoint and three assistants – Albert Pierrepoint, Stanley Cross and Thomas Phillips …. Sir Bernard Spilsbury subsequently making a special examination of Frederick Parker's heart. He found no apparent physical reason for the prisoner's collapses. But wouldn't anyone be liable to faint, with his life on the line as he was tried for murder? ….

Case 6
"The Case
Of
The Buried Girl"

Patrick KINGSTON
MURDER
Of
Sheila Wilson (11)
[1942]

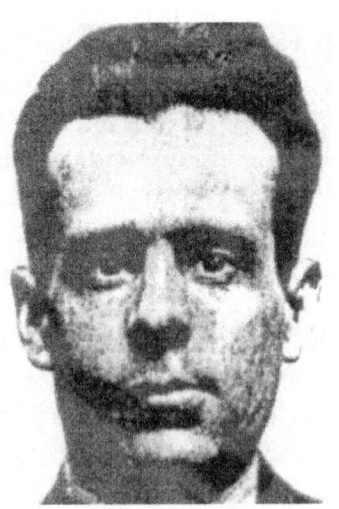

Patrick Kingston

The Grahams' crippled lodger came under suspicion when he claimed not to know the victim, although he'd lived twenty-three doors away from her for eight years ….

"Your little girl passed into the spirit world with a terrific shock. I have a feeling of constriction around the throat. Your little girl was strangled," the medium Mrs. Estelle Roberts told the child's mother. "This spirit passed over only a short time ago. She has been dead less than six months. It is difficult for her to communicate – she has not yet adjusted herself to her new life. After her death you went to see your little daughter, but you only saw her through glass." The mother nodded. "Your daughter is asking what you have done with her coloured shoes. You took them out of the cupboard downstairs." Wide-eyed with amazement, Mrs. Edith Wilson said she had taken out her child's red dancing shoes and given them away. She lived in Leahurst Road, in the Manor Park area of Lewisham, south-east London, and she had lost her 11-year-old daughter Sheila three months earlier ….

In the Sunday Pictorial she had subsequently read that to test spiritualists' claims that they could communicate with dead children, one of the paper's reporters was going to take bereaved mothers to seances without revealing their names or anything about them to the mediums. So Mrs. Wilson had written to the newspaper: "If it is possible that you can speak with your loved one who has gone, will you please tell me where to go?" As a result, without disclosing anything of her story, the reporter had taken her to a seance with Mrs. Roberts, who in spiritualist circles was acknowledged to be the leading medium of her day. On **Wednesday, July 15th, 1942**, Edith Wilson had returned home from her job at a munitions factory at her usual time of 7.55 pm. She had given Sheila and her eight-year-old brother Derek a shilling to buy a penny lemonade each at the corner shop, and when Sheila returned with the change she also had another twopence. She said a man had given her this for fetching him some cigarettes, and he wanted her to get him the evening newspaper.

After eating her supper, she had gone out again for the paper, her mother telling her not to be long because it was now 8.35 and her bedtime was 9 o'clock. Sheila didn't return, so Mrs. Wilson called on everyone in the street, asking if they had seen her ….

Nobody had, and she also spoke to Patrick Kingston, a crippled 38-year-old Air Raid Precautions stretcher-bearer who lodged with Mr. and Mrs. Leslie Graham at their home at 19, Leahurst Road, where he had spent all that evening. Mrs. Eva Graham had gone to the local pub where she worked part-time as a barmaid, and her husband had gone to the pub, too, leaving their three sons playing in the street. When the boys went home, Kingston had kept them out of the kitchen, telling them he was bathing his lame leg in the sink because he had knocked it on a chair, making it bleed. "I don't know her," he told Mrs. Wilson when she asked if he had seen her daughter. "I've never seen her. If
I wanted a paper, one of Eva's boys would fetch it. I'm sorry I can't help you – I only wish I could." At 11 pm. Mrs. Wilson had gone to Lee Road police station to report Sheila missing. She also sent a telegram to her husband who was doing war work in Wiltshire. But the wire went astray, and he did not learn that his daughter was missing until he read a report of her disappearance in an evening newspaper. He last heard from Sheila a few days earlier, when she wrote telling him she had seen a second-hand bicycle for sale at £4 10s., and she was saving up for it. "When Sheila had not returned an hour after going out, I did not worry at first because I thought she was playing with other children in the street," Mrs. Wilson told reporters. "I know she would not have gone with anyone she did not know well. She is a very sensible girl." Four days after Sheila disappeared, the police were reported to be seeking a man posing as a mute ….

One of the Wilsons' neighbours had told detectives that such a man had offered money to one of her children. He pretended to be deaf and dumb when she spoke to him, and he rode away on his bicycle. The police had meanwhile questioned Patrick Kingston, who told them he walked with a limp because of a shrapnel injury he had received to his leg during an air raid in 1940. When Eva Graham expressed her anxiety about Sheila two days after her disappearance,

Kingston told her husband, "I wonder if it was that chap who had the kiddies up an alley. Leslie, you were a fool when you saw him not to give him a bloody good bashing." Kingston had then crossed the street to ask Mrs. Wilson if she had any news. On Monday, July 20th, Scotland Yard's Detective Chief Inspector Edward Greeno became suspicious on learning that although Kingston had lodged with the Grahams for eight years, he claimed not to know the missing girl who lived only 23 doors away. So Greeno gave orders for him to be brought in for further questioning. Shortly afterwards, however, Leslie Graham informed the police that his lodger had disappeared. Kingston had left the house on Saturday evening saying he was going to hospital to have his bad leg treated, that he also hoped to go to a wedding, and that if he wasn't back that evening the Grahams were not to worry. But he had not returned on the Sunday evening either, and he hadn't reported for duty at the ARP centre that Monday morning. Greeno ordered an immediate search of the Grahams' house. One earlier had found nothing, but when he learned that a trap-door in the hallway opened onto a space four feet deep beneath the house, he ordered the hole searched again. The floor of the space was covered with rubble about two feet deep, and Greeno ordered two constables to remove it. In the process, they found the stub of a yellow pencil, its shiny condition showing it hadn't been there long. Was it Kingston's? ….

They would have to find out, Greeno told Detective Inspector William Chapman. Shortly afterwards Mrs. Graham was telling the detectives she had never suspected her lodger, when they were startled by a strange noise from beneath the open trap-door. "Suddenly, one of the constables down the hole made a sound in his throat as if he were choking," Greeno later recalled in his memoirs. "I thought he was going to vomit. He had cleared away most of the rubble, and a child's arm was sticking through what was left. It didn't take long to uncover the body. Sheila had been strangled with a length of window cord wrapped round her neck tightly three times. There were other things, too – the stamp of the sex killer." Sheila had been raped as well as murdered, and a full-scale hunt was launched for Patrick Kingston; the investigators learning that he had a police record for robbing church-collection boxes, receiving stolen property, thefts from motor cars, and most relevant of all for sexual offences against children. Experience had taught Greeno that killers sometimes return to the scene of their crime, so he had the Grahams' house placed under round-the clock surveillance. In the early hours of the following Wednesday morning, two police officers were in the house when one of them heard the limping lodger tapping his way along the pavement outside with his walking-stick. A key clicked in the front-door lock, and the light was switched on to reveal Kingston standing in the hallway. He had returned, he said, to repay a pound that Leslie Graham had lent him ….

One-thirty a.m. seemed a strange time to repay a debt, and Kingston was taken to Lee Road police station. He admitted the murder when he was questioned there at 2.10 a.m. by Detective Inspector Chapman. "I don't know why I done it," he said. "I don't want sympathy. I know it was wrong, terribly wrong, and I must suffer for it. I had been on the drink practically all week. When she came back and said what paper did I want, I said I didn't want a paper at all, I just wanted to kiss and cuddle her. She started to scream and I caught her by the arm to try to stop her screaming and I went mad." He had dragged Sheila through the hall to the kitchen, where he strangled and then raped her, he confessed. Then he had taken up the lino in the hall, opened the trap-door, and buried her in the space beneath. It was while he was climbing out of the hole that he'd knocked his bad leg. Washing his wound at the kitchen sink, he had tried to remove all traces of the crime, but cement dust from the rubble was found in his trouser turn-ups. Kingston pleaded guilty when he appeared at the Old Bailey in a trial that lasted only five minutes on September 14th before Judge Hugh Hallett. He was sentenced to death, and on Wednesday, October 6th, 1942, he was hanged at Wandsworth Prison by Albert Pierrepoint and Herbert Morris at 9:00 am …. Mrs. Wilson's visit to the medium took place a fortnight later. "Your little girl sends you all her love," Estelle Roberts told her. "Also her love to Baby, Rosie, Jim, Peter, John, May, Nelly, Margery, Vi, Ruby, Doreen, and to 'The Three.'" ….

Mrs. Wilson instantly recognised all the names as those of Sheila's friends and relations. "'Kiss Derek for me,' she says," Mrs. Roberts went on. "Listen!" she added, after a pause. "The child is telling me that you keep holding in your mind a picture of her as having suffered a great deal, but you are wrong. She did not suffer. She was unconscious when she passed." For a while Edith Wilson was too overwhelmed to speak. Slowly, she adjusted herself to this astonishing experience. And when they parted, the reporter recorded, she was happier than she had ever been since her daughter's murder ….

Case 7
"The Old Curiosity Shop-Murder"

"I was going past the shop when I heard the old lady talking and making strange noises. I rapped at the door. She opened it partly and I pushed my way in. I struck her several times and she fell down" ….

Andrew BROWN
MURDER
Of
Amelia Knowles (69)
[1945]

"Get Out Of Here, You Beast!" The eccentric victim screamed ....

It was a milkman who raised the alarm. At midday on **Monday, September 18th, 1944**, he noticed that elderly Miss Amelia Elizabeth Ann Knowles had not taken in her morning's supply at the shop which was also her home – the Old Curiosity Shop in Arundel, Sussex. Police called to the scene found that the shop's front door was not locked. Inside, Miss Knowles lay dead in a passage, wearing only her night-clothes. She had been struck several times, and the police surgeon, Dr. R.W. Pearson, estimated that she had died at around midnight. Aged 69, Amelia Knowles was the daughter of a local character known as "Knocker" Knowles. She had looked after her father in his old age, and after his death had continued to run the family junk shop which occupied the front room of their cottage at 20, Tarrant Street .... She had also become increasingly eccentric. Her neighbours had become accustomed to the cries, shrieks, groans and angry monologues which came at night from her home. Whatever ghosts visited the white-haired recluse in the dim depths of her shop were her own affair, they said. They were satisfied that all was well when she appeared each morning, ready for the day's business. But now the old lady was dead and there was a killer in their midst. Her body was removed for a post-mortem examination to be conducted by Dr. L.R. Janes, a Brighton pathologist, and the assistance of Scotland Yard was sought by the local police ....

Within hours the Yard's Detective Superintendent Frederick Cherrill arrived in Arundel, where he was briefed by Superintendent Peel. "Any clues?" Cherrill asked. Peel produced a small flannel bag, opening it to display a roll of 37 ten-shilling notes. "This was found pinned to Miss Knowles's dress," he said. "At first we thought the motive was robbery. Then we found this money. Now we don't know what to think." Cherrill nodded. "I won't form any opinions until I look around," he said. "Lead on." At the Old Curiosity Shop he found the shutters still firmly secured, the windows closed. "Miss Knowles apparently retreated as far as she could before she was attacked," he observed. "I don't understand why her cries didn't attract help from the neighbours." Peel told him of the victim's nocturnal shrieks. "From her shouts at night, anyone would think murder was being done," he said. Officers had been called half a dozen times, only to find Miss Knowles alive and well, indignant that her cries and conversations should attract investigation. It had been decided that she was simply given to weird outbursts at night because of her loneliness and her age. "So the affair is like the boy in the story," Peel concluded. "He cried 'Wolf!' when there wasn't any, and then when real danger threatened he got no help." "So any cries from here would have been ignored?" "Exactly." ....

The shop had been left undisturbed to await the Scotland Yard detective's examination. "What's this?" he asked, pulling a flannel bag from beneath an old table and opening it to reveal another roll of ten-shilling notes. In silence, he counted them on the table. They totalled 63. "If robbery was the motive," he remarked, "the killer certainly overlooked the loot." While a fingerprint officer began dusting the shop, other investigators pursued various lines of inquiry. When had Miss Knowles last been seen alive? Had she had any mysterious visitors? Had she ever expressed fear of anybody? If the murder motive were robbery, why had the killer left behind so much money? The body had not been discovered for hours, so had he been frightened off by some noise outside? Or had he taken only part of the victim's cash in order to confuse the police? And there were other possibilities. It was wartime, and enemy agents parachuted occasionally into outlying areas at night. Had one forced his way into the shop and silenced Miss Knowles to stop her screaming for help? Such a killer, already provided with English currency, would not be interested in robbery ....

A neighbour two doors away nodded vigorously when detectives asked if she had heard any disturbance. "Last night?" she said. "This morning, you mean. We certainly did hear cries coming from the shop." These had been sudden, she continued, and they were heard at 12.30 a.m. Miss Knowles had shouted, "Get out of here, you beast! You cannot come in here! Help! Murder!" Recognising the voice, the neighbours had turned over in their beds and resumed their sleep. It was only silly old Miss Knowles with another imaginary tormentor .... "Poor old lady," said Cherrill. "What chance have you got when people go back to sleep on hearing you cry 'Murder'? But who can blame them?" "I can't," said a colleague. "I dare say I'd have done the same under the circumstances. But at least we now know the time of the murder." Miss Knowles had cried out no name, so whether or not she knew her attacker remained a mystery. The neighbours said she had never addressed anyone by name in her nightly ramblings. Some recalled that years before they had asked her whom she quarrelled with at nights. She had smiled at them pityingly, telling them they must be imagining things ….

The fingerprint officer gave a hopeless look when asked what progress he was making. "Everyone who comes into a curiosity shop must have plenty of curiosity already," he commented. "They all handled things on display. There are enough prints on the vases alone to remand the whole county!" Cherrill smiled thinly. "Keep at it," he said. "If I can get a combination of a fingerprint and a man who can't tell me where he was at twelve-thirty this morning, I'll feel we're getting somewhere." The next day Cherrill and other detectives began the task of examining the victim's correspondence and records for whatever leads they might offer. Elderly women sometimes became involved in bitter feuds. There was also the possibility that at some time Miss Knowles might have informed on a lawbreaker or might have accused someone of pilfering. It was the investigators' job to find out. They were absorbed in her correspondence when there was a knock at the door and a constable thrust his head inside. "Lady as wants to see you, sir," he told Cherrill. "Says it's about the Knowles business." "Show her in," said the superintendent. An attractive young woman entered the room, identifying herself as an Arundel resident. "I just got back today and heard about Miss Knowles," she said. "I saw something last week which might interest you." Cherrill offered a chair. "Please sit down and tell us about it." ….

The woman said that at 11 p.m. on the previous Thursday, September 14th, she was passing the Old Curiosity Shop on her way home. It was a clear night, and despite the blackout she saw a man at the side of the premises. "It gave me a start," she continued. "He was bending down as though trying to look into the window. I flashed my torch at him and he jumped. I asked him what he was doing there." She said the man had replied, "I want to get in. I owe the lady some money but she won't answer the door." "I hesitated for a moment," she went on, "and I got a good look at him in the light of the torch. Then another man's voice came from across the street. He shouted, 'Come on, Paddy, let's go.'" "Did you get a good look at the second chap?" asked Cherrill. The witness said she didn't. The man at the window turned and walked quickly away towards his companion. 'Paddy' was a dark, powerfully built young man in the uniform of an aircraftman. Feeling that Miss Knowles was in no danger, the woman had continued her walk home. "It is possible, of course, that the young man was telling you the truth," said Cherrill. "But he might have been looking over the place, planning to break in. Your appearance may have given Miss Knowles five more days of life." ….

The district, like much of southern England during the war, had no shortage of airfields. If Paddy were short for Patrick, there would be scores of airmen so named in the area. Each would have to be checked out, and their alibis for the night of September 17th-18th investigated. Furthermore, 'Paddy' might have no connection with the murder. But with no other lead, Cherrill asked those in charge of local RAF bases to check their men for all Patricks. Any unable to account satisfactorily for their whereabouts on the night in question were to be detained until Cherrill could interrogate them. Three airmen named Patrick were soon under detention, Cherrill going from one airfield to another to interview them. Under pressure, each man revealed where he had been on the night of September 17th-18th. Each had been breaking regulations, and had been unwilling to admit this when first questioned. Cherrill soon loosened their tongues with the word "murder," and each then turned out to have an alibi which could be corroborated. So the lead had yielded nothing. Then another detective recalled his schooldays. "There was a lad named Clarence," he reminisced, "who made everybody call him 'Jack'. He hated his real name, and was ready to use his fists to change it. After a while we almost forgot what his real name was." "That's it!" cried Cherrill. "We'll get all the camps to check everyone known as Paddy, regardless of the names on their enlistment papers. Most of them will probably be Irish." The investigators spent the next 48 hours questioning dozens of "Paddys" without result. They were beginning to become dispirited when 26-year-old Northern Irishman Andrew Brown was marched into the office where Cherrill waited to question him. Brown was dark and powerfully built. "Hello, Andrew," said the detective. "If you don't mind, sir, I'd rather be called Paddy," Brown replied. "I don't like Andrew." "To be sure," Cherrill said affably. "They told me that and I forgot. Paddy, where were you on the night of September seventeenth? Or I should say, about twelve-thirty on the morning of the eighteenth?" "I was drinking with a couple of friends," Brown told him. "We were at a pub in Arundel and we all came back to the camp together." "Fine," said Cherrill. "What are the others' names?" Brown told him and he was then dismissed. If he noticed that he was thereafter kept under surveillance, he gave no sign of it. The companions he had named were called in. "We're investigating a murder," Cherrill told them. "Andrew Brown says he was with you on the morning of September eighteenth." "Paddy was with us that night," said one of the men, "but he didn't come back to the camp with us. He stayed on at the pub after we left." From further inquiries the investigators learned the name of a girl with whom Brown was sometimes seen in Arundel. They found her at home. She too was startled when told the nature of the inquiry ….

Twisting a handkerchief in her hands, she said that Paddy Brown had taken her to Arundel's Arun Cinema on the night of Monday, September 18th, some 20 hours after Miss Knowles had been strangled. "I saw him pay with a ten-shilling note," she told the detectives. Cherrill and another officer went to the Arundel tavern which had been mentioned by Brown's companions as a favourite hangout. They found the landlord watching a game of darts, but they soon turned his attention to more serious matters. "Aye, Paddy Brown's a good customer," he confirmed. "Come into money, he has – he was waving a fistful of ten-shilling notes the other night and saying he had plenty more." It was midnight when the detectives returned to the airfield. Brown was paraded before them again. Item by item, Cherrill told him of the evidence that linked him with the murder. Brown blinked when he heard how he had been seen trying to peer into the Old Curiosity Shop after dark. He heard what his girl had said and what the pub landlord had recalled. "You've had too many ten-shilling notes," Cherrill told him. "And your friends say you didn't come back to the camp with them that night. What about that?" Brown's head drooped, his forehead perspiring. For a moment he made no reply. Then he said, "I'm sorry. That bit's untrue. I did it." ….

After dawn he led the investigators to a bridge over a nearby stream. He had hidden items stolen from the shop beneath it. On a road near the camp he moved several large stones under which he had concealed some of the stolen money. "I was on my way to the camp that night," he said, "and I was going past the shop when I heard the old lady talking and making strange noises. I'd been caught looking into the shop at night before, but I peered in again and saw her. I thought she must have a lot of money. I rapped at the door. She opened it partly and I pushed my way in. I struck her several times and she fell down." He went on to say that he became frightened when he thought she was dead so he left, taking some money. Tried at Lewes Assizes on December 7th, 1944, he pleaded not guilty to murder but guilty to manslaughter, and his defence counsel also claimed that Brown was insane. Dr. A. Baldy, a Metropolitan Police surgeon, told the court that on examining Brown at Lewes Prison on November 25th he had concluded that he was sane. It was possible, however, that he had experienced a form of epilepsy at the time of the crime. Dr. Baldy said he believed Brown was suffering from petit mal or some other disorder. There were medical records of petit mal lasting for hours, it could be intensified by drinking, and it was often followed by epilepsy. In cases of petit mal sufferers were unconscious of what they were doing at the moment, but awareness of what they had done could come afterwards through a process of reconstruction. Two other doctors testified that they had found Brown to be sane. His own doctor in Ireland had written to say that Brown was subject to apoplectic fits. After a brief retirement of just 11 minutes the jury returned to find Andrew Brown guilty of murder. Sentenced to death by Justice Travers Humphreys, an appeal was rejected on January 12th, and he was hanged at Wandsworth Prison on Tuesday, January 30th,1945 by Albert Pierrepoint and Steve Wade ….

Case 8
"The Last Dance Before The Gallows"

John LEATHERBERRY
MURDER
Of
Henry Hailstone
[1944]

John Leatherberry

A photograph was taken - it was truly remarkable – because only hours after it was taken in a London night-club, an American serviceman booked himself a date with the hangman. How did it happen? ….

A dance was being held at London's West Indies Club that night, and someone had taken along a camera. Click! Early in the evening the shutter was triggered, and the image of John "J.C." Leatherberry dancing with a girl was captured for posterity ....

It was his last dance, but he didn't know it. He left the club shortly afterwards, and just hours after the photo was taken he booked a date with the hangman. In his office at Chelmsford police headquarters the next day, **Wednesday, December 8th, 1943**, Detective Chief Inspector G. H. Totterdell was told that the police in Colchester wanted to speak to him. They had found a taxi abandoned in mysterious circumstances. "It was left in Haynes Green Lane, in the village of Layer Marney near Colchester. A local Bobby spotted it there and took a look inside it. He found a man's jacket, as well as a bloodstained mac, so he reported in," Totterdell was told. "All right," he said. "I'm on my way." With Detective Inspector Draper he drove out to Copford police station, just up the road from Layer Marney, where they found Sergeant Garrett awaiting them. He indicated some clothing on a table. "I've been out to Haynes Green Lane," he said. "I brought these back to save time." When Totterdell and Draper examined the jacket and mackintosh, they noted that the jacket's sleeves had been turned inside-out and joined together. As Totterdell later explained: "It was as if the garment had been pulled off the wearer from behind." Holding up the mackintosh, the detectives saw bloodstains on the back, close to the collar. The raincoat looked new – and neither garment had been torn in any struggle. In the pockets was an assortment of articles, including a driving licence in the name of Henry Claude Hailstone. The address given on the licence was 127, Maldon Road, Colchester. "It looks bad," said Totterdell, frowning at the stains. Draper agreed. Their next move was to make for Maldon Road, where no. 127 proved to be the home of a Mrs.

Pearce. After the officers identified themselves and explained why they were calling, she told them that the stained mac belonged to her lodger Henry Hailstone, who drove a taxi. She had last seen him at about 11.10 p.m. the previous day. She recalled the time, because Hailstone had looked in to tell her he would have to put off his supper for half an hour. "I've got to take a couple of fares to the Yankee camp at Birch – a couple of coloured men," he said using the language of the day. "One of them's an officer. Still, I don't expect I'll be longer than half an hour." Mrs. Pearce had waited up for him until after midnight. Then she left his supper between two plates, turned off the gas stove and went up to bed. Now, as she stared at the clothing with a worried frown, she said, "I dread to think what's happened to him." ….

The detectives asked some more questions. Mrs. Pearce said that Henry Hailstone, 28, was single and was employed by a Colchester firm. She also confirmed that the number of his cab was CPU 602. So far as she knew, his health was good and he drank only in moderation. But he had bad hands, the result of an accident years ago, although this disability didn't affect his driving. Asked how much money he was likely to have had on him, she replied: "Probably not a lot." When he hadn't returned the previous night, she'd supposed that he'd run out of petrol. "It's happened before in these days of rationing," she added. She listed some possessions he might have had on him. Then she added quickly: "Oh, yes – there was his Canadian cigarette lighter. He was very attached to that." Thanking Mrs. Pearce for her help, Totterdell and Draper next headed for the little village of Layer Marney. The taxi, a Vauxhall, had its windows closed. But the lights were on, as was the handbrake, although the ignition had been switched off. Petrol was low, the tank containing less than a gallon, and the car had sustained some minor damage. The nearside rear bumper had a bolt missing, causing the metal to hang down. And the rear number plate had been cracked, probably when reversing ….

The taxi's interior showed evidence of a strenuous struggle. Hailstone's papers lay scattered on the floorboards, and the upholstery was badly scratched. Next to the running-board was a sixpence, but there was no sign of Hailstone's wallet or its contents.

There were some spots of blood on the rear seat and the offside rear window. It seemed clear to the Essex detectives that the missing driver had been attacked and his cab later driven to where it was found abandoned. The evidence suggested that the attack had been sudden, with Hailstone being lifted from the driver's seat and dumped in the back, where the blood was found. Early the next morning a forensic team went into action. The cab was photographed inside and out, but a dusting of graphite powder produced little in the way of fingerprints, save some smudges. The rear seat was dispatched to the Metropolitan Police lab at Hendon in north London. Because the taxi had been found parked on the wrong side of the road at night, the investigators suspected it had been hijacked by someone more accustomed to left-hand-drive vehicles – possibly an American. There were five US camps near Birch, just south of Colchester, and a phone call to the garrison's adjutant resulted in a score of military policemen being sent to assist in the search for the missing taxi-driver. It was almost 1 o'clock on the afternoon of Thursday, December 9th, when a constable from Copford found Henry Hailstone's body on a grassy bank close to a blackberry bush in the grounds of Birch Rectory. Totterdell hurried to the scene, where he saw that Hailstone's left trouser pocket had been turned inside-out, and the left side of his face was caked in dried blood. The detective was shown two strands of barbed wire which extended along the top of the bank. The lower strand was bloodstained, but there was no sign of a struggle and there were no tyre tracks. As Hailstone weighed nearly 12 stone, it had obviously taken more than one person to carry him to where his body had been found. Totterdell believed that the body had been carried to the top of the bank and then pushed over, leaving it to roll until it was brought to a halt by the blackberry bush. The post-mortem was carried out by Dr. Francis Camps, who found the cause of death to be manual strangulation. There was bruising – the result of at least three heavy blows. And marks on the taxi-driver's neck indicated someone having squeezed it with a tight left-handed grip ….

Then the first leads started to come in. A black GI told the local police that on the night of December 7th, while he was passing through the village of Messing on his way back to camp, he'd seen a man wearing a light raincoat making a phone call outside the Crown

Inn. A few hundred yards farther on, he'd noticed a taxi, without lights, parked just off the road. He'd seen no one in it, however. And by the time he'd reached his hut, the taxi had disappeared, though he recalled hearing footsteps and thought they might have been made by the man in the call box. That lead fizzled out, as did a few others. But then the police received one concerning a Captain Weber – a Canadian. On December 5th he'd arrived in camp with a black American GI. The American had left his gas-mask there through an oversight. Written on the flap of the gas-mask container was the name "J. Hill." Below that was an "H," followed by four figures – "1031." Inquiries established that the gas-mask belonged to a soldier stationed at Birch, who soon confirmed that it was indeed his. He said that, a week before, he'd lent it to another black GI named Fowler. It didn't take long to trace George Fowler (22), who said he'd borrowed the gas-mask when going to London on leave. Asked to be more specific, Fowler said he'd booked in at the Liberty Club in Euston. Then he'd met "several women" and gone on a pub crawl, later spending the night with another woman. That had been on December 5th. He claimed he couldn't remember how he arrived back at Birch on December 8th. He thought he might have been drugged, because when he woke up, he was wearing a sergeant's tunic. Fowler was detained by the police while his hut was searched ….

They saw a uniform with blood on it hanging above his bed. When Fowler's kitbag was emptied, they found some papers, plus a pawn ticket issued by a W. P. Hyde of London E1 for a Rolex wristwatch. Asked about the pawn ticket, Fowler hesitated, and after some thought he agreed to make a statement, in which he described borrowing Hill's gas-mask. He was escorted to Colchester, where his story was gone over again in detail. On the back of the envelope containing the pawn ticket was a name – Charlie Huntly. He turned out to be another black soldier, and he admitted that he had recently been in London, where he'd encountered a Private Leatherberry. They were both in a group of black GIs who'd gone to the West Indies Club, where Leatherberry had given him the Rolex and he had pawned it for three pounds. The police soon recovered the watch, which was identified by Captain Weber as his property. He said he'd left it in the pocket of his mac, which had been stolen by a black

American soldier. The captain's mac was later found in a gutter near Tollesbury, some six miles from Haynes Green Lane. It bore a Canadian maker's name and some bloodstains down the front ....

The pieces were being fitted into an intricate jigsaw, as Totterdell and the other detectives realised. But some of the bits were still missing. These dealt with times and places. Meanwhile, Fowler was making a further statement to the police. He said he'd gone to Liverpool Street Station on December 5th to catch the train to Colchester. During the journey, he'd got into conversation with a British captain, who invited him back to his camp when they reached Colchester. The private and the captain had left Colchester by taxi around 4.30 that afternoon. Almost two hours later, Fowler said, he declined an invitation to stay overnight, saying that he had to get back. However, he accepted the offer of his host's raincoat. The time, he claimed, was around 6.15 p.m. At that time, there'd been nothing in the mac's pockets. "And I didn't take nothin' from the room!" he added. Wearing the captain's mac, he'd then left for his own camp at Birch, he now claimed. On the bus journey, he'd fallen in with some members of his own unit. The black GIs had all gone into the White Horse at Birch for a last drink. And one of them – "a guy called Leatherberry" – had persuaded him to cut camp and head back for London, although Fowler knew he had already overstayed his leave by two days. "I reckoned that it was in for a penny, in for a pound, as you Limeys say," Fowler shrugged. So he and Leatherberry had gone together back to London. And there, the next day, Fowler found himself short of cash. So he went to the Rainbow Club, borrowed 10 shillings, and then boozed it away in various West End pubs. Then he met up with Leatherberry again at a dance at the West Indies Club early on the evening of December 7th. ....

That was when he picked up an envelope containing the pawn ticket. They didn't stay long, having decided to return to Colchester. They had both drunk a good deal and Leatherberry had a scheme for hiring a local taxi and robbing the driver at night. "That way, we get some ready cash," he had told Fowler, who said he'd more or less gone along with the idea. When they arrived at Colchester at around 10.45 that night, they flagged down a taxi. After they'd covered about four miles on the way to Birch, Fowler had asked the driver to stop, so that he could get out and relieve himself. Leatherberry had sat waiting in the cab. Suddenly, Fowler said, he was surprised to hear Leatherberry calling out to him urgently. He hurried back to the taxi, where he found Leatherberry and the driver fighting. The GI was calling to Fowler to help him as he sat in the rear, holding the driver with his left hand and punching with his right fist. Then the taxi-driver collapsed and went limp, after which Leatherberry went through the man's pockets, removing cash and a lighter, as well as some papers. "We're in this together, man," Leatherberry had told him, Fowler said. "And now we've got to get rid of him." He was in a dazed state, Fowler said, as he took hold of the man's feet, while Leatherberry grabbed his shoulders. In this fashion they carried the man's body over the road and thrust it under a barbed-wire fence, where it rolled down a slope in the dark. He had handed the captain's mac to Leatherberry, who was complaining of the winter cold, Fowler added, saying that he had never meant to rob the cabbie, but Leatherberry went ahead with the scheme, so he could not pull back ….

After the body had been dumped in the rectory grounds, he had got behind the taxi's wheel and started for camp, with Leatherberry all the while arguing that they should head for London. Leatherberry had changed places with him, pushing him aside, but when they drew up in Maldon they found that the last train to London had left. So they again changed places, Fowler driving the taxi back towards Birch. When they reached the camp, after abandoning the cab he went to his hut and fell asleep. The time, he thought, would have been an hour and half after midnight. The next morning he'd searched for Leatherberry, but could not find him. Once more, Totterdell and his men went over Fowler's story, paying special attention to the subject of clothes. Fowler claimed that he could not say what had happened to the captain's raincoat. He also insisted that he had not made any phone calls on the night of the murder. "But I can't say whether Leatherberry made any," he added. He denied leaving the Vauxhall parked on the road near his company's area. "If someone saw it parked there, then I don't know who it was that moved it," he said. Leatherberry was interviewed on December 13th, after being cautioned. He told of meeting George Fowler – whom he called "Funely" – and going with him to London, where they had separated. They met up again later, but Leatherberry denied being with Fowler on the night of Henry Hailstone's death. When his locker was searched, however, some bloodstained underclothing and a shirt were found and he was placed under arrest. The following day he was fingerprinted, but he now refused to say anything. That same day an identity parade was held in Birch, and Leatherberry was pointed out by Fowler as the GI whom he'd helped in killing Henry Hailstone. Five days later the accused pair were handed over to their regimental commander and duly charged – Fowler with murder, robbery and theft and Leatherberry with murder and robbery ….

On January 19th, 1944, they both appeared before a two-day court-martial at the Town Hall in Ipswich. Predictably, Fowler put the blame for the killing on Leatherberry, who stuck to his own story, although his nail parings showed that his hands at the time were bloody. Both men were convicted of murder. Fowler, having made a plea-bargain, was given a life sentence in return for testifying against his accomplice. He would be released in 1960, having served 16 years. Leatherberry was sentenced to death. Instead of taking part in the Normandy landings with his unit on D-Day, he was hanged at Shepton Mallet US Military Prison on Tuesday, May 16th, 1944, aged twenty-two by Thomas and Albert Pierrepoint ….

Case 9
"Murder For A

Story"

"The strangling itself was quite easily accomplished," this man told a packed courtroom. "I was pleased. I think I did it rather well" ....

Herbert MILLS
MURDER
Of
Mabel Tattershaw
[1951]

"I'm Herbert Mills and I'm ringing you from a call-box in Nottingham. About this murder I'm reporting. I was thinking of two hundred and fifty pounds" ....

It was about 4 o'clock in the afternoon of August 9th, 1951, that the switchboard operator of the large Sunday newspaper the News of the World, with offices just off Fleet Street, received a call from a public call-box in Nottingham. "I want to speak to someone about a murder – an exclusive murder," he said. "Just a moment," said the switchboard operator. A short while later the call from Nottingham was transferred to crime reporter Norman Rae's extension. "Hallo," said Rae. "Which murder are you referring to?" The voice in Nottingham had a surprise to deliver. "One the police don't know about yet. If you want it exclusive, how much are you prepared to pay?" The crime reporter sat a little stunned at this fantastic proposition. It might be a hoax, but there was something about the caller's voice that was too eager to suggest a hoax. Young and very eager, Norman Rae was already experienced. He had interviewed a good many criminals, and knew how some people thought of newspapers as open-handed purchasers of news scraps. The lure of easy money attracted the genuine and the phony. Especially the phony. He was cautious ....

"It's a real story all right. A woman's murder." "You say the police don't know about it?" "That's right. I'm offering it to you exclusive." "I'll have to know who you are." "I'm Herbert Mills, and I'm ringing you from a call-box in Nottingham. About this murder I'm reporting. I was thinking of two hundred and fifty pounds." "Look," the crime reporter responded, "we might be interested. I can't say without speaking to the editor. Can you ring back in half an hour?" The reporter was in a quandary. He wanted time to inform the police, and he also wanted to make sure the caller did not disappear into the blue. If the man had discovered the body of a woman who had been murdered, there was certainly a story. Possibly it was one worth paying for, but the police had to be brought in without delay. So he stalled. In half an hour he could do what was necessary. He felt considerable relief when the caller said, "All right, I'll ring back in half an hour." The man who claimed to be Herbert Mills rang off. Rae lost no time getting on to Nottingham Police, telling them of Mills's strange proposal, and explaining what he had arranged. "Keep him talking when he comes on," a Nottingham detective requested. "We'll have the exchange check the call to your London number and notify us. We'll let you know when we've picked him up." So the stage was set for the second call to London from Nottingham by a man who had a murder for sale. He was anxious to make this exclusive sale, for the second call was early. Reporter Norman Rae was expecting him, however, and ready with a number of general questions ....

If the questions seemed to be wasting time, he was mistaken, for Nottingham Police were soon on their way to the telephone kiosk from which the call to Fleet Street was being made. The young man in the call-box was plainly agitated. Herbert Mills was finding Rae a most difficult man to pin down in the matter of a simple yes or no to his exclusive proposition. In fact, he was getting quite irate with the reporter – and then the door of the call-box opened and a hand caught his shoulder. He pulled his head away from the handset and looked round. "Cops?" The one who held his shoulder nodded. The eager note abruptly left the young man's voice. He put the phone down. "Where are we going?" "City headquarters. There are some questions we want you to answer." At the Nottingham City Police headquarters the young man became frank and open in manner, and quite ready to reply to the questions put to him. He told the police his full name was Herbert Leonard Mills, he was 19 years old, and he had told the truth to the reporter in London. He did have a murder story to sell. He even repeated the price he had asked: £250. "And who's been murdered?" But that was one question he was apparently unable to answer. "I don't know her name. I found her lying on some waste ground, covered with a coat. These were on the ground." He took from his pocket a necklace of beads. It was a cheap, flashy piece of costume jewellery. The beads were tagged, dropped into an envelope, and the police were ready to be accompanied to the stretch of waste ground where a murdered woman, according to this unusual informant, was lying under a coat. The police were directed to the Sherwood Vale district. Mills walked briskly to a stretch of waste ground thickly covered with rough scrub, well-leafed in early August, and which had once been an orchard ….

In a depression on the waste ground the police came upon a sprawled coat. When they removed it they stared at the crumpled body of a woman in early middle-age. There was a bruise on her pale face. Mills stared at her in fascination. "How did you come to find her?" he was asked. "I'd been walking in the wood," he told the police. "I often walk here, especially when I want to read poetry. "I sometimes write poetry when I'm walking in the woods," he said. The artistic confidence was received in stony-faced silence by the men who had journeyed from the city with him. The marks on her throat and neck, the protuberant eyes, the lolling tongue, all pointed to the reason for her death. The life had been choked from her, possibly after she had been struck the blow that had bruised her face in her very last moments. One of the police dipped a hand into a pocket of the coat that had covered the corpse. He found a crumpled receipt. Smoothing it out, it was possible to read the name of the person to whom it was made out, and the address below the name: Mrs. Tattershaw, Longmead Drive, Nottingham. The corpse was removed after the ground around had been carefully examined. Mills was taken back to the city and asked some more questions. Again he replied with almost engaging frankness about himself and his way of life, about his friend and a young woman who was the inspiration for some of his poetry. He was allowed to leave when the replies were all recorded. In the meantime detectives had been to Longmead Drive. They had learned that Mabel Tattershaw, a housewife aged 47, had not been seen since **Friday, August 3rd**, by her neighbours. Mills was on record as having stated he had come across the body on the waste ground that morning, August 9th, and in the afternoon had phoned London. Medical evidence supported this, also the theory that she had first been struck before life was choked out of her. The police switched to a wider field of inquiry in the neighbourhood of Sherwood Vale ….

The corpse was removed to a forensic laboratory and a number of tests run. A few very significant discoveries were made. In the meantime Norman Rae had journeyed to Nottingham and met the ebullient Herbert Mills, who was full of smiles and good humour at the thought of rubbing shoulders with a working representative of Fleet Street. "You want me to write this up, don't you?" "I want you to come to London with me and write your own story of finding the body," the crime reporter told Mills. What Rae omitted to tell him was that he was acting in concert with the Nottingham Police. Mills was to be encouraged to tell his own version of the discovery as fully as he wished. But when he was in London it was found that the proximity of Fleet Street induced no special inspiration to add materially to the few facts already given. Needless to relate, the very amateurishly contrived article had little genuine news value and was not published as written by Mills. Mills seemed annoyed at what he considered the selective interest accorded his great exclusive story. With the Fleet Street crime reporter who had brought him to London, he returned, with an air of disappointment, to Nottingham ….

The police had a session with the London reporter. The facts in the article by Mills were compared with what had been told to the police in a formal statement. The few minor discrepancies were nothing for detectives to work on. For a day or so, Mills was left to his own rather empty devices and traipsed about Nottingham, watched by CID men. He seemed in a mood, as if concentrating on a personal problem. By August 12th, however, Mills seemed to have come to a decision. He once more approached Norman Rae. This time he offered what he described as "sensational information." "What's sensational about it?" he was asked. "Well, it's something I haven't told before." "You mean you suppressed it?" "I mean I didn't tell it, and it rather changes things." Mills was invited to write another article. He was told that if it was a good story and could be used, then the paper would certainly use it. Another article was written. It was a further dreary retelling, certainly not sensational, and the News of the World chose not to buy it. Even the one major difference from the previous article could not be so described. Earlier, Mills had claimed to have found the body on the 9th after walking through the woods beyond the waste ground. In this fresh article he stated that he had found the body on the 5th – four days before. Here was a manifest lie. But why should Mills suddenly indulge in such a stupid fabrication? The police began to wonder if this strange informer was subconsciously or deliberately thinking in terms of an alibi. One reason for considering the possibility was the result of the forensic laboratory tests ….

On the dead woman's body had been found several human hairs that were labelled "foreign – most likely male." Those hairs were now known to be identical with Mills's. Some textile fibres had been found under Mabel Tattershaw's first and second fingernails – the fingers a woman would use if making a clawing motion to defend herself from sudden attack. These fibres were to be checked against some taken from Mills's jacket. While the Nottingham detectives continued their inquiries Mills approached other newspapers with his story, but no one bought it. Each editor approached reported the offer of a murder story to the police. Then came the first real break in the case. The police located two people who had seen a young man they readily identified as Mills walking with a woman they were sure was Mabel Tattershaw. The date was significant: the 2nd. The day *before* the murder …. Mills's jacket was tested for fibre comparison. The minute fragments of textile fibres taken from under the dead woman's fingernails matched those of his jacket. His hair could have fallen on the body when he stooped over it, but fibres from his jacket could only have been snagged under the woman's fingernails while she was alive. It appeared that Herbert Mills had a good deal of explaining to do, especially about a meeting with Mabel Tattershaw on the 2nd …. Even the normally smiling and self-assured

Mills – who had lately lost both his smile and his self-assurance – was beginning to realise he had to find yet another exclusive story. He had completed his running circle, and was back where he had started. He approached Norman Rae once more. "This time it's the real thing," he promised. Again the reporter came to Nottingham. He wasn't very hopeful; he'd done it all before. Rae met Mills by appointment in a Nottingham hotel, and this time shock was added to surprise ….

Mills had an exclusive story to sell, and this time no less than a confession to murder. It was 7 o'clock on a warm August evening. Mills was forgetting to look cool. Fleet Street would have to print his confession! "You'd better write down what you have to say," he was advised. "Make it very clear that what you put down is an entirely voluntary statement, made at your own request, and you should sign each page." Once more Herbert Mills sat down with a pen in his hand and started to write his exclusive story. As the minutes passed he even seemed to be enjoying himself, as though fulfilling a secret desire. The latent exhibitionist was uppermost. He wasn't writing poetry. He was writing something few poets could have matched. He was writing the truth about what he considered the perfect crime. Actually it was a long way from being perfect in his sense of the word, but he wasn't prepared to engage in an academic argument. He wrote: "Of my own free will, without pressure or force of any kind whatsoever, I wish to confess to the murder of Mrs. Tattershaw." The words were like the lifting of a curtain in his mind. Once the curtain was removed he saw clearly what had to be said. He wrote for an hour, knowing that what he put down on the sheets of paper would be seen by the police. "I had always considered the possibility of the perfect crime. Here was my opportunity," he told Rae. "I have been most successful." The confession told a simple but horrible story. His meeting with Mabel Tattershaw, who was old enough to be his mother, was accidental. It occurred in the Roxy Cinema on August 7th. He claimed that she forced her attentions on him. As she was dead there was no possible way of proving or disproving that this was the case ….

They met again by agreement, and by that time he had made up his mind to commit the perfect murder that had occupied his thoughts at various times in the recent past. In fact, his plan was a curious blend of striving to attain a perverted perfection and a desire to make money from his shocking act of violence. Undoubtedly he had delusions of grandeur. The perfect crime would give them expression and reality. How much his greed for money tipped the balance no one can say. It remained a puzzle even to the young man, and he was not sure he understood himself. Herbert Mills duly appeared in the dock before Judge Lawrence Byrne at the Nottingham Assizes on a grey November day when much of the Trent Valley was shrouded in steamy mist. He took his place with the manner of an actor who knows he rates star billing. His eyes lingered on the rows of reporters. This time he didn't have to push a pen himself. Others would write about him. Every single word would be recorded. He had forced this on them. It was his triumph, and his manner conveyed as much. All the same, it was a curiously inverted triumph. From the moment the trial opened it was obvious that the prisoner was not a person meriting a great deal of sympathy. He was young and cocksure, and quite unbowed. Somewhere in the bright glaze of this terrifying young man there was a concealed chink, and through it had seeped all kindness and affection and integrity. The drama of the court unrolled with the clarity of a well-directed film, the high spot of which was the star performer's own dramatic assertions ….

Again he took pains to inform his listeners of how he had conceived the notion of making money from reporting a murder. "I was quite proud of it," he said, and the entire assembly sat in shocked silence. He had walked with Mabel Tattershaw to the woods and then climbed to the hilly waste ground, where they sat down and he casually removed her necklace. He dropped the beads into his pocket when she wasn't looking, and before she could become suspicious his hands were at her throat. The struggle was brief and entirely one-sided. "I placed the coat so that she could not gather any threads from it in her fingernails." He seemed curiously clear about this action, as though it had special importance for him. "The strangling itself was quite easily accomplished; I was very pleased. I think I did it rather well." This smug attempt at honesty set more than a few teeth on edge. He leaned across the witness-box stating without feeling of remorse that he was not sorry he had tried to make money from Mabel Tattershaw's death. "Do you not think it was very cruel?" counsel asked him. "Why, once a person's dead it doesn't make any difference." "The jury will think you're a monster," he was informed. The prospect brought no cloud to his bright eyes ….

Monster or not, he was remaining utterly consistent in his role of honest perpetrator of the perfect crime. "They can think what they like," he told the prosecutor, who didn't have to glance at the jury to know how they would take this gratuitous invitation. Counsel for the defence strove gallantly for a client who had formally pleaded not guilty. He did his best to convince the jury that the confession they had heard was a piece of adolescent invention. In fact he did everything he could for his client, short of letting him plead insanity. No jury on earth would have decided that the man who strangled Mabel Tattershaw and tried to sell the story for a fancy price was incapable of knowing he was doing wrong at the time of killing his victim. As a matter of fact, when they eventually retired, the jury found themselves with very little to debate at the end of the 4-day trial on November 22nd. They were back in court in well under half an hour, and the foreman rose to announce the expected verdict of guilty. A pathetic and tragic farce, which was Herbert Mills's wild bid for front-page glory at a cosy price, was almost over. He was returned to jail to await the day of execution – he had declined to appeal. He began composing a not particularly inspired verse that began: 'Though so many would believe This tale is most untrue, Who sells the news on Saturday On Friday that he slew.' ….

The Home Secretary, after considering the relevant papers on the case, ordered a panel of doctors to examine Mills and report their findings. They duly sent in their unanimous opinion: that Herbert Mills was *sane*. So justice had to take its course. But the young man did not seem terribly affected by his own final ordeal. Herbert Mills was hanged at Lincoln Prison by Albert Pierrepoint and Herbert Allen on Tuesday, December 11th, 1951. It was Allen's last execution and it appears he was 'sacked' …. The drop ensured that Mills' spinal column was instantly dislocated, which would normally bring about an equally instant death, but in this case there is some doubt when his life actually became extinct. The medical officer reported at the inquest that the heart had continued to beat for 20 minutes after the drop ....

Case 10
"The Mysterious Case Of James Lehman – The Cyanide Poisoner"

"I'm sort of married, but I'm not really married. You see, my marriage to my so-called wife is void. She's really Mrs. Stokes" ....

"A small quantity of cyanide mixed with water and coffee reveals the sugar content. I'm naturally anxious to have the best-quality coffee" ....

"When I came back a couple of hours later she was singing the children to sleep. An hour later her face was turning purple and she was clearly very ill" ....

James LEHMAN
MURDER
Of
His Wife Margaret
[1945]

James Lehman

Handsome James Lehman was a smooth-talking con-man whose whole life had become a web of lies and deceit. And when his pregnant wife Margaret died suddenly, this Walter Mitty-type character knew it was time to disappear ....

"Come upstairs quickly! My wife is terribly ill!" The husband's plaintive cry rang through the house as his landlady came running from the kitchen. The landlady later remembered a ghastly odour as she mounted the stairs, and recalled hearing the distraught woman, who was heavily pregnant, groaning. She touched the woman's head – it was clammy and very blue. And always there was this terrible smell. "What happened?" she asked. "I brought in some rum for her, and she must have taken it while I wasn't looking," the husband blurted out. The landlady stared back hard at the agitated husband. The couple had been lodging with her for three months and although she had become a firm friend of the wife, she still couldn't quite work out who the husband was, what he did, how he lived. She wasn't exactly alone in that. No one else could fathom him out, either. Everyone said he was a regular guy – a tall, good-looking, well-mannered, snappy dresser. He made friends everywhere he went, and could always tell a good yarn. The problem was – who exactly was he? He called himself James Herbert Lehman, but that didn't really help because he called himself by seven other names as well. He said occasionally that he was American, sometimes he was Irish, sometimes Canadian, and other times he was English. He fancied himself as a rich entrepreneur but he was never more than dirt-poor, and he could deceive you with lies you couldn't fail to believe ….

James Lehman – this was just about his favourite name – was in fact a Canadian, born in Montreal in 1899. He was educated in America and joined the Canadian Army in 1916, calling himself James Martin. A year later he deserted and joined the US Army. Soon afterwards he was invalided out on medical grounds. Between the wars he was James Richman, James Hiames, James Feeley and several others. He took a law degree in Pennsylvania, got divorced after a three-year marriage, and did nothing very special after that. When the Second

World War came he was James Lehman again, back in the Canadian Army as a private (they had evidently forgotten all about his desertion during World War One) and posted to Britain. Arriving in Aldershot in 1940 he met and married NAAFI canteen worker Margaret Hayden, a 24 year old Irish girl – he was forty .... Once more he was found unfit for service. This time he injured his back on manoeuvres. Discharged, he joined Dad's Army, Britain's much-vaunted Home Guard, then, tiring of soldiering, set off for Ireland with his wife and their two young children. Ireland didn't improve Lehman's prospects in life. By Christmas, 1943, the family was destitute ....

Margaret was pregnant again, and everyone who talked to her agreed she was very unhappy, trapped in another wartime marriage that had gone wrong. In January, 1944, the Lehman family did a moonlight flit from their rooms, leaving bills and months of unpaid rent behind them. They moved to furnished rooms let by a Mrs. O'Callaghan, at 11, Leinster Road, Rathmines, a quiet south Dublin suburb. They had the bedroom at the top of the house with the use of the kitchen and sink on the floor below, and soon they were on the friendliest of terms with Mrs. O'Callaghan. Lehman had sunk to a state of financial desperation when he suddenly discovered his true metier. Having no skills, and unable to do physical work because of his back problem, he worked on his principal asset, his charm, and became a con-man. At this, at least, he was mildly successful. Very soon he had tricked people into paying him a total of £225 in return for nothing at all, and, thus capitalised, he opened a baby food shop in Ranelagh, a Dublin suburb. When it went broke within a month, he switched to selling coffee. He had no head for business, though, and it never occurred to him until too late that a shop selling coffee in a small Dublin suburb wasn't much more than a recipe for bankruptcy. The charm that had conned cash out of acquaintances was now employed in romancing. This was a dodgy business for a married man, especially in a Catholic country, but handsome, charming men are generally great believers in themselves. The focus of Lehman's wandering eye was a nurse named Mary McCaigue. "I'm sort of married, but I'm not really married," he lied to her. "You see, my marriage to my so-called wife is void. That's because I discovered she was already married to someone else, a guy called Dorset Stokes, after we went through a marriage ceremony. She's really Mrs. Stokes. I've heard that she's in a Dublin hospital after trying to commit suicide with an aspirin overdose. But that's none of my business, needless to say. I don't have anything to do with her." Of course, all this was so much moonshine ….

Whatever Lehman now thought about his wife Margaret he was still living with her and their two children, and still living in Mrs. O'Callaghan's rented rooms. But Nurse Mary was duly impressed. And who might not have been? The story was so ridiculous that it could actually have been true. So she decided it must be. She was even more impressed, even more convinced, when he gave her an expensive ring. She slipped it on her engagement finger, simpering. "I've got big plans for the future," Lehman told her, his chest swelling. "I'm going to open a chain of shops." He paused significantly. "It might be a good idea if you quit your hospital job and come and work in my business as a supervisor. Of course, you'll have a company car." To show her dedication, she would be required to "buy into" the business. That would be £25, please. Nurse Mary paid up, gratefully. Now Lehman looked around for another con victim. His advertisement for a job as manager of one of his shops was answered by a Miss Anna Finucane. "The shop is part of a vast chain retailing coffee across the width of the USA and in England," he explained to her. "Your job will be manager of our first Irish branch, which will be a vital link in our international retail chain." To show her dedication, she would be required to put up a bond for £50. "But I only have £40," Anna said, heartbroken that she was about to lose this once-in-a-lifetime opportunity to enter into management. "It's all I've got in the world." Lehman considered for a moment. "Very well, I'll try to press the other directors to accept £40," he said. Needless to say, the "other directors" raised no objections. Using the con money, Lehman rented a shop at Dun Laoghaire, and installed Anna Finucane behind the counter. He also told her his fanciful story about his marriage being null and void on account of his wife already being married. "I intend to marry Mary McCaigue in June," he confided. Then, apparently forgetting his lie about the "other directors," he added: "Mary is the real owner of the business. She has invested heavily in it." ….

Once Lehman began lying, it seems he couldn't stop adding to his stack of absurd stories. "Mrs. Stokes is really unbalanced," he said. "I was pressed to go through a marriage ceremony with her by the Canadian Army authorities, who insisted on it after I'd been on a drinking spree with some of my fellow-officers. "Now, I'm afraid, she's always ill. She takes poison, you see." One of those scenes that generally happen only in theatrical farces because they are so catastrophic in real life occurred shortly after the shop opened for business. The door was flung open and in walked Lehman's heavily pregnant wife Margaret (aka Margaret Stokes), accompanied by the Lehmans' landlady, the good-hearted Mrs. O'Callaghan. Most men would have prayed for the floor to open beneath them at such a sight. Not James Lehman. He chatted to the two women, and after they left the shop he remarked casually to Anna Finucane: "That was my ex-lady-love. She is the only person I've ever hated. I've no idea who she was with." ….

Now aged 44, a new and more sinister slant appeared in Lehman's Walter Mitty character in March, 1944, when he went into the local chemist shop and asked to buy some cyanide. When the chemist raised an eyebrow quizzically Lehman added: "I want it to test my bottled coffee for impurities." The chemist was intrigued. "I've never heard of such a test," he said. "Oh, it's well known among coffee makers," Lehman replied airily. "A small quantity of cyanide mixed with water and coffee reveals the sugar content. I'm naturally anxious to have the best-quality coffee, completely free of any impurities." The chemist, still puzzled, shook his head, but without any more questions he sold Lehman a crystal of cyanide capable of producing about 150 grains. That was enough to kill about 40 people, but that didn't worry the chemist because his customer quite clearly seemed to have no intention of killing anyone. Next day Lehman pulverised the crystal on to a piece of paper on his shop counter in front of the staff. "This is a dangerous business," he said, transferring the powder into a bottle. "It's a deadly poison, but we need it to test our bottled coffee. Notice how I clean all the instruments afterwards." "Is it hard to buy?" Anna Finucane asked. "Yes," replied Lehman. "But there are ways." ….

Next day, **Sunday, March 19th, 1944**, Margaret Lehman, whose confinement was now imminent, was up and about early. She was quite fit apart from a slight cold. The day was normal enough, and in the evening she went back to bed for a rest. "She's feeling a bit giddy," Lehman told Mrs. O'Callaghan. "If she isn't better by morning I'll get the doctor to come and see her." He went back upstairs again, and five minutes later he was screaming for help from the landing. Mrs. O'Callaghan was calm and collected as she took in the bedroom scene. She watched Margaret slip quickly into unconsciousness, remembered the rum Lehman had mentioned, and turned to the husband, who was crying and running up and down the room in distress. "She probably drank the rum, but did she take any aspirin with it?" she asked. "I don't know! I don't know!" he wailed. Tears were streaming down his face. Mrs. O'Callaghan left the room and called an ambulance. When it arrived Margaret Lehman's colour was now deep purple. "She's been looking like that for several hours," Lehman explained to the ambulance man. On the way to the hospital he asked the driver: "Is she very bad?" "Bad enough," he replied ….

That was no understatement, for by the time they reached the hospital Margaret was dead, and so too was her unborn child. Told this by a doctor, Lehman became distressed, and had to lie down and rest. Back at Leinster Road Mrs. O'Callaghan, a handkerchief held to her face, was desperately trying to locate the source of the bad smell from her lodgers' bedroom. She remembered it was like bitter almonds, and strong enough to make her gasp. There was no bottle, cup or glass anywhere in the room. At 9.30 that evening Lehman came back from the hospital. "Margaret is dead," he said simply, his eyes filling with tears. Mrs. O'Callaghan laid a comforting hand on his arm before he went upstairs to write a note summoning Anna Finucane to call at his lodgings that evening. When she arrived she listened sorrowfully as Lehman sadly recounted what had happened. "Was it the result of poison?" she asked suddenly. Lehman replied: "I'm afraid so." "What sort of poison do you think it was?" He shrugged. "Aspirin, probably." Together they went through Margaret's handbag and burned a few letters. Persuaded by Lehman, Anna made a curious phone call to Mary McCaigue on his behalf. The message was, "I am speaking on behalf of a friend of yours.

There has been a death in the family." Next day Lehman called on the chemist who sold him the cyanide. He wept when he told him the sad news. "Had she been ill for a long time?" the chemist asked sympathetically. "Since the previous day," Lehman replied. "Anyway, she was always taking something, and she didn't want any more children." While he was out Mrs. O'Callaghan went to her lodgers' kitchenette and found a rum bottle in a conspicuous place. She picked it up and looked at it meaningfully. She knew it wasn't there when she was looking the night before. That evening there was a knock on the door at Leinster Road ….

The caller was Sergeant Sheppard of the Garda, making inquiries into the death of Margaret Lehman. "The doctors are not satisfied about the cause of her death and they have suggested she might have taken poison," he said. Lehman replied at once: "She got no poison here." The sergeant searched the Lehmans' rooms and slipped the rum bottle into his pocket. "What exactly happened to your wife, sir?" he asked. "Well, she had a bad attack of flu at Christmas," Lehman recalled. "Two days ago she had a bad cold and she took some rum with cero-calcium tablets. I went out yesterday afternoon to do a few errands and when I came back a couple of hours later she was singing the children to sleep. An hour later I went up to the bedroom again. Her face was turning purple and she was clearly very ill." The sergeant left, deep in thought. There can be no doubt that at this stage Lehman, the smooth-talking con-man whose whole life had become one big lie, was wondering if he was going to get away with this one. The day they buried his wife Anna Finucane took him aside. "Do you think there will be any more police inquiries?" she asked anxiously. Lehman nodded gravely. "I think there may be," he said ….

After a pause, he added: "If they ask you anything I would like you to say that you know nothing at all about my personal life – you don't even know whether I'm single or married." Anna literally stamped her foot. "I can't and I won't be telling any lies to the police," she replied indignantly. And she added artfully: "What about those poisons you were working with at the shop?" "I got rid of them a long time ago, and anyway, you know nothing about them," he retorted sharply. Next day Lehman and his sister-in-law were packing up Margaret's clothes when he found a bottle and a crucifix in her overcoat pocket. Tears pouted from his eyes. "I wonder what she had in this bottle," he said to his sister-in-law, handing it to her. But he already knew what had been in the bottle – for it was the same bottle into which he had put the cyanide powder after scraping the crystal the chemist had sold him ….

Later that day he mentioned this "find" to Mrs. O'Callaghan, and with his penchant for embellishment he added: "I also found a suicide letter she'd written. It had such terrible things in it that I burned it for the sake of the children." Four days after Margaret's death, Lehman called on Mary McCaigue. He didn't seem prepared for the frosty reception she gave him. "Have you heard about Mrs. Stokes's death?" he inquired. "I've heard about Mrs. Lehman's death," she retorted. Unperturbed, he went on: "Where is that rascal Stokes? If only I could lay my hands on him!" "I'm surprised to hear that you went to the hospital, since you are not the dead woman's husband," Nurse McCaigue remarked. Lehman replied: "I did no more than anyone else would have done," whereupon Mary told him that their friendship was now ended. It seemed too that Lehman's great business venture was also about to end. He left town and wrote to Anna Finucane: "Dear Anna, My son is very ill, hence my absence. Please shut the shop or do with it whatever you should like or think best. I am terribly sorry. Will call at your residence when I get back. Sincerely, Jim." When he failed to return the following week she closed the shop and disposed of the fittings for cash, thereby recouping at least some of her £40 investment ….

The next time she saw her employer was in court. In the meantime Lehman had gone off to spend a few days with his in-laws in Co Kildare. He told them that Margaret had died in childbirth, that the bottle found in her coat was "foreign poison," and – this because he always had to add something unlikely – the stillborn baby was black. On April 2nd he was summoned to the Garda station at Ballytore to make a statement about Margaret's death. Five days later he called on his former landlady, Mrs. O'Callaghan. "Did you see the newspaper stories about Margaret's death?" he asked her. And then added: "Would you not think I had done it?" When she made no reply, he said cheerily, "Well, I'm off to call on my brother-in-law." A few minutes later James Lehman vanished ….

The following day an American airman named James McCaigue booked into the Oriel Hotel, Monaghan, about 80 miles north-west of Dublin, close to the Ulster border. The hotel was a favourite haunt of US servicemen stationed in Northern Ireland. "I'm on sick leave," he told the manageress. "I'll be staying a few days." While the girl filled in the paperwork, "Captain" McCaigue filled her in with a summary of his brilliant flying record. During the next few days he booked out, then returned to the hotel and booked in again. When the manageress asked him to sign the register again he said he was in a great hurry, and would she sign it for him. She did, reminding him that he had shown no identity documents. "Well, hell, I left all my papers back in Belfast," he expostulated. And then: "I expect you're wondering how I managed to cross the border without them. It's because I know all the border guards. They have a soft spot for us Canadian veterans." The slip of the tongue didn't go unnoticed by the manageress, but she said nothing. Perhaps it was because no one ever said anything that he continued unabated, piling lie upon lie until he didn't know who he was or what he had said. In Monaghan he wined and dined the local girls, masquerading as "Captain Lehman," an American serving with the Canadian Air Force. But back at the hotel he was still Captain McCaigue, and because Monaghan is a small town people started discussing his dual identity ….

On the morning of Friday, April 14th, after a well-watered night out in the town, Lehman rang down for breakfast in bed. Instead of breakfast, the door was thrown open and in walked a posse from the Garda. "I am James McCaigue," he replied in answer to their questions. "I am an American airman, currently grounded.' He didn't have his identity card with him – he had left it at his US air base in Belfast. He was taken to the Garda station and given breakfast and a newspaper to read while his suitcase was searched. The newspaper must have put him off breakfast – half of its front page was devoted to a picture of a man named James Lehman, wanted for questioning with regard to the death of his wife. When a detective pointed out the picture to him, Lehman shook his head. "I'm James McCaigue," he insisted. "I've never been married." "Have you ever been to Dublin?" the detective asked. Lehman shook his head. "Never." "Then I wonder why you have two tickets to Dublin in your suitcase?" There was no answer. The trial of James Lehman – that was how they decided to name him – began in Dublin on October 16th, 1944, before Judge Conor Maguire. The defence submission was quite simple: Margaret Lehman committed suicide. It was the prosecution's job to prove that her death was the result of murder ....

Thrilled by the prospect of salacious evidence from Mary McCaigue and Anna Finucane, and by the prisoner's good looks, women flocked to the court, crowding the public gallery. But the most dramatic evidence came when the cyanide was being discussed. Doctors explained that when someone swallows cyanide the prussic acid in the poison is released by hydrochloric acid in the stomach acting upon it. The speed with which prussic acid acts depends on the quantity of hydrochloric acid it encounters. In the case of Margaret Lehman, the quantity of cyanide ingested could not be estimated. The state pathologist said in evidence that only a minute or two, depending on the quantity consumed, would elapse before the sufferer lost the power to make voluntary movements. Another pathologist said the time would be five minutes, so that after taking the poison Mrs. Lehman might be able to wash out the cup. She had, in fact, lived about 55 minutes from the time Mrs. O'Callaghan went upstairs. The defence challenged a long statement made by Lehman at the time of his arrest – he was suffering from amnesia at the time, they suggested, and therefore it wasn't a voluntary statement. But the challenge was over-ruled by the judge. Lehman himself testified to his memory loss from the witness-box. He found himself in Mountjoy Prison from March 28th until the middle of July, and he couldn't remember a thing about it. The last thing he remembered was reading the suicide note slipped into his wife's ration book, and he thought the shock of that had caused his amnesia. His wife, he said, had been a morphine addict and had threatened to kill herself if she wasn't given supplies of the drug. Unable to obtain any morphine for her, he went back to her bedroom and found her vomiting. She told him she had taken aspirin and whisky to quell her cravings ....

Eventually he found an army medical officer who came to his room and gave Margaret two injections. He bought the cyanide, he said, after reading an article in the American News Weekly describing how to make bottled coffee from beans. The article described a test of how to determine the amount of sugar and saccharine in the coffee. The test required a solution of synthetic uric acid and sodium cyanide. He bought the cyanide as described, and bought the uric acid from another chemist. Margaret helped him conduct the experiment, after he warned her that the mix was a deadly poison. He tried the experiment two or three times without success, and found he was using too much coffee. He was also running out of cyanide. On the day she died Margaret woke up feeling dizzy and unwell. He went out for three hours until seven o'clock that afternoon, and arrived home to find his wife dying. The following day he tidied up the bedroom, removing a cup and spoon and washing them. Lehman denied the incriminating remarks attributed to him by Anna Finucane and Mary McCaigue. He claimed that Margaret wrote to him confessing she was married to a man named Dorset Stokes at the time of her marriage to him. She had once introduced him to a man named Dorset who he afterwards discovered was actually Stokes. He destroyed his wife's suicide note, he said, but he could reconstruct it from memory. In it she wrote that she could not live without morphine and was taking the rest of the cyanide left in the bottle. She begged his forgiveness. The note had so upset him, he went on, that he took four morphine tablets and some codeine and went to see a priest. Under relentless cross-examination, however, things began to look bleak for him ….

The main thrust of prosecutor George Murnaghan's questioning was that since Lehman was broke, his story of making bottled coffee was sheer fantasy. "I put it to you that there was no reality in this story about the testing of the coffee, that there was no necessity to test the coffee. What necessity was there to test the coffee at all?" he demanded. Lehman remained silent. "I put it to you that in the week before your wife died there was no question of testing the coffee because there was no coffee to test, that your business had gone?" "No, the business had not gone." "It was on the verge of collapse?" "Yes." "The wolf was at the door?" "He may have been." The prosecutor switched to Lehman's different names. "Under what name were you known in the American Army?" "Martin," said Lehman. "What was your Christian name?" "William." "What name did you use after William Martin?" "I don't remember." "Did you ever use the name of Hiames?" "Yes," said Lehman in guilty surprise. "Did you use the name Richman?" "Yes. Most of my life." "Why?" There was no answer. So the prosecutor asked: "How did you come to take the name James Herbert Lehman?" "I can't answer that," Lehman replied. A psychiatrist was called to attempt to explain Lehman's flight from justice. The defendant, he said, was a pathological liar, and his hiding himself away was the result of a morbid state, an hysterical flight from reality. The jury took only two hours to find him guilty of murder and he was sentenced to hang after the 9-day trial had ended on October 25th.... But the defence immediately went to the Appeal Court, arguing that the evidence about his use of aliases was prejudicial and should not have been allowed. On December 20th after a two-day hearing, the court agreed and ordered a re-trial. The second trial opened on January 15th, 1945, and this time Lehman chose not to go into the witness-box, thus saving himself from being exposed as a liar – a fact most Dubliners were already aware of, anyway ….

The court was told that he had three previous convictions. As William Martin he was sent to a reformatory in 1919 for robbery. As James Edward James he was jailed in Minnesota for 'grand larceny' in 1936, and as James Feeley he got six months' at Aldershot in 1941 for 11 offences of 'false pretences'. Again after a 9-day trial before Judge Andrew Overend he was found guilty of murder on January 24th, 1945, and again sentenced to death: this time the jury were out for two and a half hours .... Before the sentence was pronounced, he said: "I am satisfied that on this occasion there has been some small degree of fairness. I am innocent and my conscience is clear." Another appeal was launched and rejected – again after two days on March 1st ….

James Lehman was hanged on March 19th, 1945, exactly a year after his wife's death at Dublin's Mountjoy Prison by Albert Pierrepoint and an Irishman 'Thomas Johnston' appointed by the Irish government – his real name was James O'Sullivan from Cork and he received a fee of £20 and he died in 1978 …. Was Lehman's conscience really clear? That, of course, could have been another lie. But the case remains cloaked in doubt. It is just possible that Margaret Lehman did commit suicide. She had the means (cyanide), the motive (she was very unhappy in her marriage), and she had the opportunity. Lehman's undoing, perhaps, was that he told lies. But even liars sometimes tell the truth. Could he for once have been truthful when he said his conscience was clear ….

Case 11 "The Killer Police-Officer"

"Robertson found the evidence given by Cathy's friends harrowing. They told how she'd talked of nothing but her lover. She'd clearly been obsessed with him" ....

James ROBERTSON
MURDER
Of

Catherine McCluskey
[1950]

James Robertson

When police were called to the scene of a hit-and-run in Glasgow they were shocked by the state of the victim. Whoever was behind the wheel had come back for another go – to make certain the woman was dead ....

'Ronnie' Robertson had by far the largest cell of all, but none of the other inmates at Glasgow's Barlinnie Prison envied him. Nothing would have tempted them to change places. His cell was twice the size of the rest because it had also to provide space for two prison officers. It was the cell for the condemned. There were double doors immediately opposite, just across the passage. Ronnie guessed, correctly, that they were the entrance to the hanging chamber. Not that officialdom at Barlinnie called it anything as crude as that. It was the "execution suite." The wide doors were double to permit the passage of three men walking abreast: two officers and their prisoner, taking his last few paces to eternity. As was the custom, the two officers who kept Ronnie company in his cell were from another prison. Making conversation with the condemned man wasn't easy, but they did their best in a more than usually difficult situation. For Ronnie Robertson was no ordinary prisoner. For him the sheer horror of being where he was struck home particularly acutely. Ronnie Robertson was a policeman. He'd been in the condemned cell for more than a month, since November 13th, 1950. Games of draughts, crossword puzzles and other diversions had helped to pass the time, to take his mind off what awaited him and what had brought him to Barlinnie. "Big Ronnie," his colleagues had called the six-foot Glasgow constable ....

He was married with two children, and with his good looks, fine physique and easy charm he'd been known as a womaniser, his conquests inspiring many a wink and nudge between his fellow-officers. Some even found themselves covering up for him when affairs of the heart conflicted with duty. Surprisingly, at a time when constables were far from well paid, he acquired an Austin saloon car. "You won the pools, Ronnie?" asked his colleagues. He had friends, he'd replied, and one of them had owed him a few favours. Favours? It was a dubious explanation, coming from a policeman, but it had been accepted. Perhaps his immediate superiors turned a blind eye to his shortcomings because of his past record. He'd not been a bad copper, winning two commendations. Maybe they thought he was just going through a bad patch and he'd soon snap out of it. His wife could have confirmed that all was not as it should have been at home. He had become nervy, short-tempered and sullen. Something, she had sensed, was getting him down. Dire though his troubles had seemed at the time, however, they were nothing compared with what was to follow. Now, as he sat in the condemned cell, he reflected on the nightmare his life had become. His progress to the gallows had begun in the early hours of **Friday, July 28th, 1950**. It was then that a woman's body had been discovered lying in Prospecthill Road in the Govan Hill area of Glasgow. At first it had seemed that she was the victim of a hit-and-run driver, but a closer look convinced police that her death had been no accident ....

There was no glass from a shattered headlamp, as might have been expected. No dried mud on the road shaken from the vehicle's chassis by the impact. But there were two sets of skid marks, and they didn't make sense. They appeared to have been made by vehicles travelling in opposite directions, but there was no debris where they met. It seemed that the vehicle which had run over the victim had not then sped away, as would be the case with a hit-and-run motorist. Whoever was at the wheel had come back for another go, to make sure the woman was dead. She had "the worst injuries I've ever seen in a road accident," said a policeman who'd been at the scene. Congealed blood matted her hair, her dental plate had been smashed, her shoes lay some distance away, and the dirt, blood and oil covering her red coat made her look as if she had been put through a mangle. But who was she? And who was the driver? ....

It was reported that the police were seeking a hit-and-run motorist following the death of an unidentified woman with auburn hair in Prospecthill Road. The report was coupled with an appeal for information, and it wasn't long before a woman came forward. She told detectives that she'd been looking after a friend's baby for the night. The mother had auburn hair, and she hadn't come back to collect her child. The baby-sitter was taken to the mortuary. Yes, she confirmed tearfully, the Prospecthill Road victim was her friend Catherine McCluskey. Her worst fears confirmed, she asked what would happen to the baby. It would be looked after, she was assured. But Cathy also had an older child, the woman told the police. Cathy wasn't married, she explained, and there had been gossip about her and the baby. Anything the baby-sitter could tell them would be appreciated, said the detectives. The woman said she wasn't so sure about that. Rumour had it that the baby's father was "one of you lot," and that he'd been paying Cathy maintenance. "You mean he's a copper?" the detectives asked. The baby-sitter nodded. Cathy had been seen being driven around in the uniformed officer's car, she said. And that the man was married and his name was Robertson. It was swiftly established that the officer was Constable James Ronald Robertson, 33. A policeman for five years, he had initially done well after giving up his previous job as an aero engine inspector. In his early police career he had been a non-smoking, non-drinking, non-gambling example to others. But not any more. The detectives found that on the night of Cathy McCluskey's death, Robertson wasn't where he should have been: on his beat. His log-book at the Cumberland Street police-box contained a false entry, timed at 2.10 a.m. Cathy was believed to have been struck by an Austin saloon at about 12.50 a.m. The man at the wheel was thought to have been wearing a fawn Burberry coat. Months later, in his cell at Barlinnie Prison, that man tried not to think of the prolonged grilling he'd received from his fellow-officers. The interrogation had been given an edge by their growing suspicion that he'd let the side down – spectacularly ….

As one hour followed another, the detectives' suspicion had hardened to certainty. He could tell that by their voices, their eyes, the way they looked at him. The day before they'd been his comrades. Now they were giving him the kind of looks usually reserved for unsavoury suspects who weren't to be trusted. He was then told to change from the casual clothes he was wearing and put on his uniform to take part in an identity parade. One after another, friends of Cathy McCluskey walked slowly along the line and took a good look at him. He didn't know them, but maybe they recognised him. Then he knew the worst. He was charged with murder. Well, his colleagues were only doing their job. And he had to admit that they hadn't done it badly. Bit by bit they'd reconstructed the events of July 27th and 28th and what had led up to them. His best blue suit had hung loosely when he'd pleaded not guilty at the beginning of his trial before Lord James Keith in November. It was small wonder that his clothes no longer fitted. He guessed he must have lost nearly two stone. The charge against him was a trifle wordy, compared with what would have sufficed in an English court, but it was nothing if not to the point. It alleged that on July 28th he struck Catherine McCluskey on the head with a rubber truncheon, or rendered her insensible by other means, and then murdered her by driving over her in a car bearing false number-plates. And that wasn't all. He was also charged with breaking into a car showroom in April 1950, stealing log-books and a car radio, and with following this up in May by stealing a car. He'd found the evidence given by Cathy's friends particularly harrowing. They told how 40-year-old Cathy had talked of nothing but her lover. She'd clearly been obsessed with him ….

It transpired that Cathy had done her best to conceal the identity of her baby's father. This became clear when an official of the National Assistance Board gave evidence. The witness said that when Cathy applied for benefit, she'd declined to name the father of her second child. It had only been under pressure that she'd reluctantly revealed that a married policeman was the father. The court then heard that as a bent copper PC Robertson had been remarkably careless. The radio and log-books found during a search of his home were identified by a car-dealer as having been stolen from his showroom. And the stolen Austin was identified by its owner. Worse was to come when Robertson's fellow-constable on the night shift was called to testify against him. The court heard how Big Ronnie had given his colleague a lift when the two went on duty at 11 p.m. on the night of the murder. And how when he'd dropped his colleague off, Robertson's parting words had been, "I'm going to take home a blonde." He hadn't been seen on patrol until about 1.10 a.m., when it was noticed that his collar was saturated with perspiration. A detective inspector told the court that the stolen Austin had been found in a Gorbals Street garage, with blood and a woman's auburn hair on its chassis. And in a pocket of Big Ronnie's uniform, officers discovered a rubber cosh. There was a small stain on that truncheon which reacted positively to tests for blood, a forensic scientist told the court, but the examination was not conclusive ....

The witness – Professor John Glaister, Regius Professor of Forensic Medicine at Glasgow University – had gone on to say that Cathy had been struck, probably more than once, by a car travelling at an appreciable speed. He believed she had already been lying down when the car ran over her. An officer who had been among the first on the scene said it appeared that the killer had driven over his victim and had then turned around and driven over her again. To explain why he was sweating so heavily that night, Big Ronnie told his colleagues on the beat that his car exhaust had broken. In court he was relieved to hear that story confirmed at least in part: the Austin's exhaust had indeed been found to be broken – but by what? By driving over Cathy? In the condemned cell, Big Ronnie mentally reviewed the evidence he had given at his trial. He thought he had answered just about every point raised against him. He'd admitted he knew Cathy, telling the court that they'd first met one night during the previous year. He'd been called to deal with a brawl at her home in Nicholson Street in the Gorbals. She was attractive and she had an inviting smile. "I came across her many times since then," he told the jury, but he denied having visited her regularly at her flat. He'd not stolen the Austin, he insisted. He'd spotted it parked on waste ground early one morning while he was going off night shift. It was still there the next day, by which time he knew it had been reported stolen. This disturbed him because he should have reported spotting it, but had omitted to do so. Seeing it still there on the third day he walked past it, he decided to take it for a run. Then he prepared false numberplates, proposing to use the car just to and from work. As for the log-books and the radio found at his home, he'd explained that he'd found them lying in a backyard while he was on his beat. He'd admitted he had a date with Cathy on the night of her death. The previous evening she'd told him she'd been locked out of where she was living and had to find somewhere else or walk the streets. He was under pressure to help her, and he'd picked her up in the Austin at 11.10 p.m. on July 27th. She wanted him to take her to Neilston, but that was out of the question. It would entail a round-trip of nearly 30 miles and he was supposed to be on duty. Cathy had burst into tears when he told her he couldn't take her that distance. He remembered shouting, "Oh, for God's sake!" as he set off with her, driving aimlessly towards Prospecthill Road. There he turned round, explaining that he had to get back to Cumberland Street as he'd already missed seeing his sergeant at the appointed time ….

Cathy had lost her temper. "Well, I'm not going back!" she'd cried, getting out of the car and slamming the door. He'd driven off. But then, feeling he couldn't leave her like that, he'd reversed along the dark road, braking to a standstill when he felt a bump and his exhaust suddenly began booming. He'd told the jury how he'd opened his door and got out to see Cathy's face protruding from under the running-board, her eyes staring and her mouth filling with blood. With his torch, he saw straight away that she was dead. He'd gone on to describe how he'd struggled to drag her from under the car, but her clothing seemed to have become entangled. He'd tried to free the body by reversing and then driving forward. When he'd accomplished this after several tries he sat perspiring heavily, wondering what to do next. He'd tried to fix his exhaust and had then returned to his beat, he'd told the court. As for the policeman who was said to have given Cathy money each week, he insisted that this must be somebody else. It certainly wasn't him. Questioned by the prosecution, he denied that he had coshed Cathy and then pushed her out of the car. He'd simply reversed into her by accident, he repeated. The prosecution also wanted to know how he'd striven to drag the body from under the car without getting so much as a speck of blood on his uniform, which had been examined. He'd no convincing answer to that ….

There'd been a glimmer of hope, however, when his defence counsel, John Cameron KC, rose to tell the jury that he had himself examined the car his client had been driving. In the boot-lid he had spotted a small dent which indicated that the constable might indeed have reversed into the victim. Recalled by Harold Leslie KC, prosecuting, Professor Glaister said that if Cathy McCluskey had been knocked down in this way he would have expected to find a bruise much larger than any which the corpse had displayed. Questioned further by Mr. Cameron, however, he conceded that it was possible that Cathy had been run down in the manner the defence claimed, though he thought it unlikely. It was a small victory for the defence, but it wasn't enough. The jury spent only an hour discussing the case at the end of the 6-day trial on November 13th …. Then they returned to find James Robertson guilty of Cathy's murder, by a majority verdict. So that was that. He'd been sentenced to death. He could have done without the jeering crowd waiting outside as he was driven away from the court ….

But he hadn't lost hope, not even when his appeal was dismissed on November 28th …. His wife had petitioned for a reprieve, and he'd thought one would come. But it hadn't. And now it was Saturday, December 16th, 1950, the day of the execution at Barlinnie Prison he'd thought would never take place, the eventuality he'd mentally rejected. When your last steps on earth could be to the scaffold, it didn't bear thinking about. It was small consolation to Robertson that a life sentence in prison would have been hell for him as an ex-copper. But it was a fate he'd have gladly preferred to this, the appalling alternative. Life was never so dear as when you were about to lose it. At the appointed hour Robertson's two officer companions escorted him across the corridor and through the double doors opposite his cell. Then with gruff goodbyes they handed him over to two more prison officers, also from another gaol. He was asked his name and whether he had anything to say. Then the waiting hangman, Albert Pierrepoint, and his assistant Steve Wade pinioned the prisoner's hands behind his back with a leather strap and placed a hood over his head. It was all accomplished so swiftly that Robertson had no time to take anything in – no time to wonder about the harness worn by the two prison officers who each held one of his arms as he was positioned on the trap-door. Lines from those safety harnesses were attached to four rings in the roof of the chamber. This ensured that only the prisoner made the drop, in the event of one of the officers losing his footing when the trap-door yawned beneath the plank on which he was standing. The hangman adjusted the noose, then swiftly moved back and pulled a long-handled lever. The trap-door opened and James Robertson plummeted to his death. In the chamber below was a sandpit to absorb any excrement or body fluids, and beside it was a mortuary slab near a door to the yard outside. There Robertson's grave had been dug and lined with quicklime in readiness to receive him. But there would be no tombstone for the ex-policeman. As with others at Barlinnie, his resting-place would be marked only by his initials carved on the outside wall of the hanging chamber. Years later even that rudimentary record of burial would be obliterated, chipped away prior to the redundant "execution suite" being replaced by additional prison accommodation. So now there's no tangible reminder that Robertson took his last breath a few feet away from where his remains were interred ….

Case 12
"The Terrible Case

Of The Hanging Dog"

"Her left cheekbone was fractured, as was her skull. Both her hands were broken and bruised, indicative of the fight she put up for her life" ....

"When asked to empty his pockets, Haslam produced Miss Clarkson's silver signet ring, gold chain, brooch and spectacles" ....

Max HASLAM MURDER Of Ruth Clarkson (74) [1937]

The brutal slaying of reclusive spinster Ruth Clarkson – and her beloved pet dog – shocked the Lancashire town of Nelson in 1936. But was a diminutive suspect actually the killer? ....

Nelson nestles snugly in the Ribble Valley under the shadow of Pendle Hill, Lancashire. Cotton mill chimneys dominated the skyline like giant liner funnels. Working-class townsfolk in 1936 strove hard to keep their heads above water, but they were cheerful and honest. Burglary was uncommon despite the fact that people left their front doors open. Neighbours might wander in to exchange gossip, everyone was trusted. Few people had much to envy, still less to steal. Miss Ruth Clarkson was an exception, although she didn't look it. Her appearance suggested she hadn't a penny to her name, yet the 74-year-old spinster owned property in Thomas Street and antique jewellery, the value of which could have bought out her neighbours many times over. The ragged recluse had little use for human companionship, and depended on her dog, Roy, for friendship. But somebody must have known she had money, because at some time between **Friday, June 19th**, and Monday, June 22nd, the old woman was battered to death at her Clayton Street home, and robbed. The first inkling that all was not well in Clayton Street came when Bracewell Morville walked into Nelson police station at 3 o'clock that Monday afternoon to report that a short, crippled man was hawking stolen jewellery around the town ....

More interestingly, Morville said that in the process of stealing this jewellery, the man had killed a dog. Immediately intrigued, the sergeant despatched some men to confirm Morville's story. Local pawnshop owners admitted that a mysterious "little chap" had indeed been off-loading some valuable jewellery. Most rather wistfully showed the policemen their bargains, which the seller evidently did not fully appreciate. The items were very distinctive. Two plain-clothes officers called at 56, Clayton Street after discreet enquiries had revealed the probable target for such a burglary. Miss Clarkson, they learned, had not been seen walking her dog since the previous Friday evening. The lady next door said that she had seen Miss Clarkson, although she hadn't spoken to her. The old lady was not given to doorstep chats. What the neighbour had noticed, however, was that Miss Clarkson had been wearing a breast watch with a long chain tucked into the waistband of her skirt. She had also noted that the fox terrier, Roy, which usually barked at anything moving, had been strangely quiet ....

She had remarked earlier to a friend, "I have heard Ruth coughing in the night many a time. She could die and nobody would know." Intrigued by the neighbour's remarks, the officers knocked on Miss Clarkson's door, but all they heard from within were the hollow echoes of their shouts through the letterbox. The back door was locked, although it showed signs of forced entry. Miss Clarkson's neighbour, seeing the futility of the officers' efforts, gave them the address of the old lady's niece, Edith Edmondson. Miss Edmondson confirmed that her aunt owned a lot of valuable jewellery, and ruefully explained that her aunt would not answer her door even to close relatives. It had been nearly 15 years since she had been inside her aunt's house, although she did keep in contact. The old lady had called on her two weeks previously, Miss Edmondson said, apparently in good health. What puzzled her, she said, was the fact that the dog hadn't barked when the police knocked on the door. "He is such a good house dog, with a fierce sense of territory." Miss Edmondson went on to describe her aunt's eccentricities. "Auntie has her odd ways. She has become very reclusive since the death of her good friend Miss Jane Riley. But perhaps she didn't answer the door to you because you are in plain-clothes." At this point it was suggested that Miss Edmondson should accompany the officers to Clayton Street to try to persuade her aunt to open the door …. It was at around 8 p.m. that Detective Chief Inspector Fenton returned to the house with Miss Edmondson, but nothing stirred except the neighbours' curtains. At the back of the house, the inspector discovered the evidence of forced entry, so without further ado he gave orders for the front door to be forced. Nothing could have prepared the officers for the squalid interior, or the horror yet to come. Mountains of old clothes and rags littered every inch of the downstairs rooms ....

Empty food tins, broken furniture and bundles of newspapers lay everywhere, everything filthy. Mice scampered over the mess of mouldering food scraps lying on every raised surface in the kitchen. Officers stumbling over milk bottles and crockery on the floor found Miss Clarkson's body in the midst of it all. Such were the rags she wore, it was difficult to spot her in the mounds of junk that lined the walls. Only the bloodstained tyre-lever, picked out by an alert constable, indicated violence. Despite the squalor, officers determined that the house had been systematically ransacked. Drawers pulled out onto the floor spilled their contents. Bloodstains splattered the walls and ceiling. Even the faded pictures on the walls had not escaped spattering. No jewellery could be found, not even on Miss Clarkson. Officers who elbowed their way upstairs discovered the maggot-infested dog on an unmade bed. The fox terrier had been strung up by the neck from the headboard rail. The Manchester pathologist with the unenviable task of examining the body estimated the time of death as between two and three days previously. There were 17 massive head wounds, any of which might have been fatal, inflicted with a blunt instrument. Bruises were apparent on her left shoulder, elbows, hands and head. Miss Clarkson's upper jaw fracture was so extreme that it left her gums freely movable. Her left cheekbone was fractured, as was her skull. Both her hands were broken and bruised, indicative of the fight she put up for her life. As for the dog, he had been killed at around the same time, his death being due to hanging rather than to the ferocious kicking he had taken in protecting his mistress ....

When Miss Clarkson's body was removed to the mortuary, her clothing was listed for posterity: Two patched gaberdine coats, an old grey knitted shawl, a bloodstained cotton chemise, black corset and a red flannel body belt. She wore no underwear. Within minutes of leaving the murdered woman's house detectives had apprehended the man they had been seeking – his description made that easy. He was arrested in Pendle Street at 8.40 p.m., and made no resistance. His name was Max Mayer Haslam, 23, and he claimed he had owned the jewellery for years. He went on to insist that he had never heard of Miss Clarkson, or been in a house in Clayton Street. Given the good grounds for suspicion which the police had, Haslam's explanation was not believed. A former co-lodger of Haslam's stated that, far from not knowing Miss Clarkson, he had mentioned her name a month before the murder shortly after their release from prison. Saying that he was related to the woman, Haslam had spoken of his intention of asking her for a handout. "If she doesn't come across I will do something to her that she will be sorry for," he'd bragged. "She's a miser, and it's about time she gave me something. All she can think about is that bit of a dog." For the police, the co-lodger's statement was enough. They charged Haslam with handling stolen jewellery as a temporary measure to hold him on ....

Meanwhile, they investigated his background and criminal record. Born into a large family in 1913, Haslam had from birth suffered a disease of the bones which prevented him from walking until he was nine. Full adulthood gave him a height of just four foot eight inches, which contributed to his resentment of the world. In 1934, the Oldham mill where he worked as a "reacher-over" closed, and it was then that his life of crime began. Reduced to National Assistance handouts, he turned to thieving and went to prison for six months. A 12-month stretch in Strangeways Prison in Manchester did nothing to deter him from further criminal activities, and it was on his release that he moved to Nelson. There he cultivated friendships which were to eventually lead to his downfall. James Davieson, who lodged with Haslam at Vernon Street, revealed that he and Thomas Barlow had befriended Haslam at the beginning of June that year. On one of their many walks together, the three had encountered Miss Clarkson walking her dog in the town centre. Barlow had remarked bitterly, "Look at that dirty bugger, and she has more money than any of us." "How do you know that?" Haslam had demanded, evidently excited by the thought. "I used to live back-door to her," Barlow had said, but the other man was not convinced. "She doesn't look too prosperous to me," Davieson retorted, and as far as he was concerned that was the end of the matter. A few days later, on June 15th, the three were walking down Scotland Road when Haslam suddenly expressed his desire to own a tyre-lever. He darted into a hardware shop and came out clutching the tool, very pleased with himself. Their next meeting was to be on June 19th, when Haslam remarked that he didn't know how he was going to pay his rent. "She won't let me keep living on credit," he said, before announcing that he wanted to take a look at the market. It was said in such a way that his friends knew they were not invited along. Suspecting that he was about to go "freelance," Barlow and Davieson followed him through Market Square, where he hardly glanced at the stalls, and on up to Clayton Street. As he knocked on the door of 56, Barlow and Davieson watched from a discreet distance. Haslam walked round to the back of the house, at which point his two friends departed in case he spotted them. A few hours later all three met up again in the town centre. "There was nothing in the market," Max had volunteered, and Barlow and Davieson exchanged smirking glances. Their little friend was lying to them! ….

Within 24 hours of his visit to Clayton Street, Haslam's fortunes seemed to have taken a turn for the better. He'd asked Davieson and Barlow where he could sell some jewellery, adding that he had killed a dog to get it. "I strung it up and pinched it with a screwdriver to see if it was dead." He described the burgled house as very dirty, like a rag shop inside. Later, when Barlow and Davieson suggested going to the Nelson Hotel for a drink, Haslam was suddenly reluctant, fearing someone there, another regular customer, might notice his new-found wealth. Davieson recalled that Haslam had washed and sponged down his clothes that night, and said, "Do you know where I could get rid of a corpse?" Barlow had also been asked some odd questions and been offered £200 to help take a body to Caldwell Bog. "I've done a woman in," confessed the little chap without emotion. Barlow and Davieson had decided to inform on their friend before the police closed in, but they were too late. Max Haslam was already cooling his heels in the interview room by the time they'd made their statements. When asked to empty his pockets, Haslam produced Miss Clarkson's silver signet ring, gold chain, brooch and spectacles. He remained adamant that the jewellery was his. However, a key which he claimed belonged to his father's back door fitted Miss Clarkson's door. Dog hairs were found on the caps of his boots and the patterns of the soles matched footprints on the grubby doorstep of 56, Clayton Street. Having been charged with the murder of Miss Clarkson, Haslam replied, "Not guilty, that is all I have to say." ….

Max Haslam's trial began in December 1936 before Judge Geoffrey Lawrence at the Manchester Assizes …. The defendant stood to attention as the judge came in, straining to see over the brass rail around the dock. His childlike stature was highlighted by the policemen at either side. Counsel for the defence had little to offer in the face of such overwhelming evidence. Haslam had been seen knocking on Ruth's door in Clayton Street, prior to which his financial situation had been shaky. A pawnbroker in Leeds Road testified that Haslam had wanted to pawn a pair of brown shoes on June 15th. He'd been given 4s 3d for them, and put his name down as Haslam of 55, Clayton Street. Why pawn your shoes if you owned valuable jewellery? Haslam's landlady said that he'd been behind with his rent until June 19th, after which he'd paid off his arrears. Most importantly, the tyre-lever was traced back to the shop in Scotland Road. The shopkeeper particularly remembered the customer who'd bought it as Haslam's diminutive stature made him a memorable visitor. In the same road a man reported having seen a "small man" drop something down a grating. Investigators lifted the grating and found a watch-case nestling at the bottom of the drain. Miss Clarkson had owned such a case, containing a silver watch. On June 25th at Nelson police station, police had managed to assemble nine men roughly resembling Haslam – something of a feat in itself. Out of nine witnesses, five picked Haslam out at an identity parade. But was Haslam actually the killer? Could he have had an accomplice or accomplices who had in fact also taken part in the burglary and committed the murder? Were his friends Thomas Barlow and James Davieson really as innocent as they seemed? Such considerations were immaterial, however, for after one hour of deliberations, the jury found Haslam guilty of murder at the end of the 3-day trial on December 10th, 1936 .... In their opinion the squat, bow-legged fellow was perfectly capable of battering an old lady to death with a tyre-lever – his tremendously strong upper body compensated for his lack of height and weak legs. An appeal was rejected on January 19th and to the strains of "Abide With Me," Max Haslam swung ignominiously from the gallows at Strangeways Prison, Manchester on Thursday, February 4th, 1937, hanged by Thomas and Albert Pierrepoint less than eight months after being released from the same gaol ....

Case 13
"The Mystery

Of The Missing Brother"

"Officers found small fragments of bone in the furnace but nothing was proven" ....

"Bernard went on Radio Eireann to appeal to his brother to return home" ....

"He would not have walked the six miles to return the flour sack, because he had a car" ....

"You burned your brother's arms, legs and head in the furnace, didn't you?" ....

Bernard KIRWAN
MURDER
Of
His Brother Lawrence
[1943]

The police were not surprised when the man's torso turned up in a bog. They had been expecting something like that for several months, and they had a good idea whose torso it was.

They had been looking for 31-year-old Lawrence Kirwan ever since his disappearance ….

Two labourers cutting turf in Ballincura Bog made the discovery on Friday, May 29th, 1942. A sack submerged in water was caught by the prongs of a fork, and on being lifted it smelled revolting. One of the men retched when a rope securing the sack was removed, revealing the gruesome contents. His companion went for the police. Lawrence Kirwan had vanished from his family's 70-acre farm at Ballycloughan, near Rahan, in Co Offaly, on **Saturday, November 22nd, 1941**. There had been six children in the Kirwan family, but four had left the farm years earlier to marry or find work elsewhere. The farm was still home to only Lawrence and his elder brother Bernard when their mother died in 1937. Since she had made no will, the two brothers remained in possession of the farm as her practical heirs. Lawrence was left by himself at the time of his mother's death, however, because Bernard was then in prison. In January 1936, the elder brother, wearing a mask, had held up a postman near Rahan. Threatening him with a sawn-off shotgun, he had robbed the postman of cash intended to pay old-age pensions at the local post office. Although he didn't injure the postman, he had blasted the man's bicycle wheels to prevent him from riding for help. Then Bernard had fled across the fields to Ballycloughan. But despite his mask he was recognised, and his swift arrest had been followed by a sentence of seven years' ….

In his brother's absence Lawrence happily ran the farm with the help of a young labourer named John Foran. Then in June 1941 Bernard was released on licence. Back at the farm he had been less than welcome, as the police were to learn from Foran. Lawrence had enjoyed being in sole charge and he resented his brother's return. And Bernard resented playing second-fiddle to a brother four years his junior. At first Bernard lodged with his sister who lived nearby. Then he moved into the farm, reasserting his rights. The house had only one habitable bedroom in which Bernard reoccupied his own bed, while Lawrence had to share the other bed with the labourer. The younger brother's resentment intensified when he found that

Bernard expected to be fed without doing much on the farm. One night in October Bernard went out drinking. On his return he found the door locked against him. It was raining heavily and there was no reply to his shouts, so he burst the door open to exchange angry words with his brother. The next morning they fought in the yard, Lawrence receiving a deep knife-gash on one hand. He claimed that Bernard had stabbed him, while Bernard said that he himself had been cut on both hands. Neither spoke to the other again, Bernard telling a neighbour, "He has escaped me this time, but the next will be a clear cut!" Lawrence responded by refusing to provide his brother with further food, so Bernard now had his meals at their sister's home. Locking the food cupboard, Lawrence kept the key in his wallet along with his car key. He didn't feed jailbirds, he told Foran in Bernard's hearing. So all that Bernard had of his inheritance was the use of his bed ….

On Friday, November 21st, 1941, Lawrence and Foran went to the cattle fair at Tullamore to sell some of the farm's herd. Stuffing the proceeds of several hundred pounds into his wallet after the sale, Lawrence then bought a sack of flour at the fair and gave Foran the money to buy two pairs of wellingtons. The next day Lawrence emptied the flour into a tea-chest, because he wanted to take the sack back to Tullamore to claim the five shillings' deposit. He tied the empty bag to the carrier on his bicycle and told Foran to clean out the boiler in the out-house to cook some animal feed while he was away. The boiler had not been seen to since it was last used the previous winter, but when Foran went to attend to it he found it had already been scrubbed. At around noon Bernard asked the labourer to go to Clara, a village a few miles away, to collect a watch he had left there for repair. It had been damaged in the fight with his brother. He gave Foran two shillings to pay for it and lent him his bicycle. Foran set out at about 5.15 p.m., leaving the two brothers alone. Lawrence had two appointments that evening – one with a man at 7.30, and another with his girlfriend, Miss Flannery, whom he was to meet later. Neighbours saw him around the farm, still in his working clothes and new wellingtons, at about 6.30. He kept neither appointment and that was the last that was seen of him. Returning around midnight, Foran was surprised to see Bernard wearing his brother's overalls and wellingtons, and with food on the table. He asked Bernard why Lawrence hadn't locked up the food as usual. Bernard mumbled something about his brother having gone away and gave Foran a cup of cocoa. Foran's sleep that night was unusually deep. He didn't wake until 9.30, and detectives were later to suspect that his cocoa had been drugged. He again asked Bernard where Lawrence was. Bernard replied that he had gone to Kildare to look after an aunt's farm, or so he had been given to understand by his sister at that morning's 6 o'clock Mass. He also said his brother might have gone to visit a relative in Birr. When Foran asked why Lawrence hadn't taken his car, Bernard said this was because there was "a chain on the wheel." Later that day, Sunday, November 23rd, Bernard sent Foran to Clara again, asking him to buy some whisky and telling him to take his time ….

So Foran took the afternoon off, returning at 6.p.m. when he had a snack and went out again, this time to a dance a few miles away. It was 3 a.m. when he got back to the farm on the Monday. His first job that day was to go to a spot two miles away to cut some scollops – reeds used for thatching. This seemed odd to him, because the roof had been thatched only a year ago. "What will Larry say if he comes home and finds I'm cutting scollops and not pulling turnips?" he asked. "I am the boss here," said Bernard, telling him to take some food with him as he expected him to be away all day. It was around 4 p.m. when Foran returned. No cooked meal had been fed to the pigs, and on Tuesday he gave them raw potatoes. But during his absence on the Sunday and Monday neighbours had seen smoke coming from the boiler-house. The labourer noticed that Bernard had taken the chain off Lawrence's car and that he was spending money freely. Three days after his brother's disappearance he paid a rates bill of £6, spent £6 10s. on a suit and settled several debts. In the following month he changed a £10 note for two of £5, yet he had left jail apparently penniless. Gossip about Lawrence Kirwan's disappearance soon reached the ears of the Garda. Foran, becoming increasingly uneasy about what might have happened, left the farm for another job on December 3rd. ….

On the previous day an officer had called and asked Bernard about his brother's whereabouts. "He is inside," Bernard had replied. Then, quickly correcting himself: "Well, no, someone told me he has gone to his aunt's in Kildare.'' Visibly shaken by the visit from the police, he had leant against a wall during the interview as if for support. "When Lawrence comes home, tell him to call at the barracks,'' the garda instructed. "We want to see him.'' A sergeant and two detectives arrived at the farm the next day to repeat their colleague's question. They received much the same reply. Asked if he had recently paid the rates on the farm, Bernard said he thought so. He was then asked to account for his movements on the day of his brother's disappearance. He made a statement which he later refused to sign. He said that on the evening of November 22nd he had left the farm between 8 and 9 o'clock, departing as Lawrence was brushing his hair in preparation for going out himself. Bernard went on to say he had gone to his sister's house where he remained until after the 10 p.m. news on the wireless. Then he went back to the farm, finding the house empty. He denied wearing the new wellingtons that night. Asked why he hadn't reported his brother's disappearance, he said he didn't see why he should. It was none of his business ....

Searching the premises, the officers found no sign of Lawrence. But they noted that ashes in the boiler appeared to contain some small fragments of bone. They suggested that Bernard should broadcast an SOS on Radio Eireann. "Why should I?'' he asked. "I'd be the last one he'd reply to.'' Nevertheless he recorded such a message, which was broadcast on December 5th – not that he listened to it. He said his radio was broken. The Garda made repeated visits to the farm. Bernard told one officer that he thought his brother might have ridden his bicycle into the canal and drowned. The canal was dragged. There was no sign of Lawrence. When the Garda accused Bernard of making no attempt to trace his brother, he shrugged and said nothing. Officers had found two petrol cans in Lawrence's car. They had been filled a few days earlier, but now both were empty. As the search for the missing farmer continued, neighbours asked Bernard why the police were digging at the farm. He said he supposed they thought something had happened to his brother. Encountering Miss Flannery, Lawrence's girlfriend, in early December he wept as he told her he had no news of his brother, saying that he only wished he could say where Lawrence was. When he saw Miss Flannery again later, however, he said he had good news: a man named Gilsen had seen Lawrence in Tullamore on the night of November 22nd ….

Another neighbour asked why Lawrence hadn't taken his cycling trousers with him as he never rode anywhere without them. Bernard said the trousers had still been wet through from Lawrence's time at the fair the previous night. But it hadn't rained on that day. Lawrence would soon be found if he were still alive, commented another acquaintance. "He'd be found a lot quicker if he were dead!" Bernard replied. Showing another neighbour a letter from a woman in England, addressed to Lawrence, he suggested that his brother might have gone there to see her. In late December a neighbour remarked that things now looked serious for Lawrence. "I think we may forget all about him," Bernard replied. "If he is under land or water, he won't be known in a month's time." A man with money could go anywhere, he added. Meanwhile a description of Lawrence had been circulated to police forces throughout Ireland and Britain. It had produced no result. Officers went to the farm again in January, taking away several items of Lawrence's clothing and forcing open the cupboard where the food had been kept. Inside it were the missing farmer's pipe, watch and empty wallet, all of which he would have taken with him had he gone away. Despite their strong suspicions, the police had insufficient evidence to charge Bernard with Lawrence's murder. On February 18th, 1942, however, he was charged with an unrelated offence, his parole was revoked and he was returned to prison. He paid his solicitor £73 in cash for his appeal, and on his release from custody the police asked him to account for having the money. As an old lag, he knew the ropes. Aware that he wasn't obliged to say anything, he refused to answer the officers' questions. On April 30th, however, one of the Kirwans' farming neighbours found Lawrence's bicycle. It had been hidden under straw in his hay-loft. He called the police, and Detective Sergeant McNulty promptly went to see Bernard whom he found working in the fields. Told of the bicycle's discovery and asked to identify it, the suspect paled and said he had to milk the cows. "Is that more important to you than your brother?" asked the sergeant. Bernard made no reply ….

Offered a lift in the officer's car in order to examine the bicycle, he refused to go. His farm was searched again. This time Lawrence's empty flour sack was found in the loft. It had not been there when the previous search was made. Its discovery indicated that Lawrence had not left the farm on November 22nd. He would not have walked the six miles to Tullamore to return the sack because he had a car. He hadn't cycled there either, because by then he was dead. Bernard was then seen in Tullamore one night, wearing his brother's overcoat which had been dyed a dark colour. Arrested and taken to the police station for questioning, he insisted that the coat was his. He'd had it for years, he said, and if Lawrence had been seen wearing it this must have been during his own absence in prison. The search for Lawrence's body continued, the police now concentrating on bogs and ditches. Displaying some interest at last, Bernard asked which bogs were being dug. If Lawrence were not found soon, he told a neighbour, he would have nothing to worry about ….

Then came the turf-cutters' discovery. Although the torso could not be positively identified as Lawrence's, the sack in which it was found was identical with two others at the farm. On August 14th Bernard Kirwan was arrested and charged with his brother's murder. True to form, he said nothing. When his trial began in Dublin in January 1943, the prosecution sought to have the customary rules of evidence set aside. In normal circumstances the jury could not be told that a defendant had a criminal record, but Kirwan's case was exceptional. The prosecution needed to show that Kirwan had obtained a lot of money following his brother's disappearance, whereas he'd had no source of income prior to June 1941 as he had been behind bars. The prosecution also needed to establish that Kirwan had been prescribed the drug luminal for insomnia while he was in prison, for it was to be alleged that he had drugged Foran with it on the night of the murder. Mr. Justice Conor Maguire decided that the normal rules of evidence could be breached – a ruling upheld on appeal. So even before a word of evidence was given concerning the murder, the jury knew that Bernard Kirwan had been "inside." ….

As the principal witness for the prosecution, John Foran was frequently tripped up under cross-examination by the defence counsel. He was shown to have "recognised" a cardigan as Lawrence's, whereas it had belonged to someone else, and his memory of times and dates turned out to be unreliable. But his testimony was not to be shaken when he described Bernard's threats to his brother and his actions before and after Lawrence's disappearance. A near neighbour of the Kirwans told how she had heard Bernard threaten, "Next time it will be a clear cut." In September, she told the court, she had borrowed a bar of soap from Lawrence. It bore the impression of a car ignition key, to which she drew Lawrence's attention. He had tried his key in the impression and it fitted perfectly. She also recalled Bernard giving her luminal tablets when she complained of being unable to sleep. The defendant's alibi fell apart when his sister told the court that on the day of Lawrence's disappearance Bernard had been at her home in the afternoon but not in the evening. The next morning at Mass he had worn new wellingtons which he said were Foran's. The jury then heard that while in prison awaiting trial, Kirwan had smuggled out a letter to a friend. This asked the friend to fabricate an alibi for him, and it went on to suggest that they "get Foran twelve or eighteen months for perjury. Wouldn't it be a gas?" The aunt in Kildare testified that she had not expected a visit from Lawrence. She had not asked him to look after her farm, and she was unable to account for how Bernard could have got that idea. The court heard how Bernard had begun driving his brother's car shortly after Lawrence's disappearance. The defence produced witnesses who said they had seen Bernard with money before November 22nd, but a prosecution witness testified that he had begged her to say she had given him £50 if questions were asked about his finances. She had refused. After the court was told that the police had found 77 luminal tablets in Kirwan's possession, a former girlfriend stepped into the witness box. She testified that he had told her he had been prescribed the tablets in prison and had saved them in case he ever wished to commit suicide ….

The police said that nobody had been reported missing in the district apart from Lawrence Kirwan and a man who had been traced to the French Foreign Legion. There was therefore a strong presumption that the torso found in the bog was Lawrence's. Bernard had been the last person to see him alive, and he'd had the motive and the opportunity for his murder. Dr. McGrath, the state pathologist, told the court that an attempt had been made to skin part of the torso. There was a thin coating of lime on it and it had been in the bog for three to 18 months. The breadth of the shoulders corresponded with the shoulder-width of Lawrence Kirwan's suits. In the dismemberment a sharp knife had been used to cut through the cartilage and spine segments, and a small hatchet had been employed to chop out the spine and ribs. The cuts appeared to have been made by someone familiar with butchering, and the court heard that Bernard Kirwan had often killed and dismembered pigs for local farmers. In prison he had worked in the butcher's shop, cutting up carcases. At this point the defence submitted that the case should be dismissed because Lawrence Kirwan's death had not been proved and the torso had not been positively identified. The judge ruled, however, that the court had heard sufficient evidence from which Lawrence's death could be inferred. The powerfully built 35-year-old defendant now strode confidently to the witness-box to claim that he had received money in prison unknown to the authorities. On his release, he said, Lawrence had given him £16. He had been on good terms with his brother until the night he was locked out, but the following morning Lawrence had attacked him with a pocket-knife. Bernard admitted making a duplicate ignition key for Lawrence's car, but he said he had done this after his brother's disappearance ....

Cross-examining for the prosecution, George Murnaghan asked Kirwan to account for his movements on November 22nd. "That is a tall order," the defendant smiled, going on to describe getting up and milking the cows. "Were the other two in bed when you got up?" "I believe they were." "Did they get up?" "They probably did." Asked to be more precise, Kirwan replied: "Well, they are hardly there still." Asked about the flour sack, he said that Foran had been wrong in testifying that Lawrence had emptied its entire contents into the tea-chest. Only half of the flour had been emptied on November 21st, and two weeks later he himself had emptied the rest. There had been no question of reclaiming a five-shilling deposit on the sack. Asked about eating arrangements at the farm, Kirwan said he'd had his meals with the others "if I felt like it." "What do you mean when you say, 'If I felt like it'?" asked Mr. Murnaghan. "I suggest it would depend on whether your brother would allow you or not." Kirwan made no reply, so the prosecuting counsel asked: "You heard my question?" 'I heard no question. I heard a suggestion.'" "Had Lawrence for some considerable time been locking up the food?" "He did occasionally." "Why?" "That was a matter for himself, an opinion of himself. It often struck me that he didn't know what he was doing." Kirwan denied he had sent Foran to Clara to collect his watch. He was then asked: "Do you realise that it is of vital importance to you to be out of the house in Ballycloughan on Saturday night, the twenty-second of November?" "Perhaps it is," Kirwan replied. Denying attempting to fabricate an alibi, he said he had not bothered to find witnesses to testify where he had been because the matter was of indifference to him. Asked when he first realised he was a suspect, he replied, "Right from the start." ….

From his description of his last sight of his brother brushing his hair in front of a mirror, it was apparent that he had been standing behind Lawrence. "Was it at that time, sir, that you struck him from behind?" asked the prosecutor. Kirwan remained silent, so the judge pressed him to answer. "I didn't think I had to answer such an absurdity," Kirwan replied. "I never struck the man." For the first time, however, his composure had been shaken. He had paled and then reddened as he dealt with the question. He conceded that he had lit the boiler on the Sunday and Monday, but was unable to explain why he had cooked nothing for the pigs. "You burned your brother's arms, legs and head in that furnace, didn't you?" charged prosecution counsel. But Kirwan quietly denied the claim. Asked why he had not reported Lawrence's disappearance, Kirwan said he would never approach the police on any matter. He was then reminded that in March 1942 he had reported the theft of his coat to the police ….

For the defence, Dr. Dockery maintained that Foran could not have been drugged with luminal. Six grains would be required for this, said the witness, and two grains would be detectable in cocoa, whereas Foran had testified that there had been nothing wrong with the drink. Dr. Flood, a surgeon, challenged the state pathologist's conclusion that the torso was that of a man, which was based on the observation of a single remaining nipple. That, Dr. Flood contended, was no indication of gender. He had seen such nipples on spinsters.

Summing-up, Justice Maguire cautioned the jury not to allow Kirwan's prison record to prejudice them against him. Furthermore, they should not convict him unless they were satisfied that the torso was that of his brother. It was now February 5th, the 17th day of the trial. The jury retired at 12.50 p.m., returning three hours and 20 minutes later to find Bernard Kirwan guilty of murder. Pale and shaking, he was asked if he had anything to say before he was sentenced to death. "At the outset of this case I pleaded not guilty," he told the court. "Throughout the trial I pleaded the same. That is all I have to say. For all and any sins of my life I ask God's forgiveness, but I ask no forgiveness from any man." His appeal dismissed on May 19th, he was hanged by Thomas and Albert Pierrepoint in Mountjoy Prison, Dublin, on Wednesday, June 2nd, 1943, leaving behind another mystery. How could a man bright enough to give almost as good as he got under cross-examination otherwise behave so stupidly? And if Bernard was not his brother's killer, who was? Foran? But what motive would the labourer have to kill either brother? ….

Case 14
"A Murder Plot In

Co Waterford"

"At about midnight the young mother awoke to find the cottage on fire" ....

"I believe it was me they wanted to get, and they'll get me some other time" ....

William O'SHEA
MURDER
Of
His Wife, Maureen
[1943]

At a prearranged signal he murdered Maureen with a shotgun blast ….

Maureen O'Shea stirred rabbit stew and sat down to wait for her husband William to come home at the Highways Gate in Ballyhane, Co Waterford. To make it special, she'd added wild garlic and borage from the woods nearby. He liked a hot meal when he came in, and she wanted to please him – even though she felt she could never make him really happy. As she prodded the iron pot, their baby gurgled in his crib beside the fire. They'd married in 1940 two-miles away in Cappoquin, when he was 20 and she was only 17. As a bachelor, he'd lived with his mother and step-father Michael Byrne, making a precarious living from trapping rabbits and odd jobbing for local farmers. He could barely provide for himself, let alone a wife, but they moved into a thatched cottage half a mile away and it looked as though he might settle down. Maureen was pretty as well as good-hearted, and people said William was lucky to have wooed and won her. They added that William had never seemed the marrying kind, as he spent all his time hanging out with young Thomas White, a young lad who followed him about like a devoted dog. The pair were inseparable, and there'd even been a few sniggers about them behind closed doors. When they got married, Maureen assumed William would cut down his evenings with Tommy. But, after a few weeks, she found herself alone night after night in a peat-heated cottage with no gas or electricity. She missed her family, and often cried herself to sleep in a cold, lonely bed. Their rows became predictable. She wanted him to get a secure factory job with a regular income. But he'd spent his life outdoors, and refused to be confined. Besides, he said, Tommy and I work well together. Why should I give that up? When she pointed out that he seemed to prefer Tommy's company to hers, he shouted that she was a jealous cur and it was no wonder he enjoyed the pub more than evenings spent with a 'sour-faced, nagging witch'. "You're a devil and you'll rot in hell!" Maureen screamed as he slammed the door behind him ....

During their occasional truces, William seemed remorseful and sad and she hoped things might change. But next day his manner would harden again, and she wouldn't see him till late at night. When she was heavily pregnant with their first child, he left her to go and fetch the milk from a farm across rough tracks, fences and fields – a journey that proved exhausting even for the fit young neighbour who offered to go instead. "William is hoping I'll die giving birth," she told him bitterly. On February 19th, 1943, she and the baby came home from hospital. William had at least lit the fire, bought some bread, jam and cheese, and seemed gentler than usual. But it was enough for Maureen to hope things might be different between them, and a few days later she decided to cook him a stew. By 10 o'clock, it was congealed and cold. William had not come home, and she cuddled the baby for comfort as she lay in bed listening to the wind howling round the cottage. At midnight, an acrid smell awakened her. The cottage was on fire. She heard the sound of splitting timbers and felt the heat of the flames roaring through the thatch above her. She grabbed the baby and stumbled outside. Looking back, she saw her home ablaze like a beacon in the blackness of the night. She ran the half-mile to her mother-in-law's house, and panted out her story. Several hours later, William arrived to find his wife and child safe, but the cottage a smouldering ruin. Michael Byrne had always thought his step-son strange, but never more so than that night when he seemed oddly unconcerned at what might have been a double tragedy. He'd noticed the unusually intense relationship between O'Shea and White and wondered if the youth might have torched the cottage because he was jealous of Maureen and the baby. Taking Maureen aside, he said: "D'you think the fire was started deliberately?" "Yes, I do," she said quietly. "I believe it was me they wanted to get, and they'll get me some other time." ….

Byrne was shocked and took his suspicions to the Garda, who hauled White in for questioning. In his statement, White, now 17, said he had indeed called at the cottage that evening to collect some tools he'd left there. But Maureen was out, and the place was in darkness, so he'd pulled a branch from the fire – which was still alight – and used it to find his things in the yard. "The cottage was not on fire when I left," he told the police firmly. Sergeant John Browne had to be satisfied with the statement because it was entirely possible that White had accidentally caught the thatch with a spark from his burning branch, and that it had flared up after he left. But he also knew about the intimacy between the two young men, and felt uneasy. Over the next three weeks, the O'Sheas lived with the Byrnes and their marital quarrels subsided. William was on his best behaviour in front of his mother, and Maureen welcomed the warmth and company. He even got a job as a quarryman with the local council, and the family had a meal together to celebrate his first day's work. It was mid-March and the weather had been unusually warm and dry for that time of year, so in the evenings William and Maureen took to leaving the baby with his grandma while they went out for a walk together, arm in arm. It had been William's idea, and Maureen was delighted at the change in him. At last, it looked as if she wouldn't come second to Tommy White. Now and again, however, she had a curious feeling that they were being followed. Once she saw a figure disappear behind a hedge; another time she heard footsteps in the undergrowth. She couldn't explain it. It was just a sense of something amiss. William teased her about it, and told her to put it out of her mind ….

On **Monday, March 15th, 1943**, they set off around eight for their usual stroll, passing neighbours on the way and exchanging greetings. Along the route, Tommy White pedalled past them on his bike without a word. "What's up with him, then?" asked Maureen. But William just shrugged. After calling at a farmhouse to get a light for Maureen's cigarette, they turned and headed for home, The Hill House. It was dark by now, and the narrow country lanes were bordered with dense hedgerows. A hunter's moon flickered in and out of the clouds, and Maureen snuggled closer to William as they walked. "Think we can be happy, Will?" she asked. She never heard his reply. Nor did she see the barefoot figure creep up behind her and fire his shotgun through her left shoulder from three inches away. The blast was so close it penetrated the two overcoats she was wearing, and killed her instantly, almost severing her body in two. Her hand slid from William's arm as she crumpled to the ground breathing a faint "Oh, Jesus." Her husband laid her out on the stony road, and whispered the Act of Contrition in her ear. It was past 9 o'clock when he ran into his mother's house babbling incoherently that something had happened to Maureen. Getting no sense from him, the woman hurried out into the night, calling in vain for her daughter-in-law. Returning to the house, she found William crouching in front of the fire. "She's at Highways Gate," he whispered. "Someone fired a shot at us." "But why aren't you with her?" asked his mother. "I was frightened. I thought I might get killed, too." Mrs. Byrne roused her other son John out of bed, and the pair of them ran to Highways Gate where they found Maureen lying in a pool of blood. Michael Byrne was playing the fiddle at a local ceilidh when he got the news, and he and the other musicians arrived at Highways Gate to find the Garda and a priest already there. Half an hour later, the Byrnes went home and found the baby howling in his crib and William weeping by the fire. Michael had been fond of Maureen, and his contempt for William exploded. "So you're after spilling blood tonight, are you?" "Are you mad?" said William. "You think I shot her?" He leapt up from his stool and stood menacingly in front of his step-father. "Strike me, would you?" said Byrne. "I never shot her," said William, suddenly limp. "It wasn't me." As soon as he heard about the murder, Sergeant Browne went to Tommy White's house and got him out of bed. He found that as a member of the Local Defence Force (the Irish equivalent of the

British Home Guard), White had been issued with a shotgun, though not with ammunition. Ammunition was provided only if an invasion proved imminent. Browne noted that the gun had been freshly cleaned with paraffin, but White told him he needed it clean for the parade on Saturday. Still niggled by doubts, Browne took White to the Byrnes' house to question him and O'Shea together. "Have you heard about Maureen?" Mrs. Byrne asked White as soon as they arrived. "It was a fright," he replied. "I was in bed and now I've been arrested." "If you've been arrested, what are you doing here?" asked William. The question seemed to confuse White and he answered bizarrely: "I got a cigarette from some man and smoked only half of it. It was drugged." ….

No one knew what he was talking about. After giving Sergeant Browne his version of events, William got up and went to sit next to White at the fireside while the rest of the family argued about whether the shooting was accidental, whether Maureen had any enemies, and how lucky William had been to escape being shot himself. When Browne asked O'Shea and White to return to the death scene, O'Shea shook his head vehemently. "Why?" "What should you be scared of?" asked Browne. "I'm afraid the shot was meant for me," said O'Shea. Eventually, they agreed to accompany Browne and another garda to Highways Gate, and O'Shea mentioned that his wife had felt someone was stalking them. As both men knelt by Maureen's body to pray, Browne noticed that White's shoes and socks were sodden and muddy, even though the weather had been dry for weeks. He sent White home and ordered O'Shea to be taken to the police station at Cappoquin to make a formal statement to Garda Patrick Maloney who had known the O'Shea family for many years. After a few minutes, Maloney asked casually: "So who did fire the shot, Willie?" O'Shea was quiet for a while, as if deep in thought. Finally he said: "It's hard to tell you. If I tell you, I can never go home and live among my people. I would as life die now myself. I had nothing to do with it, but I know who did it." Maloney pressed him: "Aach, Willie. You've known me a long time. If somebody shot your wife, don't save them. Tell the truth." O'Shea fidgeted and threw his head in his hands. "I will tell you," he said at last. "I don't know what to do. My heart is broke. I will tell. But I can't live out there again." While O'Shea continued to agonise,

Maloney called in Browne. The level-headed sergeant took out his notebook and waited patiently, pencil poised, for the killer's name ….

The story that emerged shocked and revolted both men. Sick of his marriage, William O'Shea, now 23, had plotted with Thomas White to kill Maureen. The youth was so besotted with him that he'd agreed to start the fire at the cottage that had so nearly burned the mother and baby to death. When it failed, however, the pair hatched another plan while they were out in the woods together setting snares. "I can do it with the gun," said White. "You just need to take her out where it's quiet, and get me some cartridges. I'll do the rest." O'Shea borrowed a shotgun from a neighbour on the pretext of shooting rabbits, and returned it minus the cartridge. He gave this to White saying: "It's up to you now." While William feigned romance with his young wife on their evening walks, White was busy trying to find the right spot from which to shoot her. When Maureen complained of seeing someone behind the hedge, it had been White practising his aim. On the pretence of looking for the mystery stalker, O'Shea had gone over and whispered: "Why didn't you fire?" "I couldn't hit her," said White. "It was too dark." By March 15th, they'd agreed a different ambush spot and the murder was set for that night. White would creep up behind them, and touch O'Shea's shoulder with the gun when he was ready to shoot. The killing, said O'Shea coldly, went according to plan. With one confession on record, Browne hauled in White for questioning. He denied discussing any murder with O'Shea, and said he'd been going home on his bike when he passed the couple on the road. He added that he spent the rest of the evening reading at home, and at 9 o'clock his mother came in to tell him Maureen O'Shea had been shot. "Why didn't you go to the scene of the shooting, as all your neighbours did?" asked Browne. "Especially as O'Shea was your friend." White shrugged, and replied that he went to bed at 11 o'clock, shortly before he was called in for questioning the first time. "Why were your shoes and socks so wet?" asked Browne. "I'd been out snaring rabbits in the dewy grass," he replied. ….

But Browne knew there was only one field in the neighbourhood, which was always waterlogged – the field where the killer had awaited in ambush. White denied being in the field, and said O'Shea had never given him a cartridge for his shotgun. Homosexuality was rarely mentioned in Ireland in the 1940s, but Browne had always sensed a bond between O'Shea and White. Now he brought in O'Shea to read his statement directly to White to try and trigger an emotional reaction in the younger man. It worked. White was clearly shaken and blurted out: "I'm afraid of him. It was O'Shea who first suggested the gun." This was followed by his own version of the murder – which agreed substantially with O'Shea's – and he led police to the ambush spot where his footprints were still visible in the mud. When they were charged with killing Maureen, William O'Shea remained silent, but White said: "I'm not at fault. I ran blind into it." At the preliminary hearing, O'Shea whispered to a court official: "We're guilty. It was a terrible crime to commit. She was very young. But I couldn't get away from her. She wouldn't let me join the army or go to England." ....

The trial began on June 7th, 1943 in Dublin before Judge Andrew Overend .... To their surprise, the jury heard evidence from the superintendent of a mental hospital and Limerick Prison's medical officer that Thomas White was "subnormal," and he was duly found unfit to plead. He never had to stand trial, and was sent instead to a hospital for the criminally insane. William O'Shea was therefore left to stand trial alone, even though he hadn't actually pulled the trigger. Since he'd made a full confession, the only option open to the defence was to claim the confession had been made involuntarily. But the garda denied any harassment and refuted the idea that O'Shea had been so exhausted by questioning that he didn't know what he was saying. His lawyer then argued that as a suspected person, he should have been immune from questioning unless cautioned. But the submission failed. In an unsworn statement from the dock, O'Shea said: "I never arranged to have my wife shot. I don't remember ever saying I did." The defence finally alleged that O'Shea was not guilty by reason of insanity himself, and called a psychiatrist to testify. "This is a case of mental abnormality," he said. "No normal man would act that way. I'm absolutely satisfied about that." He went on to claim that O'Shea was a man of low intelligence and education, was incapable of any deep feeling, and could not tell the difference between right and wrong. He later admitted that O'Shea knew his actions were punishable, and under the legal definition of insanity, it was enough to demolish the defence's attempt to have O'Shea declared guilty but insane. Two prosecution doctors were also firm in their belief that O'Shea was sane and malingering. The jury took an hour to decide that he was guilty of murder on June 8th .... In sentencing him to death, the judge was scathing about his hypocrisy, especially in saying the Act of Contrition over his dying wife. An appeal was dismissed on July 26th ....

On Thursday, August 12th, 1943, William O'Shea was hanged at Mountjoy Prison, Dublin, by Thomas and Albert Pierrepoint. No one will ever know whether William O'Shea frightened Thomas White into killing for him, or whether the men had feelings for each other they were aware of, but afraid to admit in the repressive atmosphere of rural Ireland in this era. Confronted by the law, however, they were quick to betray each other. But it remained a strange paradox that the man who loyally pulled the trigger didn't hang, yet the man who asked him to kill was himself killed by the law .... White was released after 14 years in 1957 moving to England where he married and where he died in 2001 in Wolverhampton in the West Midlands ....

Case 15
"The Extraordinary
Case
Of

'The Monocled Man'"

"Never mind the family. This is between you and me, Harold. Man to man. Will you take it and go? Believe me, it'll be for the best" ....

"I should like, as a man who is standing at the door of death, to say that I have no knowledge of this lady's death" ....

Harold TREVOR
MURDER
Of
Theodora Greenhill (65)
[1942]

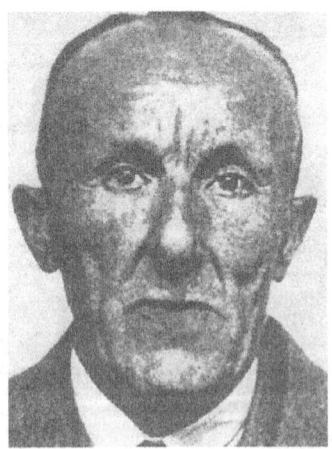

Harold Trevor

"If I am called upon to take my stand in the cold, grey dawn of the early morning I pray that God in His mercy will gently turn my mother's face away as I pass into the shadows. No fear touches my heart. My heart is dead. It died when my mother left me." ….

With these solemn words, spoken in cultured tones, ringing through the tense silence of Court No. 1 at the Old Bailey, a man who had spent most of his life in prison spoke the last words he ever uttered in public. He had come of good family, he had brains, but those brains had a kink in them. He hated work. He believed his wits were sharper than the next man's and decided they should keep him. Well, they kept him – in jail for the most part. Out of the 62 years that "Lord Reggie" graced the earth, he spent 40 years behind bars. His name was Harold Dorian Trevor. Scotland Yard knew him for many years as the 'Monocled Man'. He was probably the most unlucky crook who refused to go straight on principle. He did almost nothing right, and throughout his entire life was his own worst enemy, and knew it, which is the astounding part. He seemed driven by a veritable compulsion to crime which burned in him like a fever from an early age. Yet as a criminal he was not only unlucky, he was thoroughly incompetent. Had he really been intelligent he should have allowed the failure of his early years to scare him into going straight. Yet his early years held promise. He won a scholarship to a famous public school. He began his career in a bank, and the sight of so much money belonging to other people apparently unnerved him. He threw up his job and decided to be an architect. He applied himself to his first studies, took his preliminary examinations, and passed them. His family heaved a sigh of relief. They heaved it far too soon. He forsook his books and Gunter's chain and joined the Royal Marines. Apparently he had decided he needed a wider horizon than afforded by life in a midland town. He quickly changed his mind again. The discipline demanded of a Marine was irksome. Too irksome for Harold Dorian Trevor to endure it for very long. He deserted. In place of his uniform he blossomed out in a morning coat and grey trousers with a faint black stripe. He bought a white carnation for his buttonhole and a gold-headed cane to tuck under his arm. He acquired a gold-rimmed monocle, and when he arrived in London garbed to resemble his own notion of a member of the aristocracy, he spent some time choosing a new name. Lord Reginald Herbert. He was taken by its lilt and fancied quality. It took only a little imagination to look upon himself as veritably the man he had wished to be. London fascinated him. Its lights, its swirling gaiety in the years of the 1890s, its women, its songs, its food and drink and music and colour. London provided a rich diet for a man with a desire to live riotously ….

The capital, he was sure, would also provide the means of lining the pockets of his well-tailored clothes. London would look after Lord Reggie. His first escapade began when, with empty pockets but dressed to kill, he hired a brougham and two attendants and drove to a country hotel, where he lunched well and cashed a sizeable cheque. Rather in the manner of one bestowing a reward for good service, he suggested to the landlord of the comfortable but small country hotel that, as it was a delightful afternoon, he take his wife for a drive in the brougham that was hired for the whole day. It was all suggested with a grand air. So grand, that the landlord felt refusal would be tantamount to outright discourtesy. So he went for a drive with his wife. They were out basking in the sunshine for a couple of hours, and when they returned it was to find their benefactor had left during their absence. With him had gone any ready cash in the hotel, the wife's jewellery-box, and some of mine host's most expensive French brandy. Moreover, the landlord was left with the brougham and its attendants, and an outstanding bill to cover their hire for the day. The police were soon looking for Lord Reggie, but London is a big place, and Harold Trevor had already found a few discreet corners in which he could lurk at his ease. Especially when his pockets were not empty. He had nerve and insolence in those first halcyon days of his criminal apprenticeship. With his monocle jammed in his eye he could outstare a policeman on the beat and ensure his freedom to saunter away from a fleeting suspicion. His role of aristocrat, however, demanded a constant upkeep of appearances in days when the difference between the social classes was more readily discernible than it sometimes is today. So the money he won by conniving and cheating, by quick dramatic frauds and double-dealing, went out of his pockets faster than it arrived. He found himself with a taste for the good things money purchased, and became tricked into putting on a show for others. After all, he didn't wear a white carnation or sport a monocle for his own pleasure entirely. His real pleasure came from others looking up to him, accepting him as genuine, instead of bogus. That way, he felt he was getting something out of life to which he had never been entitled, and to him such a victory spelled success. It was the kind of success that blinded him to the cost ….

However, he became sharper and more of a rogue as he piled up experience. There came the time when he invited a large number of people to a champagne supper and forgot to pay for it. He is said to have paid court to a certain gaiety girl who specially pleased him. He sent her a lavish bouquet from a West End florist's. Only at the end of the month did she discover that the flowers had been charged to her account. Before that month was up, he took her to supper, having booked a table at Ciro's. He settled the bill, but he went off with her handbag. His smooth tongue served him well, but it could not protect him from all the trouble his bad intentions and nimble fingers earned him. Twice he was arrested and appeared before a police court magistrate. Twice he spoke in a cultured accent and offered for the court's consideration the façade of a gentleman of some circumstance and substance. Twice he received a gentle lecture. Twice he extricated himself and was bound over. He left London, regretfully, but feeling that it was the course of wisdom to allow his image to fade in the eyes of authority. He did not go far. To a country hotel, but the law of averages proved skittish. Someone he had fleeced recognised him, and this time there was no avoiding the police or the consequences of a charge by an outraged dupe. He was not bound over this time. He exchanged his morning coat and Ascot trousers for a cotton uniform and was taken to a place where a monocle was not deemed necessary to ensure that he could sew regulation stitches in mail sacks. When his morning coat, grey trousers and monocle were returned to him, he was an old lag, a veteran enemy of society. He proved it by very quickly returning to jail. Harold Trevor was now on the merry-go-round that sadly whirled him to the end of his days. He was a marked man and the police were on to him. But he refused to give himself a break. Instead, he went on his travels ....

In Paris he skipped just before the gendarmes arrived, unwilling to believe that an English milord could be roaming their city with empty pockets and a will to empty those of any confiding and friendly citizen foolish enough to be taken in by sartorial appearances. He arrived on the Riviera with a flock of new names, and his way of life ensured that he stayed only a short while in one place. With France no longer wearing a hospitable look, he returned to England and began a one-man crime wave in the Home Counties. With his margin of safety growing alarmingly narrow he returned to London, pulled a job, and was caught. The Monocled Man was back. The news brought grins to hard-faced detectives at the Yard. The men on the beat had their own rough humour to mark their appreciation of an old lag's return. Trevor was put on a train with a guard. He tricked the man and wrenched open the door of the carriage while the train was travelling at speed. Before the guard could prevent him he jumped. He could have broken his neck, but he scarcely gave a thought to the consequences of his impetuous act. One Yard man who recalled that occasion was Detective Chief Inspector Sydney Birch. "I remember the hue and cry that followed," he said. "Trevor's way of making himself inconspicuous was to call himself Rudolph Marjoribanks, and in grey sports suit with canary-yellow waistcoat, high fashionable collar and swagger cane, he ogled a young society girl in the West End, drove her in stolen carriage and pair to Hampton Court, and left her without her jewellery." ....

It is doubtful if Harold Trevor knew it, but he was a man running in circles. Sometimes the circle widened, at other times it contracted, but he was constantly in danger of running over the same well-trodden ground. As his spells of time in jail increased and the years crept up on him, slowing his speed and forcibly reducing his intrepid insolence, he became more set in his ways, more a creature of habit, more of a petty criminal whose modus operandi was too well known to plain-clothes men for him ever to hope to remain at large for long. He still tried to cut a dash. He continued to screw a monocle into his eye and to see the world very darkly through it, looking for credulous women to be his easy dupes and to provide him with the ready cash he was too indolent to attempt to earn honestly. His circumstances became more reduced each time he returned from a visit to jail. His list of false names grew impressively. The original Lord Reginald Herbert became at various intervals known to the police as Commander Herbert and Commander Crichton, Captain Gurney, Sir Francis Ford, and even Sir Charles Warren. On one occasion his revolt against society produced a more active rebellion ….

In 1912, while serving a sentence of five years in Maidstone Gaol, he headed a prison mutiny. Perhaps it was to mark the passing of 10 years since he had received his first sentence of penal servitude, in 1902. The mutiny was serious enough for the governor to ask for aid from the military. Troops arrived and fixed bayonets. For some anxious moments it was touch and go whether the spark that had suddenly burned fiercely in Harold Trevor would spring to consuming flame. He looked at those fixed bayonets, and remembered wryly that he had once bragged that he was not a man of violence because no educated man could ever really be that. Remembering, he gave up a struggle that had become hopeless and the mutiny was over. For the remainder of his prison term in Maidstone he was cowed and pliable. But not because he was anxiously considering how he could mend his life when he left prison, as the sequel revealed. On the day of his release he found a familiar figure waiting for him at the prison gates. "Hallo, Harold." He stared into his brother's face, and came to a halt, not dropping his eyes. "Why did you come?" he asked. "I've brought you money, Harold." "Why?" "So you can make a fresh start. Go abroad somewhere." "The family want me out of the way, don't they?" The brother kept his temper and said patiently, "Never mind the family. This is between you and me, Harold. Man to man. Will you take it and go? Believe me, it'll be for the best." ….

Perhaps Harold Trevor was a cynic as well as a crook. Perhaps he saw no reason why he shouldn't fleece a member of his own family equally with members of the general public. He took the money. He caught a train out of London. But he did not go abroad. He arrived in Brighton, fixed himself up comfortably in a room in a boarding-house, and began a systematic plundering of local shopkeepers by the simple process of obtaining goods on approval and, when his suitcase was full, leaving for London, where a few visits to well spaced pawnshops reduced the weight of his luggage and established him in funds. He was back to the former pattern of conniving and cheating. It had become a way of life. He was located by detectives following his trail of theft, and again he went to prison. In fact, the balance of his life was changed. He was spending more time in jail than out of it. By the end of his life he achieved something like a record for an old lag. Detective Chief Superintendent Frederick Cherrill, who helped to trace him on his last job by an overlooked fingerprint, had this to say of him: "At various times he stole anything from a walking-stick to a string of beads. His method was somewhat primitive. On release from jail he would, by a trick, manage to get some clothes, and then call at a boarding-house on the pretext of engaging a room. When the landlady's back was turned he would make off with anything that was handy." He was not a compulsive thief. He stole originally from inclination and a sense of challenge, and later from habit. He cannot be written off as a kleptomaniac. He was a product of a good home environment, who deliberately chose crime as a way of life, and who stubbornly refused to mend his ways when he had a lifetime to stare back over and perceive that the choice had been a bad one. His shabby life was swamped by a final irony ....

Harold Trevor had no thought of killing anyone when he murdered Mrs. Theodora Greenhill. Mrs. Greenhill, 65, lived in West Kensington, which had been a not so happy hunting ground for him in the past. Indeed, on one occasion, the Kensington area had provided the setting for an almost comic contretemps. With his monocle screwed firmly, almost aggressively, into his eye, he pushed open the door of a Kensington pawnshop and paraded rather than walked across to the counter, where a man was leaning forward, talking to the shopkeeper. The man turned, and mutual recognition flowed between the newcomer and the Yard detective who had been talking to the pawnbroker. "Well, I'll be damned," said the detective. He had been going over with the pawnbroker a list of articles that might be offered by the Monocled Man. Some of them were in Trevor's pocket. "I think we'd better step outside," Trevor suggested mildly. The Yard man grinned. "It's going to be inside again for you, old fellow," he retorted, matching the Monocled Man's accent, which was one that went with a single eyeglass. Kensington was a place of memories for Harold Trevor. But he was a self-induced snob, and the royal borough drew him like steel to a magnet ....

In October 1941 he had been released from prison only 10 days when he conceived a new way of getting money. He was 62 and superficially a gentleman, despite long years in prison. From a study of local advertisements he knew that Mrs. Greenhill occupied a self-contained flat at 71a, Elsham Road, off Holland Road and that she had placed part of it in the hands of house agents for letting furnished. Trevor proposed to call at the flat and explain that he had come from the house agents. It was a sure way of gaining entry, and his purpose was to soft-talk Mrs. Greenhill while he looked around, and then collect any worthwhile objects that could be slipped into his pocket when her back was turned. An unambitious criminal excursion that justified Frederick Cherrill's observation: "His exploits were petty rather than spectacular, and enabled him to live only in comparatively poor circumstances, strongly in contrast with his grandiloquent impostures." In his carefully brushed clothes that were becoming a little shiny at the seams he walked up the half-dozen broad steps of the address in Elsham Road and told the smiling woman who answered his ring that he had come from the house agents about the accommodation she was advertising ....

And so on **Tuesday, October 14th, 1941,** Mrs. Greenhill showed him into her lounge, and her visitor's eye behind its monocle brightened perceptibly as he took in the quality of the furnishings. Mrs. Greenhill was the widow of an army officer, and lived alone. She explained that it was not her flat she wished to let, but a basement room, furnished, for a weekly rent of 30 shillings. Trevor was shown the room. It looked like a poor relation of the remainder of the flat, and Mrs. Greenhill felt compelled to sound a little apologetic about it. But her visitor was smiling graciously, and telling her that he found the room just what he was looking for, and was prepared to take it and give her a week's rent in advance. She sat down at a rosewood bureau and prepared to make out a receipt for the first week's rent. Trevor had noticed an empty quart-size stout bottle. He acted on impulse, believing that if he stunned her he could have more time for picking up the articles that would be most profitable in a pawnshop. It was a case of the man who did not believe in violence stepping out of character. He snatched up the empty bottle and brought it heavily down on Mrs. Greenhill's bowed head. The act of mere instants. The thief who had been out of luck all his life was still out of luck when he chanced his arm and tried violence. Mrs. Greenhill had an abnormally thin skull. The blow from the bottle cracked it, and she died. Harold Trevor had become a murderer. That week there were three other murders in London. Of the four killers only Trevor was caught. Those seemed to be the odds against him all his life, from that day in 1896 when he first came to London ....

Only for some unsteady seconds did he panic as he stood looking down at his latest handiwork, then habit came to his temporary rescue and provided him with work. He slipped a glittering ring from the dead woman's hand, but because he was not by instinct a ghoul he left her wedding ring. He moved through the flat, picking up whatever cash he came across and pocketing any small article of value his ample pockets could accommodate. He could not have spent long on his brisk mission of pillage, then he left. A passer-by in the street saw him as he came down the steps into Elsham Road, and noticed the carnation in his buttonhole and the monocle glazing his seamed face. He realised that he should make some effort to fool the Yard men who would arrive and begin an investigation. He had not been very successful in such manoeuvring in the past, but this time his luck might have changed. He flagged down a cruising taxi, and told the driver, "King's Cross, as fast as you can make it." His intention was to lay a false trail. His luck had not changed. Within an hour Scotland Yard were searching for him after Mrs. Greenhill's daughter, a Miss Tattersall, had called to see her mother ....

On receiving no answer to her ringing of the doorbell she let herself in and found her mother's dead body beside the bureau. She called the police and the passer-by who had seen Trevor leave the house, a council worker named Levy, was still in Elsham Road when Detective Chief Inspector William Salisbury of the Murder Squad arrived. Following Salisbury came a Humber car carrying Fred

Cherrill and Syd Birch with their fingerprint equipment. They found fingerprints on four pieces of glass from the broken stout bottle and on a money-box that had been forcibly opened with a nail-file. They also found a thumbprint in blood on a small side-table. At Scotland Yard those prints were on record. They proved to be the fingerprints of Harold Dorian Trevor. By that time Trevor had reached the comparative quiet of the North Wales seaside resort of Rhyl, where he took a room in a guest-house. When he went to bed that night, Yard men had already traced the taxi-driver who had taken him to King's Cross and decided that journey had been a bluff. A nationwide description of the wanted Trevor went out. He was traced to Rhyl, and detectives hurried to arrest him. It was mid-morning, and he had gone out, when they arrived and were shown to his room. Looking for some of Mrs. Greenhill's property, they turned over the mattress, to stare with amazement at bundles of banknotes held securely by the bedsprings. There was a sharp exclamation behind them, and turning they saw the landlady in the doorway, with her hands to her mouth. "I clean forgot about the money," she said. "I put it there to be safe during the air raids." ….

A young war-time reserve constable arrested Trevor as the fugitive was leaving a telephone kiosk. He had read the wanted description earlier, and knew he couldn't be mistaken. Characters such as Harold Trevor were not seen in the streets of Rhyl every day of the week out of the holiday season, even in peacetime. When detectives searched Trevor at the local police station he had in his pockets five shillings in small change and his gold-rimmed monocle, which he had clung to throughout his incredible life as a talisman that supplied some deficiency in his personality. When he was told of the store of currency on which he had slept, Trevor smiled one-sidedly. "All my life," he confessed, "I had one hopeful dream, to make enough from one robbery to keep me for the rest of my days. When opportunity knocked I was asleep." ….

Harold Trevor was charged with Mrs. Greenhill's murder, and in due course stood in the dock at the Old Bailey. It was in the following January that he saw Justice Cyril Asquith take his seat and heard counsel open the battle for his life in a two-day trial. In his memoirs Detective Chief Superintendent Cherrill went as far as to say of the trial: "Because of his finely phrased speech, made with all the tricks of the practised orator – the subtle pauses, hushed tones, and eloquent gestures – the trial of Harold Dorian Trevor will always stand out in my memory as the most dramatic of all those it has been my lot to attend." From the first, it was clear that the evidence brought by the prosecution could not be assailed or refuted. It was late in the winter's day when the jury retired on January 29th, 1942. They filed back to their seats and their foreman delivered the verdict of guilty of murder ....

The clerk of the court asked the stiff-faced prisoner if he had anything to say before sentence was passed on him. Harold Trevor gave a brief nod and cleared his throat. He then delivered himself of a dramatic speech that was not intended to be believed, but to be remembered. "If I am called upon to take my stand in the cold, grey dawn of the early morning..." he went on, during which time the court was silent. "I speak to you tonight," the prisoner continued, "the last speech I shall ever make. Even as I speak, the moving finger writes and, once written, the words will never be recalled. I sincerely hope that each one of you, gentlemen of the jury and judge alike, will remember these words – that when each one of you, as you surely must some day, yourselves stand before a higher tribunal, you will receive a greater measure of mercy than has been meted out to me in this world." His voice became husky. "My life has been all winter." Those who were present say the silence continued noticeably after he had finished with that pathetic admission. Earlier he had declaimed, presumably more for the benefit of the record than for any useful reason, "I should like, once and for all, as a man who is standing himself at the door of death, to say that I have no knowledge of this lady's death." The judge waited while the square of black silk was adjusted on his wig, and then he gravely pronounced the sentence of death .... An appeal was dismissed on February 23rd ....

Harold Trevor was hanged on Wednesday, March 11th, 1942, by Albert Pierrepoint and Herbert Morris at Wandsworth Prison, a man whose life had been a monument to the folly of dishonesty as a foundation for building a career. He was 62 when he stood on the gallows. In 42 years as a career criminal he had known only 48 weeks of freedom. His life had indeed been all winter. Perhaps it was symbolic that he died as spring was about to arrive ….

Case 16
"The Killer Who Fled To Spain"

William HEPPER
MURDER
Of
Margaret Spevick (11)
[1954]

"I have for some time a special interest to paint an oil portrait of your daughter" …. *The first British case to successfully mount a manhunt using television was that of William*

Sanchez de Pina Hepper (who held a British passport issued in Gibraltar) who was traced to Spain and extradited after protracted consideration by the Spanish authorities ….

Not only has Crimewatch UK been one of the most popular programmes on television for the past decades, it has become a highly successful medium in the fight against crime in Britain. But for the very first appeal for a wanted man made on television we have to go back 70 or so years, to Monday, February 8th, 1954. Five million television viewers watched as the announcer Donald Gray read the description of the man in the photograph on screen. He was aged between 50 and 60, about 5 feet 10 inches tall and of medium build, and had grey hair and brown eyes. His complexion was sallow and angular, and he was described in the polite period vernacular as "having the appearance of a foreigner," although he spoke fluent English with no accent. The photograph on screen had been snapped at one of the Thames Embankment open-air art shows some time previously, but it was a good likeness, even capturing his poor posture. Gray gravely told viewers across Britain that this man was urgently wanted by the police. His name was William Hepper. "Police are anxious to trace this man," the announcer explained, "whom it is believed can assist inquiries in connection with the death of an 11-year-old girl at Hove." ….

The missing man was 62 years old and an artist. Like his looks, he was not quite English. His full name was William Sanchez de Pina Hepper. While Donald Gray was speaking on screen detectives waited outside his home at Ormonde Gate, Chelsea, in south-west London, in case the wanted man should return. Other detectives were watching a flat in Hove, Brighton; but the vigils in London and Sussex were fruitless that night. Yet minutes after the face vanished from the television screens of the nation, phones had started ringing at both the BBC and Scotland Yard. Apparently William Hepper's face was jerking a few memories. In the one-room flat rented by Hepper at 112, Western Road, Hove, the strangled body of Margaret Spevick, an 11-year-old London schoolgirl had been discovered,

killed on February 5th. She was known as Margot to her family and close friends her own age, such as Pearl Hepper. Now detectives waited in vain for Pearl's father to return to one of his two homes. William Hepper was wanted for murder. He had little stability in his life. It was his artistic temperament, his family supposed. William Hepper was a drifter who would arrive in their midst quite unexpectedly and unannounced. After staying for a while, he would vanish again without explanation or warning. They had become accustomed to such intervals, and in truth he was a difficult man to have around. Margaret had come to the notice of William Hepper literally by accident ….

On Christmas Eve she had fallen from a wall and landed on her arm, which was broken. She lived in Embankment Gardens, Chelsea, with her parents, and was a pupil at a secondary school in the Victoria district, also attended by Pearl Hepper. Ormonde Gate, where the Heppers lived, was only a short distance north-west of Embankment Gardens. It was only natural that her friend Pearl should be concerned about her during that Christmas in 1953, while Margaret's fractured arm mended, and that Pearl's father should become interested in the little girl in the cast. But Margaret's mother was more than a little surprised when on January 17th she received a letter from Pearl's father inviting Margaret to join Pearl's family in Brighton. It read: "I wonder whether you would like Margaret to spend a fortnight convalescing with us here? I have for some time a special interest to paint an oil portrait of your daughter (16 x 20 inches) for an exhibition to take place here, and I think this is an excellent opportunity, when she can't go to school for some weeks yet. There is an old nurse sharing the flat who could look after Margaret in case she needs any medical attention, such as new bandages etc., the food is good and plentiful here and when she is not sitting for me we can spend long hours at the sea-front around the coast where I usually sketch." ….

Margaret's mother found nothing suspicious in the letter and there was another letter for Margaret herself, explaining that he wanted to paint "a nice canvas" of her and another of his daughter. He even offered to pay Margaret three shillings an hour for her time spent modelling. Mrs. Spevick replied to the invitation. She said that while

Margaret's arm had been taken out of plaster, her daughter had to attend the doctor for remedial exercises. Hepper was both insistent and practical in his own reply to this. Margaret, he pointed out, could have similar exercises daily at a local hospital in Brighton. Mrs. Spevick was still debating whether to agree when she received a visitor. It was William Hepper, smiling and full of cheer. "I'm going to Hove today," he explained, "and I thought it would be an excellent opportunity for Margaret to come with me." Mrs. Spevick explained that she would have to get some things ready for her daughter if she was to go away. "I can't possibly get her ready before tomorrow," she pointed out. Hepper was very accommodating. "In that case," he said, "I'll put off going myself until tomorrow." He was acting like a man who wasn't prepared to take no for an answer. Mrs. Spevick eventually agreed that Margaret should accompany him to join the Hepper family in Hove ….

The next day, Wednesday, February 3rd, 1954, Elizabeth Spevick kissed Margaret goodbye. Her daughter left holding William Hepper's hand. If she had any misgivings the postcard she received the next day from Brighton would have allayed them: "Enjoying myself. Having a splendid time, Love Margaret." About the time the postcard was delivered to Embankment Gardens, Hepper arrived at the Sussex County Hospital in Brighton with Margaret. He explained her accident and made arrangements for her to attend the hospital for remedial treatment. Mrs. Spevick had arranged to visit her daughter on the following Sunday, but upon her arrival at Brighton station there was no one to meet her. She waited for two hours but unable to recall the precise address of the Hepper flat in Hove she returned to London angry and perplexed. Back in Chelsea, she went to Ormonde Gate, but the Hepper studio was closed and nobody answered her ring. Now alarmed, she made inquiries and finally procured the Hove address from a neighbour and returned to Brighton. She stood outside the front door of a one-room flat pressing the doorbell for several hours, getting no response. But she refused to leave. Another tenant, Mrs. Holly, asked her into her own flat to wait but as midnight came the anxious mother realised that she had missed the last train back to Victoria. She asked Mrs. Holly to introduce her to the caretaker. When she explained to him the circumstances in which she found herself, he agreed to let her into the Hepper flat. He brought his passkey and followed the two women to the Hepper front door, which he unlocked. The women entered. Later the caretaker told the police, "I heard a call from Mrs. Holly, and found her sitting white-faced on the stairs. I went into the flat and saw a foot sticking out from the bottom of the bed. I pulled back the blankets and saw the little girl lying naked. She was dead." Within a short while, Detective Superintendent Nicholson of Brighton had taken over a grim inquiry. It was he who told reporters about the visit and how it came to be made. "Apparently it was suggested," he told them, "that a holiday by the sea would help her to recuperate." ….

The bed on which Margaret lay was a divan. The only clothes she wore were a pair of rumpled socks. The doctor who examined her told the police she had been dead for at least 24 hours. She had been sexually assaulted, raped and strangled. The hand that had led her from her mother's home had brutally crushed out her life. A truly nauseating touch to the horrible tableau discovered by Mrs. Holly and Mrs. Spevick was an unfinished canvas, a lifelike head-and-shoulders portrait of Margaret in oil paints that was still tacky. Her clothes were in a neatly-folded pile, together with the books she had brought with her and a jigsaw puzzle. On the jigsaw puzzle was Hepper's rent book, which showed that the rent had been paid up to that very weekend. A mammoth police inquiry began in the Brighton area and along the Sussex coast. It was established that the murdered child had last been seen alive two days before, on the Friday. Mrs. Holly had called at the flat on the Friday evening and at 8 o'clock a man on the staff of a local newspaper had visited the artist. He told the police that Hepper had mentioned leaving the country – that he was going to Gibraltar and had been to a travel agency to inquire about fares. While he talked to the artist, Margaret had been seated in an armchair. She had been reading one of her books ….

The mention of Hepper's inquiry about going abroad initiated conferences at Scotland Yard, discussions about using television to trace the missing man. The first Sussex inquiry had drawn blanks in both Brighton and Newhaven, where the Channel ferries leave for Dieppe, so Hepper's description had been passed to Interpol in Paris and from there through the police networks of Europe. By the next day, the newspapers had dubbed the wanted man "the Stooping Artist," from his habit of leaning forward to peer, as seen in the photo described by Donald Gray. For the second night running, Hepper's face was shown on television screens in millions of British homes. On the Thursday, Hepper made the front pages of the national newspapers again, this time with pictures and large headlines. The previous day, there had been some excitement in the Spanish (French) frontier town of Irun and detectives, headed by Chief of Police Don Frederico Iglesias, called at the modest Pension España [guest-house] in that town. By 2 o'clock that afternoon they had collected the man for whom all the police in Britain and a great many throughout Europe were hunting. The man was taken to the town jail, where he spent a night awaiting the arrival of a suitable police escort to take him to the nearest large town, which was San Sebastian ….

In the meantime, the British vice-consul there was endeavouring to make arrangements for the civil governor to be requested to issue a warrant for Hepper's extradition to Britain. The charge on the warrant would be alleged murder. In the Spanish capital, the sealed diplomatic bag delivered to the British Embassy contained a necessary British warrant signed by a Hove magistrate. A second warrant held an application for extradition, issued and signed by the chief magistrates at Bow Street in London. This was done under the terms of the Anglo-Spanish Extradition Treaty (1878). Half a day and a night passed and then armed detectives, with a police motorcycle escort, collected the man from the cold jail cell and took him 15 miles along the Spanish N1 highway to Martitene Prison. While Hepper sat in his cell, the remains of the murdered child he had raped and brutalised were lowered into a narrow grave dug from frozen ground. Detective Inspector Bidgood from Hove, accompanied by Detective Sergeant Lane of Scotland Yard, arrived in Madrid and the meticulous game of protocol continued. On February 19th, it was announced that a fresh Hove warrant was being sent to Spain, backed up this time by a number of sworn affidavits. Days dragged with Hepper in Spanish custody then, suddenly, after a month he was taken from San Sebastian's forbidding prison and put on a train for Vigo. When he arrived, he was handed over with no ceremony to Bidgood and Lane ….

The two detectives and their prisoner took passage for Britain in the Alcantara, which arrived at Southampton on Tuesday, March 23rd. Hepper was driven along the south coast and, on the next day – Wednesday – appeared before the Hove Magistrates' Court, where formalities were concluded in eight minutes flat. He stood still as he was remanded in custody for a week and charged with the murder of Margaret Rose Louise Spevick. Arthur Jolly, the chairman of the magistrates, asked Hepper the formal question as to whether he had anything to say. Speaking with a markedly *foreign* accent, he responded. "All I say at this stage is that I did not do it." "You do not want to ask any questions?" Mr. Jolly had inquired in order to clarify the situation. Hepper had lifted his head. "I have no questions to ask. The only thing I say is I lost my memory," he said huskily, "and I lost my consciousness." He was driven to Brixton Prison, where he was to be held during the week's remand. On April 5th he was back in Hove for the rehearing before the magistrates' court. He was asked if he could account for the body of Margaret Spevick being found in his flat. Once again he denied the charge. "That is impossible," he cried. "I cannot remember anything since I lost my memory in Brighton, until I came round again a few days ago." He was duly committed for trial at the Lewes Assizes ….

In July, Hepper appeared in the dock before Justice Austin Jones, and the case for the Crown was opened by R.F. Levy, Q.C., who began by reading a couple of letters written by the prisoner in Spanish, which suggested that Hepper had thought he was attacking his wife at the Hove flat. Mr. Levy turned to the jury of 10 men and two women. "You may come to the conclusion," he said, "that he did think, under some curious sort of delusion, he was attacking his wife and not this little girl. He appeared to be saying that he thought the person he left on the bed was his wife. It may be that he was inventing this for the purpose of trying to cover up the consequences of what he knew he had done." The Crown referred to a statement made by Hepper to the British vice-consul in San Sebastian, in which he claimed to be in a confused state from which he was just awakening. "You may well think that by this time," Mr. Levy continued, "Hepper was taking the view that it would be safer to claim complete loss of memory for everything that had occurred."

Mr. Levy then read the statement Hepper had made in San Sebastian to a silent courtroom. "I hardly remember anything," it said. "The last thing I do remember is that the BBC sent me at home in Brighton the passage money to spend a holiday in southern Spain, but I remember that I lost the money, possibly while sleeping in a cinema." It was a warm summer but the hot courtroom was crowded to capacity every day, holidaymakers from along the south coast swelling the numbers, drawn to Lewes by the case ....

Whatever shabby roles he had played throughout his three-score years, the man in the dock was a star feature during those July days of his appearance before Justice Jones. To all he had flatly denied ever being alone with Margaret Spevick and had related the circumstances of a car accident in London which, he claimed, had affected his health so badly that he had been left subject to recurring attacks of intense depression which reduced him to contemplating suicide. The medical evidence would be of prime importance in persuading the jury as to the prisoner's capabilities – or lack of them. When the medical evidence offered by the Crown attested that the victim had been strangled and sexually assaulted, the defence sought a qualification and obtained it when it was admitted that what had happened to Margaret Spevick could conceivably have occurred during a period of unconsciousness on the part of the child's attacker. The next day, Derek Curtis-Bennett, Q.C., for the defence, wrung the admission that William Hepper was a man of good character, apart from a known conviction for theft which had occurred nearly 40 years before, from Detective Inspector Bidgood. He then presented the defence that the ghastly events had been the result of insanity: "We say, whether this man did it or not, that certainly between February 3rd and 7th, and probably long before that date and even now, he is mad in the eyes of the law." ....

However, the testimony swung to and fro, and Maxwell Turner, for the Crown, offered in evidence the text of a translated letter taken from Hepper at the time of his arrest. The original letter had been in Spanish and addressed to the Spanish ambassador in London. The translation of this letter was read in court, in which the prisoner claimed to be a Spanish citizen who had at one time believed he was British because his father had been a Gibraltarian. "When I entered here [the prison at San Sebastian] I was in a serious condition, and since I left London I was no more than an automaton that did not know what it was doing, nor what it was saying or writing. Consequently, I am going to make a confession in writing to your excellency that, with the help of God, will clearly reveal, so all may understand, the motives which incurred in my transforming myself from a cultured and mild as well as industrious youth into almost a madman. On the night of my wedding, I bore an enormous disillusion. She was not what I believed before. I continued to love my wife madly as on the first day, but she treated me coldly." After his car accident, when his wife believed he was on the point of death, she had confided that she had never loved him and told him. "My heart always belonged to a man whom I loved with passion. I always hated you." But Hepper had his own store of resilience. This admission did not complete what the accident had started. Perhaps he was a very obstinate man ….

Anyway, he recovered, almost, as it were, to spite the wife who hated him. He had told the Spanish ambassador: "She admitted she had not always been faithful. She told me, 'I have not always received from you the consolations necessary for a young and beautiful woman.' This put my head in a whirl. She had waited to tell me it for 30 years, believing that I was about to die." Had the letter to the Spanish ambassador been a bluff? And had the translation been retained so that it would be found by Detective Inspector Bidgood, or whoever came from England to collect the wanted man? Those became vital questions for the jury. Especially when the prisoner was suffering from paranoia, which is frequently accompanied by delusions of persecution. However, there was one thing William Hepper had not done during his testimony, or while in prison under remand. He had made no confession to killing Margaret Spevick. Because of this his counsel was able to take a chance and have Hepper give evidence on his own behalf. There was a tension that could be felt when the stooping prisoner moved from the dock to the witness-box and took the oath. By this time he had recovered his lost cultured English accent. He was in the witness-box for three hours. The man who might be mad, according to his counsel, had some very pat answers. "Are you fond of children?" Mr. Curtis-Bennett asked him. "Yes, very fond," was the prompt reply. "Have you ever had any desire to do anything wrong with one?" "No sir. It is inconsistent with my qualities." "Did you kill this little girl Margaret?" "Not at all, I could never do it." Hepper described a hallucinatory dream he'd had – the main features of which corresponded with claims made in the letters already read out in court by counsel for the prosecution ….

A difficult poser was being erected for the jury. Half-remembered imaginary thoughts, half-recalled dreams, half-dreamed reality – it would be extremely difficult to unravel such a tangled web of conjecture and improbability to determine a motive. Justice Jones was anxious to clear up a point that had arisen, and Hepper readily explained he had been impotent for a year. When Mr. Levy tried to clarify arrangements made about the little girl staying with him, he denied telling the mother that there was a nurse available. When the prosecution told him that a nurse who lived in the flats had agreed that she had made arrangements to take in the child, he denied that also. "Do you know why she should tell falsehoods about you?" the Crown asked sharply. "No," Hepper muttered. "You knew," he was pressed, "that Mrs. Spevick would never have agreed to let her child go if she knew she had to sleep in that room with you?" "The child never did," he insisted. He claimed that when he reached the flat, he found a letter from his sister asking him to join her in Spain, as his brother was dying. He translated the letter for Margaret and they both cried, since this letter had interrupted the painting of her portrait. He told the court, "I gave the girl a spare key to come into the room and leave when she liked. I gave her a 10 shilling note to get her home, as I was going to Spain." It sounded distinctly odd, and the prosecution asked him, in that case, why had he not notified Margaret's mother about his change of plans? His reply was more than odd. It was distinctly lame. "I did not do things properly, because I was not in a normal condition." ….

The next day seven doctors appeared for the defence, among them Dr. Richard Curran, a noted specialist in mental disorders for more than 20 years, who had given evidence in the Christie case. "When I saw him in 1952," Dr. Curran informed the court. "I believed he was in a paranoiac state, but not certifiably insane." Justice Jones put a question to the witness. "You think that such a person suffering from paranoia may be mentally responsible?" "Yes," Dr. Curran agreed, "for certain things." "You take the view," the judge went on, "that they are better treated in hospital, rather than in prison?" "Yes, My lord." When Mr. Levy, trying to pinpoint the prisoner's flight and its motive, said Hepper might have fled from a sense of guilt, Dr. Watt, a Hove psychiatrist, corrected him. "Not a sense, but a feeling of guilt." "You're making rather a fine distinction," counsel told him. Again Justice Jones interrupted to get the point, and its inference, cleared up. "If he dreamt he strangled his wife," the judge said, "and awoke and found she was not there, why should he go away with a feeling of guilt?" Dr. Watt was very frank. "I cannot give you or myself an explanation of this," he admitted. But Mr. Levy didn't refrain from suggesting one. "There is one simple explanation," he said bluntly. "And that is that he knew he had murdered a little child and wanted to escape when nobody was about." The effect of this kind of parry and thrust on the prisoner became evident when he collapsed in the dock just before being called to the witness-box for further cross-examination. Mr. Levy tried to bring the uncertainty to a clear point of understanding by suggesting he thought that he had either killed someone or left someone unconscious. The prisoner began shaking his head. "No. I had to go to Spain to see my brother," he maintained. Reference had been made to the fact that the letter Hepper claimed came from his sister had not been produced, and Justice Jones had something to say about this fact in his summing-up, which occurred the next day ….

Critical evidence from yet another of these many letters, one which had been produced and certainly did exist from Hepper to his uncle in Gibraltar requesting money, was instrumental in trapping him. The letter was sent from Irun, in Spain. Hepper had arrived there practically penniless and needed £10 from his uncle, intending to make for Portugal and lose himself in that country. He could have been confident of achieving this, having worked for the United States consul in Portugal, as well as for the American Intelligence Service during the Spanish Civil War, when he had helped refugees to escape. It did not appear that his mind had wandered on that particular subject, or that his delusions interfered with his rational and intelligent assessment of how to elude capture. Had he been in funds, Detective Inspector Bidgood and Detective Sergeant Lane might have had a fruitless journey. Without money, Hepper was anchored. The evidence produced in the Lewes courtroom established that much. It also proved how very rational his escape route was, despite the unusual circumstances. He went as directly as his meagre funds allowed. A bus from Brighton could have deposited him at Newhaven, where he was known to have caught the 10.30 morning boat for Dieppe, which connected with the Paris train. He booked a first-class ticket to Paris at Newhaven, and in Paris a second-class ticket to the Spanish frontier town of Irun. But, at the French frontier town of Hendaye, he had only enough money to purchase a visa. Justice Jones took two hours over his summing-up. He came to the alleged letter from Spain, supposedly received by Hepper on the day he arrived in Hove with the little girl ….

"You may think," the judge told the jury, "that he made it up, and that no such letter was received. If so, you may derive some assistance in coming to a conclusion as to whether the rest of his evidence was accurate." Continuing on this same subject, Justice Jones referred to a postcard Hepper was known to have sent to Mrs. Spevick on the Thursday morning, while he was with Margaret in Brighton. He had written. "Dear friends. We are writing sitting on a deckchair at West Pier head. It is like a summer day. Margaret is happy about it." "When he wrote that postcard to the parents of the little girl on Thursday," the judge pointed out to the members of the jury, "he never said a word about going to Spain. That is an important matter." Possibly, it was the coldly factual quality of the judge's summing-up that turned the tables on the man in the dock. For his part, Mr. Curtis-Bennett had told the jury in his final address that the worst they ought to do was say that Hepper was guilty but insane, although the main defence remained that he did not do the murder act at all. A subtle reminder, in case they had forgotten in the ensuing days, that on the first day of the trial the prisoner had very quietly pleaded not guilty. On the other hand, Mr. Levy, in his final address, chose to be scathing about the defence of insanity. With a touch of aloof scorn he said reflectively, "I've been wondering if these courts have ever known such a flimsy allegation for insanity as in this case." The jury wondered too, and after 90 minutes deliberations returned a verdict of guilty of murder on July 22nd at the end of the 4-day trial. Justice Jones had a black square of silk placed on his wig and soberly passed the sentence of death. There was no appeal and the execution was duly carried out at Wandsworth Prison on the morning of Wednesday, August 11th, 1954, by Albert Pierrepoint and Royston Rickard. The first British screening of a killer on the run had brought a man to the gallows. It is perhaps no surprise given the effectiveness of the appeal, that first Police 5 and much later Crimewatch UK came to out television screens ….

Case 17
"The Revenge
Of
The Sacked
Chauffeur"

"The sheer ferocity of the attack suggested the hate motive. The intruder used the logs to knock Alice unconscious from behind." ....

Leslie GREEN

MURDER
Of
Alice Wiltshaw (62)
[1952]

Leslie Green's employers – a husband and wife – had plenty of money and lived the high life. Yet she had thrown him out of his job, and now he had nothing. He knew when she would be on her own – and that was the time to get his own back .... The prosecutor pointed out that before the day of the murder Green was short of money, and after the murder he had plenty ....

It's perhaps hard to imagine these days that people once fell in love with teacups. These were the brightly coloured teacups – as were the plates and saucers and vases that went with them – called Carlton Ware, made by Wiltshaw and Robinson in Stoke-on-Trent in the first half of the 20th century and today much prized by collectors. The company's managing-director was Frederick Cuthbert Wiltshaw, a tall, distinguished-looking man of 62 who was the son of the founder. He was rich, a local dignitary, married with four daughters and he employed servants to minister to his domestic needs. Frederick Wiltshaw and his wife Alice, also 62, lived in a 14-roomed mansion called Estoril, named after a romantic holiday they had spent in Portugal. The sumptuous home in Station Road, Barlaston, Staffordshire, six miles south from Stoke, had extensive grounds and overlooked the valley of the Trent. At 4.30 pm on **Wednesday, July 16th, 1952**, the two domestic servants had gone home, which wasn't unusual because Alice liked to cook the evening meal herself. And notwithstanding the fact that she was a little crippled because there was something wrong with her left arm, that's what she was doing around 5.15 p.m. when her kitchen door was stealthily opened and an intruder wearing gloves came in. Absorbed in her cooking, Alice probably didn't look up ....

She probably didn't even hear the man. All she would have known was the searing pain as he brought a heavy log crashing down on her head. In what were to be the last few seconds of her life the killer attacked her ferociously with a hammer and an antique steel poker with a barb in the end. She fought back as best she could, crawling out of the kitchen into the hall, blinded by her own blood, as the blows rained down on her. Vegetables and cooking utensils were scattered, broken china littered the floor, and blood spattered the walls and tablecloth. Alice went down fighting valiantly, clawing at her aggressor. The top of her head was caved in; her nose was smashed and both jaws were shattered. Blows from the poker left a deep wound in her face and two more in her abdomen. She fell dying just inside her own front door in a pool of blood. This was the horrific sight that met Frederick Wiltshaw when, at 6.20 p.m., he arrived home from work. Aghast, he fetched a neighbour, a doctor, who made a brief examination of the body and then called the police. The body of Alice was still warm when they arrived. Case-hardened detectives were shocked by the vicious, cruel and determined manner in which the elderly victim was battered to death. She had been hit so often and so brutally that her features were almost unrecognisable. This was a pin-fresh crime scene, and required detailed examination ….

The first clue found was a pair of doeskin gloves, discarded in the garden. One glove's button was missing – it was quickly found alongside Alice's body. Both gloves had several holes in them and were heavily bloodstained. The left glove had a slit in the thumb that was later to prove of some importance. Next day Detective Superintendent Reginald Spooner arrived from Scotland Yard. He was a police-officer with a fearsome reputation. Very quickly he made up his mind that Alice must have known her killer. Spooner noticed that during the brutal beating the intruder left an indelible footprint on the tiled floor of the kitchen, where it was clearly defined in a puddle of water spilled from one of the overturned saucepans. It was made by a distinctively soled shoe, and there were no shoes at Estoril that were similar in pattern. The detective was so fascinated by the footprint that he had it cut out of the floor and transported to police headquarters for future evidence. The exhibit weighed about two hundredweight. Then it was time to start asking questions. People in the area reported that a young man dressed in grey and acting in a suspicious manner was seen lurking around the vicinity shortly after the murder. He was probably in his 20s, and he looked dazed. Was this the killer? No one knew what had happened to him. No one had recognised him. He was seen near the villa, and then he seemed to vanish. Spooner asked Frederick Wiltshaw: "Has anyone been dismissed by you recently? Someone who might bear a grudge?" ….

Wiltshaw nodded. There was a chauffeur-gardener named Leslie Green. He had been with the couple for nearly two years. Alice threw him out when he was found to be using one of their cars for his private purposes. What was missing, Spooner wanted to know? A check revealed that apart from Wiltshaw's raincoat, all that was gone was Alice's jewellery, whose value was estimated at more than £3,000. Among the prize pieces were a 20-inch graduated pearl necklace worth £200, a diamond and emerald studied bracelet, and a diamond eternity ring. An expensive silver cigarette case of a distinctive design had also been taken. The jewellery was obviously recognisable. So too was the raincoat. Frederick Wiltshaw remembered that he had burnt three holes in it with his cigarettes. Although the stolen jewellery would have been a good haul for a professional burglar, the image of a killer smouldering with hate and bent on revenge was at the forefront of Spooner's mind. The sheer ferocity of the attack suggested the hate motive. The detective deduced the intruder came into the house through the kitchen, wearing the doeskin gloves. He used the logs to knock Alice unconscious from behind. Then, knowing where to find the jewellery, he scooped it up and just as he was about to make his getaway he found Alice recovering from the attack. At that point she probably recognised him and crawled into the hall, where the phone was. The intruder now had to kill her. He battered her with a china vase and, knocking her to the floor, finished her off with the poker. Then, to cover the blood on his clothes, he grabbed the raincoat from a hook in the lobby and threw the gloves away as he exited through the garden ….

It might have occurred to the detective chief at this stage that he wasn't looking for the cleverest of killers. This one had left behind his gloves and an imprint of his shoe. It was almost as if he had decided to give the police a helping hand. One man stood out in all this – the sacked chauffeur Leslie Green. Routine police checks on the former chauffeur revealed some interesting facts. Green was employed at Estoril for nearly two years and while he was there he had had the run of the mansion. Apart from being the chauffeur and gardener, he cleaned all the windows, inside and out, cleaned out the fire grates and stacked up the fuel bin with logs. He also had a criminal record – he had spent three years in a Borstal institution and had served a short prison sentence. He left Borstal with an encouraging report: "There is a reasonable probability that Green will abstain from crime and lead a useful and industrious life." He then joined the army and served in the last part of the Second World War, soldiering on until 1949. As Spooner read about Green, he became more and more anxious to interview this suspect. He might have been mildly baffled if he had known Green's movements ….

On July 10th, six days before the murder, the suspect had booked into the Metropole Hotel in Leeds. He signed in at reception under an assumed name. Incredibly, the name he chose was Frederick Wiltshaw, of Estoril, Barlaston. He stayed at the hotel until July 13th, by which time he had run up a debt of £9, which he couldn't pay. So he had a word with the manager, who rather generously agreed he could pay the bill when he promised to return on July 17th. On July 16th, the day of the murder, he had lunch at the Station Hotel in Stafford and spent some time there after lunch. He returned to the Metropole in Leeds in the early hours of July 17th. Next day a hotel porter, Kenneth Beasley, read about the murder of Alice Wiltshaw and asked Green: "Are you any relation to the murdered woman?" "Yes," replied Green. "She was my aunt." He then went to the reception desk and paid off his account of £9. He told the receptionist, Gwyneth Jenkins: "Someone's stolen my raincoat. I had my wallet in the pocket with £40 in it." Miss Jenkins clucked sympathetically, but she later recalled, "He didn't seem very worried." Green went out to buy a newspaper. Back at the hotel he said: "I've just read this report about my aunt being murdered. It looks like I'll have to go back." In fact, he didn't go back anywhere.

He went off to meet the woman he called his fiancée, Nora Lammey, who had flown in from Northern Ireland and spent the night with her at a flat owned by a friend of Nora's. He never told Nora that he was already married. Nor did he tell her his real name. He called himself Terry and bizarrely proposed marriage to her. He told her he was a travelling representative for a pottery firm – his job took him to America. Clearly in love, the unfortunate Nora arranged a marriage licence – the date was fixed for August 9th. Green hadn't actually officially left his wife – he was going through what she described as one of his disappearing acts ….

Leslie Green had met Nora, a nurse, three months ago at a dance hall in Leeds. He later flew to Belfast, where her parents lived, and stayed with her there. He seemed to spend a lot of time on his own, travelling around the country on trains for no apparent reason. Two days after the savage murder of Alice Wiltshaw, Nora received a letter from her sister in Belfast, telling her that the local police were inquiring about a man named Leslie Green. The sister had linked the description of Green that the police gave her with "Terry," and her letter was a warning. Nora saw her rosy future crumbling in front of her. Confused, and full of doubts, she handed back to Green the two rings he had just given her. These, it was later established, were stolen from the Wiltshaws' home. The lovebirds still met, however, and next evening they went to the cinema to see the latest movie called, ironically, It Won't Be a Stylish Marriage. Although baffled by her beau, Nora was still besotted with him. She even asked a colleague at her workplace – Nurse Greta Davies – if Green could use her flat in Leeds while Miss Davies was away for the weekend. Miss Davies agreed, not realising, she said later, that Nora was going to spend the night with him there. If Green was on the run, he was certainly not doing much about covering his tracks. In fact, he seemed to be laying down a trail, laced with ridiculous lies that even a village bobby would be able to follow. The trail led police to his wife Constance, living in Elmore Avenue, Blurton, Stoke, with their six-year-old daughter. Constance didn't seem too surprised by their interest. "He's in the habit of going off without telling me," she told them. "I reckon he must have a girlfriend somewhere." ….

On July 23rd, seven days after the murder of Alice Wiltshaw, Green walked into Longton police station and told the astonished woman police officer behind the counter: "I am Leslie Green, the man you are all shouting after." Brought before Spooner he said: "I saw in the papers that you wanted to see me." The story he then told was as ill thought out as the discarded gloves and the indelible footprint. The day after the murder, he said, he was staying at the Metropole Hotel in Leeds, where he read about the murder. He told the receptionist that as he was a relative of the victim he would have to leave at once. He didn't explain in his story why he had suddenly become a relative of the Wiltshaws. As he was leaving the hotel he met two men he knew as Lorenzo and Charles. He had last seen them a week earlier, when he asked them to get him two rings, an engagement ring and a wedding ring, for his fiancée Nora. They gave him the rings on July 17th (the day after the murder). He then asked them for money and they gave him £15. So, with the rings, which he apparently got for nothing, plus £15 in cash, the obvious question was, what sort of transaction was this? Why did they give him money? Green's answer to that was: "For no special reason." He went on: "I had a drink and then went to meet Nora. I gave her the rings and she said they were very nice, and that was all. Next day she said she'd heard from her sister that the police were looking for me. She gave me the rings back. I had a walk round and threw the rings away in the canal from the bridge just opposite the Golden Lion." He hadn't seen Lorenzo or Charles again, but remembered that a couple of months ago Lorenzo asked him where he was working, and if the house was worth breaking into. Lorenzo wanted to know if there was any jewellery there, and Green replied, "I suppose so." It had since "passed through his mind" that Lorenzo might have been the intruder who killed Alice Wiltshaw ….

Later Green was to add, even more curiously perhaps, that he didn't do the murder, but knew that he was involved and "perhaps was responsible for the events in some way." He was able to account for almost every minute he lived up to and after the murder, but what, he was asked, was he doing at the crucial time between 5 p.m. and 5.45 p.m., the time Alice Wiltshaw was murdered, on that key date of July 16th? "I am clear in my mind about that," he replied. "It was Wednesday. I arrived at Stafford railway station about ten in the morning and about 1.30 I went to the Station Hotel and got into conversation with four men. We had lunch there and then we went to the upstairs lounge at around 4.30. "We stayed for a quarter of an hour and then I began to feel dizzy from the drink. I left the hotel and went across the road to the park, where I must have dozed off, because it was about a quarter to six when I got back to the hotel." The detail was all there – except for that vital period between 5 p.m. and 5.45 p.m. By his own statement he was never more than a few yards away from Stafford station ....

The 5.10 p.m. train from Stafford arrived at Barlaston at 5.35 p.m., and the murder villa was just 200 yards from Barlaston station. There was a return train from Barlaston at 6.05 p.m., arriving at Stafford at 6.26 p.m. It was clear then what Green was doing when he claimed to have been asleep on the park bench. He was arrested and brought to trial on December 1st, 1952, at the Stafford Assizes before Judge Wintringham Stable .... Some 40 witnesses spoke for the prosecution. The footprint was in court, together with a pair of Green's crepe-soled shoes. So were the discarded gloves. The cut in the thumb of one of the gloves, it was pointed out, was identical to a recent cut on Green's hand. Nora Lammey told the court that Green had twice visited her in Northern Ireland. He had proposed marriage and she accepted him. She thought he was quite wealthy. Green did himself no good in the witness-box. The court was told that the raincoat that Mr. Wiltshaw recognised as his own was found on a train at Holyhead that had stopped at Barlaston late that afternoon. Green vehemently denied ever having seen it before. He continued to claim that Lorenzo had given him two rings, a distinctive gold cigarette case and other items on July 17th. He hid the two rings in Greta Davies's flat in Leeds, he said, and sold the other pieces. But hadn't he said once before that he had thrown the rings into the canal? Ah, yes, he was sorry he had sent Detective Superintendent Spooner on a wild goose chase with that story. It was also untrue, he now agreed, that his wallet was stolen with £40 in it. "Aren't you rather an accomplished liar?" the prosecutor, Ryder Richardson QC, suggested. "Wouldn't consistent be a better word than accomplished?" asked Justice Stable. Green agreed with that ....

The prosecutor pointed out that before the day of the murder he was short of money, and after the murder he had plenty. Where did it come from? "I got it by stealing," Green replied. So would he now explain why Lorenzo and Charles so generously gave him money? Well, they no doubt hoped that he, Green, would join them in a bit of burglary, he suggested. He was asked: "Did you tell Nurse Greta Davies that Alice Wiltshaw was killed with an old-fashioned poker?" "I don't remember that," Green replied. "But Nurse Davies said that you did say that. How did you know that Alice Wiltshaw was killed with a poker like that?" "If I did say that, I must have read about it in a paper," Green replied. The prosecution refused to give up. Copies of newspapers dated July 17th and 18th were brought into court and studied by the Judge and by Green. It was agreed that no mention had appeared in the media that Alice was killed by a poker. For Green, this was another bad mistake to add to his long list of bad mistakes. Yes, he was a liar, he agreed. He had lied to his girlfriend Nora; he had lied to the police about how he had disposed of the rings. But, he insisted, that didn't mean he was a murderer. The prosecutor asked him: "You knew Mrs. Wiltshaw would be alone in her house between 5 and 6 p.m?" "Yes." "You knew that if she caught you in the act of stealing, she would have to be silenced for ever if you were to escape conviction?" "That is an obvious fact." "You knew, did you not, that if you went to the house you would have to wear gloves?" "I would have to wear gloves during criminal activity if I was to avoid detection, yes." "You went to that house that day and killed Mrs. Wiltshaw?" "No." He stuck rigidly to his story, that the two men Lorenzo and Charles gave him the rings and the other jewellery. The jury didn't believe him. They were out for only 28 minutes before finding him guilty of murder, and he was sentenced to hang at the end of the 5-day trial on December 5th. He did not appeal and there was no reprieve ….

Leslie Green, 29, was executed at Winson Green Prison, Birmingham, on Wednesday, December 23rd, 1952, by Albert Pierrepoint and Syd Dernley – this being Dernley's last execution. Forty years later there was a curious epilogue to the case of Leslie Green, when an MP put down a written question to the Home Secretary asking, "What steps are being taken to reopen the case of Leslie Green, and if the Minister would make a statement." A Home

Office minister replied that there were no recent representations about Green's conviction, and neither had any new evidence been presented. There were no grounds to reopen the case. So why, one wonders, was the question asked? Did the MP know something we didn't? ….

Case 18
"Belfast's Easter Gun-Battle And The Trial Of Six"

Thomas WILLIAMS MURDER Of RUC Constable Patrick Murphy

[1942]

Thomas Williams

Constable Patrick Murphy

Wartime Belfast was tense but quiet. It was Easter Sunday, 1942, time for Republican anniversary celebrations of the 1916 Easter Rising in Dublin. Although the IRA was now largely dormant in Northern Ireland, its armed struggle currently suspended, minor trouble was expected ….

But by the day's end history of another kind was in the making. What happened on **Sunday, April 5th, 1942**, was to result in six men being sentenced to death for the murder of one victim, a very unusual event in the annals of crime. Republican celebrations were banned, and it was this which gave 19-year-old Thomas Joseph Williams his role in the events of that day. With fellow-members of the IRA's "C" Company in Belfast's Clonard district in the Falls in the west of the city, he was to create a diversion keeping police away from a Republican parade. The plan was for Williams and his comrades to fire shots in the air over a police patrol in Kashmir Road, attracting enough RUC men to the area to allow the parade to take place elsewhere. Williams's comrades were 21-year-old Joseph Cahill, William James Perry and John Terence Oliver, both 20, together with 19-year-old Henry Cordner and Patrick Simpson, 18. They shot their bullets over the heads of the police, who to their surprise returned their fire and pursued them as they fled down Kashmir Road and into Cawnpore Street, a "safe" area for the IRA. There the six hoped to pass their guns to some local women. But as the fugitives dashed down the street with the police behind them, the women panicked. The six men and two of the women forced their way into 53, Cawnpore Street, where Francis O'Brien and his wife were having lunch. The couple were ordered to get under their kitchen table. Together with the two women, the six decided to leave by the back door, unaware that police reinforcements had already arrived and that the whole street was surrounded ….

A police van containing four officers had drawn up outside the house, and Constable Patrick Murphy, a 38-year-old father of nine, had been sent round the back while his three colleagues prepared to storm in through the front door. In case they were caught, the six had given their guns to the two women. They now took the weapons back and Williams crept through the kitchen and opened the back door – to find Constable Murphy facing him. Both had their guns drawn, and as Murphy opened fire Williams fell back into the kitchen. Shots were exchanged, the policeman shooting Williams again, once in the thigh and once in the arm. Only slightly injured, Murphy stepped into the kitchen, but his gun jammed as he aimed it at Williams's head. Meanwhile, the other five had crowded into the kitchen. More shots were fired and Murphy was killed instantly by a bullet in the head. Williams's comrades carried him upstairs and put him on a bed. Thinking he was dying, he told them he would say it was he who had shot Constable Murphy. As the O'Briens heard this "confession," 20 officers entered the house and the six surrendered with no further shots being fired. Thomas Williams was taken to hospital where he told the police that he had shot their colleague, but detectives were far from convinced, although Williams also wrote and signed a statement later which read: "I ran into the scullery. There is a little glass enclosure in the yard and from the scullery window I could see a policeman coming into this enclosure with his gun drawn. When he was about three yards from me and beside the kitchen window, I pointed my revolver at his body and fired one shot. He staggered and fired back and I fired four or five more shots at his body." …. This was against the IRA's rules to co-operate with the police, but Williams had done so to save the lives of his colleagues …. A post-mortem found that Constable Murphy had been shot five times. In all seven guns – including the policeman's – had been fired 19 times. The RUC contacted Scotland Yard and the celebrated gunsmith Robert Churchill was despatched to Belfast from London. He established that Constable Murphy had been shot with two guns, three of his five wounds being inflicted with one of them. All six suspects were charged with the policeman's murder; their two women companions with firearms offences – both later receiving suspended prison-sentences, although one woman was interred as a member of the IRA. Legal history in Northern Ireland was made when the 3-day trial of the six began on July 28th, 1942 at the Belfast City Commission ....

Not in the recent history of Britain and Ireland had six men been charged with the murder of one and been tried by an ordinary civil court and a jury .... The prosecution maintained that the question of who had fired the fatal bullet was irrelevant, as all six defendants had resolved to use violence to escape arrest – it was what was known as the 'felony-murder' rule or the doctrine of 'constructive malice' – the felony was both attempting to evade arrest and the death of the policeman .... For the six it was claimed that Williams alone killed Constable Murphy, and that he had fired in self-defence .... Summing-up, the judge, Justice Edward Murphy, told the jury that Williams's confession was only one aspect of the case. If the jury was satisfied that all six defendants knew that violence was to be or might be used to further their escape, then everything else was secondary, in the eyes of the law they had committed murder. Whoever actually killed or shot at Constable Murphy was of no consequence. After retiring for just over two hours the jury returned to find all six guilty of murder, and all were sentenced to death, although in the case of Simpson they recommended mercy on account of his age .... An execution date was set for August 18th but this was postponed when the men all appealed ....

A reprieve committee was promptly established, receiving strong support from sympathisers in Ireland, Britain and the United States. Within a week over 200,000 in Northern Ireland had signed a petition. They included many who were not Republicans, but were residents who feared a return of political violence. On August 21st, the Northern Ireland appeal court rejected after a two-day hearing the contention that the trial judge had misdirected the jury on the question of "common intent." The three appeal judges were satisfied that all six defendants were equally responsible for the constable's death, and a new execution date was set for Wednesday, September 2nd, 1942 at Belfast Prison .... Telegrams urging clemency flooded into Downing Street, but the government responded that the fate of the six was a matter for the Northern Ireland authorities, although behind the scenes London had a major say in what was to follow – they were particularly concerned how the case was seen in

Washington .... The six had been placed in three death cells; Tom Williams sharing one with Joe Cahill. On August 30th, the Prison Governor, Captain T. Moore-Stuart, stepped into that cell with D. P. Marrinan, the men's solicitor. "I have very good news for one of you," said the lawyer. "I am sorry, Tom." All had been reprieved with the exception of Williams. Regarding himself as a soldier, he stood to attention. "Thank you," he said. "It's the way I wanted it." .... Four of the men's death sentences were commuted to life-terms, whilst Simpson had his death sentence commuted to 15 years ....

At 7.15 a.m. on September 2nd Thomas Williams took Mass, and at a minute before eight he was pinioned by hangmen Thomas and Albert Pierrepoint, who then walked him the few yards to the gallows to become the 15th man to be executed in the city's prison on the Crumlin Road in the north of the city – had all six gone to the gallows – a third hangman Harry Kirk had also been contacted .... The whole process took only 12 seconds. "Williams was praying all the time as he walked to the scaffold," said the priest who attended him. "He seemed to be quite resigned to his fate. The condemned man went calmly to his death without a tremor." Large crowds of rival demonstrators – Republicans and Unionists – had assembled outside the prison kept apart by the police, and Dublin marked Williams's execution by closing down for an hour. Although hanged inmates were usually buried quickly in the prison, Williams was permitted a "military" interment. In a ceremony which lasted only a couple of minutes, several prison officers and the governor saluted the body as it was lowered into its grave ....

Four days later, two policemen were fatally shot in the border village of Clady in County Tyrone – Samuel Hamilton (32) of the USC and James Laird (46) of the RUC .... Tom Williams's five reprieved comrades were released in October 1949 – a political decision by the Northern Irish government after the government in Dublin created the Republic of Ireland in the 26 counties of the South. Joe Cahill had, meanwhile, got to know a fellow-prisoner, a doctor jailed for performing an abortion. The two became good friends, the physician inviting Cahill to visit him after his release. When the doctor eventually left the prison, Cahill remarked to a prison-officer how unfortunate it was that such a professional man had been in jail. The officer expressed surprise at Cahill's sympathy. The doctor, he told Cahill, had been the foreman of the jury which convicted the six! ….

Although Thomas Williams was dead and buried, he was far from forgotten and certainly not to Irish Republicans .... For 53 years a campaign was waged by the Republican National Graves Association [NGA] to have his remains exhumed from his unmarked grave and re-interred elsewhere with the honours traditionally accorded IRA Volunteers. However the Northern Ireland Secretary said he had no authority to permit the exhumation. Three High Court judges in Belfast disagreed, exercise of the Royal Prerogative of Mercy was recommended and consent for the reburial was finally received in 1995, when it was proposed to transfer Williams's remains to the Republican area in Milltown Cemetery in West Belfast. That outcome was not achieved, however, without a hitch. The Northern Ireland Office claimed that Williams's prison grave would be impossible to locate after so many years: Williams was buried near the prison hospital. Inmates later scratched initials and the date of the execution - September 2nd 1942 - on a nearby wall. They were obliterated over the years – however with the Peace Process moving rapidly to the Good Friday Agreement in 1998, Williams's body was found after the prison closed in 1996 in August 1999, although it was not moved until January 2000: attempts to pinpoint the grave had failed a number of times when 40 people, including retired prison officers, failed to agree where it was. It is thought that Joseph Cahill had also returned to the gaol to help identify the site …. Four prison-officers removed the body in a coffin …. The funeral held on January 19th, 2000 was attended by thousands, with Thomas Williams buried in Milltown …. Cahill, a life-long Republican and later Chief of Staff of the IRA in the 1970's died in 2004 aged 84 …. of the 1998 Agreement Cahill said at the time: "If Tom Williams were alive today, he would be very much in favour of the course we are taking now. I have no doubts that anybody I know who has made the supreme sacrifice would have the same thinking. I was four weeks in the condemned cell with Tom. I expected to be hanged then, you know, and we talked about life after our death, what we would like to see for the future. To me, it's like yesterday we were in the condemned cell, and I can vividly remember the conversations we had." ….

Before Williams was executed he inscribed some messages on the backs of some playing cards. On one he wrote "To ever who receives this to pray for me always & pray for the cause for which I am dying. God Save Ireland …." Williams also sent a message to the IRA Chief of Staff in which he told his comrades "To carry on, no matter what the odds are against you, carry on no matter what torments are inflicted on you. The road to freedom is paved with suffering, hardships and torture, carry on my gallant and brave comrades until that certain day." But Ireland and particularly Northern Ireland was a divided society, others like Constable Patrick Murphy had a different view – and in June 1993 Constable Patrick Murphy's grandson, John (38) – himself an ex-RUC officer –was shot dead by the Republican INLA in a hotel in Belfast …. the *York Hotel* on Botanic Avenue …. in the same hotel in the previous October the Unionist UVF had shot dead a member of Sinn Fein – Sheena Campbell (29) ….

Case 19
"Interrogation"

"Is that evidence on which you would hang a dog? asked the defence, challenging the reputation, methods and the probity of the experienced and high-ranking officers." ….

John DAND

MURDER
Of
Walter Wyld (72)
[1951]

Capstick noted that Dand chain-smoked throughout the interrogation, yet his fingers bore no signs of nicotine .... Told that his story was not believed, Dand put his hands over his eyes, leant forward and said: "I admit that we had a row about money. It was an accident and I left him there" ….

"The toughest case I ever had to tackle" – that was how Scotland Yard's Detective Chief Superintendent John Capstick described the slaying of one of York's most popular citizens. A 72-year-old widower, Walter Wyld had been a Rugby League player in his younger days, and for 25 years he had been gateman and steward at York Rugby League Club's ground. A retired joiner and jobbing gardener, he was comfortably off and always ready to lend a few pounds to a neighbour in need – without interest. And his pockets invariably contained a few sweets for any child he might meet on his walks around town. Playing whist was one of his pastimes, and he was at a whist drive at the Rugby League club's social club on the last night of his life. It was 9.45 p.m. on **Saturday, January 27th, 1951**, when he left to catch a bus to his Huntington Road home at number 199 .... About an hour and a quarter later, his next-door neighbour Mrs. Eva Clark went out to her back garden to bin some rubbish. Walter Wyld's kitchen light was on. She was to remember this because the curtains were drawn. It struck her as odd because Walter always left them open. At lunchtime the next day the curtains were still drawn, so she called across the back gardens to Wyld's neighbour on the other side – her sister Mrs. E. Raby. Wondering if the old man was all right, they knocked on his front and back doors but got no response. They found that Mrs. Clark's house-key fitted the lock on Mr. Wyld's front door, so Mrs. Clark's son Eric opened it and stepped inside with Mrs. Raby. With the curtains still drawn, the house was in darkness. They made their way to the kitchen where Mrs. Raby had seen the light switched on. Walter Wyld was stretched out on the floor at their feet. He lay on his back, with blood on his shirt and a bloodstained cushion covering his face. Eric Clark and his aunt hurried round to her house and phoned the police. The first officers to arrive noted defensive wounds on the dead man's hands. His fingers were gashed and he had a chest-injury. One of his trouser pockets had been pulled inside-out, and a bloodstained towel lay beneath a couch near the kitchen window ....

In the front-room, part of a false tooth, a pair of horn-rimmed spectacles and a framed photograph lay on the floor. It seemed that this was where Walter Wyld's fight for his life had started. There was no sign of a forced entry so it appeared that the victim had known his killer and had admitted him to the house. Robbery did not seem to be the motive, unless the attacker had been disturbed and had fled. The police soon found a tin box containing £73 in the oven of an old cooker in a cupboard. As they had easily discovered it, so would have any thief. Because Wyld was known to have often lent money, the investigators wondered if the killer was a caller angered by being refused a loan. The police knew that when he left the house, as he closed the front door it had locked itself behind him – its key had been found in the drawer where Wyld always kept it. Scotland Yard's assistance was sought, and Capstick and Detective Sergeant Joseph Plater arrived on January 29th to find the local police dragging the River Foss for the murder weapon. The river flowed past the bottom of the garden, and some small islands 200 yards from Wyld's home were also searched without success. A post-mortem examination revealed that Wyld had received three stab wounds to the chest, one of them penetrating to a depth of seven inches – all the way to his backbone. In his efforts to save his life he had ruptured his arm muscles. As a matter of routine the police questioned hundreds of soldiers based at the nearby Strensall army camp. A description was issued of a man seen near the victim's home on the Saturday night. Wanted for questioning, he was said to have a pronounced Yorkshire accent and to be about 30 and clean-shaven, wearing a suit with ragged trouser turn-ups, a dirty raincoat and a brown trilby hat. The police were reported to believe that the man might be able to assist them in describing Wyld's movements after he left the whist drive. Capstick, however, was more interested in the victim's correspondence ….

Letters found in Wyld's kitchen included one posted on January 9th in Kirkcaldy, Fife in Scotland. It was from a Mrs. Dand, writing to say she had been pleased to hear from Wyld, her former neighbour, "until I read about the money." She went on to say that she had repaid the sum he had lent her, and she was sorry to learn that he thought she had moved from York to Kirkcaldy without settling the debt. Her letter concluded: "I had to come home in a hurry because my mother had an accident or else I would have been to see you. Jock is back in York now, so whenever I get his address I will tell him to come and see you." It was learned that Mrs. Dand and her husband John had formerly lived in Huntington Road, later moving to St. Paul's Square but still keeping in touch with Walter Wyld. They had gone to Kirkcaldy the previous November, the husband returning to York by himself on January 7th. Further inquiries established that Dand was a 32-year-old ex-soldier, awarded the Military Medal in the Second World War but since discharged from the army on medical grounds. He continued to frequent military circles, however, often visiting the sergeants' mess at Fulford Barracks in York as a guest. He was now living in digs in Burlington Avenue, and four days after the murder Capstick had him brought in for questioning. Dark-haired and slim, he still had the straight-backed bearing of a soldier despite the stomach ulcers which had led to his being invalided out of the army ….

Dand said he had last seen Wyld on or about January 8th, calling on him to repay £3 he owed him and having a chat with him in his kitchen. Asked about his movements after 10 o'clock on the night of January 27th, he said he had gone out drinking with his friend Sergeant James McIrvine, who was stationed at Fulford Barracks and with whom he had served in the Western Desert. After they visited several pubs, Dand's statement concluded, he left McIrvine around 10.45 and went straight back to his digs. He appeared unruffled by the interview, as if he had no worries. But Capstick noted that he chain-smoked throughout the interrogation, yet his fingers bore no signs of nicotine .... Dand was given a lift back to

Burlington Avenue, and on arriving at his digs he handed Detective Sergeant Plater the clothes he had worn on the night of the murder. The sergeant also took away some correspondence he found in a drawer of Dand's dressing table. A letter from Dand's wife indicated that the couple's relationship was strained. She wrote to say she was enclosing two letters received from Wyld, "addressed to Mr. and Mrs. – I still have the envelope if you don't believe me. I have told Walter that you are in York so I expect he will be looking out for you. I hope you are very proud of yourself." In his letter to Dand, Walter Wyld said he had been surprised to learn that he had gone back to Scotland without seeing him. "I shall be pleased if you will send me the money I loaned you as soon as possible," the note continued. "I can just do with it as my rates are due now." Wyld's letter to Mrs. Dand acknowledged that she had paid back the money he had loaned her, but said that her husband had since borrowed £3 which had not been repaid. Further inquiries revealed that John Dand also owed money to others and was living beyond his known means. Detectives interviewed Sergeant McIrvine and another man with whom Dand had gone drinking on the night of the murder. They said he had left them around 9.20, telling them he had a date with a woman who was going to find him employment. Dand had added that he would rejoin them later if he had time, but that was the last they saw of him that evening. From Dand's landlady the police learned that he had come home at about midnight. Analysis of stains on the suspect's clothes detected Group A blood like that of the victim. Dand's blood was Group O. On February 3rd, John Dand was brought in again for further questioning by Capstick, in the presence of York's Detective Inspector Ernest Wild. What ensued was one of the strangest interviews in Capstick's long experience ....

When Dand was told that his friend Sergeant McIrvine had said they had parted much earlier than 10.45 on the night of the murder he replied, "Yes, that's right. I'll tell you the truth." He then said nothing for 10 minutes. Even Capstick found the silence disconcerting. Finally Dand said that after leaving his friends he had picked up a woman with whom he had gone to the river bank. After spending some time with her, he had walked back to Burlington Avenue, arriving at his digs about 11.30. Asked to account for the blood on his clothes, he said it must be the woman's. Asked her name and where she could be found, he relapsed into silence. After five minutes in which not a word was spoken, Detective Inspector Wild left the room to speak to officers awaiting instructions outside, and Capstick was joined by Plater. The superintendent then asked Dand if he could name anyone who had seen him between 9.30 and midnight on the night in question. Dand said he couldn't – there was only the woman whose name he didn't know. Told that his story was not believed, Dand put his hands over his eyes, leant forward and said: "I admit that we had a row about money. It was an accident and I left him there." Cautioned, he then made a statement which Plater took down in writing. "About the first statement I made to the police," he began, "there is something I missed out of it and I want to tell you what it was. The truth is that I left my pal Sergeant McIrvine in the Golden Fleece at about ten past or quarter past nine last Saturday night. I told him I had a date on and I walked along to the Three Cranes pub near the market." He then claimed that after drinking at another pub he picked up a woman. She was in her mid to late 30s and he met her near the Elephant and Castle. All he could remember of her by way of description was that she was wearing a brown coat. As Dand continued to make his statement Capstick and Plater sat confidently awaiting his confession. Instead he concluded: "I now deny going to Walter Wyld's house on the Saturday night he was murdered. There is nothing more I can say." "I was flabbergasted," Capstick admitted in his memoirs. John Dand had looked him straight in the eye and told him the opposite of what he had said only minutes earlier. Charged with Walter Wyld's murder and described as a press operator, Dand made his first appearance in court on February 5th when he was remanded in custody. He was in court again on February 21st when York Magistrates were told of his alleged confession. They also heard that Walter Wyld, in addition to his chest and hand wounds, had been stabbed in the back. Dand was said to have told Capstick "I can prove I didn't kill him." ….

Committed for trial, he pleaded not guilty when he appeared before Justice William Gorman at Leeds Assizes in April, 1951. It soon became clear that the defence was intent on discrediting the prosecution's account of Dand's alleged confession. Capstick was questioned closely about how he had written down the questions he had asked Dand, and how Dand's answers had been noted. "It must have taken rather a long time," suggested H.R.B. Shepherd KC. defending. "Was your pal – I beg your pardon, was your fellow-Scotland Yard man, Sergeant Plater, doing the same thing?" "Well, he could only do it right off in one go," he replied. "Yes, he was writing it down." "What do you mean by 'He could only do it right off in one go'?" "Well, I was writing my question in my pocket-book before I spoke such to the accused. Then when I had written it down, I asked the accused that question slowly, and the sergeant would have to write that down and write the reply." "And then you got his answer and you wrote that down?" "Yes. As he answered, I wrote that in my book." The defence counsel then read from Capstick's notebook: "'He remained silent for about ten minutes and no one spoke.' That is in this notebook, is it not? And then he told you about this woman, did he not?" "If you give me my notebook," the superintendent replied, "I will give you the exact words he said." This prompted laughter, which was quickly quelled by the judge "If there is the slightest merriment of any kind, I shall have the court completely closed. This is far too serious a case for anything of that kind. It is not a public performance .... "Was Inspector Wild in the office still?" asked Mr. Shepherd. "The inspector was there, yes." "Was Plater still there?" "No. There was only the inspector and I in the office with him." "Plater had not been in up to that statement'?" "He was in the outer office." "Was there the conversation about the woman's name and where you could find her? And then more silence?" "Yes." "That was the moment which Inspector Wild chose to leave the office, was it not? Was it arranged between you and Wild that Wild should go out?" "No. I had no arrangement with him about going out. I did not know at the time that he wanted to go out." "Then he came out and Plater came in? Did you tell Wild to send Plater in?" "Yes." "There were you two there, and Wild presumably outside in the office. There were just you two and Dand in the room when he said, 'I admit we had a row about money. It was an accident and I left him there'?" "That is so, yes." "He never said anything of the sort, did he?" the defence counsel challenged. "They are the exact words he said," Capstick replied. "I immediately cautioned him, to take particulars of the accident, and he made the written statement under caution." "At what stage did Inspector Wild come back into the room?" "He was there all the time the statement was taken." "There were the three of you in that room while Dand made the statement. Were you watching or were you listening or what?" Capstick replied: "I sat in front of the accused and the sergeant wrote it down as he said it. He saw us get the pen and paper and he signed the caution before we started writing." Mr. Shepherd wasn't satisfied. "Would this be right?" he continued. "He made his statement by saying his sentence, whatever it was. You, as it were, repeated that to Sergeant Plater, and Sergeant Plater wrote it down. And on two occasions at least he had to check you over something which you had repeated wrongly? So that it may not be said that I have not put the thing properly to you, is this the way in which this sentence, 'I now deny going to Walter Wyld's house on the Saturday night he was murdered' – is this the way in which that statement came into the sentence? You or somebody else repeated as part of his statement to Sergeant Plater: 'Now it is up to you to try and prove I was at the house at that time.' He then stopped that and said: 'I never said anything of the sort.' …. And that is how that sentence came into the statement – 'I now deny going there'?" "That is not so," Capstick replied. "There was no question put to him at all." Going on to cross-examine Inspector Wild and Sergeant Plater, the defence counsel implied that the trio had colluded to distort Dand's statement. In the witness-box Dand told the jury that he was an army pensioner, having been discharged in 1949 through ill-health after serving in most battle areas except Burma. He had never had a cross word with Walter Wyld. They had borrowed books from each other and played dominoes together every Sunday night ....

Wyld had lent Mrs. Dand money to buy overalls when she was working at Rowntree's chocolate factory, and he had lent Dand £3 in September. Dand said that when he offered to repay the money, Wyld had said that as he was moving to Kirkcaldy he would need the cash, and he [Wyld] was in no hurry for its return. Claiming he was never short of money, Dand went on to repeat the story he had told the police. "Were you at any time that night in the neighbourhood of Huntington Road?" asked his defence counsel. "No, sir." In his final address to the jury Mr. Shepherd claimed that Wyld had been overpowered by someone much bigger, more powerful and much fitter than John Dand. Walter Wyld was an ex-athlete who kept himself fit, although he was slightly deaf and his sight was said to be slightly imperfect. For his age he was no weakling, and his biceps had burst because he was attacked by somebody of greater strength. But John Dand, the defence counsel submitted, was a man of poor muscular development and had a 30 per cent army disability pension. The prosecution had suggested that the murder had been committed for the sum of £3, Mr. Shepherd continued. "Is it suggested," he asked, "that a man in good work with a pension is going to commit an offence like this for three pounds plus whatever he might be able to find?" The defence counsel went on to remind the jury that Dand had been faced by "three officers of great experience and high rank, two from the mythically famous – actually famous – New Scotland Yard. When I say "mythically," all I mean is that it is the sort of thing you read about in detective stories. Two of them come up from London, both perhaps – at any rate, in the case of Capstick – of rather frightening *mien*. ….

"Members of the jury, what would you do if you were faced with that position? Would you be completely at ease? Would you know what was the right thing to say without hesitation?" The most striking thing that happened on the afternoon of February 3rd, said Mr. Shepherd, took place in Inspector Wild's office. "First of all Inspector Wild and Capstick were in the room. Plater was outside in the general office. The thing goes on with nothing particular happening. There are three pauses and in the third of those, expecting nothing, Wild thinks to himself, 'Oh, now I can go out and talk to those three pairs of officers who have been waiting since half-past two, collect their information and give them fresh instructions,' and goes out. "Within at most ten minutes, with Plater and Capstick alone in the room, this man is said to have made what they say is an admission, and within that ten minutes Dand is said to be ready to make a statement. So Wild comes in, Plater comes in, and a statement is taken – a statement which is a denial of the very thing which five minutes before he is said to have admitted." ….

The defence counsel then asked the jury, "Is that evidence on which you would hang a dog? I make no bones about it. In my submission, that evidence of the admission or the alleged admission is not truthful. It is wholly inconsistent with what happened before." Summing-up, Justice Gorman told the jury that they might think that the implication behind the defence counsel's suggestions was that the two Scotland Yard detectives got rid of their York colleague and then in his absence concocted a statement which they said was made by Dand. The prosecution, on the other hand, claimed that with one of his statements having been found to be untrue and a second statement disbelieved, Dand had realised that the police knew more than he thought. So he said, "I was there, but it was an accident." The defence had argued that it was inconceivable that this statement should be made "sandwiched between denials," the judge continued. It was for the jury to decide whether the police witnesses were telling the truth, or whether they had invented Dand's confession ….

After retiring for slightly more than an hour, the jury returned to vindicate the detectives' integrity: they convicted John Dand of murder at the end of the 4-day trial on April 26th …. An appeal was rejected on May 28th …. Who felt sorry for him? John Capstick! "Like many other fine soldiers," the superintendent wrote in his memoirs, "he was a fish out of water in civilian life. Had he been able to remain in the army, the environment which he understood and loved, his story might have had a very different and more honourable ending." Two interrogations had been paramount to this case. The questions posed and theories promulgated by the defence counsel in the examination of a senior police officer's actions may have been deemed impertinent to some – but was it plausible that there was reasonable doubt and that Dand was innocent? The jury thought not. Instead, on Tuesday, June 12th, 1951, John Dand went to the gallows at Manchester's Strangeways Prison executed by Albert Pierrepoint and Harry Allen ….

Case 20

"Murder Of 'Old Gossy'"

"His legs were bound to the foot of the bed, his jacket pulled down so that he could not move his arms, and his tormentors tried to force him to say where he kept his money." ....

"When they put the Brown brothers in an identity parade in front of 12 witnesses who had been around Old Gossy's shop at the time of the first raid no one recognised them." ....

Joseph BROWN & Edward SMITH
MURDER
Of
Frederick Gosling (79)
[1951]

Double-execution of two young men convicted of the "Old Gossy killing." There was enormous controversy and public interest in the case. Some thought the police had got the wrong men; many believed there were others involved in the crime who had not been caught; there was even a body of opinion that the death was not a murder at all …. Smith went to the scaffold with considerable bravado. He was waiting for the executioners when they entered the cell ….

Old Gossy was the local nickname of Frederick Gosling, a 79-year-old man who, despite his age and growing deafness, still ran a corner grocery and newsagents shop at Clay Corner, in Addlestone Moor, Chertsey, Surrey; the sign over the shop door proudly proclaimed: "Est. 1902." Early on in an evening in January, 1951, Old Gossy made a call to his local police station; they had the greatest trouble trying to make out what the excited old man was saying, but it appeared that there had been trouble at the shop and some men had threatened him. A single policeman was despatched and he found the old man in such a state that he was not able to give a coherent account of what had happened. Fortunately, two young schoolgirls were able to help the policeman. They said that they had gone into the shop, heard Old Gossy cry out in the back-room and then two 'scruffy' men suddenly appeared and fled. The policeman established that, apart from being shaken, Old Gossy had not been hurt and nothing had been stolen. That seemed to be that. The constable went back to make his report ….

At 9 o'clock the next morning, **Friday, January 12th**, the milkman found the shop door locked and no sign of the proprietor. That was most unusual, so he went round to a side-door which he found was open. Now thoroughly alarmed, he crept into the house and found the old man in the bedroom. He was tied to the bed, gagged – and dead. The pathologist's report showed that Mr. Gosling had died through suffocation because he had been clumsily gagged with a duster. Reporters briefed by murder squad detectives later that morning were told that it was a senseless and unnecessary killing; by no stretch of the imagination could the old man have posed any sort of threat to anyone. The story which lay behind the death of Old Gossy was a tale of greed and stupidity and sheer incompetence. As the story was played out in public, it was to display betrayal in the sordid world of minor 'gang-related' crime; thief accusing thief in desperate attempts to escape the noose, and a man giving evidence which could only send his brother to the gallows. Old Gossy was eccentric about money. He did not have a till in the shop but kept his cash in a back-room. Even a sale involving a one-pound note meant he disappeared through the back to get the change. The secretive behaviour led to rumours that he was rich, and there were soon stories that he kept "all his money" hidden somewhere on the premises ….

The idle chatter was picked up by dishonest ears. The man who planned the robbery was a 27-year-old labourer called Frederick Brown from nearby Ashford. He first involved his older brother, Joseph, 30, and together they recruited a lorry-driver called Edward Smith, another 30-year-old; he had not been involved in crime before but was tempted by the Brown brothers, who said they could put him on to some easy money if he was prepared to join them on a job. The plan was simple: Frederick Brown was to keep watch outside Old Gossy's shop while Joseph Brown and Smith were to enter and carry out the robbery. Inside they would buy something small and give the old man a pound note; when he went to get the change, he would lead them to the money. As soon as Old Gossy, followed by Smith and Brown, went into the back-room Frederick Brown was to enter the shop and lock the door so that no one could get in while the robbery was in progress. At 6 o'clock one evening in January 1951 the plan was put into effect, and it came within an ace of success. When Old Gossy was given the pound note he duly disappeared into the back-room; from the doorway Smith and Brown watched him go to a bureau in a corner and open a drawer. The two robbers were entering the back-room when there was a racket from the shop doorbell. Brown looked over his shoulder, expecting to see his brother. Instead there were two schoolgirls coming in – and no Frederick! The bell had also attracted the attention of the half-deaf old shopkeeper, who turned from the bureau, saw Smith and Brown, and started shouting his head off. "Keep him quiet!" snapped Brown. Smith moved over, grabbed hold of the old man, and tried to get a hand over his mouth, but Old Gossy carried on struggling and Smith's nerve broke. "Let's get out!" he urged. The two men ran for it, bursting out of the back-room, past the girls and out of the shop ….

When they were eventually able to question their "lookout man" to find out what had gone wrong, Frederick claimed that someone he knew had come up to him in the street and started talking; it had been impossible for him to get inside the shop and lock the door. The police, meanwhile, were now getting their confused call from the shopkeeper. About the story this far there is no dispute. All three men were to admit the attempted robbery and their part in it. What happened next is quite a different matter. Far from being scared off by the close call at the shop, some appetites had merely been whetted, and someone decided to go back and try again – that night. Old Gossy was woken in his bed and trussed up. His legs were bound to the foot of the bed, his jacket pulled down so that he could not move his arms, and his tormentors tried to force him to say where he kept his money. It took a long time to get it out of Old Gossy – 13 cigarette ends were found in the hearth. Eventually either the old man gave in or the raiders struck it lucky, but the safe key was found in his trouser pocket and the safe was cleaned out. It is thought there was between £40 and £60 in notes and silver. Before they left, Old Gossy was gagged; an action which was to open the road to the gallows. For a week the murder squad found their investigation was going nowhere, but then they had some lucky breaks. First there was a tip off that it was "the Brown brothers" who had done the job. They did not even know which of the Brown brothers they were after, but by a fluke they happened to pick Frederick up first, and he turned out to be the weak link in the chain. Unaware of how little the police had, Frederick cracked. "All right," he told them, "I arranged it. It's not George, it's my other brother Joe." Frederick and Joseph were put before magistrates on a holding charge of assaulting Mr. Gosling with intent to rob him, but the police case was still looking fragile. When they put the Brown brothers in an identity parade before 12 witnesses who had been around Old Gossy's shop at the time of the first raid no one recognised them. At some stage a deal was done and Frederick really started throwing everyone to the wolves to save his own skin. He fingered Smith, gave what he claimed was a full confession, agreed to testify in a murder trial which he knew could send the other two to the gallows, and the charge against him was dropped ....

Edward Smith and Joseph Brown went on trial at the Kingston-u-Thames Assizes accused of murder in the following March. The prosecution's star witness was Frederick. In the witness-box he admitted formulating the original plan and confessed that he had been involved in the *first* attempt to rob the shopkeeper, but he said that he had not gone back in the night. He claimed that he was unaware that Smith and his brother were planning to return until the next morning when they told him they had done the job. They said they had tied up the old man but he had been all right. The defence mounted a massive counter-attack on him but he stuck doggedly to his story. He had not gone back to the shop. The defence produced a surprise witness, a man who was serving six months in Brixton Gaol, who claimed to have had a conversation with Frederick while he was being held on remand there. The prisoner swore that Frederick had revealed he planned the job and that he had gone back with a friend, *not Smith and Joseph*. "He said his solicitor told him to keep quiet and he was going to be discharged." Smith and Joseph fought for their lives and both of them pointed the finger at Frederick – sitting, a free man, a few feet away from them in the courtroom. At the end of the 4-day trial on March 5th, the jury was out for three and a half hours before the verdict of guilty of murder was returned. Brown's mother collapsed in the courtroom and had to be taken by ambulance to hospital when the judge, Justice Hubert Parker, pronounced the sentence of death on the two young men ....

As an appeal was dismissed on April 9th, and the controversy surrounding the Old Gossy case was still raging, the execution approached on Wednesday, April 25th, 1951 at Wandsworth Prison in south-west London .... The Sunday Dispatch had carried a story that Frederick Brown had been forced to quit his job and leave his sister's home in Ashford after threats. He was trying to start a new life where he was not known, and he told the newspaper that when his new workmates talked about the murder trial in the canteen, he just kept quiet. His sister, who had stood by him, had been compelled to abandon her job in a department store; she had also been threatened in the street and told that she would be waylaid some night. "I know what people are saying behind my back," he told the Dispatch. "They believe I hanged my brother to save my own neck. It's just not true." Despite the circumstances there was no discussion about the rights or wrongs of the case by the executioners – Albert Pierrepoint and three assistants: Harry Allen, Syd Dernley and Herbert Allen – on the eve of the execution .... That was a problem which had been dealt with by other people. Edward Smith and Joseph Brown were to hang in the morning; there was no point in talking about it. Smith went to the scaffold with considerable bravado. He was waiting for the men when they entered the death-cell and offered no resistance when they pinioned his arms, but he snapped at Dernley when he tried to guide him. Pierrepoint had turned to lead the way through the door into the execution chamber and took hold of Smith's arm to make him follow, but he growled, "Leave me alone – I'll walk on my own!" Two prison-officers started to move in on Smith, but when the executioners let go of his arm he turned and walked quickly through. On the trap Dernley strapped his legs, and was just straightening up when Brown was brought in. Harry Allen stood back and Herbert Allen did his part with the leg-strap and they both went down. It was quite a quick job for a double. Just over an hour later, outside the prison gates, Pierrepoint and Dernley said goodbye to the two Allens. Their job was done and the first two executioners were heading into London to see the sites and meet up with acquaintances. They were never to work with Herbert again – it was his last execution ....

[This write-up is based mainly on a report of the case in "The Hangman's Tale: Memoirs of a Public Executioner" by Syd Dernley [Assistant Executioner] and David Newman (1989); and is by far the best book on the genre of accounts written by and about hangmen in Britain ....]

Case 21
"The Murderous Mother-in-Law"

"Three pieces of burnt material tied together to form a noose were found in the dustbin. They were the remains of a scarf…. Hella had been strangled to death." ….

"Mrs. Christofi's counsel had urged her to plead guilty but insane. This advice had been angrily rejected. After hearing the verdict she asked to speak, but her request was ignored." ….

Styllou CHRISTOFI
MURDER
Of
Her daughter-in-Law Hella
[1954]

Mrs Styllou Christofi had her pride. Murderess she might be – though she denied it. But mad? Never! Plead guilty but insane? She wouldn't hear of it. "I am a poor woman of no education," she told her son, "but I am not a mad woman. Never, never, never." ….

The mad usually insist they are sane. It is part of their delusion. Ironically, if Mrs. Christofi had come to her senses and pleaded insanity she might not have become the first woman to be hanged in London for 30 years. A London restaurateur, Mr. Burstoff, was out late with his wife on the night Mrs. Christofi's story began. It was 1 a.m. on **Thursday, July 29th, 1954**, and the Burstoffs were driving slowly past Hampstead Railway Station in north-west London when Mrs. Christofi ran up to their car. "Please come! Fire burning! Children sleeping!" she cried. They went with her to her home at 11, South Hill Park, Hampstead Heath, but could see no sign of a fire. Where was the blaze, asked Mr. Burstoff. "Shush! Babies sleeping!" said Mrs. Christofi. Then she opened the French windows of the flat. "Look!" cried Mrs. Burstoff "There's somebody on the ground." Mr. Burstoff saw the head of a nearly naked body covered in blood. "I told Mrs. Christofi that I must telephone the police," he said later, "and she pointed to a telephone in the room." Just as he was about to dial 999 all the lights in the house went out. Nevertheless, he managed to get through to the police, and while he and his wife awaited them with Mrs. Christofi at the front door, Mrs. Christofi told them: "Me smell burning. Me come down. Me pour water, but she died." "Isn't that your son lying there?" asked Mrs. Burstoff. "My son married German girl he like," Mrs. Christofi replied. "Plenty clothes, plenty shoes. Babies going to Germany." ….

In fact the body was that of her daughter-in-law. When Mrs. Christofi had gone upstairs to bed, she told the Burstoffs, she had left her son's wife downstairs, sewing. Police found that Mrs. Christofi's bed had not been slept in, and there were bloodstains in the kitchen which someone seemed to have tried to wipe away. Outside by the charred body of her daughter-in-law Hella, Mrs. Christofi's 36-year-old German daughter-in-law, there was burned newspaper and wood which had been soaked in paraffin. The body was completely unclothed, in a supine position, and seemed to be burned black. The face and hair were covered with blood and there was a "band" strip all round the neck. When Home Office pathologist Dr. Francis Camps turned the body over he saw that it was really a mixture of black and white – black where the charring had taken place on the front of the body and white on the buttocks, calves and shoulders which, touching the stone floor, had escaped scorching by the fire. Hella's husband, Stavros Christofi, had left the house at about 8.30 p.m. on July 28th, going to his work as a waiter in a West End restaurant. Now he told the police that he had never seen his wife without her tight-fitting wedding ring, which was engraved with his name. It was not on the charred corpse, however. It was found wrapped in a piece of paper and tucked behind a china ornament in the mother-in-law's bedroom. A superficial view would have been that death was due to burning, deliberate burning. However, the back of Hella's skull was fractured and the wound was consistent with a blow from the ash-plate of the boiler, which was bloodstained. Furthermore, three pieces of burnt material tied together to form a noose were found in the dustbin. They were the remains of a scarf belonging to one of Hella's three children. Hella had also been strangled to death. ….

The police learned that Stavros Christofi, a member of a Greek family in Cyprus, had arrived in Britain in 1937. In 1942 he had married Hella, a tall, attractive brown-haired young woman from the Ruhr, who proved to be a good mother and an excellent housewife. In 1953, however, Stavros's mother had come to stay with the family, ostensibly just long enough to earn enough money to buy some land on her return to Cyprus. A year later, however, she was still at her son's Hampstead home, disapproving of her daughter-in-law who could do nothing to please her. By now Hella was showing such signs of stress that Stavros arranged for her to take the children on holiday to her parents' home in Germany. Upon Hella's return, it was decided, Stavros's 53-year-old mother would go back to Cyprus because of her health and the onset of winter. Stavros and Hella told her as tactfully as they could. "If you feel like that about it, I shall go back," said Mrs. Christofi. She had got the message. Now, questioned by detectives, she said: "I wake up, smell burning, go downstairs. Hella burning. Throw water, touch her face. Not move. Run out. Get help." Shown the material which the police believed had been tied round Hella's neck, she said: "I was so afraid. I did not even notice anything round her neck." And the wedding ring? "I found it on the stairs," said Mrs. Christofi. "I wrapped it up because I thought it was a curtain ring." She told the detectives: "I came to this country in July, 1953, and lived with my son and his wife for a little while, but owing to the language difficulty we didn't get along very well together and I went to live elsewhere for about two months. "I then returned to my son's house and had been away on two more occasions owing to the same difficulty. I have now been with my son for about three or four months and have been getting along much better with my daughter-in-law during the last week or two. When I went to bed Hella and I were on perfectly good terms and she said that she was going to do some washing. I do not know whether she meant clothes or whether she was going to wash herself. Every evening Hella washes the whole of her body with water." Mrs. Christofi went on to say that at 12.55 a.m. she got up and saw smoke. Hella was lying in the garden. I saw little flames at the ankles, around the knees, on both arms and the back of the head. I put some water in a bowl and splashed it over her with my hand. I called her by name, and touched her face and hand, and then I got some more water and threw it over her." ….

This account, however, did not square with evidence given by John Young, a neighbour. He told the police that at about 11.30 on the night of Hella's death, he had taken his dog into his garden. "When I got out there, I noticed that the whole of the back of number eleven was aglow as though from the light of a fire," he said. Crossing the garden, he peered into the back yard of the house next door and saw what looked like a wax model lying on a bonfire. Looking through the French windows, he saw Mrs. Christofi come round a table and go out into the yard, apparently to stir the fire .... It was no surprise when, at Mrs. Christofi's trial in the Autumn, the jury found her guilty of murder after a 4-day trial on October 28th .... The jury had been out for just under two hours and there was no recommendation to mercy. Before them had been someone from a different culture, someone from a background in which the matriarch of a peasant family was accustomed to reigning supreme. Her crime must have seemed as foreign to the jury as was Mrs. Christofi herself. To deprive one's grandchildren of their mother, one's son of his wife, in such a horrific way was not only dastardly; it was also unnatural.

And if any member of the jury had any lingering doubts these must have been dispelled when it subsequently became known that this was not the first time Mrs. Christofi had been charged with a killing. Ironically, as a young woman she had herself experienced mother-in-law trouble. In 1925 she had been tried but acquitted of murdering her husband's mother by stuffing a burning torch down her throat in what was an 'honour-killing', itself related to another honour-based murder on the island in 1911 ....

After Mrs. Christofi's arrest for Hella's murder, her counsel had urged her to plead guilty but insane. This advice had been angrily rejected. In court, with little English, but accompanied by an interpreter, she had not had much to say. After hearing the verdict she asked to speak, but her request was ignored, and Justice Patrick Devlin pronounced the death sentence in a language she could not fully understand. Back in prison Mrs. Christofi was visited by her son, who was torn between grief for his murdered wife and horror at the fate awaiting his mother, who now seemed to blame him for her plight. From her death-cell, she wrote to Stavros: "I hope you are all right as well as your children. I hope that you will always be well, with God's help. It doesn't matter what is going to happen to me. You have tried too hard to hang me, in order to put around my neck the noose, so that you may rest. I am not obliging you to come to see me, my son." She recalled the days when the family was together in Cyprus, working in the fields; she, the matriarch, taking her place alongside them as well as baking the bread. She had come to England, she wrote, because she could no longer bear to be apart from Stavros, although she had four other children ....

Dr. Thomas Christie, the medical officer at Holloway Prison, had some understanding of her situation. He realised how, finding herself in an alien society, Mrs. Christofi had come to resent the comparatively sophisticated daughter-in-law who had taken her son's love, and who chatted with him in a language Mrs. Christofi could not comprehend. She resented the daughter-in-law who, instead of staying at home where a mother ought to be with her children, went out each day because she had a job. Although Hella's work enabled the children to have nice clothes, for Mrs. Christofi this was no way to bring up a family. That resentment had festered, developing into an insane jealousy which had culminated in the symbolic removal of Hella's wedding ring: a mother had reclaimed her son. Dr. Christie had studied Mrs. Christofi in prison and he had written a report. Mrs. Christofi, he believed, was suffering from a mental disorder. "In my opinion," he wrote, "the fear that her grandchildren would not be brought up properly induced a defect of reason …. whereby however much she may have been capable of appreciating the nature and quality of the acts she was doing, at the time of the acts, the defect of reason was such that she was incapable of knowing that what she was doing was wrong." This report could have been quoted in her defence at Mrs. Christofi's trial, but she refused to allow her counsel to mention it ….

After her conviction, and an appeal that was rejected on November 29th, she was examined by a panel of medical experts who – doubtless to her satisfaction – found her to be sane. Then, the day before Mrs. Christofi's execution, the prison doctor's report was published by the newspapers. Three Queen's Counsel were among those who now tried on that last day to save Mrs. Christofi's life. They applied unsuccessfully to see the Home Secretary. His mind was made up: there was to be no last-minute reprieve. Mrs. Christofi was duly hanged by Albert Pierrepoint and Harry Allen at Holloway Prison in north London on Wednesday, December 15th, 1954, and with her execution the final curtain descended on a drama which for many had all the ingredients of a classic Greek tragedy. …. While in the condemned cell, Mrs. Christofi requested that a Greek Christian Orthodox cross be put on the wall of the execution chamber, which was granted. It remained there until the gallows was dismantled in 1967 when the Home Office ordered that all execution-chambers in England & Wales be dismantled except one at Wandsworth Prison in south-west London following the abolition of the death penalty for murder in Britain in November 1965 ….

The murder took place at 11, South Hill Park; at 2a in the same road was and still is the Magdala Tavern – here four months after the execution of Styllou Christofi …. Ruth Ellis shot and murdered her boyfriend …. She was the last of just 18 women executed in Britain and Ireland after January 1st, 1900 ….

Case 22
"Murder & Mystery At Ashcombe Gardens"

"I could not believe what they said about Danny. It was not like him. He was a gentle boy" ....

Daniel RAVEN
MURDERS
Of
His Parents-in-Law Leopold & Esther Goodman
[1950]

It isn't enough for a crime reporter to take down the facts from the police and then type out his story for the next edition. He has to do much more than that. He has to get behind the story, find out all about the bit-part players, probe and discover the background of the killer, his victim, and anyone else involved. Duncan Webb, undoubtedly

Britain's most renowned crime reporter of the mid 20th century, knew all about this. A few weeks after Mrs. Marie Raven, a petite, auburn-haired Jewish woman of 23, gave birth to her first child, Webb went to see her. "I would like to write your personal story," he said. Many would have regarded this as a brazen proposition. For the young mother was in deep shock. Her husband was about to be hanged for the murder of her parents – a murder which didn't seem to have any logic attached to it at all ….

Shortly after the child's birth, Daniel Raven, her husband and also Jewish and aged 23, had visited her at Muswell Hill Nursing Home in north London. The date was Saturday, October 8th, 1949, and Raven was accompanied by her parents, Mr. and Mrs. Leopold Goodman, aged 49 and 47, both Russian Jews. Two days later **[Monday, October 10th]** Raven and the Goodmans made another visit to the proud mother. Another happy family occasion? There was no reason why it should have been anything else. That's why the events that followed that second visit to the nursing home, on October 10th, were both sinister and inexplicable. On this second occasion Mr. and Mrs. Goodman left their daughter's private room a few minutes before Daniel Raven. He followed them shortly afterwards, and his wife heard the three of them talking outside the nursing home. The time, she reckoned, was about 9.45 p.m. Apparently the Goodmans went to their home at 8, Ashcombe Gardens, in the Stone Grove area of Edgware, north London. Raven was to say later that he accompanied them to their front door, then went to his own home, about 500 yards away. Later that night Mr. and Mrs. Frederick Fraiman called to see their relatives the Goodmans ….

When they received no reply to their knocks on the door, Fred Fraiman, who was a partner in Mr. Goodman's radio business, entered the house by a back window. He found Mr. and Mrs. Goodman lying in pools of blood, both apparently bludgeoned to death by an intruder. When the police arrived they summoned Daniel

Raven from his home. Seemingly distressed, he told Detective Inspector John Diller: "Why didn't they let me stop? Why did they tell me to go?" Diller was convinced from the start that the young man's behaviour was suspicious. He noticed that Raven was wearing a newly-pressed suit, that his shirt and collar were meticulously clean. They did not seem to have been exposed to a day's dust and grime in London. Without telling Raven, Inspector Diller phoned the Muswell Hill Nursing Home and asked if anyone there could describe the colour of the suit Raven was wearing on his last visit there a few hours earlier. The subsequent description proved that Raven had changed his suit, tie and shirt after he got home that night. Diller put down the phone and looked hard at the pale, pinched face of Daniel Raven. "May I have your house keys?" he said. Raven handed the police officer his keys, then immediately tried to snatch them back. He wasn't successful. At 11.45 p.m. Inspector Diller went to Raven's house. The first thing he heard was the roar of a domestic boiler burning. "There was a gas poker in the lower part," he said later. "I disconnected the tube." ….

Inside the boiler he found one of Raven's suits. It wasn't completely burned because it had been packed in too tightly to allow a draught. Diller asked Raven if the suit he was wearing was the same one he had worn earlier in the day. Raven said it was not. He'd had a bath at his home and left his suit on the floor in the bedroom. He was asked how he accounted for the gas poker being alight. Raven replied: "I don't know anything about that. Do you think I murdered them?" The suit was taken away for analysis, during which technicians discovered splashes of blood group AB, which was the same group as the Goodmans', on the trousers. A blood clot of the same group was also found on one of Raven's shoes which had been washed and hidden in the garage. Next day Raven was seen by another police officer. Asked how his clothes and shoes had become bloodstained he said, "Yes, they are mine. I wore them last night. How the blood got on them I don't know." Detective Inspector Diller asked Raven about his relations with his in-laws. Raven said: "I did not get on with Mr. Goodman too badly, although we quarrelled at times. But Mrs. Goodman and I didn't get on well at all. She did not like me, and I did not like her very much. Neither did I like Mr. Goodman, although he has been very good to me." ….

Raven was arrested and charged with the murder of his in-laws while their daughter Marie and the new-born baby slept peacefully at the nursing home. The staff there told her at first that her husband and parents had been involved in a car crash – she learned the truth from someone else. "The initial shock, and the deep grief she afterwards sustained, beggar words," Webb recalls. The day after Raven appeared at Wealdstone Magistrates' Court Mrs. Raven left the nursing home against doctor's orders, accompanied by Raven's parents, and went to see her husband in Brixton Prison. She spent some days after that at the Ravens' home. Why should young Daniel Raven, middle-class and apparently well-heeled, want to murder his wealthy in-laws only hours after becoming a father? His defence was that he didn't do it. He claimed that on the night of the murder he left the Goodmans outside their house and went home. He then went to visit some cousins who lived nearby, but they weren't in. On the way back to his house he passed the Goodmans' home and decided to call on them because he thought the Fraimans might be there. There was no answer to his knocking, so he went in and found the corpses of Mr. and Mrs. Goodman. The body of Mrs. Goodman was in the dining-room and her head was so split down that there was a huge crack in the middle of the skull, and the brain was showing. He knelt by the body, but couldn't remember if his knee touched the ground or not. Looking around in panic and desperation, he saw the body of his father-in-law. He fled the house in terror. ....

Duncan Webb described Raven's 3-day trial at the Old Bailey in November before Judge James Cassels as "spectacular." Raven was defended by John Maude QC, an erudite and brilliant advocate who had a reputation for fighting to the last ditch for his client. In this case he fought so well that even today there are still some who think Raven was innocent. "I am not one of them," Webb clarified. Marie Raven was subpoenaed as a defence witness, but there wasn't much she could contribute. She knew nothing about what happened to her parents, or about her husband's ability to prove that he did not murder them – for the prosecution led by Edward Hawke it was very simple case .... On November 24th, 1949, Daniel Raven was found guilty of murder and sentenced to death after the jury had retired for just 48 minutes. His appeal on December 20th, was almost as fascinating as his trial, because it was contended on his behalf that one of the jurors was Jewish who had taken the oath on the New Testament. The judges set little store by that. The Appeal Court said that the reason the trial judge's summing-up was 'unfavourable' to Raven was that the evidence against him was overwhelming. Raven made four different statements and "four times he told lies." ….While Raven languished in the condemned cell, Webb got to know Marie Raven. He wrote: "So far no one had provided a motive for the double-murder. The fact that he had been tried and found guilty was, to some extent, proof that he did it. After the trial and the appeal, more can be said about someone involved in a murder charge than is permissible before. "From Mrs. Raven I learned a lot about her husband and I was in a better position than anyone to ferret out the reason for the double-murder." Webb expected to meet a grief-stricken young mother, too distraught to discuss the case. He sat next to her during the trial and they only exchanged niceties. ….

The day after the trial Mrs Raven was pale and wan, and did not want to talk to him. But Webb persisted gently. "I brought her round to the subject of her husband, who she called Danny. Then I discreetly mentioned her mother and father. I was trying to find out what was in her mind regarding her husband. A reporter sees many people in positions similar to that of Mrs. Raven, and experience will have taught him that often such people do not say exactly what they wish to say, and sometimes they imply things they do not exactly wish to imply." During their first half hour of conversation Mrs. Raven said practically nothing. Of one thing though, she was sure. That was that the trial was a perfectly fair one. "In her demeanour and attitude I clearly could not discover any regret at the verdict. She said, 'Justice has been done and I do not complain.'" A little later, though, she told Webb, "I could not believe what they said about Danny. It was not like him. He was a gentle boy." Webb had difficulty in fathoming her out. "There was a mixture of emotions, the confusion of loyalties, the bewilderment of facts. I came to the conclusion that this stark and horrible tragedy had completely passed her by. Our nervous systems can assimilate so much sorrow and grief, but beyond the limit we give up and our minds say, 'no more.' So it was with Mrs. Raven. Her young mind, her hitherto happy outlook on life, her naïve immaturity could not cope with this singular and unique tragedy. Mrs. Raven was a woman overwhelmed. Now there was only her son, named after his grandparents, whom as yet she hardly knew. This was all she had left. I went back to my office and thought deeply about her before I began writing my article." Webb didn't have to show his article to Marie Raven, but he thought it was only fair to do so. She read it, and so did Mr. Fraiman, her Uncle Fred. Mrs. Raven didn't like all of it. Some parts she crossed out, and Webb allowed her view to stand. Re-reading what remained she said, "I like that. It makes me want to cry. It's so touching." ….

This is what Webb wrote next day in The People: "Mrs. Gertrude Marie Raven, 23-year-old wife of a man condemned to die for the murder of her parents, is determined that her baby son shall never hear of the tragedy, overwhelming and complete, that blasted her life in its hour of fulfilment. "'My baby has my father's name and he will live as my father did – honestly, decently, and with kindness in his heart,' she said. 'I will not tell him why he does not remember his grandparents, nor will he ever know the truth about his father.' "In one of the most poignant interviews ever given to a newspaper, she told me of the conflict which has racked her mind and spirit from the moment they told her of the murder until Daniel Raven – he was a gentle boy, she said – was led from the dock. But last night Daniel Raven was still fighting for his life. His solicitor, announcing an appeal, said, 'Raven persists in his innocence.' "I asked Mrs. Raven what were her thoughts when she made her decision to help establish that innocence by giving evidence. "'I looked at my child,' she said, 'and I felt that Danny alone was fighting for his life. For the sake of my baby I felt that I must help his father. I did all that I could. "'There is no use in living on bitterness,' she exclaimed. 'I have my youth and my son. I am alone in the world now, except for him. So long as I live he will never be alone.'" Towards the end of the article Webb included Mrs. Raven's "Justice has been done" quote. He said afterwards that the article might have led some people to think that Marie Raven was not displeased with the jury's verdict. After the article appeared Raven's appeal was dismissed and the execution date was fixed. As the countdown began Raven's solicitor, Mr. Rutter, did an extraordinary thing ….

At midnight on January 3rd, 1950, he called 10 reporters and two photographers to a media conference in his book-lined office and announced: "Daniel Raven is mad. Home Office experts have confirmed his mental condition. I am horrified to tell you that the Home Secretary has nonetheless decided against any interference with the course of the law." Webb, one of the reporters present, said, "He sat behind his desk beneath a standard lamp, the light shining directly on his face, with his hands clasped together in front of him." Rutter was calm and deliberate. He said: "Gentlemen, it is obvious that if Raven committed this murder, he must be insane." He then read out paragraphs from a pile of documents which, he said, "prove that in the view of the most eminent psychiatrists in this country it would be absolutely wrong to hang this man." Why, he was asked, wasn't all this said in court? "It would have prejudiced Raven's case," Mr. Rutter replied. Duncan Webb didn't like that argument at all. "If he was innocent of the murder but insane, then he should have made that clear at his trial," he wrote in his notes. But the solicitor didn't discover "this alarming state of insanity" until after the appeal had failed. The midnight press conference certainly succeeded in getting plenty of publicity for the Raven case. And Mr. Rutter wouldn't give up. Turning to Duncan Webb he asked the reporter to use his powers of persuasion on Mrs. Marie Raven to get her to write to the King asking for clemency. "He even promised to get me Raven's permission to publish his personal letters." ….

The solicitor was, of course, only doing his job – and doing it exceedingly well. Webb was happy to oblige because at heart he was deeply opposed to capital punishment. The solicitor phoned Webb every two hours until 3 o'clock the following morning to ask if he had managed to persuade Marie Raven to write to the Queen. Webb was certainly doing his best, even going somewhat beyond the line of duty. "I went to see Mrs. Raven. I pointed out to her that one day she might regret not taking all the steps she could to save her husband's life. I added that, in my view, whatever she did at this stage no reprieve would be granted, and in view of that perhaps it would be as well, if only for the record, that she took some steps in order to have it said that she did not flinch from trying to save a human life." Mrs. Raven didn't agree. She told Webb: "Sentiment will not change anything. Nothing I could say or do will alter the law that found Danny guilty." That, says Webb, summed-up her state of mind in a nutshell. Not only did she refuse to write to the King, she also refused to sign the petition which was raised for her husband's reprieve. "For that," she told Webb, "they call me heartless. Why should I have signed that petition? Do people realise what I have been through? He killed my mother and father. He wasn't insane. There are stories about brainstorms and blackouts, but so far as my life with him is concerned, I don't know about them." Duncan Webb's account of that meeting with the wife the hangman was about to make a widow is straightforward and unsensational. But reading between the lines of the conversation Webb and Mrs. Raven were having together, it becomes clear that despite the recent birth of their first child, all was not well with the Ravens. Webb says, for instance, that while she talked, Marie Raven picked up her child – "then similar in looks to his father." ….

As she hugged her son she murmured, "My love for Danny isn't completely dead. I wrote to him regularly while he was in prison – until I found that he had willed my property to his own relatives. "Up to that point I wrote to him from the bottom of my heart. I told him I still loved him, and I told him all about his baby. Since he murdered my parents I have learned why he didn't write to me from the condemned cell. I now know that on the night of the murders he said, 'After this I cannot live with Marie any more.' "It's strange that he said that. In the waiting-room at the Old Bailey we had shed tears together. My tears were real. They were for the man I loved, although even then I knew in my heart what he had done. Danny's fate had to be. I knew all along that I had to accept it." On the day that the appeal was heard Webb had lunch with her. They talked about all sorts of things. Only over the coffee did the talk come round to the subject of Daniel Raven's appeal. Webb asked her then, "What would you do if the sentence and the verdict were quashed and he walked out of the law courts this afternoon a free man?" For a moment she looked intently down at her snakeskin shoes before replying: "I suppose I would have to go home and make him a cup of tea." That didn't happen, of course, but the story wasn't over then. Some days after that lunch, in his capacity as a private citizen, Duncan Webb wrote to the Home Secretary pleading for clemency for Daniel Raven. Did he thereby break the golden rule of all investigative journalists not to get personally emotionally involved in the story? He doesn't tell us. What he does say is that after considering the case, "I had doubts about Raven's state of mind at the time. And I still have those doubts even to this day." The execution was carried out by Albert Pierrepoint and Harry Kirk at Pentonville Prison in north London on Friday, January 6th, 1950 ….

The morning after Daniel Raven's execution Webb went to see Marie Raven again. "She did not give way to tears. And now, that strange look of bewilderment was no longer present in her eyes. There was just wistfulness, and that soft, maternal smile that hovers on the faces of all loving mothers." She then had to face a gruelling ordeal of legal wrangles over the property which was said to have belonged to her husband. "In fact, it did not belong to him," Webb says. "She retained possession of her home. And she retained, at all times, complete possession of her gentle poise." Almost a year after the execution he met Marie Raven for the final time. She had changed her name, and she was about to change it yet again. She told Webb: "Tomorrow I am shutting the door on the past. I am getting married. Please don't publish the name of my husband." Mrs. Raven was married the next day. Webb says: "If I ever see her again, she will always be Mrs. Raven to me. I never did quite catch that new name of hers." ….

Cases 23 and 24
"Two Hanged

"For Separate Southend-on-Sea War-Time Murders"

John YOUNG
MURDERS
Of
Frederick & Cissie Lucas
&
Sgt James McNICOL
MURDER
Of
Sgt Donald Kirkaldie
[1945]

At the end of the Second World War a double-murder in a bungalow on the first anniversary of D-Day and a shooting at an army camp on VJ night celebrations saw two men hanged on the same day in north London for murders committed along the Essex coast ….

It was the evening of **Thursday, August 16th, 1945**, and Japan had surrendered the day before. All over Britain there were celebrations at the ending of the war. Many army units were holding their own parties and dances, and personnel at a Royal Artillery anti-aircraft gun-site at Thorpe Bay, Southend-on-Sea, were no exception. But there was one big difference between the high jinks everywhere else and the celebration at this ack-ack camp. Elsewhere hostilities were over. But not at the gun-site off St. Augustine's Avenue in Thorpe Bay. Here, before the night was over, the peace was shattered by shooting. Having survived the war, one sergeant lay dead – another was rushed to hospital, seriously wounded; a third had disappeared. All this had nothing to do with enemy action, but a lot to do with a woman .... and it was Southend's third killing in three months. On **Wednesday, June 6th, 1945**, a married couple had been battered to death at their bungalow in the Leigh-on-Sea area of Southend .... Detectives were still investigating this when they found they had another murder case on their hands: the killing at Thorpe Bay. The crimes were not connected, but both were to have sequels at the same Chelmsford Assizes ....

On the evening of August 16th, 1945, men of the 494th Heavy Anti-Aircraft Battery had celebrated peace with a bonfire and a dance. Everybody seemed to be enjoying themselves, except for one disgruntled sergeant who'd had too much to drink. At 3.15 the following morning **[Friday, August 17th]** Captain John Owen was called to a Nissen hut occupied by several sergeants. On entering the hut he saw 27-year-old Sergeant Donald Kirkaldie slumped in a half-sitting position on his bed. His lower jaw had been shattered by a rifle bullet and he was dead. Lying nearby on the floor was Sergeant Leonard Cox, seriously wounded by another bullet. The police were called and Sergeant Cox was rushed to Southend General Hospital. As a result of what they were told, detectives instituted a search for 27-year-old Sergeant James McNicol, from Motherwell, Scotland, who shared the Nissen hut with Kirkaldie, Cox and other NCOs. At 4 a.m. he had been seen by a police constable on the esplanade, and shortly afterwards he was traced, arrested and taken to Southend Central police station at 5.50 a.m. Following questioning, McNicol was charged with Kirkaldie's murder. "All I say is I didn't know I killed Kirkaldie," he replied. Three days later, at the inquest on the slain sergeant, a police surgeon said Kirkaldie had died instantly from shock and haemorrhage following gunshot wounds to his neck and the lower part of his face. His lower jaw had been reduced to fragments. The court was told that Kirkaldie's home was in Ramsgate. He left a widow and a child. Meanwhile police and troops had searched a field at Thorpe Bay. Using metal-detectors, they had unearthed an army rifle. Events leading up to the shooting were described when McNicol's trial for his fellow-sergeant's murder began at the Chelmsford Assizes on November 12th, 1945. He pleaded "not guilty." Cecil Havers KC, prosecuting, said that some days before the shooting McNicol had become acquainted with a female private, but on August 15th she'd had a tiff with him, telling him their relationship was over ....

The following day had been set aside for VJ celebrations, and a dance was held at the Thorpe Bay gun-site. Prior to the dance Sergeants McNicol and Cox had some beer at a local pub, where they were joined by an RAF leading aircraftman who was in civilian clothing. Afterwards the woman private and the RAF man were standing at the door of the dance hall when McNicol threw a glass of beer over the leading aircraftman. Bystanders had to intervene to prevent a fight. Sergeants Kirkaldie and Cox subsequently went to their sleeping quarters. Before they went to bed Kirkaldie secured the door of the hut with a piece of rope. At about 3 a.m. Cox heard a window being broken. Somebody switched on the light, there was a shot and Cox was wounded in the chest. Following another shot it was discovered that Kirkaldie was dead in his bed, with rifle wounds in his head. A policeman later saw McNicol walking in stockinged feet along the esplanade. He told the constable he had got drunk at a dance. Interviewed after his arrest, McNicol claimed that Cox had threatened to kill him the next day. "I thought I would have a good hit at him that night," he told detectives, "or the men would think I was afraid of him. They knew I was looking for him. I was thinking about his words that he would kill me. I thought he would beat me up in the morning. I took a rifle and took it to the camp. I had no intention of killing him, but I wanted to wound him. I broke the window and could not draw back. I tried to shoot Cox in the leg. I tried the rifle two or three times. I was dazed then. I knew I had done wrong. I ran from the camp and found myself in a field with the rifle still in my hand." McNicol had concluded his statement by saying he had buried the rifle where it was found ....

Sergeant Cox told the court that he had intended to take McNicol before his commanding officer because of his behaviour at the dance.

Describing the shooting, he said: "I saw the muzzle of a rifle put through the window and then I heard an explosion. It felt as if I had been kicked by a horse." The woman private was next to give evidence. Questioned by Tristram Beresford KC, defending, she said that she had been out with McNicol on four occasions. On the night of August 15th he met her when she came off duty and they stood chatting for some time. He wanted her to go with him into an empty hut, but she refused. "The suggestion was that you should go with him into the hut and have a flirtation?" asked Mr. Beresford. "Yes," said the private, adding that when she refused to accompany him McNicol lost his temper and threw her handbag on the ground. She told him she had finished with him and went to her billet. When she saw him at the dance the following night she thought he was drunk. He had no cause to be jealous of either Cox or Kirkaldie on her account. Another sergeant and a bombardier told the court that they didn't think McNicol was drunk at the dance, although the bombardier said McNicol "had a strange grin on his face." The constable who had seen McNicol on the esplanade at 4 a.m. said that the sergeant appeared to be recovering from the effects of drink but was quite self-possessed. James McNicol, short, stocky, fair-haired and speaking with a strong Scottish accent, told the court that he had been on good terms with both Cox and Kirkaldie prior to August 16th ....

On that evening he had six pints of beer at the Halfway House, and some more when he returned to the camp. Questioned about the beer-throwing incident, he told why he had thrown the contents of his glass into the face of the RAF man. When he saw him with the woman private, "I had a sudden desire to break up their partnership." Cox then arrived and there were words between them. They tried to get at each other but were restrained. McNicol said that he had more drink and subsequently went to the sergeants' hut where he took a short bayonet from his kitbag and put it in his pocket, thinking that if Cox "got nasty" again he might have to use it. At the same time he overturned Cox's bed. Then he went back to the dance where he saw Cox and told him he would see him outside. He wanted to fight him when the dance finished. He told the court that later, in the sergeants' hut, Cox asked him if he thought the overturned bed was a joke. He wanted to fight Cox in the boxing ring but Cox refused. He went back to the mess, had some more drink, and on returning to the hut he saw Cox there with some other soldiers. Someone called out that he (McNicol) was mad ....

Wandering around the camp, he found himself at the armoury, which was unlocked. He went in and took a rifle and a clip of five rounds which he put in the magazine, also fixing the bayonet. "What was the idea of arming yourself in this way?" asked Mr. Beresford. "If Cox had started anything against me I might have used it to frighten him," McNicol replied. "When you took the rifle did you intend to kill or harm Kirkaldie?" "No intention at all. I went to the sergeants' hut and found the door was locked. That made me angry. I broke the glass in the window and switched on the light. I pushed the rifle through the window. I fired a shot, but did not aim at anyone. Then I just stepped back and took a blind shot at the hut." "What was the idea of that?" asked Mr. Beresford. "Just to frighten them," said McNicol, adding that after running away he realised he had done wrong. He buried the rifle and went to the sea front where he took off his shoes, walked into the water and washed his hand, which was cut. He also bathed his face and then threw his shoes over a hedge for no reason. Cross-examined by Mr. Havers, McNicol said: "I dare say I had the intention of shooting Sergeant Cox, but not killing him." It was by chance that he found himself at the armoury, he continued. It was then that the idea of taking the rifle occurred to him. When he went with it to the hut he intended to go to bed and "forget the whole trouble." He was only going to use the gun if Cox started anything. "How?" asked Mr. Havers. "By firing at his legs." "Why did you switch on the light?" "So that I should not hit him in a dangerous spot." "Why did you fire a second shot?" "To scare the others in the hut." "You deliberately fired a shot into a hut in which there were six men?" "Yes." "Didn't it occur to you that you might hit one of them?" "No." "In his concluding speech for the defence Mr. Beresford argued that this was a case of manslaughter, not murder, as McNicol was drunk when he fired the fatal shot. The jury thought otherwise. After deliberating for an hour they found James McNicol guilty of Sergeant Kirkaldie's murder .... but the stress of bringing in that verdict was too much for one juryman, who collapsed and had to be helped from the court. "Thank you, my lord," said McNicol as Justice Lewis sentenced him to death on the second day of the trial

November 13th .... Then he turned smartly and ran down the dock steps to the cells below ....

Five days earlier on November 8th the court had heard details of the double killing at Leigh, when John Riley Young, a 40-year-old builder of Belmont Road, Ilford, east London, was tried for the murder of Frederick Benjamin Lucas, a 52-year-old travelling jeweller, at "Cranham," his bungalow in Undercliff Gardens. Young had been committed for trial by Southend magistrates, charged with murdering both Mr. Lucas and his wife Cissie Clara Lucas, also 52 and at the same Assizes and the same judge as McNicol .... Pleading "not guilty," Young admitted battering the couple to death but claimed he had been temporarily insane at the time. The murders had been discovered by the couple's daughter Eva on her return home from her work as a hairdresser in Leytonstone, east London. "I found mother lying in the hall," she said later. "She was covered by an eiderdown and she was on her back with a black coat over her head. I pulled her right arm out of the sleeve. She was cold. I left by the front door .... and sent a woman for the police. I then saw the postman and he and I went into the bungalow. I noticed the dining-room door was slightly opened. I went into the dining-room and found my father lying on the floor. He was covered by a carpet and there was a green cushion from his bedroom over his face."
Furniture in the dining-room had been smashed and overturned. Part of the table had been broken off and fragments of chairs were strewn around. Crockery also littered the floor, and blood was spattered everywhere. Cissie Lucas's skull had been fractured and she had suffered contusion of the brain, dying from her injuries, it was believed, some hours after the attack had taken place. That was put at 9 a.m., the time at which her husband's watch had stopped. Frederick Lucas had received seven head wounds, dying from a fractured skull and lacerated brain. At 10 a.m. a short, stocky man had called at the home of the Lucases' next-door neighbour, asking her if she knew where the couple were. He said he had been delayed by his car breaking down. When the neighbour said she didn't know where the Lucases were, the man asked her to tell them that a Mr. James had called and would return in the evening. He was in fact John Young ....

The following morning he left his lodgings and went to the Barking home of his married sister, in east London, saying he'd had a row with his landlady and he wanted to get away from her for a few days. That evening his sister was surprised to hear him give the name 'James' when he made a telephone call. That night, making up a bed in the kitchen, he tried to gas himself, but the bid was thwarted when his sister's brother-in-law found him lying on the floor with his head in the oven, dragged him out and revived him. Young next went into an air raid shelter and slashed his wrists, but that didn't work either. Returning to his sister's, he made a second attempt to gas himself. This time he was found lying on a bedroom floor with a fractured gas pipe in his mouth. He was taken to hospital, unconscious. The previous morning he had phoned his landlady. She had told him that the police had called, asking for him. He had said he would return later that day, but didn't. Detectives wanted to interview him because he was known to have had recent dealings with Lucas. They also wanted to see if he had a trouser button missing – a button, complete with thread, which had been found between the legs of the murdered man but had not belonged to him. Officers had also found a heel-print in blood at the scene, and in that print the word BARD could be read. So the detectives also wanted to take a look at Young's shoes. "I have been expecting you," he said when officers arrived at his bedside. "It was me. I want to get it off my chest." The rubber heel of his shoe matched the footprint found at the crime scene, and the button discovered beside Mr. Lucas's body had come from Young's trousers ….

At his trial he said that he and a partner had been in business as builders for about four years. In May he had some rings to sell. Mr. Lucas had been introduced to him as a prospective buyer and he had gone to his office to view the jewellery. He had not bought the rings, but had spoken of his home at Leigh, saying he might need some repairs done. Then Mr. Lucas had asked Young if he could get some gold sovereigns, for which he would pay £4 each as he could get £5 or £6 for them. Young said he told Mr. Lucas that he could obtain some sovereigns, and Mr. Lucas later phoned him, asking if he needed any cash for the sovereigns' purchase and inviting him to call at his home to collect some money for this purpose. Young told the court that he went to Mr. Lucas's bungalow on June 3rd, when Mr.

Lucas handed him a packet, telling him it contained £900 and saying he didn't want a receipt as he could "recognise honesty when he saw it." Admitting that he used some of this money, Young told the court that he became worried and wanted to make a clean breast of it, but when Mr. Lucas called to see him he could not bring himself to tell him. Mr. Lucas then left him a further £2,000 in notes. Young said he redoubled his efforts to obtain sovereigns, without success. "It is a relief," he told the jury, "that I have at last come here today to be tried for a crime that I have lived with for six months in mental agony. I want you to realise that I am not afraid to die. In fact, I have prayed for death on a great number of occasions during the past six months. I would like you to believe that the man who stands before you charged with this murder is not really the man who committed the murder, but the frame of a man into whose being a demon entered that morning. The demon was created as a result of a blow in the struggle. I told Mr. Lucas that the golden sovereigns were a myth. He changed from the man I had known, and got into a terrible temper. He called me a dirty twister, as he was entitled to. He said he would put me in the hands of the police. I said, 'I am sorry,' and turned as if to go. As I turned he rushed at me. I felt an impact on the back of my head. I felt his arms holding me. I went into a frenzy. Mere words cannot express what happened inside me. I want you to believe I am not really a murderer. We struggled and I struck him again and again. Hearing a noise from outside the room, I rushed out and saw a woman in the hall. I struck blindly. I felt as if I was striking an army." Why had he called on the next-door neighbour? "I went next door with the idea of taking the people in and showing them what I had done," he said. "When I knocked at the door a very dear old lady answered. I didn't have the heart to tell her or frighten her, so I made the pretext of asking if Mr. Lucas was home." ….

Questioned by John Flowers KC, prosecuting, Young agreed that the bank account of his building partnership had an *overdraft* of more than £1,200 and that he had only a few pounds of his own. Yet on June 2nd he had bought a car for £1,333, paying for it with a cheque. For the defence, a Harley Street nerve specialist told the court that Young had a degree of mental instability and might, under certain circumstances, become temporarily insane for a few minutes or longer. Young himself told the jury that he had been knocked down by a tram-car in Cardiff when he was 12, sustaining head injuries, and had received a further head injury in an accident at school. An aunt, an uncle and two brothers, he said, also suffered from mental trouble. But the medical officers of Chelmsford Prison and Brixton Prison both told the court that Young had shown no sign of insanity while he was in their care, and the jury took only just over an hour to reach their verdict after the two-day hearing on November 9th .... They found John Young guilty of murder, and he was sentenced to hang ....

Both men had appeals rejected on December 5th .... So it was that two men, the overspent builder and the disgruntled sergeant, sat petrified in condemned cells at Pentonville Prison in north London as dawn broke on the morning of Friday, December 21st, 1945. It was the day of their execution: John Young was the first to keep his appointment with the scaffold. He was executed at 8 a.m. by Albert Pierrepoint and Steve Wade .... James McNicol followed him to the gallows 90 minutes later, despite a petition for a reprieve signed by 20,000: he was executed by Pierrepoint and a different assistant, Herbert Morris .... It was 9.30 a.m. when he plunged to oblivion, his penalty for celebrating VJ Day by killing a comrade ....

Case 25
"The Full Picture?"

Eric NORCLIFFE
MURDER
Of
His Wife Kathleen
[1952]

One minute a neighbour, a young coal miner, was sitting in the front room of his home in the Nottinghamshire town of Warsop, five miles to the north east of Mansfield. It was the fine afternoon of <u>Wednesday, June 25th, 1952</u>, and at a house opposite at 59, Hammerwater Drive another female neighbour was pegging out blankets. A moment later, both were startled by chilling screams ....

Looking through his window, the man saw Mrs. Kathleen Norcliffe stagger out of her house just across the road. She was covered in blood, and as she collapsed he dashed out to her in his stockinged feet. Her husband had thrashed her, she groaned as the miner carried her into her kitchen and laid her on a mat. As he ran out for help, the female neighbour hurried round from next door, saw Mrs. Norcliffe on the floor, and rushed to another neighbour to call an ambulance. Meanwhile the miner spotted a crew of workmen. Returning to the house with them, he saw a trail of blood leading from the kitchen to the front room. Following it, he found Mrs. Norcliffe's 30-year-old husband Eric lying on the hearth rug with a deep cut in his left forearm. Helped by one of the workmen, the miner bandaged it, and when this didn't stop the flow of blood they applied a tourniquet. At 4.20 p.m., two hours later, Kathleen Norcliffe died in Mansfield General Hospital from multiple stab wounds. In another room at the hospital, a policeman sat at her husband's bedside. The Norcliffes had always seemed a happy couple, said neighbours. But they were known to be hard-up, and they were believed to be facing notice to quit their council house because of rent arrears. Eric Norcliffe, an unemployed miner, had spent the Second World War in the Far East where he was wounded twice while serving as an RAF sergeant. His wife, a slim, dark-haired 23-year-old mother of three, had died just five days short of their fifth wedding anniversary ....

Norcliffe had been sitting in the house all that Wednesday morning while Mrs. Norcliffe was out, reporters were told. She had come back at about 1.45, the female neighbour recalled, and a gas meter collector doing his rounds had then called at the house, leaving shortly before Mrs. Norcliffe began screaming. On June 27th, two days after her death, Eric Norcliffe was discharged from hospital and taken into custody, charged with murder. At the inquest on June 30th the coroner was told that the cause of Kathleen Norcliffe's death was shock and haemorrhage following stabs which had punctured both lungs. The next day a small number of women filled the back pews of Warsop parish church at the funeral. A bus taking miners to Welbeck Colliery stopped to let the cortège pass, the miners removing their hats. In addition to suffering chest wounds, Mrs. Norcliffe had been stabbed three times in the back and several times in the arms, a Nottingham Assizes jury was told at her husband's trial on November 20th, which lasted just one-day ....

Two of the stabs in her back had been delivered so forcefully that they had gone through her ribs, piercing her lungs, and both sides of her chest had filled with blood, the Home Office pathologist Professor J.M. Webster testified. "Kathleen Norcliffe had been a healthy young woman, but at the time of her death she was in a condition of early pregnancy," he added. The court also heard that when Norcliffe was told at the crime scene and in hospital that his wife's state was worse than his, on both occasions he replied, "I wish she'd die." Police Sergeant Sydney Barlow testified that after being called to the crime scene, he saw Norcliffe in hospital at 4.10 p.m. that day. "I said to him, 'Your wife has been admitted to this hospital with injuries. I have reason to believe that you inflicted them.' I cautioned him and he said: 'Yes, I did it with my sheath knife. We had been falling out. It has been going on for some time now. Look after the kiddies for me.'" The sergeant went on to say that after re-examining the crime scene an hour later and attending the victim's autopsy the following morning, he saw Norcliffe again in the hospital. "I said, 'I have to tell you that your wife has now died from her injuries.' I cautioned him, and he replied: 'So she's dead. I have nothing to say.'" Continuing his evidence, Sergeant Barlow told the jury that he subsequently arrested Norcliffe and took him to Mansfield police station. "I said, 'I have reason to believe that you have been responsible for the death of your wife by stabbing her in the back with a knife.' I showed him the knife, cautioning him, and he replied: 'That's right. The meter man had just been and found the meter broken. The wife did not know about it but I had done it two days before. We had a fall out. I had a knife in my hand but what I did was not intentional.'" The next witness, the meter inspector-collector, told the court: "As soon as I touched the meter the lock dropped off. The contents of the meter had all gone. I found no money there. I spoke to the accused about it and then left the house." "I heard the gas man say 'Good afternoon' as he left the Norcliffes," the female neighbour testified. "Not many minutes after that I heard Mrs. Norcliffe say, 'Oh, Eric, what are you doing?' Then there were screams and she shouted my name. I ran round to their house and through the back door. I saw Mrs. Norcliffe on the floor in the scullery, I noticed there was some blood about and I ran for help." ....

Seeking a verdict of "Guilty but insane," W.H. Fearnley-Whittingstall QC, defending, said he would call evidence to show that at the time of the stabbing Norcliffe did not know what he was doing. Norcliffe's father then told the court that his son and daughter-in-law had lived apart for considerable periods after their marriage, due to difficulties in finding accommodation. In both 1951 and part of 1952 his son had lived with him, suffering from melancholia and sometimes sitting with his head in his hands, his mind a complete blank. Dr. G.M. Woddis, a consultant psychiatrist, said he thought Norcliffe suffered not only from melancholia but also from temporary amnesia, during which he was unaware of his actions. Towards the end of a three-hour interview he had suddenly become upset, talking of his "contemplated suicide and the destruction of the entire family." A conflicting opinion, however, was given by Dr. R.R. Prewer, the medical officer at Lincoln Prison. "Is the accused a person of unsound mind?" asked the prosecutor, Richard O'Sullivan QC. "No, sir," the doctor replied, saying he did not think there was any defect of the mind at the time of Mrs. Norcliffe's death. Sharing this view, the jury found Eric Norcliffe guilty as charged after just 30 minutes retirement ....

Asked if he had anything to say before he was sentenced, he told Justice Hugh Hallet: "I have had to keep quiet during the case, but as far as I can see you have heard how I did it, and where I did it, but no one seems bothered about why I did it." His wife had called him a bastard, he said, but there was more to it than that. There are two or three witnesses who could have been brought forward who have not appeared." Sentencing him to death, the judge told him: "Whenever the sanity of a murderer has been or may be questioned, it is usual for further medical investigation to be made after sentence has been passed and before the Home Secretary decides whether it ought to be carried out. I have no doubt that this procedure will be carried out in the present case." An appeal was rejected on November 30th, but despite the judge's observations, there was to be no reprieve. On December 10th the Home Secretary Sir David Maxwell Fyfe announced that there were insufficient grounds to justify any interference with the course of the law. Two days later, on Friday, December 12th, 1952, Eric Norcliffe was hanged by Albert Pierrepoint and Robert Stewart at Lincoln Prison at 9:00 am – there were just three members of the public outside the prison ….

Case 26
"The Murderous Nurse"

"His diagnosis of a cerebral haemorrhage was based on the symptoms described to him by Nurse Waddingham" ….

"If ever again you cross my path you will get to know me better. There is nothing but straightforwardness carried on here" ….

"Ada had made the new will before her mother died. And Mrs. Baguley hadn't lasted a week after the new will was signed" ....

"This nurse premeditated both the Baguley murders and callously withheld the prescribed painkilling tablets" ....

"Dr. Manfield's testimony was damning. There had never been an occasion for the use of morphia tablets in Ada's case" ....

Dorothea WADDINGHAM
MURDER
Of
Ada & Louisa Baguley
[1936]

The pride that Albert Pierrepoint felt at assisting his Uncle Thomas at a hanging is a matter of record. It perhaps gave him a relatively easy way into that most forbidding of professions before actually pulling the lever as number one on a hanging job. There was, however, another significant hurdle to be cleared: hanging a member of what was then still referred to as "the weaker sex." In 1934 he'd passed the test with flying colours at the execution of Ethel Major at Hull; but 1936 would see him face the challenge again – and this time the woman on the gallows was a nurse ....

At the first soft rap on her bedroom door, Nurse Dorothea Waddingham awoke instantly, for the ailing patients in her nursing home depended on her.

There was a chill in the air on that September night in 1935, and she threw on a warm quilted dressing-gown before opening her door. In the corridor stood her assistant-cum-lover Ronald Sullivan. He was fully dressed and he looked worried. "I'm sorry to disturb you," he began apologetically. "Which one is it?" "Miss Ada," he said. "It looks like she's been taken pretty bad." "I'll come and see to her at once," the nurse told him. All the patients at the nursing home in Sherwood, Nottingham, were women, most of them quite elderly. However, Miss Ada Baguley was only 50, but looked older. She now lay with her eyes wide open, her breathing was heavy and her face flushed. Nurse Waddingham felt for her pulse. "It looks like a stroke," she said. "Yes, that must be it." She stood beside the bed, a picture of solicitude although she herself was not in the best of health. She was 36 and eight months pregnant. If all went well, the child would be born some time around the middle of October. Today was September 11th. Sullivan, 39, was without experience in medicine. He told Nurse Waddingham: "I came in quietly so as not to wake Miss Ada, but straight away I saw how sick she looked. I'd better go and ring up Dr. Manfield." "No, wait," said the nurse. "I can handle this. The doctor, I happen to know, has been out tonight on a confinement case. I hate to have Dr. Manfield called out in the middle of the night." "You're always so thoughtful, Dot," said Sullivan. "But suppose Miss Ada is dying?" "No," said Dorothea. "I know these cases. She may hang on like this for days. There's nothing much to be done for her. It will be quite all right to call Dr. Manfield in the morning. He'll do all the better by her, if there's anything he can do, after a good night's sleep." ….

It was shortly before 9 a.m. when Nurse Waddingham told Sullivan he had better phone at once for Dr. Manfield. The physician had been attending Ada Baguley and had attended her mother, Mrs. Louisa Baguley, prior to her death the preceding May, at the age of 89. Dr. George Manfield arrived at the nursing home at 32, Devon Drive in the Sherwood area of the city a few minutes after 10 a.m. "It's a sad thing, doctor," Nurse Waddingham told him. "Miss Baguley took a turn for the worse during the night. I hesitated to call you out then. Now I wish I had." "Has her condition deteriorated?" the doctor asked. "She's dead." "When?" "Only a few minutes after Ronald phoned you. I never left her for a moment. But with a stroke you can never tell." Neither of them said any more until the physician stood by Miss Baguley's bed. He then asked a number of routine questions and nodded when the nurse's answers were what he had expected. "Cerebral haemorrhage," he decided. "I'll make out the death certificate as soon as I get back to my surgery." "We shall need it right away, I expect," the nurse said. "I'll get Ron to call in and pick it up. And he'll have to arrange the cremation." "Was that Miss Baguley's wish? She didn't want to be buried beside her mother in Caunton?" "No, she didn't. Does it seem strange to you, doctor? It did to me. But poor Ada was very insistent about it," Dorothea explained. "Had us set it all down in writing." She took a folded half-sheet of notepaper from a pocket of her uniform and showed it to the physician, who looked at it briefly. "I see," he said. "Well, I'll have to make out the application form for cremation too. Then Ronald will have to take the papers to Dr. Banks." Dr. Cyril Banks was the medical officer of health for Nottingham. He received the application for the cremation of the body of the late Ada Baguley on Thursday, September 12th. There was a half-sheet of notepaper attached to the form. "This is the signature of the deceased?" Dr. Banks asked Sullivan. "Yes, sir." "But this is not the same handwriting." "No, sir. It's mine." "You mean you wrote this note?" "Miss Baguley was dependent on me," Sullivan explained. "She dictated what she wanted said, and I wrote it down for her. She read it over and then she signed it." ….

The note was dated August 29th – 14 days earlier. Dr. Banks read: "It is my desire to be cremated at my death, and it is my wish to remain with Nurse until I die. It is my last wish that my relatives shall not know of my death. Ada Baguley." "This woman anticipated her death on the 29th of last month," said Dr. Banks. "And she died yesterday, **[Wednesday] September 11th**, of cerebral haemorrhage. Am I to assume that your patient expected to suffer a sudden stroke?" "She was not my patient," Sullivan told him, explaining that he was not a qualified nurse and had only done odd jobs around the nursing home. He said he had felt sorry for Ada Baguley, as he had for her mother before her, and so he had tried to show them little attentions and do them kindnesses, such as writing an occasional letter to a relative or friend. "And you say you were kind to Miss Baguley's mother. That was at the nursing home too, I presume. When did Mrs.

Baguley die?" "She was very old – eighty-seven [*sic*]. She died last May. It was a Sunday, I remember, but I'll have to look up the date." "I can look it up," said Dr. Banks. "Now about the cremation. I shall have to refer it to the coroner. So kindly inform your employer, Nurse Waddingham, that I cannot grant the requested permission to cremate until I have the coroner's confirmation." Sullivan went back to Devon Drive, while in due course Dr. Banks called at the office of Wilfred Rothera, the Nottingham city coroner. The medical officer described his problem, mentioning the "last wish" in the note Ada Baguley had supposedly dictated and signed. "I declined to authorise immediate cremation," said Banks. "You were quite right," the coroner told him. "I shall have to question Nurse Waddingham." He acted at once, sending a message to the nursing home asking the nurse to call him. But because of her pregnancy, she sent Sullivan instead. He said that neither he nor Nurse Waddingham could account for Ada Baguley's hostility towards her relatives, and he gave the names and addresses of some of them. He told of a chiding letter he had written for Ada to a cousin living in Scotland. "Neither Dr. Banks nor I will authorise cremation in this instance until we have at least discussed the matter with a relative of the deceased," said the coroner ….

Detective Chief Superintendent Downs was informed of the situation. He duly reported to the coroner that officers in Aberdeen had located Ada Baguley's cousin and had questioned him about his invalid relative. The cousin did not believe that Ada, in her right mind, would ever have expressed a desire to be cremated, let alone insist upon it. The whole family had been opposed to cremation, he said, and he thought Ada would have wished to be buried beside her mother. The cousin also said, Downs added, that on calling at the nursing home he had been made to feel unwelcome. This had been early the previous spring, before the death of old Mrs. Baguley. "I have a transcript of the cousin's exact words," said Downs. He read from it: "There was a fellow there named Ronald. He seemed to exercise the greatest influence upon Ada. When I got back to Scotland I sent her a registered letter, to make certain that she received it. The reply I got from Ada was written for her by Ronald. He added to Ada's letter a postscript of his own. It was not only offensive, but threatening. Of course, I had no idea that cousin Ada was dying." "I'd be obliged," the coroner said, "if her cousin sends us that particular letter as soon as he can." Detective Chief Superintendent Downs promised to wire this request to the Aberdeen Police. The coroner then telephoned Dr. L. Owen Taylor, the Nottingham police surgeon. "I have spoken to the attending physician, Dr. Manfield," Rothera explained. "He tells me that Ada Baguley was afflicted with creeping paralysis. He admits that his diagnosis of a cerebral haemorrhage was based on the symptoms described to him by Nurse Waddingham." "You think there ought to be a post-mortem?" the police surgeon asked. "I do. I authorise you to conduct a post-mortem on Miss Ada Baguley," Rothera said. This decision disposed for the time being of the request for cremation. Nurse Waddingham, still using Sullivan as her spokesman because of her own delicate health, sent word that she had no objection to the post-mortem. As for cremation, she had merely been trying to follow the expressed wish of her patient ….

Dr. Taylor, the police surgeon, called at the coroner's office on Wednesday afternoon, September 18th. He was accompanied by William Taylor, the chief assistant to the city analyst. "Here is the report of the autopsy," said the surgeon. "The woman didn't die of a stroke. There was no cerebral haemorrhage." Rothera studied the report. "Morphine?" he inquired. "Just a little matter of 3.192 grains in her organs," said the analyst. An accumulation of more than three grains of morphine could not, in any circumstances, be mistaken for an overdose, even if the last sufferings of Ada Baguley had warranted regular and medically prescribed administration of the drug. The analyst's report cast a new and sinister light on the situation at the nursing home. And Nurse Waddingham would have to be questioned. She went to the coroner's office on Friday, September 20th, accompanied by Ronald Sullivan. The coroner explained the serious situation confronting them and said there were questions he had to ask. "I am quite ready to do anything I can to be of help," Dorothea said. "Thank you," Rothera said, going to the door of an adjoining office and opening it. He beckoned, Detective Chief Superintendent Downs walked in, and Rothera introduced him. Sullivan appeared puzzled. Nurse Waddingham, however, seemed unperturbed. "I have been greatly helped by Mr. Downs in getting in touch with relatives of your deceased patient, Miss Ada Baguley," the coroner explained. "He has obtained a letter from one of her cousins." "Oh, that one!" said Dorothea. Sullivan hastily interposed: "Nurse is naturally upset. That cousin made her a lot of trouble at the time of the death and burial of Miss Ada's poor old mother." "He seems to have had no quarrel with Nurse Waddingham," Downs said. "It's you who appear to have threatened a relative of one of her patients." Sullivan looked shocked. "Did that nosey little bloke tell you I threatened him?" "After reading his letter, the coroner and I find that we agree with him," Downs said. The letter which Ada had asked Sullivan to write for her was casual and only faintly complaining. But in his own private postscript Sullivan had let fly at the patient's cousin. "I should like to know what you mean by calling me 'that fellow Ron,'" he had written. "If ever again you cross my path you will get to know me better. There is nothing but straightforwardness carried on here. We know what you have been trying to do, but if you are not careful you will regret it. So keep your eyes open in future. Miss Baguley is quite aware of me writing you this." ….

"The whole thing's a lying forgery!" Dorothea Waddingham protested. "It was he who threatened us, and he sent it by registered post to make sure," Sullivan said. Dorothea said quietly: "I took in the old lady and Ada for thirty shillings a week. That was last January. But I soon had to tell them their thirty shillings didn't pay for the keep of one, and Miss Ada was understanding. The new rate we fixed, five pounds a week, gave me something to turn around on. Both Ada and her mother needed the most nourishing meals and everything of the best," said Nurse Waddingham. "On five pounds a week I could manage this. But Ada's cousin implied that I was fleecing two helpless sick people. I had to tell the Baguleys plainly that it was either to be the agreed-on five pounds weekly, or they must find another nursing home." "When was this?" Downs asked. "In April. Not long after the old lady passed away. With just Miss Ada alone, there was no trouble." "What did you charge Ada Baguley alone?" "Oh, we'd made a new arrangement for that, which was satisfactory to both of us," the nurse answered. When the coroner moved onto the matter of *morphine* poisoning, Sullivan looked bewildered. Nurse Waddingham insisted that she had never given a patient anything not prescribed by the patient's own physician. She said emphatically that she had never administered any drug like morphine to any patient. She just gave medicines prescribed by the doctors and dispensed by a chemist. She explained that Dr. Manfield was her personal physician, as well as a long-time friend. He had attended both Mrs. Baguley and Ada ever since they came to the nursing home from Southwell, and no medicines or drugs, other than those prescribed by him, had been given to either patient. When the questioning finished, Nurse Waddingham looked flushed and exhausted. "I'm sorry to have to subject you to this," the coroner said. "But you incur a special responsibility when you take people into your home and accept payment to care for them. Miss Ada Baguley's death is under investigation." "I understand," she replied. "If you'll excuse me now, I'll go to my home." Sullivan then escorted her out of the office ….

On September 25th Detective Chief Superintendent Downs obtained a warrant, and he and Detective Inspector Albert Pentland searched the nursing home. They found no lethal drugs of any description. Dr. Roche Lynch, acting for the Home Office, had been called upon to check the findings of Dr. Taylor, the police surgeon, and William Taylor, the analyst. He confirmed that Ada Baguley had died from an excessive dose of morphine. On September 30th the Home Office had the body of Mrs. Louisa Baguley exhumed. The examination and analysis which followed on October 1st was directed by Dr. Roche Lynch, with the two Taylors assisting. Mrs. Baguley had died on **Sunday, May 12th, 1935**, four months earlier. However, the examiners found traces of an alkaloid which indicated poisoning. "During that period of time after death any morphia or heroin in the body would be converted into this alkaloid," William Taylor told the coroner. The coroner asked if any other substance in the body could be converted over a period of 20 weeks into this alkaloid. "No, sir. It is known as pseudomorphia, and derives from morphine or heroin," said the analyst. Detective Inspector Pentland went to Scotland early in October and questioned Miss Baguley's cousin. He explained that he had visited the nursing home only from a sense of duty. He added that he was not seeking his relatives' money. He had never considered it, but when he received so cool a welcome at the nursing home it occurred to him that the Baguleys' money was the reason. Pentland asked: "Did they have much money?" "Possibly two thousand pounds," the cousin replied. "Enough to awaken the greed of a certain type of person." On October 20th Pentland reported to Downs that he had followed up the information obtained from the cousin and had interviewed Ada Baguley's solicitor in Nottingham. Ada had requested a new will to be drawn up for her to sign, and it had been validated on May 7th last. ….

The significant fact, Pentland pointed out, was that Ada had made the new will before her mother died. And Mrs. Baguley, succumbing to what Dr. Roche Lynch had said was either morphine or heroin, hadn't lasted a week after the new will was signed. Ada's solicitor told Pentland that the will of May 7th left everything Ada Baguley possessed to Nurse Dorothea Waddingham – in consideration of which the nurse had bound herself to take care of Ada for as long as Ada lived. Downs asked: "But the old mother was then alive. What about care for her?" "I asked the lawyer. He says it wasn't alluded to." "Poor old Louisa's number was already up," Downs commented. Dorothea Waddingham had to be questioned again, but she was now in hospital expecting her baby. The inquest was adjourned and Detective Inspector Pentland continued his investigation. He learned that Dorothea was not a qualified nurse. What little training she had was acquired as a maid at a workhouse infirmary. She had acquired a small amount of capital and established a nursing home. That was 11 years ago, before her marriage to a Thomas Leach. She had borne him three children, and when he died suddenly she had resumed her maiden name. Pentland believed that the key to the poisoning mystery would be found among the records of her patients as kept by Nurse Waddingham, but Sullivan said there were none. He and the nurse had been much too busy to keep records, he said. Only the attending physicians would have recorded case histories ….

Pentland learned that on February 25th, 1935, a Mrs. Kemp died at the nursing home. Five weeks later, an elderly Mrs. Harewood had also died there. The doctors who had attended Mrs. Kemp and Mrs. Harewood told the detective that both women had been terminally ill and suffering intense pain. Alleviating narcotics had been regularly prescribed for each of them. Both doctors prescribed morphine. Together they had provided Nurse Waddingham with a more-than-ample supply of half-grain morphine tablets. So she had lied when claiming that she neither possessed any morphine, nor had been required to give it to any of her patients. Pentland then interviewed relatives and friends of Mrs. Kemp and Mrs. Harewood, and the agonising last days of both women were recounted to him with painful clarity. Pentland summed-up his findings for Downs. "For the two dying patients Nurse Waddingham received from the two physicians more than 250 half-grain morphine tablets. She returned twelve tablets after Mrs. Kemp's death, six after Mrs. Harewood's. "In my opinion, this nurse premeditated both the Baguley murders and callously withheld the prescribed pain-killing tablets, allowing Mrs. Kemp and Mrs. Harewood to suffer in order to be sure to have enough morphine available when she needed them. Ada's will being validated simply set in motion the murder of Mrs. Louisa Baguley." "And what," asked Downs, "set off Ada's murder?" "The expected birth of her child," Pentland said. "And, I suppose, an ever-pressing need for more money. Also the fact that the longer Ada Baguley was allowed to live, the less money she'd have to bequeath." "How much does Dorothea Waddingham stand to inherit under the terms of Ada's will?" "The net estate, I understand, should be about £1,600," said Pentland. ….

On January 10th, 1936, four months after the death of Ada Baguley, the coroner learned that Dorothea Waddingham was now sufficiently recovered to appear in court. So on January 16th the inquest was resumed, Dorothea bringing along her 12-week-old baby. Apart from her display of motherhood, she mainly distinguished the proceedings with cries of outrage and denunciation of Ada's cousin as he testified. With tears streaming down her face she cried: "You are a liar! You are a wicked man and you know it!" On January 30th Detective Inspector Pentland went to the nursing home and confronted Dorothea and Sullivan. "I hold," he told them, "two coroner's warrants charging you both with the murder of Ada Baguley. I must warn you that anything you say may be taken down and used against you." Each of the accused said the same thing: "I am not guilty." Nurse Waddingham and Sullivan were then lodged in jail. Dorothea, for a time, was permitted to keep her baby with her. Her other children were taken into care ….

On February 6th the pair were further charged with the murder of Mrs. Louisa Baguley, but only the case of her daughter was proceeded with when the couple's trial began at Nottingham Assizes on February 24th. The prosecutor, Norman Birkett KC, said the Crown would show that the pair had conspired to poison Mrs. Baguley and Ada in order to benefit from Ada's will. In order to secure Sullivan's conviction, the prosecution had to prove he was a party to the murders; and Birkett conceded that the prosecution did not know "the exact and precise parts played by each prisoner in the running of the nursing home." Justice Rayner Goddard asked what evidence the Crown had against Sullivan. There was no direct evidence against him "of either the possession or the administering of morphine," the prosecutor replied, but there was "evidence against the female prisoner of both possession and administration, and evidence that the administration by the female prisoner was part of a common design and a common purpose." "The only evidence against Sullivan," said Justice Goddard, "is that he was in the house assisting in the taking about of the patients, raising them in and out of bed, wheeling them about and doing household work. The sum total of evidence against Sullivan comes to no more than that Sullivan may have been a participant, not that he must have been." The judge then ruled that "there is not sufficient evidence to justify me leaving the case against Sullivan to the jury." ….

A verdict of not guilty was entered and Ronald Sullivan left the dock. Dr. Manfield's testimony was the most damning evidence against Dorothea Waddingham. There had never, he said, been an occasion for the use of morphia tablets in Ada's case. She had not been in severe pain. Mr. Birkett asked him: "At the date you changed the medicine in August did you leave any tablets for Ada?" "No." "Or at any other date did you leave tablets?" "No. I never prescribed them. I never gave them." In the witness-box Nurse Waddingham denied that she had not returned all the morphia tablets left with her when Mrs. Kemp died. She said that on August 27th she told Dr. Manfield that Ada was in pain. He prescribed another medicine and also gave her six tablets to give Ada if her pain intensified – two each night with her medicine. On September 2nd, she continued, the doctor asked if she had used the tablets. She told him she hadn't and he gave her four more from a bottle in his pocket. He did not say what they were. "I took them to be half-grain morphine tablets, because some were given to me when I had pneumonia." She had "administered morphia to Ada in accordance with the doctor who left ten tablets with me for that purpose." Cross-examining, Mr. Birkett asked her why she had not told Detective Inspector Pentland she had given Ada morphia tablets when he questioned her at the nursing home. "I didn't say so because Dr. Manfield told me not to," she replied. "Why should Dr. Manfield do that?" asked the prosecutor. The nurse's reply was inaudible. Norman Birkett continued: "Dr. Manfield says he didn't give you any tablets. Do I understand you to say it is not true?" "It is not true." Dr. Manfield was recalled. He repeated that he had not given morphine in any form to Ada Baguley ....

Summing-up, Justice Goddard said it was in Dorothea Waddingham's favour that she had not sought out the Baguleys, who had been on a month's trial and could have left at the end of that time; nor had Ada Baguley complained that she was not well looked after. But there were "grave and serious matters which might be said to tell against the prisoner." In particular the judge drew attention to Nurse Waddingham's testimony that on the day before she died Ada had a breakfast of mushrooms; a lunch of two helpings of roast pork with apple sauce, baked potatoes and kidney beans, and Bakewell tart and tea. "Can you, as men of common sense," the judge asked the jury, "think that anybody in their senses would give a woman suffering from such sharp abdominal pains that morphia had to be given for three nights, two helpings of pork, baked potatoes and fruit pie?" When the trial ended after four days on February 27th, after just over two hours deliberation the jury returned a verdict of guilty, with a strong recommendation for mercy[2]. "I am innocent," Nurse Waddingham insisted as she was sentenced to death ....

Removed from her Nottingham cell to another at Winson Green Prison, Birmingham, she cast about for some hope of relief or appeal – the appeal was rejected on March 30th. Her defence counsel J. F. Eales KC besieged the authorities in London until he had exhausted

---

[2] On the grounds that her accomplice Sullivan had been discharged by the court ....

every avenue leading to mitigation of the death sentence. The Home Secretary ruled that a premeditated murder had been committed. A trust had been grievously violated, and the responsibility and integrity of a great profession sullied. If a person charged with the care of sick and dependent patients was not to be trusted, then society had lost something invaluable. It seems that hangman Albert Pierrepoint had felt some anxiety the first time he assisted at the hanging of a woman. It was 1934, and the woman in question was husband-killer Ethel Major. The worry that gnawed at him concerned whether a woman faced with death would break down and make a swift, clean execution impossible. The night before the hanging, Albert anxiously asked his uncle: "What are women like? What do you have to do, anything special?" Smiling slowly, his uncle asked, "Why lad, you're not afraid, are you?" "No," he replied. "I was just wondering." Tom put his hand on his nephew's shoulder and reassured him there was nothing to worry about: "I shall be very surprised if Mrs. Major isn't calmer than any man you have seen so far." So she proved to be, and so too did Nurse Waddingham two years later. Despite some public feeling against her hanging – and despite the presence outside the prison of demonstrators led by Mrs. Violet Van der Elst – there was no reprieve. On the morning of Thursday, April 16th, 1936, the woman who had hoarded up death half a grain at a time was taken from her cell and walked to the gallows, where the Pierrepoints, Thomas and Albert, did their bit to ease her passage into the next world ….

Case 27
"The Thames Towpath Murders"

"Everyone who knew him said he couldn't be the killer. Yet Whiteway was a knife and axe thrower." ....

"At Oxshott a 14-year-old girl had been struck on the head with the side of an axe by a cyclist who then raped her." ....

"It looks like me, I grant you. But when the job was done I was with my wife. You are wasting your time" ....

"If Whiteway never made that statement, the only explanation is that the statement was fabricated" ....

"Do you believe that any officer would be so fantastically murderous as to forfeit the whole of his career by plain, wilful forgery and foul, murderous perjury against an innocent man?" ....

Alfred WHITEWAY
MURDERS
Of
Barbara Songhurst (16) & Christine Reed (18)
[1953]

It was a shaken Chief Superintendent William Rudkin, of the Metropolitan Police, who emerged from Richmond-u-Thames Mortuary at the end of the 18-year-old girl's post-mortem examination. "I've seen a few bad 'uns," he said. "In my twenty-eight years on the job, I've watched the PMs on a few murdered bodies. But this is the work of a maniac. This murderer is a monster. He must be as strong as an ape. We've got to get him." ....

The autopsy Chief Superintendent Rudkin had just watched had been carried out on Christine Reed of Teddington, south-west London. And she wasn't the killer's only victim. Slain with her on the River Thames towpath at Teddington on the night of **<u>Sunday, May 31st, 1953</u>**, had been her friend, 16-year-old Barbara Songhurst, also of Teddington. Both girls had been virgins until their murderer raped and butchered them and tossed them into the Thames. On June 1st Barbara's body had been found floating two miles down-river at Twickenham. Three stab wounds in her back, inflicted with a double-edged knife, had punctured one of her lungs. Her skull and one of her cheekbones had been fractured, and she also had numerous scalp wounds. Five days later, on June 6th, Christine's body was spotted bobbing in the river near Grover's Island, a mile or so from Richmond Bridge. She'd been stabbed six times in the chest, apparently with the same knife, and her skull had two fractures, together with several lacerations. On the day of their disappearance the girls had set out from home together on their bicycles. Christine's blue and silver sports model was discovered lying in mud near Teddington Lock off the Twickenham Road on June 2nd, the day of the Queen's Coronation. Barbara's bike has still never been found. How could one man have raped and killed the two girls almost at the same time? This must have been the case, otherwise one of the victims would have escaped. The feat seemed almost impossible, yet both murders showed every sign of having been committed by the same hand ….

By coincidence, the ace crime reporter Duncan Webb had stood near the bridge at Teddington Lock on the evening of May 31st, gazing at the spot where the murders were committed about 90 minutes after he departed. So he had more than just a professional interest in the case. He also had some theories, and he later wrote an in-depth study of the crime, to which this account is in part based on. The killings could not have been committed by a stranger, Webb reasoned, because someone who didn't know the area intimately could never have made his escape without being spotted. Plenty of people would have been around late that spring night, because the Thames towpath near Teddington Lock was a popular area. The killer must have had blood on his hands and clothes, yet somehow he had vanished unseen. He must have known precisely which route to take to avoid observation: probably a short cut across country to his home, or an indirect way on which he would not be seen by anyone who knew him. Knowing the area so well, the killer would also be acquainted with its people. That would account for the murders. He had to kill the girls he'd raped because one or perhaps both of them knew him. But this didn't explain how the double slaying had been accomplished, or how the two girls had been immobilised if not killed outright at virtually one and the same time. Webb thought it over. What if the murderer had been a skilled knife-thrower? That would enable him to kill or disable one girl within seconds of dealing with the other. The crime reporter passed his ideas on to the police, who to their credit took them seriously and acted upon them. With the investigation coinciding with the Coronation, it meant that Superintendent Rudkin was heavily engaged in other duties in London ….

So Scotland Yard's Superintendent Herbert Hannam was drafted in to lead the on-the-spot hunt for the killer. Hannam was nothing if not thorough. Taking a map, he drew a ring round a wide area encircling the crime scene. Then he instructed his murder squad to interview every man who had been there at the time of the killings. Thousands of statements were taken. Servicemen based in the district were checked out. Lock gates were closed and the Thames was drained in the search for the murder weapon. As a result, Richmond police station acquired seven dustbins full of odds and ends recovered from the river bed; items which might or might not tell the detectives something. As things turned out, the exercise was fruitless. But it had to be done. Interviews established that the girls had last been seen on their bikes on the towpath at 11.30 p.m. That put the time of their deaths at around midnight. Following up Webb's notion, the police checked whether any theatrical turns or circus acts featuring knife-throwers had been appearing in the area. There had been none. Nevertheless, the theory was to prove valid …. Continuing to ponder the case, Webb concluded that the killer had to be local. Anyone making a getaway by public transport or by car would have been seen. And why should a stranger go to Teddington Lock anyway at that time of night? It was much more likely that the murderer was someone from nearby who habitually mooched around there, the spot being practically on his doorstep. Twenty-one days into the investigation, Hannam seemed to be getting nowhere. But he was no quitter. Taking a closer look at all the reports that had come in, he examined the file on Barbara Songhurst a second time. Who were her friends and neighbours? Apart from the Songhursts themselves, the names of two other families kept recurring: the Knights and the Whiteways ....

Barbara's 24-year-old brother had married one of the Knight girls, who had earlier been courted by a young man called Alfred Whiteway .... Now Whiteway was married, with one child and another expected. He wasn't living with his wife because they couldn't find accommodation. Anyway, he had apparently been with his wife in Kingston-u-Thames at the time of the murders, and everyone who knew him said he couldn't be the killer. He just wasn't the type. His former fiancée, for one, said he was far too considerate. True, he had form ....

Currently unemployed, he'd done time for theft, but that didn't make him a killer – let alone a homicidal maniac. When Hannam had asked Barbara's brother if he knew anyone who carried a knife, Whiteway had been mentioned but dismissed in the same breath as the last person to be suspected. Yet Whiteway, now 22, did have a reputation for his ability as a knife and axe thrower. He'd taken this up as a hobby as a schoolboy, practising until he could split a matchbox with a knife at 30 yards, and with an axe strike a line chalked on a tree 40 yards away. And what was it that Bill Rudkin had said about the killer's physique? "He must be as strong as an ape." As a child, Whiteway had played at being Tarzan in trees near the towpath. As a teenager, he had taken up bodybuilding. But nobody thought him dangerous. All his acquaintances said he had quite the wrong disposition to be a killer. "Even now," one of his former girlfriends mused affectionately in 1953, "I still think of the time when I wanted to be the mother of his children." Hannam next studied reports of other recent sex attacks in the district, seeking anything which might suggest a connection with the towpath murders ....

Ten miles away to the south at Oxshott, a 14-year-old girl had been struck on the head with the side of an axe by a cyclist who had then raped her. In Windsor Great Park – 15 miles to the west – a middle-aged woman had been sexually assaulted by a knife-wielding cyclist. Both victims said their attacker had a cleft chin and wore gloves, and the descriptions they gave of him appeared in local newspapers. A schoolteacher reported seeing such a man throwing meat choppers and knives at a tree not far from the murder site. And a few days later, some builders saw a man who attracted their attention because he was wearing gloves despite the hot weather. He also had a cleft chin. The builders had called the police, and the man had been taken by car to Kingston police station, where he was released after inconclusive questioning. His name was Alfred Charles Whiteway. The detective inspector who interviewed him thought him an unlikely rape suspect as he had been married less than a year and had a child with another on the way. This was an odd conclusion for the inspector to draw. Pregnancy is a turn-off for many men, and pregnant women often reject their partners' advances. In such a situation, a highly sexed, frustrated husband would be more likely than ever to look elsewhere for 'satisfaction'. He might even become a rapist ....

The policemen who apprehended Whiteway at Weybridge had put him in the back of their car when they took him in for questioning. Cleaning the vehicle the next day, a constable found an axe under one of the front seats. Failing to connect it with the murder weapon being sought by his colleagues, he put it in his locker, awaiting anyone claiming to have lost it. Then he was off sick. On his return to duty five days later, he took the axe home. It came in handy for chopping wood. Whiteway was brought in again on June 28th, put on an identity parade, and picked out by the Windsor Great Park victim. He was charged with that sexual-assault, and also with the rape of the 14-year-old girl on Oxshott Common. Told of Whiteway's arrest, Hannam hastened to Chertsey police station to ask him about the towpath murders. "I guessed this would come before long," Whiteway told him. "It looks like me, I grant you. But I can save you a lot of time by telling you now that when the job was done I was with my wife at her home ....You are wasting your time. The bloke who did that job was mad." He added that while he was cycling home to Sydney Road, Teddington, after visiting his wife in Kingston that night, he had seen a policeman near Bushey Park, Teddington. Subsequent inquiries established that no officer had been in the vicinity of Bushey Park within hours of the time at which Whiteway claimed he had seen one. Several days passed, and then Hannam saw the suspect again. Whiteway had now admitted the Windsor Great Park and Oxshott offences, but he continued to deny responsibility for the towpath murders. However, he said he had an axe. He kept it in a cupboard at his home. The superintendent now told him that the police had been there, and no axe had been found – officers had even searched the garden with metal detectors. "Kingston police have got it," said Whiteway. "When I was in the police car I put it under the seat. When they picked me up I had it tucked in my shirt. In the car I was sitting in the back on my own. I pushed the axe under the seat with my foot. I watched the driver in the mirror …. At Kingston police station I was alone in the car for some time, and I wedged it further under with my hand." Hannam was horrified ….

Allowing a suspect to sit alone in the back of a police car went against one of the most basic rules of officers' training. As for the chopper …. The superintendent had spent hours personally examining enough axes to stock a wholesale ironmonger's. He'd lost count of them. And all the time the suspected murder weapon had been in the police's own possession! It took only minutes to trace it to the hapless constable who had taken it home, and who now shamefacedly produced it – covered with his fingerprints, all traces of its involvement in anything other than chopping wood long since obliterated. This was one of those aberrations that occur from time to time despite all precautions against them. Many years later, a victim's handbag sought during the hunt for the Yorkshire Ripper was to be belatedly discovered tucked away at a police station, where it had been handed in by someone and pigeon-holed as lost property. Although the chopper was now of little use as evidence it still had a role to play. It was to become a prop in a typical piece of Hannam stage-management. ….

Interviewing Whiteway again on July 30th, the superintendent casually produced the axe from his briefcase and placed it on the table at which the two were sitting. For a moment there was no response. Then, "Blimey, that's it!" cried Whiteway. "It's been buggered about. It was sharp when I had it. I sharpened it with a file." Next, the still apparently casual superintendent referred to some blood detected on one of Whiteway's shoes. "What blood?" asked the suspect. Hannam said it had shown up under microscopic examination. "You're not kidding, are you?" The detective repeated that laboratory tests had revealed heavy bloodstains. Whiteway rose from the table, shaking. Hannam replaced the axe in his briefcase in a manner which implied that as far as he was concerned, that was that: everything was sewn-up, and there was little more to be said. Tucking the briefcase under his arm, he patted it as he rose to leave, as if his business had been concluded. Whiteway, pushed to breaking-point by the detective's quiet confidence, could take no more. "You know bloody well it was me!" he cried. The superintendent paused at the door. He hadn't been bluffing about the bloodstains, although they alone would not have secured a conviction. By introducing them as he had, however, Hannam was unnerving the suspect into making a confession. "I didn't mean to kill 'em," Whiteway went on. "I never meant to hurt anyone." ….

Returning to the table without a word, Hannam sat down, opened his briefcase, took out the axe again, and produced some paper. The time had come to get it all down in writing. Cautioning Whiteway that anything he said might be used in evidence against him, the superintendent proceeded to record the suspect's statement, not in "policeman's English," but just as it was spoken. "It's all up," Whiteway began. "You know bloody well I done it. That shoe's buggered me. What a bloody mess. I'm mental. I must 'ave a bloody woman. I can't stop meself. I'm not a bloody murderer. I only see one girl. She came round the tree where I stood and I bashed her and she was down like a log. Then the other screamed out down by the lock. Never saw 'er until then, I didn't. I nipped over and shut 'er up. Two of them and then I tumbled the other one knew me. If it hadn't been for that, it wouldn't have 'appened. Put that bloody chopper away. It haunts yer. What more do they want to know? Why don't the doctors do something? It will be mental, won't it? It must be. I can't stop it. Give us it. I'll sign it." Whiteway seemed relieved to have it all over and done with. Then something else occurred to him.

"Have you got the bike?" he asked, referring to Barbara Songhurst's cycle. "No," Hannam replied. Not only had the bike not been found, the murder knife had also yet to be discovered. Whiteway sprang to his feet, enraged. "So you've done it on me!" he stormed. "I'll say it's all lies, like the blood. You can tear that last one up. I didn't give it." But by now, signed by the suspect, the statement was secure in Hannam's briefcase. And it was upon its authenticity that the fate of Alfred Whiteway was to hinge ….

Alfred Whiteway's Old Bailey trial for Barbara Songhurst's murder followed in October and was to last 6-days and when, repudiating his alleged confession, he relied on his alibi to clear him. But Whiteway wasn't the only one in trouble. The unfortunate constable who had taken the murder axe home also had a rough time. Why, he was asked, had he put it away in his locker without reporting it? "The practice among drivers is that anything found in the car is claimed by the driver finding it," the constable replied. "You are not suggesting," said Justice Malcolm Hilbery, "that if a man leaves a jemmy in a car the officer claims that?" "No, sir." Whiteway's sister told the court that she had seen her brother with a sheath knife, but she could not say when she had last observed it in his possession. Confirmation of Hannam's account of the bloodstained shoe came from the head of Scotland Yard's forensic laboratory. "On the right shoe," he said, "I found there was a strong reaction for blood round the sewing near the lace tags, and also round the outside edge of the junction of the sole and the upper, and also on the inside edge. I took the shoe to pieces and in the dust which was round the stitching holding the upper to the sole, I identified the presence of human blood." Whiteway's 18-year-old wife, by now the mother of two, was questioned closely about her husband's whereabouts on the night of the murders …. She said he had been with her until 11.30 p.m., when he had left on his bike. As the murders were believed to have been committed half an hour later, this made his alibi somewhat shaky. ….

Then came what was to be the crux of the trial: the prosecution's claim that Whiteway had confessed, and they had his signed statement to prove it. This was countered by the contention of the defence that the statement was a police fabrication. Superintendent Hannam denied that he had concocted Whiteway's statement, and that he had addressed the suspect as "Alf." "Did you say to him, 'How is our stubborn Mr. Alf?'" asked Peter Rawlinson QC, defending. "No, sir." "And did he reply, 'As stubborn as ever'?" "No, sir." "I suggest," Mr. Rawlinson continued, "that exhibit twenty-four (the confession) is a statement manufactured by you." "That is absolutely untrue." "I suggest that no such words were ever used by Whiteway on the thirtieth of July or at any other time." Hannam replied that they were Whiteway's "own words, from his own lips." He said he found Mr. Rawlinson's suggestion shocking, and he was pleased to deny it. In the witness-box Whiteway said that while he was cycling home on the night of the murders he noticed that a clock on a department store showed 11.35. He denied that he had told Superintendent Hannam that he left his wife's home before 11.30 p.m. and that he had not arrived home until after midnight. Christmas Humphreys, prosecuting, asked him if he carried an axe in his bicycle's saddlebag. "Yes." "Had you the axe with you on the thirty-first of May?" "No, sir." ….

Mr. Humphreys moved on to the bloodstained footwear. "You remember suddenly shaking when Superintendent Hannam mentioned about the blood on your shoes?" "Yes." "And you turned very pale and were trembling?" "No." Turning to the disputed statement, Mr. Humphreys said: "You are alleging that these two officers forged that statement and committed perjury in putting it before the jury?" "I am saying I never said it." "Are you saying you were asked to sign a blank piece of paper?" "No, there was writing on it." "What did you think you were signing?" "I did not read it." Summing-up for the defence, Mr. Rawlinson told the jury that nobody knew exactly what had happened to the two girls, or at what time they were killed. It could have been as late as 1 a.m., and Whiteway had been back at home since 11.55 p.m. "There is going to be one issue, and you may think perhaps the most vital and important issue: was the confession ever made?" Mr. Rawlinson continued. Without that "confession" there would certainly be an acquittal, he claimed. "If Whiteway never made that statement, as he says he never made it, the only explanation is that the statement was fabricated by somebody, and it is suggested his signature was put on it by means of a trick." He went on to say that Whiteway's alleged confession was "a completely manufactured piece of fiction without the slightest speck of truth." We have heard a lot about blood, but there is no evidence of blood on this man's clothes. There were nineteen wounds on Christine Reed and at least seven on Barbara Songhurst, yet there was no blood on this man." ….

Concluding for the prosecution, Mr. Humphreys said that the Crown was satisfied that Whiteway was guilty even without his confession. But he asked the jury: "Do you believe that any officer would be so fantastically murderous as to forfeit the whole of his career by plain, wilful forgery and foul murderous perjury against an innocent man, as to write out this statement and fake and fool him into signing it?" Of course, today we know of many instances of police witnesses "sticking in the crippler," or giving falsified evidence to secure a conviction. But in 1953 the reputation of the police was still whiter-than-white, and the very idea that Hannam was attempting to "fit up" Whiteway was astonishing. Hannam's reputation was permanently dented. Dealing with the absence of blood on Whiteway's clothes, Mr. Humphreys said that the garments taken from him for examination were not necessarily those he had worn on May 31st. He might subsequently have had the clothing in question cleaned, or he could have got rid of it. ….

In his summing-up, Justice Hilbery told the jury that it was important for them to remember that Whiteway had said there was writing on the paper which he had signed. "If that is so," said the judge, "and if it is a concoction from beginning to end by police officers, when did they concoct and write it? Is the theory that this imaginative police officer had written this piece already before he went to the interview, taking it with him with a determination first of all to get another statement from the accused so he could fraudulently insert this statement somewhere, and induce the prisoner to sign it without observing what he was signing? Whiteway denies there is a word of truth in the statement. If he did say it, it is a confession, and he is guilty. There is no escaping from that." On November 2nd, after 50 minutes deliberation the jury found Alfred Whiteway guilty of murder and he was sentenced to death; the indictments for the murder of Christine Reed and the rape and sexual assault of the two other females remaining on file. His appeal dismissed, on December 7th, Alfred Whiteway was hanged on Tuesday, December 22nd, 1953, at Wandsworth Prison by Albert Pierrepoint and Joseph Broadbent. Such was the strength of the circumstantial evidence against him that it is unlikely that there was a miscarriage of justice, whatever the truth about his confession. That could be debated forever. Hannam was already noted for sailing close to the wind. And although he was vindicated by the verdict on this occasion, his credibility had been seriously put into question ….

Case 28
"The Evil Neighbour"

Horace CARTER
MURDER
Of
Sheila Attwood (11)
[1952]

Horace Carter

It is every police-officer's nightmare; a missing-child report. When the police receive one of those, everything else gets put on the back burner. An all-out effort has to be made to find the missing child quickly ....

On the evening of **Wednesday, August 1st, 1951**, in the Birmingham suburb of Kingstanding, police received a report that an 11-year-old schoolgirl had gone missing. She was Sheila Ethel Attwood, who lived with her parents at 36, Caversham Road. Sheila, one of a large family, was described as being four feet tall, with dark brown hair and grey eyes. She had been seen wearing a grey gymslip, black pumps and a green mackintosh. Neighbours and police made an all-night search, but without result. The next day at lunchtime Mrs. Ada Ford, of 32, Caversham Road, went into the garden to hang out her washing. Just under the privet hedge which separated her garden from a public works maintenance yard in Binstead Road, a pair of bare legs protruded. Sheila Attwood had been found. Recoiling at her ghastly discovery, Mrs. Ford ran screaming to a neighbour to blurt out, her find, and this neighbour called the police. Detective Sergeant Hancock was the first police officer to see the body, which was partially obscured by the privet hedge. A piece of string had been wrapped tightly round the child's neck several times. There was a belt from a blue mackintosh across the top of the privet hedge. Scene-of-crime technicians arrived, together with Home Office pathologist Professor James Webster, who made a cursory examination on site. It was obvious that the child had been sexually-assaulted and raped. On Thursday, August 2nd, Detective Superintendent John Davies, head of Birmingham's CID in company with Superintendent Mulloy, the divisional superintendent, and other officers, descended on 30-year-old labourer Horace Carter at an engineering company where he worked. He lived at 34, Caversham Road, next door to the Attwoods ....

Superintendent Davies told Carter who they were and explained that they were making inquiries into the death of Sheila Attwood. They said they believed Carter could assist them with their investigation and that they would like to question him. Carter said he knew nothing about the little girl's death and that his conscience was clear. "We want you to come along with us," Superintendent Davies said. "Okay. Sure," Carter said. While travelling to his home in the police car, Carter adopted a merry attitude, but as they drove along Tame Road, his mood abruptly changed. Shaking and apparently overcome with emotion, he murmured to Detective Superintendent John Davies, "I never really intended to hurt the girl." "You have the right to remain silent," Superintendent Davies said curtly. Carter nodded. "If you will take me home, I will show you how I did it and where she is." When they arrived at 34, Caversham Road, Carter led the detectives to the front bedroom. "This is where I did it. This is some of the string," he said, and pointed to a length of string on the bed. "Follow me," Carter said, walking towards the stairs. He led the officers into the back garden, lifted the lid off the dustbin and pointed to more lengths of string. "That is some of it." The detectives watched closely as Carter, demonstrating, carried a ladder to the bottom of the garden and laid it against the privet hedge. He produced a blue mackintosh without a belt and said, "That is what I put over her and carried her away in." Detective Chief Inspector Harris stepped forward and formally arrested Carter for murder ....

In the house, detectives found two volumes entitled, "Famous Detective Stories," the first of which contained several short stories about murders, and the second with a story entitled, "Mistress of Murder." When they arrived at Kingstanding police station, Carter wrote out a statement. The next day, Friday, August 3rd, Horace Carter made an appearance in the dock at Birmingham Magistrates' Court charged with the murder of Sheila Ethel Attwood. The court was crowded, many people having been unable to get in, when Carter, wearing an open-necked white sports shirt, a dark sports jacket and flannel trousers, came briskly up the stairs into the dock from the cells beneath. Several times during the brief proceedings, before he was remanded in custody for seven days, his face broke into a wide smile as he stared around the court. Mr. Pugh, prosecuting, outlined the case and finished by saying that Horace Carter had written out a statement which it was not proposed to produce in court at that time. It would be produced at a later stage. The police were now asking for a remand, as they still had extensive inquiries to make. Superintendent John Davies corroborated Mr. Pugh's statement. Handcuffed to a detective, Horace Carter attended the opening of the inquest on Sheila Attwood after his brief appearance in court. Professor Webster, who had conducted the post-mortem examination on August 2nd, was asked to give cause of death and said, "This girl died from asphyxia due to combined manual strangulation and strangulation by ligature." ….

Evidence of the arrest and of the prisoner's appearance in court was given by Detective Superintendent John Davies. The city coroner, Mr. Billington, told the jury that was as far as the proceedings could go at that stage. He had to adjourn the inquest until after the criminal proceedings, which had been started. Formally discharging the jury, he said he would adjourn the inquest until September 28th. "I shall probably have to adjourn it again," he added. On the afternoon of August 9th, crowds of spectators watched the funeral cortège of the murdered schoolgirl. Blinds were drawn at practically all the houses in Caversham Road, including Horace Carter's. Over 200 people filled St Luke's Church, where the funeral service was held, and between 400 and 500 more stood outside. The majority were women and children, many of whom had previously clustered round the dead girl's home, waiting for the cortège to leave for Witton Cemetery. On September 6th, Horace Carter, looking quite composed, appeared in court for committal proceedings. The police had now completed their case against him and Mr. Pugh asked that he should stand trial at the next Birmingham Assizes. He said the evidence would show that the motive for the crime was 'lust', followed by the fears that the girl might tell somebody what he had done ….

Horace Carter's statement, read out by Pugh, stated that on August 1st he had asked Sheila into his front room and he had given her some sweets. He'd then urged her into his bedroom where he committed a 'serious offence' against her. The statement continued,

"Fearing that she would tell, I got a pillow and shoved it under her head. After that I knelt on her arms and whipped the pillow from underneath her head and shoved it over her face. She struggled for a bit, so to finish her off more quickly I shoved my fingers around her throat. After that she stopped struggling, but she was still breathing so I decided to use string. As she was unconscious I left her and hunted for some string. I found some in a drawer, went back upstairs and tied it around her throat. Either I was weak, or did not like doing it, or she was tougher than I thought. She was still breathing, so I got some cloth and my handkerchief and tied them around her mouth and her nostrils. I turned her down on her face on the bed and there she died. I tied her arms behind her back and then tied her legs and I left her in a praying position. I waited in patience for darkness to come and when it did I took her out of the house. In the shed was a pair of ladders which helped me to get her over the hedge, which finally I did; a task which caused me such distaste of one I liked as a friend. I took the gags out of her mouth and took the string off her legs and arms and put them in the dustbin. I am glad it is all over." On that note, Carter's statement ended. Mr. Pugh said the girl, born in March, 1940, lived with her parents and attended a school in Burlington Street. He went on to say that Carter's brother-in-law, Frederick Pearce, who lived in Carter's house, would give evidence that on August 1st, Horace had asked him several times when he was going out. He (Pearce) eventually left the house at 8.20 that evening and came back at 9.30 p.m. …. At half past 10, Mrs. Ford, the next-door neighbour, heard the prisoner shouting from the bottom of the garden, trying to stop a dog barking. "It may well be that that was about the time he was disposing of the body in the place where it was found," Mr. Pugh said. ….

The prisoner was then committed for trial. Horace Carter's trial took place at Birmingham Assizes on December 12th, 1951, before Justice James Cassels, and lasted just one-day. The jury comprised of nine men and three women. Walker Carter, KC, prosecuting, outlined the case for the jury and told them of the defendant's voluntary statement. Counsel then gave copies of the handwritten statement to the jury and proceeded to read it out aloud. "That statement is as complete and detailed a confession of murder as can be imagined," the prosecutor commented. Corroborative evidence of Mr. Carter's opening statement was given, and in cross-examination, Detective Chief Inspector Harris, who had made the arrest, said that the accused's elder brother had been certified in 1934 under the Mental Deficiency Act, the order having been discharged in 1941. In addition, the defendant's sister, Lily Carter, had been placed under statutory supervision as a mental defective in 1938 and remained so until her death in 1941. Opening the case for the defence, Richard Elwes, KC, said, "You have now heard the whole horrifying story of this terrible crime, and you have noticed that I have taken no steps to challenge any of the evidence put before you. It is an undisputed charge as far as the murder is concerned." He went on to say that the issue was now into the mental condition of the prisoner as related to his responsibility for the appalling crime he had undoubtedly committed. Dr William O'Conner, medical superintendent of a private mental home, called by the defence, said he found Horace Carter to be a psychopathic personality ….

While being interviewed, said the doctor, Carter had shown no interest in his near relatives except his mother. He had admitted attempting suicide by shooting himself through the chest while serving in the Forces, and when asked why he'd done it, said that it was something to do with the weather at the time. "He is quite indifferent to his own fate and to the death of others," Dr. O'Conner said. "It is my opinion that when this man committed this murder he was suffering from a life-long abnormality which, although not amounting to the better known forms of insanity, was of such a degree as profoundly to interfere with his appreciation of right and wrong and his sense of guilt and responsibility." Dr. J. J. O'Reilly, medical superintendent of Winson Green mental hospital, and Dr. J. Humphrey, principal of Winson Green Prison, however, said they had both formed the opinion that Carter had known exactly what he was doing. After a retirement of 13 minutes the jury agreed and found Horace Carter guilty of murder, Justice Cassels sentencing the prisoner to death seconds later. The condemned man made no appeal against the death sentence and the Home Secretary, Sir David Maxwell Fyfe, refused to reprieve him. Horace Carter was duly executed on Tuesday, January 1st, - New Year's Day, 1952, by Albert Pierrepoint and Syd Dernley. Fewer people than usual were outside the prison at 9 o'clock, a biting east wind probably keeping down the numbers of those waiting to read the death announcement. Three minutes after 9 o'clock, a prison-officer posted the formal notice that the execution had taken place and that death had been instantaneous. The detective who arrested Carter less than three hours after the child's body had been found, Detective Chief Inspector Harris, was among the small crowd who waited outside the prison to read the notice ….

Case 29
"The Cameo Cinema Murders"

"The man tried to tackle him and Kelly butted him. Kelly said the man then let go of him for a second, so he pulled out his gun and shot him in the chest" ....

George KELLY
Convicted of the Murders [But Conviction Quashed] Of
Leonard Thomas and John Catterall
[1950-2003]

We used to think the police could do no wrong. We now know otherwise, our view changed by cases of police corruption. Once, when a man was hanged for murder, we assumed that justice had been done. That view, too, has long since changed, due to a spate of convictions found to have been unsafe. Case in point: the conviction and execution of George Kelly, a Liverpool tearaway of the late 1940s. Kelly was destined to find more fame half a century after his death than he ever did in life, and for all the wrong reasons. He had been a small-time crook little-known outside his patch, whose reputation was inflated by the media to that of a ruthless gang-leader. One newspaper called him "The Little Caesar of Lime Street." ....

On the evening of **Saturday, March 19th, 1949**, as the audience at the Cameo Cinema in Webster Road off Smithdown Road in the Wavertree area of Liverpool watched the film Bond Street, the cinema's 43-year-old manager Leonard Thomas was shot dead in his office and his assistant John Catterall, 30, was mortally wounded. The double-murder netted only £50, and nearly six months passed with the investigation getting nowhere. Then the police received an anonymous letter: "Dear Sir," it began, "This is not a crank's letter or suchlike, nor am I turning informer for gain. It says in the papers you are looking for one man. I know three and a girl, not including myself, who heard about this plan for the robbery. I would have nothing to do with it and I don't think the girl had. There was only two men went. The man he took with him lost his nerve and would not go in with him, but said he would wait outside, which he did not." The writer added that the letter was anonymous through fear of prosecution as an accessory, and asked the police to respond with an advertisement in the personal column of the Liverpool Echo "giving me your word that I won't be charged." The police replied in the small ads.: "Letter received. Promise definitely given." But the writer failed to come forward. Detective Chief Inspector Herbert Balmer suspected that the letter was from a 'prostitute' who associated with criminals. The handwriting of all known sex-workers in the city was checked, and Balmer's hunch was confirmed. The writer was a Liverpool 'street-walker'. ….

Identified and questioned, she said she knew the names of only two of the people she had mentioned in her letter. Neither was the killer. They were another sex-worker named Jackie Dickson and her lover James "Stutty" Northam. Both had criminal records, and they were arrested and interrogated. Northam admitted being present when the raid was planned. According to the statement he made, the killer was 27-year-old George Kelly, who was already a suspect – the police had questioned him on the day after the shootings, but he had an alibi. He said he was in a pub at the time of the raid, and he named witnesses who could confirm this. Northam, however, claimed that after the raid he had asked Kelly what had gone wrong. Kelly told him he had gone to the cinema with an ex-seaman, Charles Connolly (26), who was to follow him up to the manager's office in case the assistant manager turned up unexpectedly. But at the last moment Connolly had refused to accompany Kelly beyond the cinema's side door. Northam's statement continued: "Kelly said he got to the manager's office and walked in. There was an old fellow sitting down. Kelly said he wanted the takings, and then pointed to the bag on the table. The man said, 'Don't be such a fool. Put that toy away.' And Kelly said, 'This is no toy – and I want that bag.' "The man then stood up and said, 'You can't take that bag. It belongs to the company. You can take some of my own money.' He then tried to brush the gun aside. "Kelly told me, 'I couldn't be bothered with him any more, so I shot him.' He put the gun in his pocket, picked up the bag and started to make for the door. When he was a few feet away the door opened. Another man came in and closed the door behind him. The man kept his hands behind his back and said to Kelly, 'What are you doing here?' The man then came towards him, made a grab at the bag and the cash went all over the floor. The man tried to tackle him and Kelly butted him. Kelly said the man then let go of him for a second, so he pulled out his gun and shot him in the chest. He went down screaming and tearing at his chest. The man got to his knees again and tried to tackle Kelly, so he shot him again. The man was stretched out by the door. He had to drag him away so that he could try to open the door. Kelly thought the man had locked it when he came in, so he shot the lock off. He rushed down the spiral staircase and out of the cinema." Northam went on to say that after making his getaway Kelly had boasted to him that he had a cast-iron alibi. He had made a point of being seen in nearby pubs immediately before and after the shooting. Jackie Dickson made a statement saying that she had witnessed the planning of the raid in which Kelly was to be the gunman and Connolly his accomplice ….

On September 30th, 1949, the pair were arrested and charged with the murders. Their 13-day trial in January 1950 was the longest in British criminal history to date, and in his summing-up Justice Roland Oliver told the jury they had three questions to consider. Was Kelly the gunman? Did he fire the fatal shots? And was Connolly guilty of murder if he had agreed to the raid? In law, the judge directed, if Connolly knew that Kelly was armed and would use the firearm, then he was equally guilty of murder. After five hours deliberation the jury failed to agree and a retrial was ordered ….

When this began at Liverpool Assizes a few days later in February, Justice James Cassels decided that the defendants should be tried separately. "I have come to the conclusion," he said, "that it is in the interest of justice that the jury in a long case like this, particularly a retrial and on a capital charge, should not have to dissect evidence of individual witnesses and relate it to more than one person under trial. "I don't think the defence is prejudiced. On the contrary, it may well be favoured by a separate trial in that there will be before the jury no evidence other than that relevant to the issues being tried concerning one person." Kelly was tried first, the jury hearing that the shootings had taken place at about 9.30 p.m. Dealing with Kelly's alibi, the prosecution said he left the Spofforth Hotel before 9.30, and when he appeared at the Leigh Arms some time after 9.45 he deliberately ensured that others noticed him. He tapped a taxi-driver on the shoulder, telling him, "You can have a drink with me, pal. The best in the house." The cabbie, who knew him only as a nodding acquaintance, asked, "You been in the sun?" Kelly refuted everything said by the Crown's witnesses, claiming that what he actually said to the taxi-driver was, "I've been having a go at the bevy" – a Scouse expression for going "on the beer." The court heard that while in custody during the first trial Kelly was visited by a brother accompanied by several friends. He allegedly said to them, "Don't forget, boys, if I go down it's up to you to do something about that grass." He admitted saying something to that effect in the presence of a prison officer, but claimed it was not intended to be a threat. The prosecutor William Gorman asked: "Did you mean them merely to see him and say, 'Please tell the truth'? Is that what you meant?" "All the time I've been in prison, my brothers have threatened nobody yet," Kelly insisted. "What do you mean by 'yet'?" asked Mr. Gorman. "Is that something that's still to come?" This was to prove damning, coupled with the statements of Northam and Jackie Dickson. The jury retired for only just under an hour on February 8th – this time the trial had lasted 6-days. They returned to find George Kelly guilty of murder, and he was sentenced to death. Stunned by the verdict, he had to be helped from the dock by two prison officers who took him below ….

Charles Connolly appeared in the same court five days later, to deny the two murders but to admit robbery and conspiracy to rob. The prosecutor announced that no evidence would be offered on the murder charges, and Connolly was sentenced to 10 years imprisonment for the other offences. An appeal in respect of Kelly was rejected after two days on Match 10th …. George Kelly's execution followed on Tuesday, March 28th, 1950 at Liverpool's Walton Prison carried out by Albert Pierrepoint and Harry Allen. And that was that, thought the police and public: a double-killer had got his comeuppance. The pair's friends and relatives continued to insist that Kelly and Connolly were innocent, but nobody wanted to know. "Kelly richly deserved to hang," declared the Daily Express, "and the world is the better for his removal." He became history, and remained so until his case resurfaced in 1998. The first intimation of this came with the publication of The Cameo Conspiracy, by George Skelly. Ever since the murders the author's eldest brother James had maintained that Kelly was innocent. He said he knew this because he was elsewhere with Kelly at the time the two defendants were alleged to have been with the two prosecution witnesses, plotting the raid on the cinema. But James Skelly had a criminal record, so his evidence at the first trial was discredited by Justice Oliver. For this reason the defence counsel Rose Heilbron didn't call him to testify at Kelly's second trial. George Skelly, however, was impressed by his brother's unshakeable belief in Kelly's innocence. He began his own investigation, and the more he learned, the more he became convinced that his brother was right. In Skelly's book, Detective Chief Inspector Bert Balmer is the villain of the piece. "After Kelly's execution," the author claimed, "there was an atmosphere of unashamed triumphalism in the Liverpool CID, particularly among the Murder Squad who received eulogies and commendations galore from the city's Watch Committee. In this euphoric climate a senior detective involved in the case admitted to a well-known criminal lawyer that Kelly and Connolly and been 'fitted-up', telling him, 'they were only scum anyway.'" The protests of the two convicted men's families and friends fell on deaf ears, Skelly wrote, because "the general feeling was that they would say that, wouldn't they? After all, hadn't the two villains had not one, but two trials? What could be more fair? And did anyone for one moment, in *1950*, believe the police would tell lies? Hadn't the two main prosecution witnesses been publicly complimented and financially rewarded by the trial judge for their public-spirited action? And weren't Connolly's guilty pleas to robbery and conspiracy to rob a virtual admission of the rightness of the convictions?" ….

After his release from prison in 1956, Connolly became a popular night club "greeter" on Merseyside. George Skelly first met him in 1993, and in the ensuing three years came to admire and respect him as a sociable, active and clean-living ex-amateur boxer. "During his wartime service in the Royal Navy he had an impeccable record, serving in the Pacific and on decoy duty in the Normandy landings," the author noted. True, Connolly had a criminal record .... but then, so did everyone else involved in the case, including the prosecution's key witnesses. Connolly had been urged by his counsel to admit the lesser charges in order to avoid Kelly's fate, and he died in 1997 aged 73, still tortured – said Skelly – by the belief that his guilty plea had been responsible for the other man's execution. Balmer's career had meanwhile progressed from success to success, culminating with his retirement as Liverpool's Deputy Chief Constable. But he failed to win his last two battles. The first was with officialdom which denied him the top job in Liverpool. Home Office policy precluded officers from becoming the Chief Constable of a force in which they had spent their entire service. His reputation was by now legendary, and he was piqued and retired in a huff. His second battle was with cancer, from which he died in 1970. Skelly's book claimed that Jackie Dickson didn't know George Kelly, and knew Charles Connolly only by sight as a frequenter of Lime Street. She named him as a man she thought might be involved in the murders because, like a suspect described in the newspapers, he wore a trilby ....

Northam knew neither Kelly nor Connolly. So why did Jackie Dickson and Northam make statements incriminating Kelly and Connolly? According to Skelly's book, Balmer threatened Jackie Dickson with the prospect of seven years jail for theft and jumping bail. He told Northam the police had evidence he had stolen a lorry which killed a woman in Lime Street, adding that he could also be prosecuted for 'aiding and abetting' Jackie Dickson in skipping bail. For the latter he could face 10 years in jail. And he might even go to the gallows for the case in which a woman had lost her life. Balmer allegedly told the two potential informers that their way out was to co-operate with him in providing evidence against *his* two suspects, Kelly and Connolly. If Jackie and Northam helped the police, the police would help them, dropping all other charges against them and ensuring that Jackie was conditionally discharged on the theft offence for which she had been on bail. So to stay out of jail, Skelly's book claimed, the pair agreed to become informers and signed the fabricated statements which sent one man to the scaffold and robbed another of six or so years liberty. "What can now be established," Skelly wrote, "are such grave doubts about the safety of Kelly's conviction that it must be reviewed." The witnesses' statements were uncorroborated, there was no forensic evidence against either Kelly or Connolly, no murder weapon, bloodstains or fingerprints. "No jury today would ever convict on the evidence as it stood then," Skelly argued ….

In March 1998 the solicitor acting for Kelly's daughter, Robin Makin, applied to the Criminal Cases Review Commission [CCRC] for her dad's conviction to be reviewed. Mr. Makin submitted that the evidence was unreliable because witnesses had been given inducements, and on February 8th, 2001, it was announced that the Commission had referred the case to the Court of Appeal. Mr. Makin claimed that Kelly's fate was an indictment of the justice system and policing that prevailed at a time when it was thought more important to reassure the public by securing a conviction than to investigate a case properly. After a two-day hearing on June 10th, 2003, the Court of Appeal at last overturned the convictions of Kelly and Connolly, ruling them unsafe. "However much the Cameo murders remain a mystery," said Lord Justice Bernard Rix, "we regard the circumstances of Kelly and Connolly's trials as a miscarriage of justice which must be deeply regretted." During the appeal the judges heard that a statement made by a prison inmate, claiming that a man named Donald Johnson had confessed to committing the murders, had not been disclosed at the defendants' first trial. The Crown conceded that the inmate must have spoken to Balmer. But Kelly, who always protested his innocence, seems to have been as badly treated in death as he was in life. After his conviction was quashed his family, devout Catholics, wrote to the Home Office asking to be given Kelly's remains and were told that a car park had been built over the old prison burial site ….

A Home Office spokeswoman said: "We have received an application for the exhumation of George Kelly's body. We can confirm that at HMP Liverpool a secure car parking area has been built over the body, but there are pre-concrete slabs over the grave so it is easily accessible." …. Eventually Kelly's remains were returned to his family and a service was held for him in Liverpool's Metropolitan Cathedral ….

The Condemned Man Writes

Dear, Harry, Doris has been up to see me and she has given me some very good news. But it's no good if these people don't take action about it, Harry I can't believe I am sentenced to Death, I don't know the first thing about this Murder, why these people has blamed me God only knows. Well there is a lot of people who knows I am innocent of this Crime, But what can we do about it, Tell all the Boys I was asking about them, Please do me a favour, if I get Hung for this Harry please try some day to prove me innocent, I know it will be to late then, But it will clear my family's Name, also it will get those people in trouble who blamed me for it. There is one thing I can do I can face God with a clear Conscious so why should I worry, Harry Nobody knows what it is like to be sentenced to Death when I know in my own Mind that I am a innocent man. People can only do their best for me. That Saturday night I left the Lee Arms pub, and went down to the (spoford) for a pint just to see if Doris was there, I went in there about 9.15 and stayed there till 9.20. I could not see Doris so I went back to the Lee Arms pub and stayed till 10 pm. So here I am convicted of Murder. The people who Blamed me for this I have never seen them in all my life, who the man who was charged with me, I can't understand it please write me a letter. From George Kelly. Good Luck ….

Case 30 "The Curious Affair

Of The Signed Stamp"

"Two volunteers cradled his head and shielded him from the sight of the body-shaped bag as it was lifted from the pit and carried to Jenkins's cottage" ....

"We parted on good terms at the boundary gates. Mind you, I did notice a couple of gypsies who'd called at the farm earlier asking for a cup of tea .... that's who killed him" ....

Albert JENKINS
MURDER
Of
William Llewellyn
[1950]

Mrs. Mona Llewellyn was worried. Very worried. Her 52-year-old husband William had not come home for lunch, and this was most unusual. He was a market gardener and landowner in Ellesmere, Rosemarket, near Haverfordwest, Pembrokeshire, in Wales and the previous day, Sunday, October 9th, 1949, he had received a note from the tenant of his Lower Furzehill Farm, asking him to meet him there at 11 o'clock the next morning ....

Albert Edward Jenkins, the 38-year-old tenant, had been negotiating to buy the farm. His note intimated that he was now ready for the deal to be done, so Mr. Llewellyn had set out to cycle there to see him. At about 4 o'clock Mrs. Llewellyn went to the farm to see if her husband was still there. Her married daughter accompanied her. "He was here, but only for about ten minutes," Jenkins told them, saying that Mr. Llewellyn had left just before Russell Codd, an artificial inseminator, called at the farm at about a quarter past eleven. There was still no sign of Mr. Llewellyn when his wife and daughter returned home, so they reported him missing and a search was launched by the police. About 100 volunteers took part until darkness fell, and at dawn the following day the hunt was resumed. The search concentrated on the area surrounding Jenkins's cottage, and in the afternoon Police Sergeant William Rossiter examined the bottom of a clay-pit about 400 yards from the farm. The ground appeared to have been disturbed, and a long-handled spade lay nearby. Rossiter started to dig, and when he was satisfied that the clay had recently been excavated he called to the other searchers to join him. As the digging proceeded, the silence was broken only by the clang of spades colliding and the steady thud of discarded clods. Mr. Llewellyn's son-in-law was at the forefront of the search. He'd had little sleep since his father-in-law disappeared, and he collapsed when a large tarpaulin sack was unearthed ….

Two volunteers cradled his head and shielded him from the sight of the body-shaped bag as it was lifted from the pit and carried to Jenkins's cottage, where it was found to contain the bloodied remains of William Llewellyn, his skull crushed by a heavy object. Outside the cottage, groups of shadowy figures gathered to discuss the murder. Everyone spoke in whispers, as if afraid of being overheard. And nobody wanted to have to inform the widow. "I know nothing about it," Jenkins was heard telling the police. "I made a deal with Mr. Llewellyn to buy the farm from him for a thousand pounds and he came over for the money. I gave him one thousand and fifty pounds in pound-notes because I owed him fifty pounds back rent. He put it in his wallet, signed a receipt, and left. We parted on good terms at the boundary gates. Mind you, I did notice a couple of gypsies who'd called at the farm earlier asking for a cup of tea. That's who killed him: it was the gypsies." "Where's the receipt?" asked a detective. From his pocket, Jenkins fished out his rent book, opening it to display a twopenny stamp spanned by what appeared to be Mr. Llewellyn's signature. "Strange, very strange," said the detective …. "What do you mean, 'strange'?" Jenkins asked angrily. "I said 'strange,'" the detective replied, "because yesterday was **[Monday, October 10th]**, and this receipt is dated September 29th. Where did you keep the £1,050?" "I kept it on top of a beam in the bedroom." "Let me see," said the detective. In the bedroom, Jenkins pointed to a beam beneath the ceiling, and the detective stood on a chair to take a closer look. "Are you sure it was this beam?" the policeman asked. "I'm positive." "You removed the money yesterday?" "Yes." "Well, Mr. Jenkins, if you would like to look you will see that there is a continuous film of dust the full length of the beam that hasn't been disturbed in years." ….

Outside, another officer noticed blood on the corner of a calf stall. He moved some of the manure, to reveal William Llewellyn's boots, minus their laces. Earlier, Mona Llewellyn had told the police something which now prompted them to ask Jenkins to turn out his pockets. The items he produced included a pair of laces, one of them knotted. Mrs. Llewellyn had told the police that before cycling to Lower Furzehill Farm the previous morning, her husband had broken one of his laces while putting on his boots. He'd broken it not once, but in two places. Two pieces of the lace had been long enough for him to tie them together, and the smaller piece he'd put into his pocket. This smaller piece matched exactly the laces taken from Jenkins's pocket. When he was asked to account for blood on his clothes, Jenkins said one of his animals was injured. But no such beast could be found. Arrested on suspicion of murder, Jenkins was taken to Milford Haven police station, where he made a statement in which he said he had become the tenant at Lower Furzehill Farm in 1945. "Mr. Llewellyn told me I could buy the farm for £1,000. I did not have £1,000, but I told Mr. Llewellyn that I would be in a better position in a few years' time. On Wednesday evening, September 28th, I called again on Mr. Llewellyn." ….

"We then struck the deal at his figure of £1,000. At the time he said he would call on me after he had been to Milford Haven to see his solicitors. On Sunday, October 9th, about 5.30 p.m. I sent my little boy over to Mr. Llewellyn with a letter, asking him to call at my farm about 11 a.m. the following day. The note in your possession is the one I sent to him. About 11 a.m. yesterday Mr. Llewellyn came over to me on his bicycle. My wife wanted to go to Pembroke Fair, and it was arranged that she and the children should go over early and I would follow in the early evening after finishing the work. She left the farm with my two children about 9.30 a.m., leaving me at home alone. I later took the milk to the road entrance, where I met Mr. Llewellyn on his bicycle. I was driving the tractor and he followed me down to the farmyard, riding his bicycle. On arriving in the farmyard we had a little chat over general things, and then we both went into the house. He left his bicycle by the garage door. We both went into the kitchen and each one of us sat side by side at the table. We each sat on a chair. I went upstairs to one of the bedrooms and fetched down from the beam a bundle of one-pound notes which I knew contained 1,050 notes. This bundle was tied with elastic and was got ready by me about a month or six weeks ago. The notes were blue and green, and a good many were brand new. The bundle would be about nine inches high. I put it on the table by Mr. Llewellyn, and he counted the notes out in tens and put them in fifties. After he had checked, I handed him the rent book and also a twopenny stamp which he put on the book and signed W.H. Llewellyn with my fountain pen as having received £1,000 and £50 on September 29th, 1949. The reason for the date being put as the 29th and not the 10th October is that my rent was due to Mr. Llewellyn on the September 29th, 1949. As far as I can say, there is about £20 in one-pound notes left in the house at the present time. Mr. Llewellyn told me that he was going in on the Thursday to see his solicitors in Milford Haven to get the deeds turned over to me. I accompanied him out of the house as far as the garage doors. He had a look at the pigs and a heifer in the cowshed. Then we left the cowshed, he picked up his bicycle and I accompanied him to the boundary gate. Both of us said 'So long' to one another, and we parted on good terms. After Mr. Llewellyn left I went and finished the work up, had a wash and shave and changed. I was having a cup of tea when Mrs. Llewellyn and her daughter came to the door round about 4 o'clock and asked me if I had seen Mr. Llewellyn. I told them I had seen him and he had left hours ago. They were a bit worried as he had not come home to his dinner." ….

In conclusion, Jenkins's statement said that he then went to Pembroke Fair, where he met his wife. Around 8.30 p.m. he was on his way home when he was stopped by a constable who asked him if he had seen Mr. Llewellyn, saying he was missing and a search was being made for him. A very different story was told by the prosecution, however, when Jenkins stepped into the dock at the Haverfordwest Assizes at the end of February, 1950, charged with William Llewellyn's murder. The receipt for £1,050 in his rent book, the court was told, was clearly a forgery. Jenkins had simply stuck a twopenny stamp partly over Mr. Llewellyn's signature, continuing the signature over the stamp with his own pen ….

Far from having £1,000 to buy the farm he tenanted, Jenkins was in arrears with his rent and his payments for his tractor, and his bank account was overdrawn by £136. The moment Mr. Llewellyn arrived at the farm on his bike, the Crown alleged, Jenkins bludgeoned him to death. Then he removed his victim's boots, so that if he had to drag him over soft ground there would be no telltale marks left by the heel-tips. He had already prepared Mr. Llewellyn's grave in the clay pit, and after manhandling the body into a tarpaulin sack he loaded it on to an open boxcar trailer behind his tractor. He was just setting off for the clay pit when Codd, the artificial inseminator, arrived. "I can't see you now, I'm too busy," Jenkins shouted. "The heifer's in the cowshed." And with that, he drove his rattling tractor off across a rutted field. Codd had done his work and left when Jenkins returned to the farm, having buried the body, the prosecution claimed. He later rode Mr. Llewellyn's bike to Leyland and dumped it in a derelict chapel, before taking the ferry to Pembroke Fair to join his family. When he showed the police a beam on which he claimed he had kept £1,050, the presence of undisturbed dust proved he was lying. And he lied again when he said Mr. Llewellyn had put the £1,050 in £1 notes in his wallet. The police had borrowed £1,050 in one-pound notes, tried to fit them into the wallet, and found it impossible to do so. Step by step, the Crown built up an overwhelming case, in which Russell Codd's evidence was particularly damning. When Jenkins saw him arrive at the farm, he testified, the farmer waved his arms wildly as he shouted he was too busy to speak to him. Jenkins's dramatic behaviour seemed out of character, and Codd recalled wondering what was in the tarpaulin bundle he saw on the tractor's trailer. Several points were raised by Jenkins's defence counsel. No murder weapon had been found, he pointed out. It was believed to be an iron-bar, and the prosecution suggested that Jenkins could have dropped it over the side of the ferry on his way to join his wife at the fair. The trial lasted 4-days and after less than two hours deliberation on March 2nd, the jury found Albert Jenkins guilty of murder. Wearing a blue suit, white shirt and dark, striped tie, he showed no emotion as Justice Laurence Byrne sentenced him to death. On April 3rd his appeal was dismissed, and at Swansea Prison sixteen days later on Wednesday, April 19th, 1950, he was hanged by Albert Pierrepoint and Harry Kirk ….

MARCH 2025

MATTHEW SPICER

Printed in Great Britain
by Amazon

60014331R00141